Sven Sagas

Hells Lefse

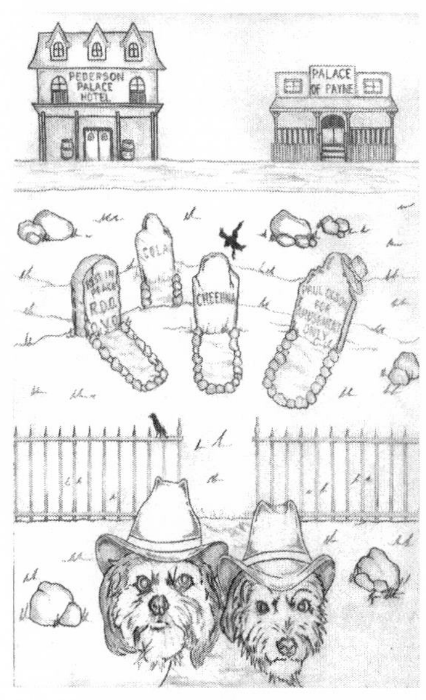

PublishAmerica
Baltimore

First printing

Hardcover 978-1-4512-9607-5
Softcover 978-1-4489-4616-7
PUBLISHED BY PUBLISHAMERICA, LLLP
www.publishamerica.com
Baltimore

Printed in the United States of America

DEDICATION

To Sven and Lena my dog children for their love and loyalty. To Einer a breed apart with a heart of gold and his human.

For the humans in my life. I thank my parents Roger and Olivia who taught me that a pet is as much family as any human. A special thanks to my cousin Kathy and Aunt Delores who have shown so much enthusiasm for my writings.

A special thanks to my daughter Valerie for the gift of a lifetime, my first grandchild, Caraline. I have learned that a baby's smile warms my heart as much as a doggies kiss.

As a last minute savior I thank Ryan the new artist extraordinaire for his drawings that now grace the cover and pages of SvenSagaS.

GRAVESEND
OR
WHO SHOT MY PAW

A SVEN & EINER ADVENTURE

PUPPYLUDE

Humans would call this a prelude. I am not a human. I am a dog. Sven is my name, full-blooded black and white Shih-Tzu. Eighteen pounds of rough and tough western dog. This is the early American west. If you are reading this you may be aware that I have a great, great, great, well anyway put a thirteen in front of all those greats and that is heir to my name. He also is adventuresome and writes books.

I have a friend named Einstein, they call him Einer, heard he has a great heir also, 13 times removed. Einer is what you would call scruffy looking. Part Schnauzer and part Border collie. Forty pounds of black furred muscle.

I am the dog about town. Stories, I have heard them all. This particular story had its beginnings long before I came to live here. I have heard this 'tail' told and retold at saloons, around campfires, restaurants and even in peoples parlors.

Once I moved here, I witnessed the rest of the story. If you are weak of heart, do not like violence or are afraid of the dark. Stop here. Sell this book or use it to light your fireplace. You will be entering an unknown realm in America's Old West. Contrary to the popular saying: "You can only be sure of two things. Death and Taxes." In this book, you can only be sure of one thing "DEATH."

CHAPTER 1

Eighteen-fifty-one, Bohemia, a young man named Jack Payne joins the military Cossacks to insure the freedom of their county and their lifestyle. He believes in the cause of freedom for the working classes. Clashes between his group and other military groups along the Dnieper River and extending to the Volga River and across Siberia were often brutal and bloody.

Jack came from a poor family, working the ground for enough sustenance to keep them alive. He met and married a Gypsy girl whose family was camped on their small farm. The Gypsy's moved on and Jack and his young wife stayed to work the land. Their first and only child, a girl was born during the harsh winter. The Cossacks were looking for men, the pay was minimal, but the men were fed and clothed. Jack left with the Cossacks sending money home to his family. It was the best way he could think of to support them.

The political and military situation continued to worsen. Bands of outlaws, even sanctioned armies would raid small villages killing and plundering just to feed and sustain themselves. The worst killed, raped, and then burned homes to the ground. The claims of course were retaliation for helping the enemy. Often it was for greed and sport.

Jack's group was proud and brave. They did their best to defend the common people. Astride their steeds, they showed no fear. Racing to do battle, their black Cossack hats pulled tight around the chinstraps, their long flowing coats trailing in the wake of their charge. Swords swinging, metal clashing metal. In the end, it was more death and destruction. The wounded, for lack of care or the bitter climate were expected to die.

Jack Payne finally saved enough money to take his family away. He booked passage on a ship to America. Settling himself, his wife, and his daughter in Charleston, South Carolina. Jack's years in the Military had taught him well. He was an expert at handling supplies and making the best of what was at hand.

He was frugal, untrusting of others and a shrewd businessman. He soon had control of a large plantation, growing cotton and tobacco. This led to his ownership of his freight business and eventually even his own ships. He was an American success story.

His Gypsy wife was a perfect match. She had the Gypsy blood of shrewdness in her veins. The plantation workers and her household staff feared her temper. When it came to business or finance, she was a woman to be reckoned with.

She could also be charming and beguiling at the many receptions that she and Jack would attend. To them these receptions were not for pleasure, it was business only, a possibility to make contacts for more financial gain.

Then there was their daughter, Lotta M. Payne. Dark hair, blue eyes, almost skeletal slim, and pretty. She was often the bell of the ball at social gatherings. Not so much for her beauty or charm, which were more than acceptable, but for her family's money and prestige. Lotta had inherited two things from her parents. Her father's cut throat business ethics, which included trusting no one. She also had her mother's Gypsy temper. A nasty combination.

CHAPTER 2

Polar Pederson's parents came from Stavanger Norway. Proud of their Viking ancestors, they felt coming to America was another adventure for their family to undertake. They settled in the Dakota Territory to farm and make a home for future generations. Polar was born on that farm. He was a good son, always did as he was told. By the time he was sixteen years old he knew that the backbreaking life of a farmer was not for him.

He bid his family farewell. Like his Viking forbearers, he needed to discover a new land and a new life for himself. He teamed up for one winter with a trapper, working the mountain streams. A job he quickly knew was not to his liking. It was cold, hard, and lonely work. Heading west, he did some cowboy work, driving cattle, roping, branding, fixing fence and doing odd jobs. It did not take long to decide this was not his calling. Working his way east, he started working on a steamboat plying the Mighty Mississippi River. Starting as a mate, he soon worked his way up to co-pilot. In a few months, he was made Captain of his own boat the Misslisa Queen.

As captain of the Misslisa Queen, he had the position, the prestige, and enough money to enter him into the elite of society. Fancy diners, lavish parties, and gambling become his days and nights activities. Although he was a good ship's Captain, he found his true calling as a gambler. Cards soon became his new passion. Within a few short months, he amassed enough wealth to leave the river and spend a life of leisure, playing cards. No matter where it was, if the word of a high stakes poker game was in the air, Polar Pederson would be there.

Normal haunts for Polar were still the riverboats and the towns along the Mississippi. At times, he worked his way all the way up to Minneapolis, Minnesota. From there he would take a train into the Dakotas to see his family. Although his Father and Mother did not approve of his life style, he was still welcomed home. A family picnic of lutefisk, lefse, komla, and fried bread would be served the day before Polar would leave. Polar never left home without leaving a thousand dollars on the kitchen table. As a son and a man, he was loving and generous.

Trains were now starting to run on a regular schedule. Leaving the Dakotas, Polar would spend a day or two in Minneapolis gambling. Usually there was not much money to be made gambling with tight-fisted old world farmers, he liked the people and the honesty, but the cash was scarce.

Chicago was always a great place to pick up cash. The gambling was rampant and went on twenty-four hours a day. After Chicago, it was over to Boston, a conservative town in many ways. For Polar, who knew where to go there was lots of old money to be won from the wealthy aristocratic type Americans there. The young gentry of the old world families had the cash and were easy marks for a professional gambler. A week or maybe two and Polar was on his way, it was never safe to stay to long in one place.

Charleston was known to have lots of old world cash, plus the new found wealth of perceptive businessmen. Plantation owners, shipping magnets, a booming town. This would be Polar's first trip to South Carolina, hopefully it would be profitable. He had the names of important contacts from his friends is Boston. Time to make some cash and maybe spend some time relaxing with some southern hospitality. It just so happened that a large party was being held at the Jack Payne plantation. The rumor was that after the festivities a high stakes poker game was planned. Buy in was twenty-thousand dollars. Polar happened to be in a waterfront saloon playing poker. One of the players was the son of a wealthy shipping magnet. That son just happened to be holding an invitation to the Jack Payne party. By the time the game ended the shipping magnets son had lost all his cash and his invitation. Polar being a good sport bought the kid a drink and tossed him a hundred dollars on the way out.

Donning his best evening clothes, a long tailed black suit coat, robin's egg blue ruffled silk shirt and black beaver top hat, he hired a carriage to take him to the Payne Plantation. This was Polar's first trip to Charleston and the plantations were elaborate affairs compared to the farms he was used to. As the carriage was winding through the overhanging cypress trees, draped in silver strands of Spanish moss, he noticed a number of small wooden structures. There seemed to be a lot of colored folk hanging around those buildings. Polar questioned the driver about what the shacks were used for.

The driver answered. "Well, sir, thems the slave quarters. Ma'ser Payne he got over a hundred slaves just for the fields, 'dars even more if ya count da ones on the housekeeping staff. T'aint you never seen slave houses 'fore?"

Polar was still looking at the primitive conditions these folks were living in. A lump caught in his throat as he gave an answer. "I have spent very little time in the south. I of course know about slaves. This is my first experience to see how they live." What Polar said and what he thought were two different things. The conditions appalled him. Just for that, he would take this Master Payne and his southern friends for all he could get. There would be no mercy in this poker game.

Walking up the steps and looking in wonderment at the huge pillars that supported the roof, polar could only imagine how much money must be available for him to win tonight. The interior of the ballroom was two stories high, done in exotic woods, a huge crystal chandler hung from the center of the ceiling. Two hand carved wooden staircases wound their way to the upper floors along each of the walls. A fireplace on each side of the ballroom flickered its heat among the chilling night that awaited the guest when they left.

The butler announced Polar to the other guests. A gruff looking gentleman and very beautiful elderly lady approached. Their daughter followed them at a socially acceptable distance. The man held out his hand to Polar and said; "Welcome friend, I am your host Jack Payne; this is my lovely wife and my daughter Lotta. I do not believe we have met before."

"Mr. Payne it is a pleasure to meet you, my name is Captain Polar Pederson." They shook hands; Polar felt that under the circumstances it was wise to use his old steamboat title of captain. Then he took the hand of Mrs. Payne and lightly kissed it.

"This is your beautiful daughter Lotta I assume; it is a pleasure to meet you. Would you be so kind as to honor me with a dance during the evening?"

"Mr. Payne, you are so kind." Said Lotta "I would be honored to have you escort me to the dance floor."

Polar mingled with the crowd, checking out the big money players that would convene for the evening poker game. He wanted to watch their movements now. It was always good to study ones opponents before the game. Pick out the little quirks and idiosyncrasies, the things that would help him later to determine what kind of cards they might be holding.

Except one thing was bothering him. Lotta Payne. She was not a ravishing beauty, but she held a distinct fascination for Polar. When he should be studying his opponents, he found himself looking at Lotta. Dancing with her only made matters worse. The touch of her hand, his arm around her waist, he liked the feeling. He always had stayed shy of women, ever since the last two hussies' had lead him on only to take his money and disappear from his life. His rule with gamblers and women, in that game the gambler always loses.

The ball continued as a select group of men went to Jack Payne's private study. Polar was one of those men. The table was set up and ready. A colored servant kept the drinks full and the cigars lit. There was seven players plus the dealer. The game started out slow and easy, no big dollar bets hitting the table. Polar was up and down in winning. His mind kept wandering back to Lotta Payne. He really wanted to see her again. Polar never left a game early, he always played it to the end, win or lose. Right now, he was down fifteen-thousand dollars. He folded his hand, and excused himself.

"Gentleman, I am afraid my mind is just not on the game tonight. It was a pleasure meeting you all. Mr. Payne thank you for a wonderful evening. I hope we see each other again, real soon."

Polar returned to the ballroom, things were winding down; most the guests had left for the evening. Lotta was at the door, saying goodnight to a few remaining stragglers. Polar waited, the last to leave. He approached Lotta as she smiled.

"Miss Payne, I hardly know you, I hope you do not think me being to forward. I would consider it an honor if you would allow me to escort you to dinner in Charleston tomorrow evening. Shall we say five o'clock?"

It caught Lotta by surprise. Many men had approached her. She found none of them attractive. She was brought up to believe men wanted only one thing from her. The family's prestige and money. Something about Polar was different. He was not extremely handsome; he was plain, somewhat good looking. Yet, there was something about him that she found interesting.

"Why yes, Mr. Pederson I would be honored. Five o'clock it shall be."

Polar bowed and kissed Lotta's hand. The same carriage that brought him was there to return him to the city. As the bumped along the dirt road towards Charleston Polar asked the driver. "The Payne family, have you worked for them long? What are they like? What can you tell me about the daughter, Lotta?"

"Well sir, I been with the Payne's 'nigh on fifteen years. They treat most of us coloreds pretty well. The Mister he is harsh but fair 'nough I guess. Always keeps food in our mouths and wood to keep our cabins warm. Now Mrs. Payne, just 'tween you and I, she has a might appropriate name. Payne is what she likes to inflict on anyone that does not meet with her approval. Most of us do our best to stay 'way from her. Lotta, she nice 'nough. Had a few suitors, the ma'ser usually puts a quick stop to that. Figure's theys all after his money. Lotta she treats us all right but she can be contrary like her ma, her ma was a gypsy so they say, fiery temper in that woman. Now ma'sah he's as tight as a sows belly 'fore birth. Poor Lotta has a little of both in her, a good man might be what she needs to gain some trust in human folks. Ya all thinkin' along them lines Mr. Polar?

"Maybe I am. I find her mighty attractive. She has a way about her; I am not sure what it is. Nevertheless, I like her. I do not have much trust in women; you know the past has not been to kind to me. Tomorrow though I think I will give Miss Lotta a chance to see if she is what I think she is. Anyway, I just spent fifteen-thousand dollars for a chance to ask her for supper."

"Ma'sah that's a might 'spensive dinner you asked Miss Lotta to. Good luck."

CHAPTER 3

Supper went very well. Lotta gave Polar a tour of the city. They passed the old jail and courthouse. Pirates had actually been prisoners in the basement of that old building she explained to Polar. Just imagine real pirates. Then along the battery and rainbow row. Stately homes of sea captains with widow's walks where a woman could watch for her husband's ship to return. The harbor filled with sailing vessels, docks so crowded with goods it was hard to maneuver the carriage through the area. One day they visited the slave auctions. Polar could not help but comment.

"This is not right. Humans being sold to other humans as slaves. Lotta, I know your father owns a plantation, he has slaves, but is it right in your mind?"

"Polar, I grew up here; this is a way of life for the south. You have heard the talk. Mr. Lincoln, he would try to stop this way of life for us. Without the slaves, the south as we know it would crumble. All our traditions, our livelihood, they would disappear. Polar you come from the north, your lad is rich and fertile. Here it takes so much land and so much labor to produce so little. It has to remain like this."

This was a subject Polar avoided from that day on. He was falling in love with Lotta. He believed she was in love with him also. Two different lives, two different worlds, could it ever work.

Mr. Payne had taken it upon himself to start raising money for the south. Union soldiers started to dot the area in and around Charleston. The visits with Lotta were becoming strained. She could only see that her life style must not change. Her family, the plantation, the style of life, it depended on the south not changing.

Somehow, the love they shared stayed alive. Polar a man of high moral standards was about to make an error that he would regret until the day he died. The error was not that he proposed marriage to Lotta; the error was what happened afterwards. Lotta's father was not happy with the proposed union of marriage between his daughter and Polar. Although he accepted it as a fact. Then he felt he may even profit from it, Polar was a wealthy man, and his money could help the southern cause. How could Polar refuse to loan money to the south when he would be married into it?

A large party was planned. The engagement was formally announced. The food and drinks seemed endless. The talk was of war with the north. Polar felt as if he was alone in a room full of southern sympathizers, and he probably was. He drank way too much, kept his mouth shut. Lotta took him upstairs to sleep off the liquor. Then it happened. Polar a man of an iron constitution on the sins of sex before marriage. The marriage only a few weeks away. The combination of the Polar, the liquor, passion and his beautiful Lotta was too much. Lotta too, was filled with drink, she slowly undressed, and Polar could do nothing but watch in wonder. She was so beautiful, and soon to be his wife. He wanted to give her everything. The night was beautiful, she was warm and loving, and she felt like an angel in his arms, he loved her with all his heart. During the night, she had returned to her room. Polar awoke guilt ridden in the morning. Loving her more deeply than ever, but feeling his religious roots, all he could do was pray for forgiveness. Maybe with the marriage vows and the wedding so close he would be forgiven by the Lord.

They shared breakfast in the morning. Polar was running short of cash. He wanted to plan a European honeymoon. That would take money and lots of it. He had become too well know in Charleston to get into any high stakes big money games. The best bet was a short trip to Boston. In five or six days, he should be able to raise plenty of cash. The clouds of war were hanging heavily over the nation. In two weeks, Lotta and he would be married, off to Europe. War was not in the plans for Polar, the farther away he could take his wife the better.

As he boarded a train for Boston, he could see the soldier's presence had greatly increased in the last few weeks. The Union troops at Fort Sumter were no longer leaving their little island. Some of the south's cannons had actually been placed facing Fort Sumter. Lotta saw Polar off at the train station. It was April eight 1861.

The trip to Boston was not as pleasant as his trips in the past had been. The train was crowded with troops. Everyone talked of war, President Lincoln, slaves, and succession of the southern states. Polar had tried to stay out of the conflict as best he could. Yes, he was anti-slavery, yet he was in love with a woman who stood for many things that Polar disagreed with. He was blinded by this love. Only Lotta meant anything to him. Getting her out of the country would keep her safe. Let the fanatics fight their war. Polar's home was in the Dakotas, why would they ever get involved in a conflict like this. If the war lasted to long, well Polar liked it out west. Lotta and he could build a business out west. He could quit gambling, settle down, and have some children. Live a good life with his Lotta. They could open a store, or a hotel. Nice quiet little town. Not like the big cities. If only Lotta would go along with it. Whatever happened, Polar knew if he had Lotta in his life it would work out well.

Boston was not as Polar had left it. The city was crowded with union soldiers. The high roller poker players were investing their extra money in war industry. Munitions, uniforms, transportation, and food were good investments. Any item that had a government contract was sure to make money for greedy warmongers. Of course, the investors would be sitting in their lavish homes keeping an eye on their investments. The young and the poor would do the fighting.

This forced Polar to do most of his gambling at the water front saloons. Sailors just off the long voyages had money to spend. Many of the soldiers had bonus money from the army for signing up. One nice thing about saloons, drinking, and money were poor combinations when you went up against a professional gambler like Polar. He knew to keep the drinking light, just enough to be sociable, for him gambling was a business. However, he hated taking too much money from hard working people like those that frequented the waterfront. Nevertheless, the talk of war forced him to make money where it was available.

He walked the waterfront until he came to a bustling establishment. Looking into the windows, he could see at least a dozen poker games in progress. He picked the game with the most money lying about. For the next thirty minutes, he studied the players. When one of the players dropped out, Polar made his move. He entered the doors of the Dogs Breath Tavern. The smell of liquor and cloud of tobacco smoke quickly permeated his clothes and his nostrils. It was a smell gamblers had to accept as part of the job. He had purposely dressed in shabby workman's clothes. He approached the open chair of the poker table and asked rather gruffly to keep in character, if they could use another player. His invitation was accepted by all at the table.

For the first hour, he purposely lost enough money to build up the confidence of the other players. The talk around him and at his table was disconcerting. Everyone was talking only of the upcoming war between the North and South. They made it sound as if it was a sure thing. The combination of southern slavery, Mr. Lincoln as the new president and succession of the Southern states sounded to be like a time bomb ready to explode at any minute.

Being on the waterfront many of the men were sailors or dockworkers. Some were ready to volunteer just for the adventure, others thought of volunteering for the extra cash bonus that was offered, better to volunteer then to be conscripted. The need for men was so great and the politics so crooked that one subject often reared its ugly head. Organized groups of men would Shanghai unsuspecting individuals; the ruse was to let them exit a saloon, while they were drunk a well placed black jack to the back of the neck would make them very cooperative. This band of marauders would then load their victims into a waiting wagon and take them to a cohort who would be singing up army recruits. They would use the identification found on the victim's person for the sign up information. The group of ruffians was then paid ten dollars per 'volunteer' that they had delivered. When the victim finally awoke, he would find himself signed up to serve in one of the many army camps set up around Boston. Desertion was punishable by firing squad.

Polar had to admit Boston, and probably the United States was heading for disaster. The faster he could make some money and get out of the country the better. If worse came to worse Lotta and he could always head west, away from the war.

It was two in the morning as the poker game ended. April 11th, 1861 was the date on the calendar. Polar was up about three thousand dollars. It was a long way from his goal of one-hundred thousand. It was too dangerous to stay in Boston long. He decided to build his grubstake to twenty-thousand; there would naturally be card games in Europe that could sustain them once they got there. As he left the Dogs Breath Tavern, his thoughts now returned to his waiting Lotta. Then everything went black.

CHAPTER 4

The day for the wedding had come and gone. Lotta had not heard anything from Polar. War Between the States had been declared on April 12, 1861. The war started right in Lotta's hometown with the Confederate army firing the first shots at Fort Sumter in Charleston bay.

It had been a month since Lotta's wedding was to have taken place. She wall ill most of the time, refusing to eat, not leaving her bed. Her mother put it off as heartbreak. After four months, her illness was confirmed. Heartbreak? Yes. Pregnant, also yes. She kept in her room, no visitors, no contact with anyone. Only her mother, father, and doctor were aware of the pregnancy. Twin girls were born. They came with Lotta's screams of pain in the night. The first a red haired tiny bundle, soft, gentle, barely a sound in her tiny cry. Two more hours of misery for Lotta. The pain was unbearable, at midnight the child was born. Jet-black hair, already two inches long, and a voice that would startle a banshee. Both little girls were strong and healthy. Their mother had passed out. She would sleep for the next two days.

Lotta's parent's orders were strict. No compromise. The babies must go. Lotta had two choices. Her father would quietly do away with the babies, or they could be taken to the orphanage in Charleston. Lotta knew that keeping the children would only break her heart every time she looked at them. Especially the little redhead, the baby who so resembled its father Polar Pederson. The other child, its black hair, and an attitude of life that seemed to say 'here I am, nothing will stop me.' She was the spitting image of her mother. Lotta kept the babies for eight weeks, until

they were strong enough to make the trip to Charleston. S Cassie and Alvira.

In her mind, she hated Polar for abandoning her; in her not always so sure. What if he were dead? Still if he was fo to get himself killed, it was the same as abandonment in he had resigned herself that the babies must go. Although a pang in her heart let her make a small concession of a mother's love. given her a set of earring as an engagement gift. They hon heritage of both of their families. The Earrings were custom silver in the shape of a Bohemian Cossack on his horse, his lon flowing out behind him. Engraved on the back of the flowing jac a small Viking ship. Lotta's Bohemia and Polar's Norway united together forever. The night before she was to take the babies t orphanage Lotta looked closely at the earrings. By morning, she fashioned the earrings into two necklaces. One for each of the ba She would leave a note to the adopting families that these necklaces w to stay with the children forever. . She sealed the envelopes with the w seal of her family. They were to be opened on each of the children thirteen birthdays.

It was kept confidential the whole time. The doctor arrived early in the morning; he and Lotta's father accompanied her to the Charleston orphanage. The doctor had already made all the arrangements. The orphanage was told the parents of the little redhead; Cassie had died during a Yankee raid on their farm. Lotta filled in the babies name as Cassie P. Pederson. The raven-haired little girl had come from a distant cousin whose mother had died at childbirth; the Payne's did not want to keep her. With the south at war and so much to do, a baby was not welcome on the Payne Plantation. She was registered at the orphanage under the name of Alvira M. Payne. Lotta managed to separate herself from her father and the doctor to make a request of the lady who registered the babies into the orphanage. The request was that Lotta be given the names and addresses of the people who adopted Cassie and Alvira and that they are allowed to keep their given names of Cassie P Pederson and Alvira M. Payne. Lotta used the excuse that she only wanted the best for the babies and would like to be able to check up on

m occasionally to make sure they were leading good lives and get a ɔgress report on them. The lady felt Lotta was very compassionate and ve her promise to honor Lotta's request. Lotta then handed the two ax sealed envelopes to the woman; she gave strict instructions that ıese were to be given to the adopting parents.

The happenings of the last year, the disappearance of Polar, the ›regnancy, the forfeiture of her babies, and the war. This combination lestroyed any semblance of feelings, compassion, or love that Lotta ever had. Her heart was officially dead.

Charleston was a major hub for the Confederate army's supplies. Blockade-runners were still getting ships into port. The railroad was handling freight at breakneck speeds. As the war progressed, Charleston also become the staging place for the sick and wounded. Besides the regular hospital now run by the army, tent hospitals sprang up to handle the overflow.

Jack Payne spent most of his waking hours at his office located by the shipyards. His priority was to keep the south supplied with needed materials, and his ships were hauling it in as fast as the Yankee blockade would allow.

Lotta and her mother were volunteering to help at the tent hospitals. Medicine was in short supply. Morphine almost non-existent. The combination of a father who was hard and cold in his dealings and a mother who was quick to anger and even quicker to mead out her own justice finally boiled into Lotta's blood. Add the hurt and rejection of what she felt Polar had done to her and it was a lethal combination.

She tended the wounded, the sick, and the dying. Men would beg to be out put out of their misery. Some of these men were dying slow painful deaths; others were missing limbs and body parts and did not want their burdens carried onto their families. Doctor's would refuse to listen; the Hippocratic Oath came in to play. Therefore, the men suffered, some to survive others to die. A few who would later wish they had died.

Lotta had not taken a Hippocratic Oath. In her mind, she would play God. She would decide who lived and who dies. She soon figured out that by using your thumb and forefinger on just the right areas of a person's throat she could apply enough pressure that the person would quickly

stop breathing. The misery and pain for the person was over. Some of her victims asked to die, some did not, and she was judge and jury. In the next three years, her toll of victims was in the hundreds. She had hardened her heart to stone. No remorse, no question of right or wrong, she controlled the destinies of countless soldiers and their families. The doctors and staff suspected something was wrong; the death rate on her shifts was always higher than any other shift. No one took the time or had the time to investigate. Behind her back, they had a name for her. Lotta M. Payne, the M. stands for Murderous. Thus, she was known in the inner circle of the tent hospital at Lotta Murderous Payne.

For some time the Payne family all lived together in Mr. Payne's office on the waterfront. The outskirts of town had become a battlefield. The plantation lay dormant. The slaves who had not run away were conscripted by the Rebel Army to do war work behind the lines. The Union blockade of the harbor and disrupted railroad lines had left the city cut off from incoming supplies. The city was slowly starving. Even the few who still had any money left found that it was useless. There was nothing to buy. Groups of renegade soldiers and civilians alike were looting, steeling and even killing just for food.

February first, 1865. Lotta and her mother left the family office on the waterfront and headed to one of the many tent hospitals to help with the wounded. Mr. Payne stayed behind, he was broken, and in poor health, his business shattered, his health deteriorating from lack of food. As for the plantation, no one knew if it was still standing or not. The city was falling to the onslaught of the Yankees.

Lotta and her mother approached her father's office shortly after six pm. They were tired and blood stained. Lotta had hidden some bread in her skirt for her father, at least working at the tent hospitals provide meager rations for the volunteers and the staff. The door of the shop was wide open, a very unusual thing. Her father lay on the floor in a puddle of blood. It was obvious that he had been bayoneted in the stomach at least twice. Near the small cache of food they had hidden, they could tell their father had fallen. With a stomach wound, he would live for a short while, then bleed to death and die. He had crawled about ten feet to the front door. Even if a passerby had stopped to help, it would have been too late to save him. The food was gone and the office ransacked. Bayonet wounds meant that Rebel soldiers had done the killing and the looting.

Lotta's mother grabbed a large knife that was left on one of the office shelves. She ran into the street and plunged the knife into the back of a passing soldier. The soldier's companion turned in shock as she lunged at him and drove the knife into his chest. She raised the knife into the air, blood dripping down her arm and onto her clothes as she looked for her next victim. Lotta saw her mother's body give three quick jerks, before she heard the report of the gunfire. The three soldiers who fired the shots came over to make sure she was dead. They carried her body to the sidewalk and left it lay. Lotta looked at them and pointed to her father's body. The soldiers picked up her father and placed him next to her mother. Lotta was told to leave the bodies on the sidewalk, once a day a wagon came around to pick up the dead.

Lotta walked the streets until she found an abandoned fruit sellers push cart. It had large wheels, a flat bed, and two handles similar to a wheelbarrow to push it. She warped her hand around the handles lifted the rear of the cart into the air and headed back to her father's office. Some soldiers helped her load her parent's body onto the cart. She then pushed the cart along the rough cobblestone streets towards the family plantation. Exhausted, weak, tears running down her dirty cheeks, her hands bloody and callused she took three days to reach the plantation.

She lowered the cart handles down. Leaving her parents bodies alone for the first time since they left the city. She looked at the mansion that had been her home. The walls still stood, scared and blackened by fire. The roof and all the floors had caved in, the fire and heat had burned up most of the derbies, nothing worth saving was left.

The cart was left where it was next to one of the slaves cabins. Even the majority of the slave cabins had been burned. She only counted three still standing; the others were just black spots of charred wood lying on the ground. She checked all three cabins; nothing was left in any of them. Therefore, she entered the cabin closest to her parents. She went to the corner and curled herself into a ball. Then she finally slept.

When Lotta awoke the sky was grey, a light mist floated in the air. She thought of how the weather matched the fortunes of the south. Grey and downcast. She was not sure how long she had slept. Time no longer existed, the day, the month, the year, it no longer mattered. She pushed the cart with the bodies of her parents to the top of a small hill. A large willow tree would protect the graves from the heat of the summer. Her father and mother would like the view. The hill overlooked the river that flowed past the front of the plantation. The plantation itself now in ruins was also visible. She spent most of the day digging the graves. The bodies were lowered into the earth, the only coverings were the old gray army blankets that her parents were wrapped in. She piled stones as a maker at the head of each grave. Two pieces of slate stone were found on one of the garden footpaths. She scratched her parent's names and the dates of their births and deaths on the slate. On the very bottom of each piece of slate, she carved these words "Killed by Rebels."

Next, she worked her way through the ruble of the plantation that had been her home. At the base of one of the chimneys she got down on her knees and removed the little bit of rubble that remained after the fire. Her fingertips becoming raw and bloody she dug them into the loose stone at the base of the fireplace. Finally, it came loose. Pulling the stone away, she reached inside the secret hiding place and pulled out a wooden box. The edge of the box was charred from the immense heat that had been produced during the fire. Opening the box, the contents were still intact. The only items that they had bothered to hide before they left the house and moved to her father's office. Her mothers and her own jewelry, worth at least ten thousand dollars, and five thousand dollars in pre war-currency. She was thankful that they had kept Yankee currency and not Confederate money.

She tore the hem of her dress open with a rusty nail; she sewed the jewels and all but two hundred dollars of the cash into the hem of her dress. One thing Polar had told her came back into her mind. If you want to start over head west. A few miles down the road she came to a sharecropper's farm, he had two horses in the corral. She offered to buy one for twenty dollars. The sharecropper only laughed at her and said. "Lady there's more than twenty dollars worth of meat on that horse; it will feed my family for a month." She finally struck a deal for one hundred dollars for the horse, a well-worn saddle, five potatoes and some hardtack. She learned from the farmer that the date was February twelve; the war had been over for three days. The South had lost. Lotta swung herself up and into the saddle. Then she headed west.

CHAPTER 5

Polar was having one of those terrible nightmares. He was running, trying to return to Charleston for his wedding. No matter how fast or how far he ran he just could not make it to the wedding on time. Then he awoke, the sun was filtering through the window. Everything around him was white, the ceiling, the walls, the floor, even his bedding. Looking to the side, he could see rows of beds, all occupied by men he did not know. Trying to sit up, his head felt like it had been hit with a sledgehammer; he fell back onto the bed. Moments later a nurse was by his side. She was feeling his forehead for a temperature when she began talking.

"Good morning Rip Van Winkle. We were wondering if you would ever wake up. You have a nasty bump on your head, probably a mild concussion. Another day in bed and you should be up and around and ready to join your unit"

"Join my unit? What unit? Where am I? What day is this? What happened to me? Asked Polar.

The doctor had now joined the discussion.

"Let me see, ah yes, Mr. Polar Pederson, enlisted on April twelve. It says here your recruiting officer had you admitted to the hospital after you slipped and fell. Seems you and your friend were celebrating and had a little too much to drink. Nasty bump on the head you have there. I will sign your release from the hospital for tomorrow morning. Someone from your unit will be here to escort you back. Most the units are pulling out with-in the week."

"Wait a minute, I never enlisted. Someone hit me on the head. I was shanghaied. There is no way I am going in the army. Get me someone in charge. I'm getting married in two weeks!"

The doctor motioned to an army officer that was standing in the corridor. The officer had a brief discussion with the doctor before approaching Polar's bed.

"I'm Captain Griffith United State Army. I just spoke with your doctor soldier. I looked at your enlistment papers and everything is in order. You try to leave here or leave your assigned unit and you will be considered a deserter. We shoot deserters. You best serve your time and forget all this nonsense. It is too late to change your mind now. You are in the army boy."

The nurse informed Polar that the date was April fourteen. Polar had been unconscious for three days. America had already been at war for two days. Polar had the nurse bring him some stationary and a pen. He scribbled the words as best he could, his throbbing head, lying on his back and his hand shaking from anger made it hard to write.

My dear Lotta: 04-14-65

The most terrible thing has happened. I have been shanghaied into the service of the Union Army. If I try to leave, they will shoot me as a deserter. I will do my best to remedy the situation and return to you as soon as possible.

Love, Polar

The nurse gave her word to Polar that she would Post the letter for him. She also informed him that it was doubtful it would reach its destination. Nothing was moving from north to south anymore. Any letters had to be reviewed by a board of censors. If they felt it was giving information or may be in code the letter would be destroyed. This was the only choice Polar had, he hoped Lotta would understand.

Polar was escorted to his unit the next morning. A meeting with his superiors accomplished nothing. The army needed men, and they were not too particular about how they got them. The meeting with the captain of Polar's unit did yield one benefit. When the captain asked about experience, he seemed to be impressed with Polar's title of captain from his steamboat days. An instant promotion was granted. He was now Sergeant Polar Pederson. He figured if he was going to be stuck in the army for a while, the least he could do was to work his way up in rank. It would mean more money for Lotta and him. Maybe he would even have a better chance of getting word to Lotta about his whereabouts.

Being sergeant was not a good position as Polar soon found out. There was money to be made gambling in this man's army. A good amount of free time was available. A case of too many men for the jobs that needed to be done. Playing cards was a favorite pastime. The money was not much, but Polar knew he could drastically increase his income if he could get into some of these poker games. One problem stopped him. As a sergeant, he was not to fraternize with the enlisted men. Then again, as a sergeant he was not to fraternize with the officers. Talk about being stuck in a difficult situation, this was it.

It forced Polar in to action. He became the best-damned Sergeant in his company. It paid off. Within two months, he was now Lieutenant Polar Pederson. Now he was playing poker with other officers, some had come from rich families up north. Polar's income increased dramatically.

One other benefit of rank was that he could post letters more often to his darling Lotta. As an officer, the censors were not so strict, and officer's mail had first priority to be checked by the censors and posted. Still the chances of mail crossing the lines of north and south were slim. Slim or not, Polar posted a letter at least once a week. Knowing his Lotta, she would be none too happy about Polar's disappearance, and understanding and forgiveness was not one of her or her family's strong points.

Polar was transferred to what he would consider his home unit on June thirty, 1861. He was now part of the Minnesota Volunteer Infantry, although he never agreed with the volunteer part. One big difference between Lotta and Polar was that Polar was a pacifist at heart. Killing was not in his nature. A test he would have to face in the near future.

July twenty-first 1861 found Polar at the battle of First Bull Run. The Minnesota unit had 460 men killed during that battle. The Confederate army was victorious. Then the Seven Day Battles, Second Bull Run, and Fredericksburg, all Confederate victories. Antietam came next, the

Union army fared better, but the outcome was inconclusive. Then Gettysburg, a blood bath for both sides. Polar's commanding officer fell in battle, and Polar was given a filed commission to the rank of Captain. After Gettysburg Polar's unit was assigned a position in the rear. There were to be no more battles for Polar. Somehow, he had survived the carnage, and he had not had to kill anyone. Not that he did not do his duty, he just happened to be in the right place at the right time. His men respected him, he was a good leader. Although he was haunted by guilt, he survived; many of his men did not. He knew the people of the South, just as he knew the people of the North. To him dying was not winning. Too many had died for the men to stubborn to negotiate a reasonable solution to a problem.

Lieutenant Polar Pederson was to be mustered out of his unit on April fifteen, 1865. The day president Abraham Lincoln was shot and killed. Polar would have to wait five more days until April twentieth for his release. Lincoln's death slowed down most of the Union Army's plans for a few days.

As soon as his papers were approved and he was released from military duty, Polar was at the railway station. Still in a Captains uniform, he was able to secure a place on an overcrowded train heading to Charleston. Charleston was not as he had left it. The city was badly scarred from the effects of battle. Beautiful historic structures, burned, and destroyed. People scavenging for food in the streets. Union soldier's everywhere, proud and haughty in their role as conquerors. Confederate soldiers looking beaten and dejected, no weapons, roaming the streets in tattered uniforms.

He procured a horse from one of the union units and proceeded to the Payne Plantation. Not sure what to expect, in his heart he was hoping for a happy reunion. In his mind, he was prepared for the worse.

The worse was what he found. The plantation in ruins. Surveying the area from atop his horse, he saw the stone markers on the hill. He rode up as fast as his horse could travel. Stopping at the two graves, sweat beading up on his face, his heart felt as if it would burst from his chest. He read the crudely written grave makers. Mr. and Mrs. Payne, killed by Rebels. His body relaxed to the fact that Lotta's grave was not there. A good chance that she was still alive. He mounted his horse and returned to Charleston. Maybe he could find an acquaintances of the Payne's who could help him locate Lotta. One thought disturbed him, why would the Rebel army kill Mr. and Mrs. Payne? Two people who were as grey as the Confederacy that they believed in.

Polar stayed in Charleston for ten days. The few friends he found of the Payne's knew nothing of what had become of Lotta. The fact was none of them even knew the Payne's had been killed. It was the low point in his life when he rode away from Charleston. Lotta was gone, dead, alive he did not know. He had exhausted his resources to find her. It was time for him to admit defeat.

He managed to procure some provisions at the quartermaster's office; an ex-captain still had some respect. He turned his horse to the west and rode away.

CHAPTER 6

Lotta who had been brought up as a lady, with the comforts of the gentility found the travel out in the open a harsh reality to her lifestyle. The last four years of the war had hardened her. Although she had always hoped that the Confederacy would prevail and she could return to her previous lifestyle. Her past was gone, no parents, no home, no Polar. She was determined to survive. Never would she have feelings again. Never would she depend on anyone other than herself.

The territory and the towns become more hostile to her as she continued to travel. She would often arrive in a town, dirty and worn. Her clothes were shabby; she was wind-beaten and tired. Often she had to clean up as best she could in a horse trough. She still had her pride, and she would do whatever she wanted. She no longer had any rules in her life. Soon this was to become evident.

Riding into a small town late one the evening, she was tired and thirsty. The only establishment open was a small saloon. She walked in and sat at a table. About a dozen rough looking men stared at her. The bartender asked what she wanted; she ordered food and a whisky. It was unusual for a woman to come into a saloon in those days. At least unusual for a woman with any repute. The bartender was too tired to argue about her place in society and went to get her meal.

One of the cowboys in the room came to her table. He sat himself down and started to talk.

"So little lady, what brings you into a saloon? Looking for a good man I bet? Well, I'm just what you ordered."

Lotta looked at the filthy thing sitting across from her, a man no, an animal maybe. She was tired, hungry, and in no mode for this. She looked at the man and smiled.

"That is a very impressive knife in your scabbard sir. I like to see a man who knows his weapons. May I have a look at it?"

He was only too happy to hand her his knife, butt first. Looks like he was making head way with this little lady.

She took the knife, nice wood handle, a blade at least eight inches long; she ran her finger on the edge of the blade. It produced a small cut on her finger. The blood dripped onto the table. The cowboy just stared, not sure what to think.

Then Lotta lunged into the air, her hand pushed the cowboy's forehead back and she slit his throat with the knife. Blood was rushing out of the cut and down the cowboy's shirt. She wiped the blade clean on the cowboys shoulder. Then she un-did his gun belt and laid it on the table. Next she checked his pockets and took anything of value. She picked everything up and moved to another table. Before sitting down she tried on the gun belt. It was much too large for her.

She finally spoke to the room full of men who all sat in horrified silence.

"Excuse me? Bartender I have decided to move to another table." She looked at the forty dollars she had taken from the dead men. Then she tossed ten dollars onto the blood-splattered table she had just left. "My friend over there left a mess; I hope the money will help to cover the expense of cleaning it up. You other gentlemen in the room, your friend seems to be sleeping at the moment. If you would, please thank him for buying me my meal."

After eating her beef stew she ordered a beer. The next fifteen minutes she spent carving a new hole in the gun belt so that it would fit her. She stood up and strapped the gun belt around her waist. Then she left the saloon, mounted her horse, and rode away. No one in the room even considered trying to stop her.

Lotta stayed away from towns for the next month. She camped out and kept to herself. She had no destination; it was more of an aimless wandering, away from the world. Sitting by her campfire, she could here horses and riders approaching. They were much too loud to be hiding their approach. Lotta slipped her colt revolver under a blanket on her lap. She cocked the gun and kept her hand wrapped around the handle, just in case. The men tied their horses to some trees next to her horse. Walking up to her campfire the larger of two men spoke.

"Howdy there little lady. Mind if we sit a spell, that coffee smells mighty good. I see ya got only one horse tied up over yonder. All by yourself, no men folk riding with you?"

"My man is out hunting game, he should be back any time now. You can help yourself to some coffee. However, my husband is very jealous, very fast with a gun. After your coffee I would suggest you ride on."

The smaller of the men now started speaking.

'Ya know ma'm, we was looking at your tracks, been following you a good half day now. I think you might just be lyin' 'bout your having any men folk around. Your kinda skinny, but ya ain't bad lookin'. I think maybe me and my partner here might just have to warm you up a little bit."

Both the men were sitting on a log just opposite of Lotta. The larger of the two started to get up. Lotta pulled the colt from under the blanket. The first shot knocked the smaller man off the log and on his back. Her second shot hit the taller, his hand grasped at the burning hole in his chest. He staggered forward and dropped face down onto the ground. Lotta sat looking at the two men. She picked up her coffee cup and slowly finished drinking her remaining coffee. She thought to herself, why should I let these to hombres ruin a nice warm cup of coffee. After she was done with her drink, she walked over to the two men and stripped them of their valuables. The taller man had an almost new Colt 45; she would keep that one for herself. Between the two men, they had almost three-hundred dollars in cash. She left their horses tied where they were. Not a bad night's work.

Next morning she gathered up all the men's belongings and checked out their saddles and saddlebags. The taller man's red sorrel was a magnificent animal. She liked the color; it was a deep, deep red, almost like blood. The saddle was tooled Mexican leather with a Mexican silver saddle horn. This would be her new horse. She left the men lay where they fell and rode away. The first town she came to she sold the horses and all the saddles to the local stables. She kept a nice Winchester that was in the rifle boot of the horse she was now riding. The rest of the guns she sold to the local general store. Now she had a nice new supply of food and cash to keep wandering for a while. She also had a lot of time to think. She needed some excitement; she liked what had happened last night. To her, men had become animals, something to be eliminated. She did not have to hunt them; it seemed they were hunting her. From this point on, she would be ready. She stayed away from any well-traveled trails and spent her time practicing, with both the Colt 45 and the Winchester. She was even thankful to the last three men she killed, they gave her an abundance of ammunition to practice with.

Finally, she made her way into the next town she came across. She went to the local mercantile and picked out some new clothes. Men's dark blue wool shirts, a man's pair of tan pants, and a brown Stetson cowboy hat, just a few sizes bigger then she needed.

Her next stop was at the shoemakers shop. She had him design her pair of black boots; her initials "LMP" on the sides, one boot had a pocket on the outside to hold a knife. A pair of brown chaps and a brown gun belt with her initials on the holster. Before leaving town she stopped at the local café and ate her fill, it was nice to have food that did not come out of a can. She was starting to be one of those meat and potato girls. Good food that stayed with you.

That night she changed into her new outfit. With the Stetson on her head and her long hair tucked up into the hat, she could pass for a man. She was not what you call well endowed in the areas women like to be, but for what she wanted people to think this was now an asset. The only problem seemed to be the gun belt. Around her waist, it gave the impression of a nicely shaped, very slim woman. An impression she was trying to hide. Wearing her shirt loose and bulky at the waist gave the impression of more weight and a more manly look. She found that wearing the gun belt bandolero style helped to fulfill the look of a man. Here again her small top was an asset, who would have ever thought of that being an asset, it brought a smile to her mouth. She packed her dress and old clothes into her saddlebag. She left her jewels still sewed into the hem of her dress just in case she would need them for cash later.

She was very happy with her proficiency with both the Colt and the Winchester, every day she practiced. The fast draw with the bandolero style gun belt was not so good. Nevertheless, it was fair enough to get her by. Of course getting into a gunfight was something to be avoided at all costs.

She was gaining confidence and today it would come to the forefront. As she rode along a dusty road, a stagecoach was approaching. There was no thinking about it, she just did it. She flagged the coach down. Then she pulled the colt from its holster and told the driver to raise his arms in the air. She had no idea if the coach was carrying anything of value; she just figured that if you were going to be an outlaw, you had to start somewhere. In the deepest manly voice she could muster, she ordered the passenger to get out. There were two men in business suits and an elderly lady in her late sixties.

She told the man with bowler cap on to put his hat on the ground upside down. Then everyone was to put their valuables into the hat. Then she asked the driver about a strong box. He pushed one off the floor from under his feet. As she started to dismount her horse, the driver went for his gun. it surprised her, not that he went for his gun, but at how fast she reacted, her bullet left him slumped over in a heap, blood dripping from his chest. Damn, now what she thought? If I leave witness' they will come looking for me. The three passengers all had their hands in the air; sweat was running down their faces. She shot and killed both the men. The old woman was pleading for her life. Lotta hesitated, she had never killed a women. Then she fired. She got off her horse and looked at the locked strong box. Well, she had read some dime novels about the west when she was younger. She would just shoot the lock off. She stood back aimed and pulled the trigger. Something burned across the side of her forehead. She reached up, she was bleeding. Now she knew what a ricochet was.

The strong box had close to six thousand dollars in cash. She also saw a bundle of mail. Damn that was what she should do. She had saved the address of her daughter. She was in no hurry; if anyone comes along, she would shoot them. She wrote a letter to her daughter, sliced open one of the letters in the strongbox, removed its contents crossed out the address and put the new address on the envelope. She stuffed her letter into the middle of the rest of the mail, and then she gathered up her loot and rode away. It had been a long time, she had written four other letters over the years. Of course, she did not know if her daughter received them, for she never gave them a return address. For Lotta she only acknowledged the one child, which was Alvira. The other she felt belonged to Polar. Cassie and Alvira would be about five years old now.

CHAPTER 7

After the war, a lot of people were heading west. Families looking for new lives. The railroads were opening the territories and land was cheap. Others were looking to get rich. Prospectors, entrepreneurs, cattlemen, bankers, saloon owners, ladies of the evening and yes gamblers.

Polar went back to gambling for a living. He shunned his army clothes, feelings about the war were still strong, a blue or grey uniform was usually an invitation to trouble. He decided to dress as an ordinary cowboy, cloth shirt, leather vest, and brown hat and cloth pants. He wore chaps as needed; there were times the brush on the trails was sharp and devastating. Those trails he did his best to avoid, not just for his own health, but also for his horse. The black horse he procured from the army he had kept. He named him Zorro.

He soon discovered the best poker games were being held in the boomtowns near the mining camps. Miners came down from the mountains and streams, gold nuggets, gold dust, sometimes silver. They had been prospecting and away from civilization far too long. So for most a night on the town was in order. With a bath, new clothes, too much whiskey and a saloon with some ladies of the evening they were ready to celebrate. One thing in the gamblers favor was a lack of female companions. For every one woman in the saloon there might be fifty men. The trick was to lock these miners with pockets bulging with gold to the poker table before one of the women got them first. That was Polar's job. To Polar the women meant nothing, there was only one women, she was gone. In his mind Lotta would be the only one until the day he died.

He spent many years gambling and roaming form town to town. Although it was never like the old days. In the beginning, he gambled because he was good at it and he liked making money and being on his own. After Lotta, then the war, it was different. He was still a good gambler. He missed the fact that he wanted most of all to be a good husband. Now he was alone. He had not been home in years. Every few months he sent his mother and father a few thousand dollars. Maybe it was guilt money.

He stayed out of gunfights and saloon brawls. He had a silver tongue and it saved him many a black eye or worse. He was also generous, drunks and the down and out could always depend on him for a good handout. If his saddlebags had more than twenty thousand, the extra went to the local church, school, or orphanage. He loved kids, and orphanages broke his heart, so they always got a nice donation. Churches, he did not attend, but he was religious, so donations were always generous. Heck, never hurts to give to the lord, to him the domination of the church did not matter, the Lord was boss of them all, and that was all that was important.

For fifteen years Polar never settled in one place for more than six months. Being a loner was a form of punishment for what he had done to Lotta. In his mind, it was what he deserved. Now, one last time he decided to return to Charleston. If Lotta was there, she was most likely married with a bunch of kids. He just felt he had to know. If she was dead, he wanted to know that to. If he still could not locate her, well that was the worst-case scenario. Better she be happy and married then dead. Polar could live with that. He knew he could never expect her to still be thinking about him. It was just something he needed to do for himself.

Polar was still riding his jet-black army horse. Although the horse had started to show some grey in its color, then again Polar was also showing some grey in his hair and beard. He took the horse to the stables and boarded him until his return from Charleston. The stable owner was prepaid and told there would be a bonus if his horse were groomed and supplied with fresh oats every day. For Polar, loyalty, human or animal was on the top of his list. In addition, his horse never failed him, in fact in fifteen years together they had become best friends.

Polar boarded a train for Charleston and headed east. Arriving at the Charleston railroad depot he was happy to see that things looked back to normal. Then again, it had been fifteen years since the war ended. The buildings and streets had regained their southern charm. Along the street, there were carriages for hire. Polar stepped aboard the nearest carriage, the driver was an old colored gentleman. He asked the driver if he knew of the Payne plantation. The driver turned from his seat at looked at Polar. It took a few minutes before the driver answered.

"Mister Polar, is that you?"

Polar answered, "Yes, do I know you?"

"Why the saints be praised, it's me mister Polar, Amos. You knows me; I used to take you and Miss Lotta for buggy rides. I was the ma'sah Payne's driver. Where's you been?" We all thought you was dead."

"Amos, I cannot believe it is you my good man, what are the chances I would find you? I was shanghaied just as the war started. If I had tried to leave the army, they would have shot me as a deserter. I kept writing letters to Lotta, but I do not know if she ever got them. I came here after the war, but I could not find her. I went to the plantation, but all I found was the burned out building and the graves of Mr. and Mrs. Payne."

"Well mister Polar the plantation looks the same. I goes out there now and again just to think about the old days. The carpetbaggers from up north, they got the property for back taxes, stole it they did. The home is still there, just a burned out shell. Ma'sah Payne and his Misses, they left them alone up on the hill. That's all the Payne's own any more, a little hill with their graves."

"Amos, how about Lotta? Do you know where she is or what became of her? The Payne's grave, I saw it when I was here after the war. It said rebels killed them. How could that be?"

"A lot of things has changed since the war mister Polar. I heard many stories about the Payne's. I don't rightly know where to start."

"Amos, can we go somewhere and talk, could I buy you lunch or a drink?"

"Ya know things ain't changed that much, us colored ain't allowed to go into no place that white folk go."

"Ok Amos how about this, take me to a nice restaurant. Drop me off and wait for me to come back. I'll pay the regular fare so your employer does not get mad at you for not making any money."

"Ah Mister Payne, that is one thing that has changed, I own this here horse and carriage. Bought 'em myself after the war. I is a businessman now. Got me a wife, and had three young 'uns. Sent all three off to school, they got schools now just for the coloreds. All my kids is gone off now, one went all the way to Chicago, studying to be a doctor, the other one she's teachin' school now. And my baby she works at the local orphanage, can ya all believe that. We ain't slaves no more."

Polar went in to the restaurant and ordered a large picnic basket full of food, enough for three people, plus wine to drink. It took about an hour before Polar was back in the carriage.

"Amos, take me to your home and let's pick up your wife for a picnic."

"Whatever you says, Mister Polar."

They found a nice grassy field and set up under the shade of a big oak tree. Amos' wife was shy and a little reserved as to why this white man was being so nice to them.

"Amos, tell me everything you know about Lotta and the Payne's. What happened after I left for Boston? Do not let anything out, all the details you can remember, tell them all to me."

"Now you gotta realize a lot of what I heard was just gossip, old women stories and such, but I think most of it is true. After you left, they all figured you just run out on Miss Lotta. Ol' ma'sah Payne he told Lotta you were just no good, some Norwegian trash, not trustworthy. A Bohemian suitor was what she should have had. Then with the war breaking out, well some thought you was dead, killed coming home, you being a Yankee and all. Most the folks, they figured something had happened to you, we all knew'd that you loved Lotta and you was a good man. You know all Ma'sah Payne though, he and his Missus, they poisoned Miss Lotta's mind. Filled her with hate for you. Poor Miss Lotta, with parents like that she finally believed them. Then something strange happened."

"Bout four months after you left, Miss Lotta became ill. Locked her up in her room for almost a year. No one was allowed to see her 'ceptin he ma and pa and a doctor. Even old mammy Rose who brought up Miss Lotta was locked out. 'cept there was no stoppin' old mammy from snoopin' aroun' and listening. Best old mammy could figure it was nine months after you left; terrible screams came from Miss Lotta's room. The doctor was called and spent the next two days in Lotta's room. Old mammy she eavesdropped in on all the goings on. Lotta was having a baby. Old mammy she said she could hear the faint cries of the little one while she listened at the door. Two more hours went by, Lotta was screamin' as if she was trying to wake the dead. A second child was born, and it had lungs like it's mamma's."

'Old mammy she kept her ears open. Ma'sah Payne didn't want no bastard children in his home. They all knew'd you was the papa. The ol' Ma'sah he told Lotta he was gonna kill them chil'ren unless she put 'em up for 'doption. One mornin' that's just what they did, snuck Lotta and the babies away, and only Lotta came back, no babies. Never a word was said about the babies or Miss Lotta. Things went back just as they were. 'ceptin of course the war."

"Ma'sah Payne he moved out of the house and started living' at his office in Charleston. Lotta and the Missus they started having me drive 'em to Charleston everyday where they helped at the tent hospitals. The roads being so crowded with soldiers we often had trouble getting back and forth to the plantation, so Lotta and the Missus they started living with the Ma'sah in his office on the water front."

"'Then some stories 'bout Lotta started going round. They say she was killing soldiers who were too badly wounded or sick to recover. They had a name for her in the back alleys. Instead of Lotta M. Payne, they called her Lotta Murderous Payne. No one every proved she was doing the killin' but a lot of folks believed it. Some say she killed over a hundred men, strangled 'em to death. With so many die'n every day, I don't think the doctors cared, it was just that many less to worry 'bout."

"One day Lotta and the Missus returned to the Ma'sahs office, found him dead on the floor, he'd been stabbed by a rebel bayonet. Looted their place, stole what little food and valuables they had. Well the Missus she went crazy, grabbed her a knife and ran out and killed the first two rebel soldiers she saw. Then some other soldiers, they shot her dead. Told

Lotta they would pick up the bodies latter and dispose of them. Lotta, she wanted her ma and pa to be buried on the plantation where they belonged. She stole herself a little cart and she pushed her Ma and Pa all the way from Charleston back to the plantation. She dug their graves, and scratched out a marker for her ma and pa, she's the one that put the words 'killed by rebels' on them stones. Seemed kind of strange her being such a southern lady and all."

'There weren't nothin' left here for her. The plantation had been burned. The slaves, well the one's that hadn't run off and headed north, they got conscripted by the Confederates to work at labor jobs for the army. Everyone says, the rebels themselves looted and burned the plantation, guess we'll never know for sure."

The last we heard of Lotta she had stopped at a farm near the plantation, bought herself an old horse and some food and rode away. T'aint no one ever heard of her since then."

Polar just sat and contemplated the whole thing. What a hell the Payne's had gone through. His poor Lotta, abandoned and pregnant. Yet, this meant that Polar was a father.

"Amos, the children, do you have any idea which orphanage she took them to? Or any rumors of what happed to them?"

"'Theys only one orphanage in all Charleston. It would have to be that one. Ya all knows my baby girl she works there, maybe she can help us to find out about them babies. A lot of things was destroyed when the Yankees burned out most of the city, but I knows for sure the orphanage was spared. I'll get the carriage and we all can go over there."

They dropped off Amos' wife at their home. She thanked Polar for being so gracious to them. Polar told her he was just happy to meet her and wished her well. Then Amos and Polar rode to the orphanage.

Amos went inside the orphanage to speak with his daughter. He asked her to do what she could about checking on the records of the two children that Lotta had left there. His daughter said she would do what she could, but all records were confidential. She would have some type of an answer in the morning.

"Would ya all like me to take you to a hotel Mister Polar?"

"If it is all the same to you Amos, I would like to have supper at your house. If you think it will be ok with your misses?"

"Why I think she would be plum tickled pink to have ya all for supper Mister Polar."

They arrived at Amos' home and yes Amos' wife was very happy to have company. She apologized for the food, she was not expecting company, pork back, hominy greens, grits, and a fresh apple pie. Polar told her she was a fine cook; he couldn't have found a better meal in all of Charleston.

Amos offered to drive Polar to a hotel as the sun sank onto the west. Then Polar made an unexpected request.

"Amos if it's all the same to you and your misses, I sure would like to stay here overnight, I can bunk out on the couch or the floor."

"Mister Polar, we are flattered that you would even ask. This is still the south ya know. There's people that would hang a colored man like me, they might even hang you if they caught ya all sleeping here."

"Amos the last thing I would want is to put you or your family in danger. It is already getting late, no one knows I'm here, if you want you can paint me black in the morning and we will leave together."

"Mister Polar, you is a funny type of white man. You stay in our spare room where the kids used to sleep. We'll sneak you out in the morning for the sun comes up. We can find you a coat with a hood, ya just remember to keep your head down."

Early the next morning just as Amos said they left the house before sunrise. Amos gave Polar a tour of Charleston. It was nice to see the town was back to normal. A few Confederate flags still flew from many of the buildings. At least the soldiers were all gone. They arrived at the orphanage a little after nine o'clock in the morning.

Amos' daughter said she could not find out anything on her own. The office with the records was locked up shortly after Amos and Polar left. She did however talk to the orphanage administrator and she agreed to have a meeting with Mister Polar and Amos as soon as they arrived.

At least they had a foot in the door. Polar explained to the administrator why they were there.

"I sure hope you can help me with my problem. Twenty years ago I was a young a foolish man. I made a terrible error in judgment and my fiancée' became pregnant, I understand now that she had two children. I was shanghaied into military service up north two weeks before we were to be wed. For all these years I have never found my fiancée' Miss Lotta Payne. It was only yesterday that I learned of the existence of the children. I was informed that they were brought here and turned over for adoption. I never married, these children are my family, I will do whatever is necessary to see them."

"Mister Payne. I understand your plight. You must realize that adoption records are confidential. I would have to find the records and contact the adopting families before I could ever even consider giving you this information."

"I understand m'am, but the war, losing my future wife, I would have never put my kids up for adoption if I had only known what was happening. Could you see your way clear, just this once to help an old soldier."

"Mr. Payne, just how long ago was this adoption?"

"The best I can figure from the information Mr. Amos here told me it would have been right after I left for Boston. Let me see, that was in April of 1861, add about nine months, should be in late 1861 or maybe January 1862."

"Alright, that is a start, although we are talking about twenty years ago. These are not children anymore, they are adults. Were they girls or boys? What name was given when they were placed here? Or even if you can tell me the first names of the children? Seeing it has been such a long period of time and the extenuating circumstance I will see what I can do for you."

"Amos here, he knew someone inside the plantation. She told him there were two babies. We do not know if they were boys or girls. I am not sure what name Lotta would have given when she brought them here?"

"Lucky for you the records survived the war. They will be in a filing cabinet in the basement, come with me."

The basement, like the rest of the orphanage was not very inviting. It had stone walls, water seeped across the floor. The records for December 1861 and January 1862 were located and placed on a table. The administrator would not even allow Polar or Amos to touch or look at the files.

"Mr. Polar what is your last name?"

"It is Pederson, Polar Pederson."

"Mr. Pederson you are a very lucky man. I have a file here for a month old baby girl. Her name is Cassie Pederson. It says in her file that she was adopted by a couple in Florida. They could not have children of their own. They were financially stable and own an orange orchard. The little girl was adopted six days after she arrived here. A note attached to the file reads. The mother has requested that the baby's name of Cassie Pederson not be changed by the adopting parents. That should be quite a break for you Mr. Pederson. Having been twenty years since the adoption the child is now a legal adult. Here is the last known address of the adopting family. They were required to send a progress report to us every six months. Since the child reached the age of eighteen this was no longer a requirement. That is why the file is in the basement, it is considered a closed case."

"How about the second child. Is there any information on that one?"

"Mr. Pederson I have helped you far beyond what I should have. Let us leave well enough alone."

"Do you think the orphanage could use a thousand dollar donation? I have just such a donation in my pocket if you could maybe let it slip if there was another child, and if it was a girl or boy?"

The administrator looked in the one other file from the same date. Not too hard to figure that out.

"Well Mr. Pederson, you did not hear this from me. There was another girl on the same night at the same time. She does not have the same last name. The two children are listed as having different parents. Although both were brought her by the same women. That is all I can tell you."

Polar thanked her for her help and handed her the thousand dollars in cash. He left her with Amos' address in case she might ever find anything else out.

From that point Polar had Amos take him to the train station. Polar was on the first train to Florida. Arriving at the station in Florida, he hired a carriage to take him to the address he was clutching in his hand. They soon located a small well kept orange orchard. The house was nice, it looked like the folks that owned it were doing well. The last name on the mailbox matched the name of the adopting family.

Polar hesitantly made his way to the front door of the house. His breathing stopped as his hand knocked on the door. The door opened and Polar was finally able to exhale. The woman was older then Polar, must be the mother.

"M'am my name is Polar Pederson. I am not sure if this is the right place. I am looking for a long lost relative of mine. Her name is Cassie. Can you help me?"

The lady smiled and invited Polar to come in and have a seat.

"Just a moment sir, Cassie is out back I'll call her in. Can I get you some fresh orange juice? I just squeezed some this morning, right from our orchard."

"That would be nice ma'm." answered Polar.

Cassie walked into the room. She was about 5' 7" tall. Red hair that bounced off her shoulders. Small and petite like her mother. Although she had Polar's eyes and it was easy to see Polar's features in her face. Cassie's adopted mother had been sitting and visiting with Polar when Cassie entered the room.

"My gosh Mr. polar, Cassie looks like she could be your daughter, you two certainly are related"

Polar stood up, tears running down his check. He walked over to Cassie and gave her a hug, she accepted reluctantly. Finally, Polar was able to speak.

"Cassie Pederson. How do I say this. Ah, let me see, I already asked your mother here, she said you know that you were adopted when you just a baby. Well, I am your father. I never knew you even existed until two days ago. Your mother and I were separated by the war. She gave birth to you and I was never told. The war started and I have never been able to find your mother. I do not even know if she is still alive. You, you certainly are alive, and a beautiful girl."

Cassie answered. "I do not know what to say. Every adopted child hopes they will find their parents. This is my home, here with my mom and, well my dad died a few years ago. I do not even know you. Although it would be nice to have a dad again."

Polar noticed a necklace on his daughter's neck. He stepped closer. "Cassie, your necklace, may I see it?" she held it away from her neck see he could get a good look. He held the little silver Cossack between his fingers. Turning the Cossack over he could see the small Viking ship engraved on the Cossack coat. "Cassie, this necklace, where did you get it?" My mom and dad, you know my mom and dad here, they presented it to me on my thirteenth birthday. They said it was given to them when they adopted me. My real mother had sealed it an envelope and it was held in trust by my adopted parents. All the note said was 'wear it always, love mother.'

"Polar. I mean dad, do you know anything about the necklace?"

"Cassie, I gave your mother a pair of custom made earrings for our engagement. This is one of those earrings. She must have made it into a necklace for you. It certainly leaves no doubt that you are my daughter. I thank God that he let us reunite with each other."

Polar stayed with Cassie and her adopted mother for the next month. He helped with chores and picking fruit. Cassie was attending college. She was working on a degree in business. She wanted to manage a large fancy hotel like they have in the big cities.

Polar realized that he had to let her finish her schooling and get on with her life. He gave the excuse that he had to head back west on business. He neglected to tell them his profession was gambling. He called himself an investment broker. Polar promised to write at least once every two weeks. Once he was settled into one spot, he would send his address. A tearful farewell at the railway station ended their reunion.

Polar had a lot of time to think while riding the rails west. He was to an age where it would be nice to settle down. He had a daughter; maybe he could do something for her. Something a father and daughter could do together. Gambling was not a good idea. A business would be a possibility. The west was still booming. The opportunities were endless. He decided to follow the mining strikes for a few months while he mulled over his choices. Cassie still had one year of school left. He had one year to find something that he hoped would interest her.

CHAPTER 8

Since becoming a 'man,' Lotta found her life to be much simpler. She could enter saloons, ride the trails, and do as she pleased. On those occasions that she wanted to be a women, that was ok too. She bought some feminine clothes, she would get a nice hotel and spend a few days, or weeks at being the female gentry that she was raised to be.

Then she would find that her man hating side would spring back up. Usually do to the attentions of some un-wanted stranger. Most of who were married. If not married, they were poor cowboys or drifters. She needed no one, she had herself.

If cash ran low she would hit the trail, in the few cases she had to speak to someone, she would introduce herself as Larry Parks. It was a good easy to remember name. One thing that worked in her favor was that being two different people, one male and one female it was an asset to her new profession. A woman alone in a nice restaurant was sure to attract a local businessman. Finding out when payrolls were due or gold was being shipped was very easy. A man's aptitude to brag would always cost him if he were with Lotta.

Her current job was casing out a bank in a lumber town along the Mississippi River. The banker was a squirrelly little guy, spectacles, a tiny mustache and wore a bowler hat. He had a crush on Lotta. She stayed in town and had supper with the little banker almost every night. She knew the payroll would be in town on Friday night. Saturday it would be distributed to the lumberjacks. Fourteen thousand dollars in cash.

Using her best southern bell charms, she convinced the banker to show her the money. Why sweet little ol' her had never seen that much cash in her life. It would be such a thrill. She would be so grateful, with an emphasis on 'grateful.' The banker agreed to let her see the money after hours. She was to knock on the back door of the bank at nine pm. Two knocks, then wait and two more knocks.

The knocks came right a time at nine o'clock. The banker opened the door. Larry Parks stepped in. A black kerchief covered his face. In her deepest voice, she asked for the payroll money. The little banker had it laid out nice and neat on a table for his sweet Lotta to see.

Her Larry persona told the banker to turn around and get down on his knees. She grabbed a handful of his hair, pulled his head back, and slit his throat. Gathering up the money, she moved on to new business.

Banks became a good business for her. Sometimes even a local store or rich rancher traveling with a bag of cash would get her attention. Now it was getting dangerous. Larry Parks had a safe record. Never a witness left alive and as Larry, she did not commit to many crimes. However, the lady Lotta, there she made an error. There was never any witness', they were all dead. Although she was rumored to be suspect in many of the cases.

For fifteen years, she roamed the west. Even she did not know how many men she killed. It was not important anyway. She had spread her cash around into at least two dozen banks. Her net value was somewhere in the two-hundred thousand range. It was time for a vacation. In fact, maybe it was time to see if she could find Alvira.

She boarded a train and headed to Charleston. She had an address that the adoption agency had given her. The people that adopted her were wealthy cotton merchants. The address was on Rainbow Row. An affluent part of town.

Alvira would be in her twenties now. A young woman. Lotta was not even positive if she still lived at that address. For two days, Lotta sat on a bench along the battery watching the house. Finally, a young woman came out. She was beautiful, hair that shone like a black pearl. She had a body men would kill for and a face like her mother, attractive enough to draw a man's attention. Lotta followed her while she did her shopping. She went only to the most expensive stores. Clothes, jewelry, money did not seem to be a concern. She was living well, maybe it was best for Lotta to leave her be.

Then something happened on the way back to Rainbow Row. A carriage pulled up and two policeman approached Alvira. A heated discussion took place; Lotta was too far away to hear what was said. Alvira was handcuffed and taken to the police station.

Lotta never one to be afraid of confrontation entered the police station and inquired about the young lady who was just arrested. She was passing counterfeit money; this was not the first time. The police had been lenient with her the last two times. They felt sorry for her, both her parents were dead; her house was being foreclosed for back taxes. Yet she was still trying to live as she always had. Well, she will be living like before now, said the police sergeant. "Yup, we'll take care of her, she will get three meals a day, free clothes, free place to stay. Although she may not like the part where she gets to pick cotton in leg shackles for ten hours a day."

"How about bail" asked Lotta?

"Lady, this is strike three for this little lady, I don't think the judge is gonna let her out on bail."

"Sergeant you seem like a reasonable man, maybe you could overlook this little incident, say for a thousand dollars in cash."

This certainly got the Sergeants attention.

"Lady, this sounds like a bribe to me. There are two other officers involved in this. They are probably writing up their reports right now."

'Well, sergeant, maybe you could be a dear and talk to those two nice officers, I am sure they could each use a thousand dollars too. It is possible they made a tiny little mistake," she said with all the southern charm she could muster.

"Lady, wait here a minute, I'll have a talk with those two officers, I think you might just be right. Sometimes it is awful hard to tell real money from counterfeit money."

The sergeant was back in less than five minutes. Alvira was standing between the two arresting officers. She was no longer handcuffed.

"I talked to these two nice officers, looking over the evidence it seems we made a grave error. If you would like to give me the papers you have for us we can release the young lady into your custody."

Lotta slipped three thousand dollar from her purse, she cover it wither her silk kerchief as she slid it across the sergeants desk. She held Alvira's arm as they left the building.

Once outside Alvira jerked away. "Who are you ya old bitty, pulling me out like that, what do you want from me."

That Bohemian Gypsy blood was definitely in Alvira's veins. Lotta told Alvira to stand still. She picked up the locket with her fingers from around Alvira's neck. The silver Cossack with the Viking ship on his coat. It was her daughter.

"Listen lady, what do you think you're doing, let go of my necklace. Get away from me, leave me alone."

Lotta held her composure, not an easy thing for her to do. "Alvira Payne. Look at me closely. Do you notice any resemblance?"

Alvira just stood there staring. "What, what am I supposed to notice!"

"Alvira, I am your mother, your birth mother. My name is Lotta Payne. I gave that necklace to the orphanage when I was forced to leave you there. Twenty years ago."

"Please walk with me, we will go back to your house. I'll explain on the way. All I ask is that you listen. After all, I just spent three thousand dollars to talk to you. Twenty years ago I belonged to one of the wealthiest families in Charleston. My father was Jack Payne, plantation owner and shipping magnet. We had it all. I had it all, except love, men to me were shallow creatures living on the bottom of a scum-infested pond. They would court me only for the money and prestige of my family."

"Then I meet Polar. He was kind, gentle, he had his own money. He loved me for me. I was treated like a princess, Polar wanted only one thing for me, which was to make me happy. We became engaged. I seduced Polar two weeks before our wedding. That was when you were conceived. Polar had to go to Boston on business. It never occurred to me that he might not return. I do not know if he ran out on me, or maybe was killed by scoundrels or had a terrible accident. I do not know what happened to him. The war came, then my wedding came and went. I never heard from Polar again. Nine months after he left, you came into my life. Unwanted yes, un-loved, I cannot say for sure. You were a living piece of a past I wanted to forget. My father refused to even consider letting me keep you. In those days, the father ruled the house. There was no choice, either I gave you up for adoption or you would be killed and hidden away, no one would ever know you existed.

"I left Charleston after the war. I roamed the west on my own. Trying my best to bury the past. Men have no place in my life, I hate them all. The only spark of any feeling my heart ever had, is for the daughter I surrender so many years ago. Forgive me if you will. If not I will walk away right now."

"Mother, I guess that is what I should call you. I dreamed as a child that my parents would come for me some day. The people that adopted me, they were good people. Wealthy, gave me everything I wanted. Well, everything except love. They were too busy to love me. I had nannies to take care of me. As I grew older, I felt probably like you did, the men were after what I might someday inherit, they did not love me for who I was. Then my adopted parents died in a train wreck about two years ago. Because I still bore the last name of Payne, the lawyers figured out a way to say I had no legal claim to any of the inheritance. The house has been up for sale ever since then. I am allowed to live there until they sell it. Then I am out on the street."

By this time, Lotta and Alvira had entered the house and were sitting on one of the few shabby pieces of furniture that Alvira had managed to find.

Alvira, about the counterfeit money, why spend it on such expensive things, I was following you since early morning, afraid to talk to you. I saw what you were buying. I don't understand the reasoning."

"Oldest trick in the book, mom, buy it with worthless money and then sell it to one of the pawn shops along the water front."

"Just where did you come up with counterfeit money. My adopted father was not exactly an honest man. During the war, he and some other gentlemen printed up thousands of counterfeit union bills to try and wreck the north's economy. I found a stash of it hidden in my dad's office under a floorboard. You know how snoopy kids are, I just never thought of using it till the damn lawyers bilked me out of my inheritance."

" Honey, I hate to say it, but you are a child after my own heart. I think we will get along just fine."

"Before we do anything I need to find us a place to settle down. I've been out west, but I have no real place to call home. I think a mother and daughter business might just be the thing for us. I have to ask you to be patient. Let me go west and find us a place. I'll leave you with five thousand cash, which should hold you for a few months. If they kick you out of the house find a nice hotel to stay in. I prefer you stay here so I can get in touch with you."

The two of them spent the next week together. They learned a lot about each other. Alvira was as stubborn and cold hearted as her mother. Luckily for both of them they understood each other. They both had no time for men, they both were crooks at heart. As a team, they might just be the most cutthroat operators to hit the west.

The day Lotta left, she flagged down a carriage to take her to the railroad depot. The colored driver kept glancing over his should at her. Finally annoyed she chastised him.

"Driver, why do you keep looking at me. Do you have a problem? If this was still the old south I would whip you for being so forward with a lady of distinction such as myself."

The driver smiled, stopped the buggy, and turned to face his passenger.

"Miss Lotta, it's me Amos. Your daddy's old driver, ya all remembers me don't ya?"

"Amos? You're still alive? I would of thought you would be old and dead by now. Did any other of the slaves get out? I've seen the plantation, there's not much left. I buried my mother and father on the hill there. The war was a terrible thing."

"It's nice to see ya Miss Lotta. I see you still hold to your old southern ways. That's alright, I understand ya all. There's a few of us still 'round from the plantation, but most left and went north looking for work. I was a lucky one, bought me this here carriage, now I works for myself. Where ya been all this time Miss?"

"I left right after I buried my folks. Went west and been living out there ever since. I have a good job, living on my own, I make enough to live in a style I like. I had a daughter Amos. You probably did not know that. I came back here to find her. You just picked me up in front of her house. She is a darling girl twenty years old now. I'm going back out west to find us a place, then I'll send for her and we can settle down together."

"Amos. Did you ever. Well you know."

"Miss Lotta you trying' to ask 'bout mister Polar?"

"Yes."

"Funny you should ask, he was here in Charleston just two days ago. I ran into him just like I run into you. He got in my carriage, and there we were, just like old times."

"Amos. Why was he here? Was he looking for me, did he say why he abandoned me, left me at the altar."

"Ya know miss I wish you could have been here to ask him yourself. I'm not sure what I should tell ya, I guess the truth is the best. Yes, he was looking for you, again. He came right after the war he told me, looked all over for you, found out about your mammy and pappy. Said he asked all the friends he could still find, no one knew what had become of you. Miss Lotta I think you judge him to harshly. He told me when he went to Boston he was trying to raise money, wanted to take you away from here for the war broke out. Told me some one shanghaied him, and forced him into the army. Now I ain't sure what shanghaied means. But he done said once they got him in the army they told him they would shoot him as a deserter if he tried to leave."

"Miss Lotta he said he wrote to you once a week during the whole war. That war though, you all know as well as I do that no mail was crossing the lines from north to south. I really think he still loves you, never got married or nothing he said, just roams around, has no home."

"Amos I would like to believe you, but I just don't know. Amos why don't you tell me your address. Maybe I might write to you sometime. If you see Polar again. Don't tell him you saw me."

"Amos, I'm sorry I snapped at you before, I think you are a good man, you take care of yourself.'

Lotta boarded the train and headed back to the west she had grown so fond of. She would build an empire with her daughter, she was sure of that. Alvira's youth and Lotta's experience, a lethal combination.

CHAPTER 9

Back to what he considered his home territory Polar was feeling good. Since he had lost Lotta, his life had become aimless days and then years of wandering. He had honed his gambling profession so that it was more skill then luck. He was proud that he never cheated in a game. His weapon was reading other people. Their actions, words, movements told Polar all he needed to know. When to fold when to raise, when to pull out. Poker was his forte. Although his system worked in any type of card game that he was involved in.

Now he had a goal. The winning, the money had all been nice, but they never fulfilled his soul. A daughter he had never known, a child of his own, a piece of Lotta back in his life. Polar now had dreams and goals he wanted to fulfill. His life finally had meaning again. A plan was developing in his head. Cassie wanted to be in business for herself. She was smart, energetic and independent. She was looking to the future, women were moving into a man's world, a world of business and finance. To Polar there was no better place to start a new life as a family, Cassie, and he, the new breed of entrepreneurs of the west.

Prospectors, individuals, and large corporations were combing the western mountains and valleys, gold, and silver were big business. Boomtowns, little mining camps that had exploded with wealth were spawning fast growing and profitable towns. Polar was looking for town like that, a place that would grow fast, and produce huge profits right away. Yet it had to be stable enough to survive. The town would need to grow, mining could not be its only source of wealth. New business, manufacturing of goods, a solid base of citizens. These were the criteria for Polar's dream town. The town he wanted to offer Cassie for a home and life, with her father close by, but not a detriment to her life. He wanted to be a perfect dad; after all, he had a lot of time to make up for.

One nice thing about poker games, they were always a great place to gather information. Whatever you wanted to know sooner or later it would come up in conversation. From local town news, national news and everything in between. Polar was listening for news of a boomtown, one that had potential. Something with a possibility for growth and a town that would grow from within its self. Now he was in Deadwood, South Dakota. This was a boomtown that fed on crime and corruption for many years. The town' s sheriff was doing the best he could, but still murders, robbery, and corruption were commonplace. The town was large enough that it might just survive, the mines were rich and doing well. It just was not a place to make a home for his daughter.

Then talk turned to a new rich ore strike. It was located quit a distance south from Deadwood. It was located in the center of a mountain range, some folks said the mountain was in the shape of a quarter moon, but the name depicted the shape of a horn, the mountain was called Devils Horn Mountain. On the south it was more mountains and inhospitable country. To the north and west it was desert, given the name 'Desert of Death.' To the east in the center of the open valley of the mountain was a small establishment known as 'Gravesend.' The area had been prospected for a number of years already. It was harsh land, the mountains were known for freak storms, high winds, and perilous cliffs, and superstition had it, ghosts, ghouls, spirits, maybe even the Devil himself. So many deaths occurred in the area that the first establishment in what is now the town was an undertaker, named Plantem Deeps. If you could put up with the superstition, it would be a good place to settle. The mines were rich and endless, things looked well for a long-term future. Stagecoach and freight lines were already serving the town. The railroad had surveyed the area and tracks were being laid. That was the magic word for Polar, railroad. If the railroad was willing to invest money by laying tracks to the town, there was a future. Next stop would be Gravesend. A three-day ride from Deadwood.

Polar rode in to Gravesend on a nice cool autumn day. It was not what he expected. The area was green and lush; a large forested area separated the town from the base of the mountain. The Desert of Death was not visible from the town, a definite plus. He rode down the main street to the end of the town limits, turned his horse around, and rode back to the saloon.

Businesses were already setting up shop. New structures included Mamma Bunn's Bakery, Dragon's Breath Chinese restaurant, Casey's Mercantile, Dr. Pull dentist and doctor, Miss Valerie's dress shop and a midsized saloon called the Buffalo Chip.

Polar tied his horse to the rail of the saloon and went in to check it out. The wood was fresh cut and a deep aroma of pitch from the pine trees they used filled the room. It was actually a nice smell compared to the smoke and liquor smell of most saloons. A stage occupied one wall; the bar ran the length of another wall. Thirty tables filled the room. The largest buffalo head Polar ever saw hung above the bar. Another wall had a large painting of a running buffalo with a scantily clad lady riding on its back. Ten or fifteen customers loitered about, visiting, playing checkers, and three men playing what looked to be a very low stake poker game.

Polar ordered a beer and asked the poker players if he might join in their game. They gladly accepted him into their group. Two of the men were cowboys just looking for work; the other was a miner just out of the mountains. The game was a two-bit buy in; pots seldom grew to more than two or three dollars. It was relaxing and a good time to visit. The cowboys passed on stories of the news of the surrounding areas. Cattle round-ups before winter had brought them to the area, work should be easy to find. The miner he had come down from Devil's Horn yesterday. Just needed some time around people. Awful lonely in the mountains by yourself he told the group. He had been prospecting on his own for the last two months. Had a fair poke with him, enough to take a few weeks off and relax.

The saloon had a dozen rooms upstairs for rent. Polar signed in on the register and settled in for the night. The bartender told him around eight o'clock they had a floor show and the place started hopping, mostly miners and cowboys. It would be rowdy happenings, so he told Polar he might as well sleep during the day, he would get no sleep at night while the saloon was full of drunken customers.

That evening Polar went downstairs to join the festivities. The room was crowded, a man was on stage reading from Shakespeare. The crowd sat in rapt attention, it was easy to see that entertainment of a serious kind was sadly missing from the west. Polar had been around, this Shakespearian reader was one of the worst he ever heard, then again maybe the readers drunken slurring of the words was more understandable to most of the over inebriated listeners. Polar had found a spot at the crowed bar when the next act took the stage, it was a juggler, and he was actually very good at his trade, Polar tossed two bits up on the stage as did a lot of the other patrons. The only pay the acts get was the donations from the audience. The Shakespeare fellow was most likely living hand to mouth. Then the big entertainment of the night. Two sisters came on stage, one played piano the other sang. The first song was Streets of Laredo, this one left the place in a dead quit, there were even a few teary-eyed ruffians in the crowd. The music picked up and become louder and more boisterous as time went on. For the last number the ladies kicked up their heels and finished their act. Those two little gals took in more cash than many a miner saw in a weeks' worth of work.

One of the ladies approached Polar just as one of the tables was opening up. The two of them took a seat and Polar bought her the customary drink she required to visit with the clientele.

"Howdy ma'm my names Polar.,"

"Well howdy to you too, I'm Ruby, my sister over there she's Renee. You here mining, or just drifting by?"

"Well, actually I'm looking for a place to settle down, maybe open a business. Ruby how long have you been here, do you know much about this little town?"

"I've been her about a month. Must be more than five hundred people in the area. A lot of miners drift in and out of town. A few large ranchers east of here bring the cowboys around. There are even some homesteaders staking claims for farms. The stage comes through regular now, always bringing in new folks. The only thing that seems a little queer is the ghost stories, anyone been around long they have some story to tell, restless spirits, ghosts and such. Ain't seen none myself, I don't want see any either, but I hear tell of 'em. If you want all the juicy stories ya gotta hang out with Plantem the undertaker, he hears everything, and buying him a drink will loosen his tongue faster than a rattlesnakes strike. Maybe you would like to come up and see my room? Nice guy like you, I'd give ya special rate."

"Ruby I appreciate the offer, but no offense I'm the sort of guy that just doesn't do things like that, might say I'm a one woman man, I just have not found her yet. Here's ten dollars, just to show I appreciate your asking."

A spot at a poker game opened up and Polar was quick to fill in for the departing player. He played cautiously, did not want a reputation as a gambler in this town. If he decided to stay, he wanted to start on a clean slate. Polar picked a good table to play at, the players were all local citizens. The Undertaker Plantem Deeps, Casey, owner of the Mercantile, Larry owner of the café, Doc Pull and a man named George. George had just bought the land next to the undertakers; he had plans to build a hotel there. A good group to make acquaintances with.

The poker game was friendly, no high stakes. A few pots hit the one hundred mark, Polar played it easy, and he left the table with a two hundred dollar profit. Casey, Larry, Doc had been in town about three months, just about the time the big gold strikes came in. George was a speculator looking to build a hotel, he had been in town less than two weeks. Plantem had been here for over twenty years. With his shallow eye sockets and cheeks, long bony fingers, well he looked more like one of his customers then the undertaker. He was to be Polar's target for conversation.

"Plantem, you have been here a long time, it must have been a lonely twenty years all by yourself? Whatever possessed you to settle here all alone like that?"

"Actually I was an undertaker before I came west. Like a lot of men, I thought I could make a fortune in the mountains. Strike it rich, retire, and live a good life. There was a large group of men boring a tunnel in the side of one of the cliffs, following a vein of yellow, they were sure there fortune was made. One day the Devil shook his head and the mountain rumbled, thirty men died in the resulting cave in. Some of men came to me to bury the dead. Thirty graves is a lot of work. The surviving minors offered me one hundred dollars a body for burial. Hell, three thousand dollars to take up my old profession. It was more money than I was taking out of the mountain. Word spread fast, every fool that got killed mining, cow punching, gun fighting I got 'em all. Flat price one-hundred dollars a head. A pine box, a hole, a wood maker and an amen. That's what you get for your one hundred dollars."

"Made more money than ninety percent of the other folks around here. Built me a nice little home with a funeral parlor attached. Some of them that died, they had kin wanted fancy little crypts and mausoleums. Charge 'em a thousand dollars for anything fancy like that. There were even a few who showed up that pre-paid their expenses. Never knew where they came from, they just sort of appeared. These fellows would hand me five thousand dollars for a fancy crypt, wanted to be buried above ground they did. I called them the strange ones. Never knew how they died, they would show up on my doorstep, all fancied up and placed in their own coffins. I had their crypts ready and just slid 'em in and locked 'em up. Easiest money I ever made.

As for being lonely, well them fellows in the crypts, I hear them at night. Sometimes they sing, sometimes they talk. I can sit by one of them their crypts and visit all night with the occupants inside. There's some think I'm crazy. Spent too much time alone with just the dead for company. You men mark my words, someday you'll find out old Plantem ain't crazy. Them crypts will ask to be opened and those fellows will ride again. Just wait, you'll see."

The group of men didn't have much to say after that. Plantem played a decent game of poker, drank his share and other then being off his rocker was an nice fellow.

During the next two weeks, a new building was being erected. The owner came in on the stage walked around town once. Then he went to the land office bought the property and the next day he was laying out the foundation. The Cowfur Leather shop would soon be open.

Polar's poker friends from his first night in town now had a regular game going almost every night. Polar did his best to keep the game friendly and not upset his new friends with any large bets. George was unhappy, his wife and kids missed him, and his wife wanted him to go back east. She wanted her children brought up in a civilized world, not in the western frontier.

Then one night the poker game started to get out of hand. George had been drinking heavily. He announced that tonight he would decide his future. He kept raising the stakes, the games had thousand dollar pots. No one was giving in, wins, and losses see-sawed back and forth between the players. Then came the hand of fate. George and Polar where the only two left in a game that had a pot of eight thousand dollars. Polar's gambling instinct would not let him walk away, friendly game or not. He raised another two-thousand dollars. George did not have the money. Polar realized to late that George was tapped out, he just did not feel right winning be default. It would be rude to offer a loan to George, so now what? George's eyes lit up.

"Polar, I have the deed to my hotel land, it is not worth the two-thousand today, but in the future with the town growing it will be worth ten times that in a year or two, will you accept it instead of two-thousand cash?"

Polar had not really thought much about hotels since his daughter Cassie had mentioned she would like to manage a big fancy one. Maybe this was fate. Then again, he was holding a dead man's hand, aces, and eights. Let the fates decide. He accepted George's bet. George called. Polar laid out his hand: aces and eights. George sat deathly still. By now, the whole room was in silence and watching for the outcome. George laid his cards face down on the table. The he started to flip them over one at a time. Ace, ace, seven, seven, two.

"Well, Polar my friend you win. My wife and family will be happy. I'm headin' back east just as soon as I can raise some money."

"George, please accept this as a token of friendship, a present for you and your family." Said Polar as he pulled two-thousand in cash from the games pot and handed it to George. Next day George was on the stage heading home.

Polar had land, and it was plotted for a hotel. There was no telegraph in town. So Polar put a letter on the next stage to San Francisco. He had met an architect from there in one of his poker games over the years. He would have him come to Gravesend and design him the nicest hotel west of the Mississippi.

His next letter went to Cassie. He told her he found a nice town, had some land, and was building a hotel. Would she like to come and run it for him? Now he was part of the town. Finally, he was putting down roots. His only worry was Cassie, would she accept his invitation. If not, he would be back where he started.

Within the week, the architect was in Gravesend. Polar gave him the basic design ideas. The architect drew up the blueprints. Cassie's letter came almost two weeks later, having been carried by stagecoach, train and a Charleston mailman. She needed to finish her schooling in business management. If it were ok with Polar, she would be on her way to Gravesend in three months.

Polar had the information he wanted. Blueprints in hand, he hired out of work cowboys, the round-ups were over, and the ranches were laying off their extra men. Polar paid well for work well done. The men respected him, and Polar was out every day supervising and helping with the construction himself.

Polar took time to write one more letter. To Amos and his wife. He offered them both jobs in the hotel. Enclosed in their letter was three hundred dollars to cover expenses and the train and stage fare to Gravesend.

CHAPTER 10

Lotta started her search to build an empire. She donned the clothes of 'Larry' her alter ego and started her quest. She was not sure what she was looking for. Although one thing she was sure of, Alvira should not be a killer like her mother. Killing was one thing that Lotta did not want to pass down to her daughter. The hatred she harbored for men was also a detriment. To involve others in her dreams of an empire was going to be tricky, and building an empire would need people. Women of the west involved three distinct classes. Wives, whores and an occasional businesswoman. Of course, wives and successful businesswomen were out of the question. Whores, no way, any women that would let a man touch her, even for money was not a woman in Lotta's mind. As for men, in Lotta's mind two classes were known, bad, and worse. Not much to choose from there.

As Larry, she knew she had to start to mingle with others to help her find answers. Riding along a little used road one day she happened upon a large ranch, the Bar-B-Q. A hand painted sign on the fence said 'Wagon Driver Wanted, $2 day plus keep.' Heck, she could drive a wagon. The money meant nothing, but free room and food would be nice. She could mingle with the ranch hands, maybe pick up some helpful information. She rode up to the ranch, the foreman greeted her; of course, she was dressed as Larry. The ranch needed a driver to go back and forth to town for about a week; it was an all day job to town and back. Each day she would take a list of supplies to town, have the list filled and return, then unload the wagon and her day's job would be over. If all went well they might need a driver to deliver repair materials along the fence line, this would add another two or three weeks of employment. 'Larry' accepted the offer.

The work was harder then she expected. Loading fifty-pound sack of flour, barrels of nails, plus other assorted goods took every ounce of strength she could muster. Being 'Larry' a man, she could not ask for help, men of the west are expected to do their work and not complain. At night she gathered at the kitchen and lounged around the ranch yard listening to the men tell stories. Most of their talk centered on nasty cows, Indians, gunfights, drunken brawls, card games, and conquered whores. Some of them were actually quite nice and had their own conduct of behavior. Those men often thought of women as pure and things of virtue, they hoped to someday find the right women, marry, and settle down. Some did not like to see men killed, and some did not drink or gamble. It was truly a mixed lot.

In many ways, 'Larry' learned that men are just big boys. This became evident one night. The men had a large campfire burning. Coffee was the main beverage, although a few bottles of whisky were being passed around. One of the men suggested telling tales of the cowboys they knew or had heard about. These stories had to be of something unusual, maybe even a little superstitious and hard to believe. The criteria were they could not make them up; they had to pass on from another source. Everyone tossed two dollars into a hat, the men would vote on the best story when it was all over, the winning storyteller would win the pot.

The first storyteller was in his mid-twenties, always tended to brag some. He was to start the nights tale's of terror.

"Boy's, I was in a little town called Webster's Bend. I had been on the trail for a few days when I came upon this little town and it was not much of a place, but it had a saloon, and that's what I was lookin' for. The sun was already down, the place had a poker game going, so I joined in. the whiskey was bad, but at least it was wet. The cowpokes at the table was all right fella's. A few Mexicans were loitering by the bar. Weren't no women in sight."

"Then these two hombres come through the doors. They sorta' stopped the poker game for a few minutes, quite a sight they was. I picked up on their names as they was talkin' to each other. 'Cause of what happened that night I ain't never forgot those two fella's. One was called Illinois Igor; the other was a gent name Rent Field."

"Rent Field was a mousy looking dude, about 5" 6" high, pointy little nose and thin lips. He was wearing a black suit with a white shirt. His shiny black boots had a knife pocket with a red handled stiletto knife sticking out of it. Silver spurs on his boots looked out of place for this dude. His plain black gun belt had a red handled six-shooter, looked like he was trying to match the handle on his knife. He had one of them sissy looking black bowler hats on. His laugh was a hideous shrieking type, sounded like a women in pain, darn near had to cover your ears when he laughed."

"Now for his partner, Illinois Igor. He had a face that looked like a horse stomped on it, scraggly beard, and long unkempt hair. This person was a hunchback, big old bump on his right shoulder, and he walked with a bad limp. He was wearing a tan shirt and grey pants. The shirt was sorta draped over him, it was way oversize I suppose to help cover his hump. His tan cowboy hat was full of holes and the rim was tattered. He had a plain old brown gun belt with a rough looking old navy six-shooter. Spoke with a lisp, hard to understand what he was sayin"

"It wasn't that these fellows looked so strange, it was what they did that told me they weren't quite right. First off that Rent Field fella. He was a quick little bastard; he would catch a fly in mid-air. I had to wonder if he could draw his gun that fast. Now I've seen other fellows catch a fly in mid-air before. But I ain't never seen no other fellow eat 'em after he caught 'em. This here Rent Field, he just popped that fly in his mouth, then he made a big show of chewing it up and swallowing it. I had heard of Injuns and starving men eating bugs, so maybe it weren't the worst thing a man could do, 'ceptin this guy he enjoyed it."

"Now that bug eatin' Rent Filed fella, that was kinda bad, but it got worse. His pal Igor was staring in the mirror behind the bar, we was all watchin' him, he was so ugly it was hard not to stare at him. We all saw this rat creeping 'round the corner of the open saloon door. Igor fast as lightin' swung his body round, and threw his knife, skewering that rat right through the middle. Then he walked over to his knife lifted it in the air, that rat hangin' limp from the blade, blood trickling down onto Igor's hand. Igor went back to the bar by his partner Rent Filed. Then Igor he cut the rat in half. Rent Field took half of the rat, the part with its head attached and stuffed it into his mouth and ate it. Igor, he picked the other half of the rat up by its tail. He turned and faced the saloon full of cowboys. He held that rat up high by the tail. Then he tilted his head back and slowly dropped that rat into his mouth. Chewed that rat up right then and there, made a big scene of it, and kept chewing on the critter with his mouth half open, blood dribbling down his chin."

"Some of them cowboys were running outside to vomit. I had to swallow hard myself just to keep from gettin' sick. Then them two fellows had a shot of whisky, went out to their horses, and rode away. Boys that's the honest truth."

That was one hell of a story. 'Larry' was feeling a little nauseous after that one. It looked like the cowboys were going to have an early winner for their contest. Another Cowboy took his turn.

"Boys, eatin' rats is gonna be a hard story to beat. This here tale I'm gonna tell ya is about a woman with a heart as cold as ice. You boys know what I mean, ya'll have met at least a few of them ice-cold women. This one here though she takes the cake"

"The story says she come out of Charleston, South Carolina. Her pa was a mean old domineering man, ex-Cossack soldier from Bohemia. Her ma, well, she was a gypsy princess, temper like the fire of hell they say. They say she started hating men when her fiancé' jilted her. Now, this here jilted daughter of theirs, no one really knows her name but they say she had the initials LMP. To those that know of her they just knew the middle initial 'M" stood for "Murderous.' She got her start in some Rebel army hospital. Any man she felt might die, well she just up and helped him get there a little quicker, the story goes she killed them poor hurt soldiers by the hundreds. Strangled 'em all she did."

"If that weren't bad 'nough, it gets worse. Seems some Rebels killed her Ma and Pa. Drove her over the edge they say. She headed west. The first man she killed was butchered with a knife, dozen witnesses, said she was so evil that no one dared to try and stop her. There were rumors that she took up robbing stages and banks, never left a witness. If you saw what she looked like, you died. The only trail they ever found was when she would sell off her victims' belongings. They say she was a skinny looking thing, sorta attractive if ya like 'em with no meat on their bones."

"As for being scary, I would say she is, she don't kill bugs and rodents and eat 'em. She liked to kill men, just 'cause she hates them. They got wanted posters of her in the sheriff's office, just a description no pictures, but she done hid her actions well 'nough that there is no reward, she's just wanted for questioning, the most they can accuse her with right now is being a suspect. So if ya see a skinny lady on the trail, best leave her be, or you might be her next victim."

"Larry found that story very interesting. It also warned her that her reputation was more well know then she realized. It only strengthened her resolve to bring Alvira out west, settle down in a nice little town, and at least look respectable.

A third cowboy started to spin his tale.

"This story I got for you fellow's is gonna sound pretty unbelievable. I was ridin' range for a big ranch just outside the Desert of Death. We had made camp for the night, had us a nice little fire going, we were drinking coffee and softly singin' camp songs. That old Desert of Death she started abruptly about two hundred yards from our camp. It is like the trees and grass just stop at the edge of that desert, and then all you see for miles is sand, maybe a cactus or two trying to survive."

"The moon was high up in the sky, must have been near midnight. Then we saw two shadows out in the desert. We figured must be coyotes looking for rodents that would be taking advantage of the still warm desert sand. As they drew closer, we could see they was too big to be coyotes. It was two men on horseback. They rode right up to our camp and stayed on their horses just staring at us. I was standing up by now, hand on my gun. My pard,' he had a Winchester pointed right at one of the riders' bellies. The taller of the two told us they was lost and sure could use a cup of our coffee and a warm fire. So I invited 'em to sit down and join us, as a sort of friendly gesture and asked 'em to leave their guns by their horses."

"The tall fellow, his name was Boris Karl. Must have been 6" 2" or taller. He looked like one of them stereoscope pictures from Egypt; ya know where they got them pyramids and humped horses. He was wearing a round cap; it had this tassel hangin' from it that ended in a little silver coffin charm. His jacket was cut short like them fellows over in Egypt wear, and his pants and shirt were a dirty white cotton, to light of clothes for our climate. He didn't even have no boots, just open sandals, and both his feet and hands was wrapped in bandages. His face, looked like a sun dried prune, grey and wrinkled. His horse kinda matched the rider, a dirty grey color. The saddle was tooled with all kinds of Egyptian designs and the saddle horn was in the shape of one of those standing Egyptian dogs like ya see in the pharaohs' tombs. Between him and his friend, he was the only one that talked. It was a slow deliberate talking, strange accent I ain't never heard before or since. He mumbled his words like his tongue didn't work right."

"Now this other fellow, we was told his name was Mole Mann, he didn't talk at all. Kept a kerchief over his mouth and nose, lifted it up only to take a drink of coffee. His eyes were covered by some sort of dark glasses; at an angle, I could see them eyes of his. Big and round like the bottom of whisky bottles. Everything he wore was brown, torn and dirty, jacket, shirt, pants, hat, and boots. Didn't even have a holster, just a revolver with a birch bark handle stuffed in the rope that held up his pants. The knife at his side had sort of a turned up edge, like he used it for diggin' roots or something. Fingernails, damn, I almost forget to mention them, must a been two inches long, curved and dirty, they looked like the back of a turtle shell. His horse was no better, skinny run down animal, looked like it weren't groomed in months. The saddle was weather grey in color, so damp and dirty it had mushrooms growing on it."

"They told us they got lost out in the desert. Wanted to know if we knew'd 'bout some special graveyard in the area. Hell, the damn Desert of Death was a graveyard I told 'em. Then they finished their coffee, the tall guy thanked us. Got on their horses and rode right back out into the desert. Damn strangest visitors I ever had."

Larry was listening in rapt attention. It was easy to see that the stories were getting to the men. They were all looking a little jumpy, like a bunch of kids, there was not a one of them that would admit being scared. Then Larry felt something wet touch her neck. She screamed. Every cowboy in the group jumped, they were all staring at her. She turned quickly around to confront a black forty-pound mongrel dog. One of the cowboys spoke up.

"Damn Larry, if you don't scream just like a woman. Must be kinda embarrassing for ya?"

In her deepest voice she answered. "Come on guys, damn dog started me, I was just swallowing, almost choked my vocal chords right out of me."

The boys let it slide. It was a narrow escape. Then that darn burr filled, scroungey dog laid his head on Larry's lap. She felt sorry for the thing, started pettin' him. He rolled on his side and let her rub his tummy.

"Hey Larry, you start paying attention to that mutt and he's yours for keeps. Came wandering on to the range two or three days ago, half starved like that. The foreman says if he hangs around another couple days he's gonna shoot 'em. So we ain't been feedin' him or nothin', hoping he'll go back where he come from."

The fourth cowboy began talking.

"Now them other stories you boys told, hell I don't believe a one of them. Now this one I'm gonna tell ya is the gospel truth. Happened in a Saloon over in Cody, Wyoming. I was there myself and witnessed the whole thing."

"A bunch of us cowhands were just hanging around having a few drinks. The sun had just gone down. We see these two fellows riding up the street. These weren't no ordinary cowpokes. They was like something none of us had ever seen before. The smaller of the two was about 6' tall. Just sort of a regular build. We would learn latter that they called him Count Cowboy Lugosi. It was his clothes that set him apart from others. He wore a long tailed coat with a bright red lining, a black shinny vest, white shirt buttoned tight around his neck; his pants were black with a silver gray silk strip running the outside length of the leg. His boots were black and shiny as a pool of oil in the sun. The boots had silver tips on the toes, shaped like a bat in flight; the silver spurs had a three-winged bat as a star wheel for spurring on your horse. His belt buckle had a silver bat in flight for a buckle, with two red rubies for eyes. The black gun belt had no design, but the holster had a silver flying bat riveted to it that matched his belt buckle. The colt revolver was nickel plated with a black grip and yup, flying silver bats on the grip. Opposite the gun, he had a black knife sheath, the knife handle was in the shape of a bat with it wings folded in, and it also had red ruby eyes. His black Stetson had a hatband of silver bats, touching wing to wing all the way around. Hanging from his neck was a bright red ribbon, with another flying bat in silver."

"Then there was the man himself and his horse. The man had piercing black eyes, made ya afraid to have him look at ya. His skin was pale like he never saw no sunlight. His hair was slicked down like he had used a handful of buffalo grease to hold it in place. Had him a real funny accent, one of them European languages, but his English was understandable. I wouldn't say he was some dandy from out east playing cowboy. I wouldn't say he was even some European aristocrat playing cowboy. He just had this air about him that he could do whatever he pleased."

"Looking at his horse made ya feel the same way. Shiny black and groomed to perfection. Why there wasn't even any dust down by his hooves. The saddle and saddlebags were black leather with silver bat Conchos. The best part about that saddle was the saddle horn. It was like his knife handle. A big silver bat sitting up right with its wings wrapped around its body. "

"Now of the two men that just rode in, this one was the normal looking one. The other one was really strange."

"The second man's name was Frank N. Stein. Let me describe his horse first, it will give you an idea of what were dealing with. He was riding a Clydesdale. Biggest damn horse I ever did see. It had a plain brown saddle and saddle bags. The saddle horn was custom made like his friends, ceptin' this saddle horn was black ebony stone in the shape of a coffin. When that hombre stepped out of the saddle and stood by his Clydesdale, hell you would a thought that the big old horse was just a little quarter horse."

'This boy was a big 'un. 7'tall if he was an inch. He was wearing a black ten gallon hat that gave the illusion of adding another foot to his height. His black suit coat and pants were two small for him, adding a deception of more height as you could see his wrists and part of his ankle above his thick soled black boots. His gray undershirt at least looked like it fit him well enough. The plain black gun belt and holster held a sawed of shotgun, I'd swear the handle of the gun was made from a human femur bone. His belt knife had to have an 8 inch blade, the handle looked like some other type of human bone. To top it off was his hat band. Human skeleton fingers intertwined the full circle of his huge hat. If ya think the outfit was strange, ya ain't heard the worst of it yet."

"This Frank fellow was the most hideous, ugly creature I ever set eyes on. His forehead was almost square, his eyes sank in to the sockets like a dead man's, and they was two different colors, one brown and one blue. His face was scared and around his neck was a scar that looked to have been sewn up. Like someone hanged him, popped his head off his body, and sewed it back on. Then his wrists, they were like his neck, reminded me of when the Indians would tie a man's hands to two horses and pull him apart, accept the Indians never sew a man's' hands back on. This ain't even the worst of this guys looks, his skin was green. Looked like the green slime ya see on brackish water."

"Well. We watched these two come into the saloon, Frank had to duck his head just to get in the door. They sat down at a table and ordered a bottle. The Count poured himself a shot, held it up in the air to his friend, and said "cheers"; his friend picked up the bottle and the clinked the glass and the bottle together. The Count downed his shot of whiskey. Frank downed the whole bottle as if it were a shot glass."

"There was this young cowpoke, had two friends with him. They were sitting at another table, looked to have had a few too many beers. This young pup he starts tossing insults at Count Lugosi. The Count and his friend just ignore the kid. Of course, this just riles the kid up even more. The kid just keeps pushing the Count with phrases like, "Dude in the black, where ya all buy sissy clothes like that? The bats on all your hardware, they come out of your belfry? That gun, bet it's just for show, them dainty hands of yours probably couldn't even pull the trigger." Then the kid got up and walked to the Count's table. The kid looked Frank right in the eyes and said. "Damn you is one ugly brute, your friend there, he must of dug you up out of some old graveyard." Now the Count seemed ok that the kid picked on him. Picking on the Count's friend

Frank that was a different matter. The Count stood up and walked over to the bar; he turned and faced the kid. This kid he was standing right next to Frank and Frank he didn't even move a muscle just sat there still as stone. The kid spoke first. "So fancy pants finally decided he had enough. I'm gonna give you chance old man, you can draw first." The Count only said four words. "No, you draw first." The kid was fast, his gun fired three shots before the count had even drawn. The Count didn't even jerk, I swear all three shots went right into his chest. He just stood there like nothing happened, his gun slowly raised, he aimed it at the kids head, took one shot and nailed the kid through the forehead."

"Frank he still never twitched a muscle. The Count walked over to the kid who was lying on the floor, blood spurting from the hole in his head. Frank picked up the Count's shot glass and handed it to the Count. The count got down on one knee before the kid and held his empty shot glass under the kid's blood spurting wound. Once the shot glass was full of blood the count returned to his table. He ordered another bottle of whisky for Frank. Then they had a toast to the young and foolish. Frank took a long swig of whisky. The count he lifted the shot glass full of the kid's blood and drank it down."

"I tell ya right now. That Count, I know the kid put three slugs from a '45 into him. But he acted like nothing happened. At that point the saloon cleared out, none of us was waiting around to see what was going to happen next."

A fifth cowboy started talking.

"Well boys it's getting' late. I got me one of them strange stories too. But mine is pretty short and straightforward. So I'll tell it to ya quick as I can. I ain't never seen no rat eatin' blood drikin' cowboys. What I seen is true, had three folks with me at the time, and they all seen it to."

I was driving a stagecoach and we had to pass by a section of the Devils Horn Mountains. There was four passengers. Two men traveling along and a husband and wife. They all seemed nice enough. Also I had a strongbox heading for the bank, supposed to be about five thousand dollars in it."

"Word of the money must of leaked out. Got held up right at the base of the mountain pass. I ain't no coward, but then again I don't want to die. So I just tossed the box to the ground and put my hands in the air like I was told."

"They ordered the passengers out of the coach. One of the men from the coach, everyday looking fella looked like he was going to get really mad. He was about 6 foot, stocky built, didn't even carry a gun. When they started to get fresh with the woman, he stepped in. One of the robbers pushed him back and said; "what's your name fella?" The man answered "Larry Wolf." "Well Larry Wolf if you want to live, best you mind your own business." Larry didn't listen. He pushed the robber away from the girl, next thing you know the robber cracked Larry's skull with the butt of his gun. Larry went down on the ground. Then the strangest thing happened. Larry pushed himself off the ground, he was on his hands and knees shaking his head. Then I swear hair started sprouting all over his body. The back of his shirt tore apart. Then his boots split wide open. He grew claws and muscles like a huge wolf would have. Within seconds, he stood up like a man but looked like a wolf. One swipe of Larry's hand and the robber's chest split open. The other two bandits jumped on their horses and high-tailed out of there, didn't even get a dime for all their trouble."

"Then Larry, he looked at the three of us like he was sorry for what he did. Next thing we know he ran off into the mountains. Never seen him again."

It was time for a vote. Rent Field and Illinois Igor took the pot for the best story. Lotta was concerned about sharing the bunkhouse with a bunch of cowboys. So she concocted a great excuse. "Boys' she said, "I like this dog here, I think him and I are going to sleep in the freight wagon tonight. That way he'll get used to me and I can see if he's worth keeping." No one questioned the logic to the answer, so they let Larry and the dog sleep in the wagon.

The dog curled right up by Larry. She liked that dog, kept her warm during the cool night. She also was thinking about all those stories she just heard. If those characters the men talked about really existed what a gang of cutthroats they would make. A gang like that could rule the territory. They would just need a woman to lead them. Yes sir, she could lead a gang like that. Teach Alvira the ropes, let the gang do the dirty work, she and Alvira could sit back and reap the profits. If only the stories were true.

CHAPTER 11

Gravesend was growing fast. The last nine weeks saw the addition of the Slowemdown & Nevercome stage and freight office, Lorin Korn's Stables and Blacksmith shop, Larry's Eatumup Café, Cowfur Leather shop, and yes, they hired a sheriff and built him a new Sheriff's office and jail. The town was booming. Of course, construction on the largest most elaborate building was nearing completion, which would be 'Pederson's Palace Hotel.'

The hotel was to be the centerpiece for the town. Three stories high, with balconies warping around the front and both sides on every floor. In the center of the roof was cupola, which the guest could access through a circular staircase. This little addition to the building would allow anyone to view the whole town from up above. The main floor had a large dining area and a raised stage for possible future entertainment. Another room held an opulent bar and smoking lounge for business men who wanted more privacy in their dealings. The main lobby had marble floors and a marble counter for checking in guests. The second floor contained 20 private rooms while the third floor had 15 private rooms. Two of the rooms on the third floor were huge suites, one for Cassie, and one for Polar. From the main floor to the ceiling, it was open space. This allowed the rooms to all be on the outer edges of the walls. A guest could step out of any room on to the open walkway and look down to view the activities below on the main floor. No cost had been spared, from crystal chandlers, to expensive wood furnishings for every room. Even the china and silverware were given star treatment, every piece parked with a "P P H." For Pederson's Palace Hotel.

Occasionally a problem seemed to crop up at the graveyard. Usually brought on by drunken cowboys. With a sheriff now patrolling the streets at night the drunks were forced to find a place of refuge. The crypts in the graveyard seemed like a nice sheltered place to stay. Except one problem kept coming up, ghosts. The cowboys and drunks that occasionally stayed in the crypts said there were voices coming from inside the coffins and the walls.

The now weekly poker night in town had two new players Lorin the blacksmith, and Max the new sheriff. The group met every Saturday night. It was a good night to hear all the latest news. The miners and cowpokes were in town and anything that was interesting in the area around Gravesend was sure to be discussed.

One subject that was garnering more talk than it should was the ghosts in the graveyard. Stories like that were not good for business. Our little group of civic-minded leaders at the poker table felt they should put an end to all these rumors. Seeing Plantem Deeps was a regular member of the group, they elected him to give them a tour of the graveyard on Monday morning.

So far, the town's progression had been smooth and uneventful. The little group of poker players felt it was time for more organization. They could be all politically correct or just form a loose group of concerned citizens to take new matters under advisement. After a few beers and no arguments, they elected themselves as town council.

The state had already set up a temporary land office in an old army tent on one of the town's empty lots. With all the mines, ranches, new business and homesteaders filing claims it was a welcome business in Gravesend. The group decided right then and there that the Land Office Manger would be a welcome addition to the weekly poker game, if he seemed all right they might even make him a council member. This of course would be a great benefit for our little group. They could find out who was filing claims, buying land, and best of all which business were filing for permits, just in case any competitors were coming to town.

Monday morning found our hardy little group of poker players at the door of Plantem's funeral pallor. The Gravesend graveyard was just a short walk down the road. The question for Plantem was, just how did all these ornate walk in crypts come to be? Who had them built and who was interned in them?

Plantem did not want to break any professional ethics. Then again, these folks were all dead and as far as Plantem knew, they had no next of kin. Plantem had spent the previous night looking through his records on the crypts' and their occupants so he would have answers for the newly non-elected town council.

Walking along the paths of the graveyard, everyone in the group was amazed at the size of the area it encompassed. Must be five hundred graves, maybe more. The grave markers covered all kinds of professions from before the town was founded, miners, prospectors, homesteaders, cowboys, travelling salesmen, mothers, whores, unknowns and even a few children and babies. Plantem told the group that anyone that died within a hundred mile radius was usually brought here to be buried. The best part for old Plantem was, who the hell would think the first business in any town would be the graveyard.

There were actually four crypts located in the center of the graveyard. One crypt in each corner of a large area that looked like a small park except for one thing, in the center of this little park was a large stone crypt shaped like a barn. Each crypt was of a distinctive design. None of the crypts was locked so access was easy. Each crypt had been designed by the individuals who paid his five thousand dollar fee to be interned inside that specific crypt. The first crypt was heavy gray stone. Shaped like a small medieval castle, a large flying bat was carved in stone above the door. Upon entering, the room was damp and musty. The bodies had been interned into the walls. There were no visible locks on the crypts, which to the small group seemed strange, what about possible grave robbers?

Plantem Deeps finally spoke up.

"This crypt we are in right now belongs to two men, for whatever reason they designed it to hold four bodies. The two that are currently interned here came to me about two years ago. Both showed up on the lawn of the funeral home. They were both in sealed caskets with notes attached to them. The notes identified the bodies as belong to Count 'Cowboy' Lugosi and another man named Rent Field. Both of the caskets were of normal size. . The note said nothing about cause of death. The instructions were very specific. Intern the bodies within the crypt. The doors of the body compartments were to have locks on the inside of the doors only. No outside locks."

"It was as if someone thought these dead bodies were going to lock themselves into their own burial chambers. Then the note went on to give a warning. Any sounds or a noise from these crypts is to be ignored. If anybody here interned is disturbed, evil will befall the entire area. Two more large caskets will be arriving soon. These are the count Lugosi's and Rent Field's horses. You will find ten thousand dollars in a separate envelope when the horses arrive. A stable size crypt in the shape of a barn is to be erected of stone that will accommodate up to eight horses. Please make sure it is ready with-in a weeks' time. Thank you."

"Well men every note is basically the same, except after I had the stable crypt built the other horse owners only paid two thousand per horse for internment. The horses came in custom built caskets just like their owners."

"Now on to crypt number two. This crypt is in the shape of an Egyptian pyramid. You can see all the Egyptian designs carved into the stone. The body of a Mr. Boris 'Mummy' Karl arrived in one of those fancy Egyptian coffins like they use to bury royalty in. All filled with hieroglyphics and lots of gold inlays and precious stones. . If I weren't so honest, I would have been tempted to pry some of those gems off the casket. The other man's name was Mole Mann, all he had was a wood coffin, looked like somebody made it out of rotted wood that they dug out of the ground. Take a close look at the Mole Man's resting place on the wall, darndest thing the door that covers his casket sprouts mushrooms year round, summer, winter it don't matter, there's always mushrooms growing there. "

"Crypt three as you can see looks like a small stone cottage. Nothing fancy, just as ordered. Two men lay in state here, a man named Frank N. Stein and another named Illinois Igor. Nothing seemed unusual about Illinois Igor. Now Frank N. Stein must have been a giant. His casket was at least eight or nine feet long, probably a foot wider than a standard casket. It was a good thing they gave me designs for these crypts ahead of time or I would have to add on for the that gentleman."

"Crypt fours owner must have had a sense of humor. It's shaped like a stone doghouse. Look above the door and your will see a stone carving of a wolf howling at a full moon. Like all the other crypts, there's room for four bodies. This is the only crypt that has three openings left; the other three have only two unfilled spaces each. So here lies Larry Wolf all by himself."

The drunks talk about these crypts. Strange noises, talking, scratching, even sounds of horses are heard out here. Gentlemen, not to alarm you, but the stories are true. I personally believe the notes that were left with these men. Anyone ever disturbs these bodies and all hell will come to the world."

"If you want history on all these fellows, just sit around any campfire and ask them to tell you the strangest things men have seen or heard. These boys lying in state here. Their names come up a lot."

The consensus among the group was to leave well enough alone. They would start a fund to build a wrought iron fence around the cemetery, but it would take years to raise enough money. Plantem Deeps was not spending any of his cash on such a project. He lived by the cemetery and it was his livelihood, heck the ghosts kept him company on lonely nights."

The next day was a banner day for Gravesend. Surveyors were in town and were putting up markers for the railroad. If all went well the town would have rail service in two weeks. The railroad had already been granted land so no need to file at the land office. The first train in to town would have a load of building supplies to erect the Gravesend Railroad Depot.

PART TWO
WHO SHOT MY PAW

PUPPYLUDE II

This is the human equivalent to a prelude for Part two of the story of Gravesend. Things get a lot better now. Einer the dog my best friend is already at Gravesend. As for me 'Sven' the world's best looking Shih-Tzu dog, I'll be arriving on the next train. Please, read on and enjoy.

CHAPTER 1

Larry spent the next week doing her job. Whenever the opportunity would arise, she would try to sneak in questions about some of the men she had heard talked about at the campfire stories on strange happenings. Her new friend the dog was working out well. He would ride on the wagon seat by Larry and followed her everywhere. She even confided in her canine companion that her real name was Lotta and she was really a woman, not a man. The dog took it quite well.

Between what she learned around the campfire and a few more stories she picked up in town, there seemed to be a common denominator within many of the stories. The mountains called Devil's Horn, the Desert of Death and Gravesend seemed to have a connection. Some even hinted that Gravesend was where the cowboys of the stories went to die. On the other hand, if one was superstitious, the cowboys went there to rest and come back later.

Finishing her job on the Bar-B-Q ranch, she decided to take a trip to Gravesend. The most recent information was that the town had progressed from being just a graveyard to a mining boomtown.

Checking in at the railroad depot she found out that Gravesend was just about to open a train station in town. Tickets were available now, and trains were running to Gravesend twice a week, once there you were on your own, until the Railroad station was completed.

Lotta had made the change back to being a lady for the train trip to Gravesend. It was stifling hot, well over the one hundred degree mark. She and the dog were sitting on a bench outside the depot waiting patiently for the train. A gentleman approached, his coat hanging over his arm. He laid his coat on the bench and sat next to Lotta and the dog.

"Where are you heading ma'm?" he asked

"Little town called Gravesend."

"Why what a coincidence that just happens to be where I am going. The reports I have say it is a booming little town. I sure hope my information is correct. I just bought three lots of land right on the main street. The location is right across from a hotel that is under construction. They say that this new hotel will rival some of the best in San Francisco. Therefore, I speculated and bought the land sight un-seen. Did everything by wire, just wired the money over and they sent me the deed to the property. No one at Gravesend even knows my name or what I look like. It is a foolish gamble, but sometimes you have to take a risk."

"Sir, may I ask what kind of business you hope to establish when you get there?" Asked Lotta.

"Why sure you may ask little lady. A theater, and only the best, I will book class acts from around the country. Once the reputation is there the great acts of Europe will be knocking down my door to get a booking."

"A theater, what a grand ambition you have sir. Do the people of Gravesend know how lucky they are to be getting such a grand establishment?"

"No, I've kept it secret. I want to surprise the town with my news. Right now, the only thing the land office knows is that an autonomous buyer purchased the lots. I should think it should be very interesting."

"What about the deed or the blueprints for the theater? Do you have them with you?"

"Of course I have them with. Right there in my inside coat pocket, you can see them sticking out of my jacket right here beside me. I have to keep a close eye on these two envelopes. Every cent I have is tied up in this deal."

"Lotta scratched the dog's ear as she whispered under her breath. If only I could get my hands on that deed and blueprint. I could take the town by storm and look like a solid citizen."

The dog jumped down from the bench and went over by the gentleman that was sitting by them. The dog jumped on to the bench and while the man was visiting with Lotta, the dog deftly took his teeth and removed the envelopes from the man's suit coat. The dog jumped from the bench and was lying underneath with the envelopes covered by his tummy. The man excused himself for a trip to the restroom, taking his suit coat and luggage with him. That is when the dog crawled from under the bench and presented Lotta with two envelopes. A deed and blueprints for a theater. Lotta looked at the dog and said.

"I am not sure if you understood me or not. Although I would have to assume you did. You must be the smartest dog in the country. Either that or just damn lucky. Let's assume you are smart, you need a name, can't keep calling you dog."

She held the dogs face in her hands and looked deep into his brown eyes. Then she said. "Einstein, that sounds like a name with brains and class. I can call you Einer for short, yes that is a good solid name for a dog of your caliber. So now Einer I hate to have to do this, but we will have to dispose of the gentlemen you so deftly borrowed the tickets from."

The train was just pulling into the station. A beautiful American class 4-4-0 steam engine built by the Rogers Locomotive Works was slowly rolling to a stop. Its four huge driving wheels shining in the sunlight. That was when Lotta made her move. She pretended to slip and knocked the previous owner of the deed off the train platform and under the locomotives driving wheels. By the time the engine could stop, the man was in two pieces. One more time Lotta got what she wanted the easy way. By killing the only witness.

Einer and Lotta boarded the train and headed for Gravesend. Although Einer was happy to have a friend, he had doubts about her blood thristy actions at the tain station. The trip was comfortable and quiet. The conductor let Einer sit next to Lotta. Einer had to wonder if the conductor had forced him into the baggage car where animals were supposed to ride, what would Lotta have done. The railroad might just have lost a conductor. For now Einer at least felt he had someone who liked him, and it seemd like a safe haven.

Just before the train was to arrive at Gravesend Lotta went to the restroom. She changed into her Larry clothes before disembarking from the train. It was an era where men commanded much more respect in business matters. Therefore, Lotta would once again become Larry.

Larry and Einer made their first stop at a new tent business that had just set up in town. Aaron Long's Barbershop and bathhouse. Larry convinced Aaron to give Einer the whole works, haircut, bath, and shampoo for a five-dollar gold piece. After all, it had been many months, or maybe even never that Einer had had a bath.

Next stop was the land office. Larry registered the property in the name of L. Payne. No one of course asked what the 'L' stood for. This way when Lotta started operations she would be the owner. Larry received directions to the property and went to look it over. The hotel across the street was near completion, but as of yet there was no sign on the front as to a name of the establishment.

Larry rented a room at the Buffalo Chip saloon. Next stop was over to Long's barber and bath tent. Einer looked like a new dog, trimmed and clean. By the way Einer walked next to Larry, head and tail high in the air it was obvious he liked his new look. That night Larry looked over the theater blueprints. It seemed that a theater alone may have trouble surviving in such a small town. So changes were made. The three lots would share one large building with three separate entrances. Once a person entered any of the entrances, they would find that open arched doorways connected all three establishments. The center unit would house an elaborate theater with seating for up to one hundred people. On the left would be an eating establishment, serving only the best in food. The most elaborate of menus, a private dining, and meeting room would of course be available as needed. The building to the right was to be a gambling hall. It would cater to anyone who had money, rich or poor. Roulette wheels, craps, card games and even one of the new Fey slot machines she would have sent from San Francisco.

Luck was with Larry, as the hotel neared completion men were now out of work. Larry hired them as soon as they became available. Lumber was cut and construction was started with-in four days of Larry's arrival in town.

Alvira received a letter from Lotta telling her it was time. She packed what few things she still possessed and boarded a train for Gravesend. All she knew was that her mother promised her a new and exciting life.

CHAPTER 2

The hotel needed only one finishing touch, the sign. Polar planned a gala grand opening. A blanket invitation went out to the whole town. A free buffet from 10 in the morning till midnight was open to all. Tours of the hotel showing off the gas lighting and a crowning achievement for the area, indoor plumbing. He hired a local band to play music and set up a wooden platform out on the street for dancing. Of course, it was easy for him to get permission from the city council to close the street in front of the hotel for the day. Ranchers, mine officials, cowboys, and miners reserved every room in the hotel, except for one. One room was left unoccupied for guest tours, after all a room with a hand carved bed and furnishings, gas lighting, its own balcony entrance and indoor toilet and bath were something to brag about.

Amos and his wife Ruby were now settled in. Amos was to be in charge of making sure guests were comfortable and handled properly by the staff. Ruby his wife was put in charge of the admissions desk. This was another first for the area, colored people given charge over all the other staff people. A chef from San Francisco was in charge of the kitchen and dining room staff. Amos took care of the bellboys and the grounds keeping employees. Ruby hired and operated the admissions personnel.

The train depot was just nearing completion when Cassie and I stepped off the train. 'In case you are wonder who "I" am, it is me Sven, the Shih-Tzu. Remember me from the 'puppylude' well, it is time I take over and tell the story first hand, from what I have witnessed myself. Up to this time I could only repeat the story as it had been told to me. Now you will get it right from the dog's mouth.

I adopted Cassie as my human two years ago. Therefore, where she goes I go. The railroad depot was about three fourths of the way completed when we set foot off the train at Gravesend. Even as the train entered town one building was visible standing above all the rest. Although at the time, we did not know that was our destination. Pulling into town, we passed Lorin Korn's Stables and blacksmith shop. The Gravesend Land office which was operating out of a tent looked to have their permanent building started, the Aaron Long's Barber and Bath, and the Gravesend Railroad Depot. Exiting the train we noticed the Slowemdown and Nevercome Stage and Freight Station, I had to wonder how long they would survive with the railroad now in town. As we walked through the lobby of the depot and out the other side, we could see the hotel. Three stories festooned with red, white and blue bunting for the grand opening. We made our way through the construction of the lot across from the hotel and then up the hotel steps to the beautiful mahogany doors, with stained glass windows.

I could see that Cassie was sad or maybe a little hurt that no one bothered to meet her at the train station. Even if Polar was busy, he could have at least sent someone over. As we entered the lobby, a cheer went up. Must have been twenty people clapping and hollering congratulations to Cassie. A huge banner hung across the lobby proclaiming "WELCOME CASSIE, HOTEL MANAGER."

Polar appeared out of nowhere grabbed his daughter in a big bear hug and gave her a kiss on the check. Then they both stood looking at each other, tears flowing down their cheeks. Cassie introduced me to everyone. Of course Polar and I had become friends while he was visiting us in Florida. The next four hours were spent introducing Cassie to the employees, partying and just having a grand old time.

Polar escorted Cassie to her room on the third floor. No expense was spared to make Cassie comfortable; Polar even promised that a few amenities for me would be added. For now, we had a beautiful canopied bed and bedroom set of our own, the sitting room was spacious with velvet couch and chairs, and an ornate polished granite fireplace. The bathroom had an extra large bathtub to soak in, plus a flush toilet, all set off by marble floor and tiles.

I was promoted to official hotel dog, which gave me the run of the place. I found that the kitchen was my favorite room. The chef liked me and let me sample most of the dishes he was preparing for the opening day festivities.

The big day finally arrived. Cassie and Polar each stood on the third floor balcony, their hands on the ropes ready to release the canvas cover that hid the hotel sign beneath it. The covering dropped, the huge sign proclaimed "Pederson palace hotel." I was sitting right next to Cassie's leg as we watched the sea of people flow through the hotel doors. They were cheering, and most looked might hungry. I had to wonder just how much money Polar invested in this one. I doubt this town would ever see the likes of a grand opening like this again.

Cassie was beautiful in her light pink formal dress. Polar sported a brown tuxedo with a long tailed coat. As for me, I went the conservative route, just a nice white bowtie and collar around my neck.

Cassie, Polar, and I worked the crowd. Polar took the handshakes and backslapping in stride. Cassie, ever the lady, accepted slight womanly handshakes and kisses on the cheek from the ladies. From the men, she received kisses on her hand. Me, I was patted and ear scratched until my head felt raw.

Larry had let construction come to a halt for three hours so his crew could cross the street and join in the festivities. Then Larry himself stopped over. He seemed to be avoiding us. Then he was caught up in a group of people and herded into a meeting with Polar. Larry introduced himself.

"Good afternoon Mr. Pederson, 'Larry did his best at a manly handshake.' " Hello Miss Pederson" as Larry gave a light bow. He ignored me, not even a glace came my way. I looked over at Polar who had a strange look on his face. He whispered to Cassie. "Have you ever met that man before? He seems so familiar. Yet, I cannot quite place him." Cassie had never seen him before. I for one did not like the way he kept starring at Cassie. She was my human and I am responsible to keep her safe. This Larry guy looked like trouble to me.

The party lasted into the wee hours of the morning. Amos volunteered to lock up everything for the night. The guests had all retired to their rooms. Polar escorted Cassie and I to our room. Seeing a father and daughter who truly love each other is a remarkable sight. It made my tail wag as they hugged goodnight. Cassie fell onto the bed exhausted. I decided to sleep at the foot of the bed nearest the door. Part of my job was to take care of my human, so tonight I would stay alert and be the watchdog.

CHAPTER 3

Lotta now knew who owned the Hotel across the street. The only one she confided in was Einer. Now I noticed the black mongrel sitting by Larry one day, of course as a good neighbor I went over and introduced myself. It was then that I learned Einer did not consider himself a mongrel. He is a Schnauzer-Border Collie mix. Boy, did I start out on the wrong paw. Other than that little breed mix-up thing we really hit it off.

It took Cassie and Polar a little while to allow my new friend to roam the hotel at will, but they finally accepted him as part of the family. Larry, which Einer had confided in me was really Lotta the human he adopted, well, she did the same for me. It is nice to have two families to hang out with. Cassie and Lotta were total opposites, with my Cassie being sweet and nice to everyone. Larry was mean and nasty to everyone, and the Lotta side had a hatred for men like I had never seen in a human.

One day Larry asked Einer and I to accompany her to the graveyard. Seemed like a strange place to go for a walk, but we did. She acted as if she was looking for something or someone special. The next thing you know we were all entering a crypt. After the first crypt, we visited three more. Larry made notes of who was buried in each crypt and the dates they were interned. Then we took a walk around a big stone stable, from what I could figure out it was a crypt for the horses of the men Larry had made notes on. The whole thing was somewhat spooky.

Occasionally when I would sit out on the third floor balcony with Polar I could see him watching Larry as if something was very strange. Polar never said anything, but something did not seem right.

Larry's place of business was almost completed. One large building with three entrances, each entrance was for a separate part of the complex. On the left a nice middle class restaurant to cater to business people and common folk alike, this was important to make everyone feel like they belonged. That would then lend itself to the diners going to the attached theater or gambling room. Really a very novel idea.

The next train into Gravesend would have Larry's final load of furnishings and equipment. The upstairs had twelve very private rooms for visitors and two large living areas for Lotta and her daughter. Much like the Pederson hotel, gas lighting and indoor plumbing were provided.

It seemed every day we took a walk with Larry to the graveyard. Often he just sat and looked at the crypts. It was as if he was trying figure something out. Then one day we stopped at the funeral home. Larry convinced Mr. Deeps to let him look over the crypt records under the pretense that he might want to be buried in one of them. Mr. Deeps told him it would cost five-thousand dollars. Larry did not even flinch; he just said "No problem."

As Larry read the notes on the crypts current tenants, he came across the part that read, "Anyone that disturbs these bodies will bring Hell to the World." In Larry's mind, this sounded like a very interesting prospect. That night she went back to her room at the saloon. Looking over her list of names and matching them to the stories she had heard, she decided to pick out one individual as a candidate to test the written warning at the funeral parlor.

Then she had one other thing on her mind, which weighed heavily. Polar Pederson. Once she reverted to her Lotta persona, he was sure to recognize her. What were the chances that they would both settle in the same town? Was it by chance? Could it be destiny? Should she give him a chance to explain? Or should she just kill him and get it over with?

Then there was Cassie. Her other daughter, the oldest of the twins. Her long red hair shone in the sun. Such a beautiful child and so cultured compared to Alvira. Amazing how twins could look and be so different. By the end of the week, the building would be completed and Alvira would be arriving. There was no need to make any rash decisions yet.

One thing was for sure. She would not let Polar Pederson show her up with his fancy grand opening. She telegraphed San Francisco to send the best stage acts they could find to Gravesend. Her chef was brought in from New Orleans and her gambling boss was brought in from Chicago. She was ready. Let the world sit up and take notice. Lotta would not be the down trodden southern Belle the world had wanted her to be. She would be the Queen of the frontier, and her daughter Alvira would be the princess.

Alvira would be arriving in two days. It was time for Larry to disappear. That very day Larry stopped at the land office and let them know he was leaving town. The real owner of the property would be arriving the next day. She also made sure that many of the people at the saloon and all the workman knew that a new owner would be there to take over. He added that the new owner would be a woman. Larry made a brave move when he went to the Pederson Hotel. He asked to see Cassie. Then she left Einer with Cassie and me. Larry said that he was only taking care of Einer until his real owner could reclaim him. Cassie was told the owner was a lady named Lotta and she would be arriving in town tomorrow. I of course knew the truth, but it was a good bluff.

Next morning Larry boarded a train, traveling only sixty miles away to the next nearest town. Once she arrived at her destination, she changed into her new clothes. She now wore a split leg dark brown leather skirt and a white blouse. A dark brown leather jacket with fringe and dark brown boots completed her outfit. She made her way to the town stables and bought a chestnut gelding with a beautiful white star on his forehead. A used saddle and saddlebags would add to the illusion that she had spent many days on horseback to reach Gravesend. The Larry outfit was packed into the saddlebags just in case. Never know if Larry may have to return in the future. She mounted her horse and headed to Gravesend. Larry was out of the picture and Lotta was arriving.

Lotta arrived in town late in the afternoon. She did her best to look tired and trail worn. She surprised herself by going straight to the Pederson Hotel to retrieve Einer. The first time since the early days with Polar that she actually loved and missed someone, and it turns out to be a dog. She introduced herself to Cassie and quickly retreated out the door. She was not ready to confront Polar at this time.

Alvira would be arriving by train in the morning. Then they could make final preparations for the grand opening. Lotta and Einer spent the rest of the day making sure everything was going as planned. The theater acts were rehearsing on the stage. The chef had the menu and all the ingredients for the buffet. The gambling manager had dealers and pit men ready for all the games of chance in the gambling parlor. The huge sign on the front of the building was covered with canvas. The building looked great. The restaurant and gambling hall were each two stories high with second floor balconies. The center part of the building, which contained the theater, was three stories high, with a balcony on the second and third floors. The third floor also contained the living areas for Alvira and Lotta. The second floors of the restaurant and gambling hall had rooms for guests and a few of the employees. Large round pillars reminiscent of the south supported all the balconies.

Lotta was determined to rival the Pederson hotels grand opening. With one major difference. Her grand opening would make money; nothing would be given away for free. Men, they were only for one purpose, to take their money. The girls working the gambling hall were dressed like ladies, beautiful gowns, and low cut fronts to attract a man's attention. Lotta's rules were strict. The girls were ordered to flirt just enough to keep the gamblers spending their money. When a customer was broke, get him out the door, and find a new mark. Absolutely no fraternization with customers on or off duty was allowed. The male employee's had more strict rules. Any disrespectful behavior or fraternization with any women, customer, or employee would lead to immediate discharge of employment. Lotta was the queen; she made the laws in her establishment.

Lotta, Einer, and I were all at the train station to meet Alvira. Mother and daughter hugged, I'm not sure but their might have been one tear between the two of them. Emotions were not their strong point. The train depot was right behind Lotta's new establishment so we went up the back stairs and straight to Alvira's room.

The new town newspaper carried a full page advertisement for the grand opening. A teaser was put into the paper that mentioned a 'secret' room. This room holds the most marvelous invention in the west. Men, women and children will all be amazed. Not only will the name of the new establishment be revealed, but also the new owner will be present to greet guests.

It was amazing that the secret had been so well kept. The workman kept their mouths shout, if no one in town knew what was behind the wall or the name of the establishment, each worker would receive a one hundred dollar bonus. One slip of the tongue and they all lost their bonus. The un-veiling would take place at high noon the next day.

That evening Alvira, Einer, Lotta, and I were treated to a special meal in the new dining room. Einer and I were allowed to sit on the chairs just like our humans. Alvira seemed ready to accept us dogs as if we were all part of the family. I think we must be the only 'men' that were allowed to share their lives.

The grand opening was a gala affair. The first big surprise came when Lotta and Alvira released the covering from the sign, which proclaimed in huge letters with gas lights on each side. "palace OF PAYNE" in smaller letters on the bottom of the sigh was printed "FINE DINNING, THEATER, GAMBLING." The crowd surged through the three entrances like a swarm of locusts. That little room inside, well it was finally un-veiled. The first elevator in the territory. Just think a room that could you take you up three stories with no walking involved. A marvel of modern times. Every table, every seat in all three building was filled. Lotta, Alvira, and Einer were on the stage in the theater. She introduced herself and her daughter. Then the theater acts begin, jugglers, dancers, singers, comedy acts. With Lotta's establishment and the Pederson hotel Gravesend had become the 'place' for people to come to.

Polar Pederson and Cassie were there for the grand opening. Polar saw what he came for. He never said a word to Cassie. They spent some time looking over all the wonders of the new businesses and Polar retired back to the Hotel. Cassie stayed to attend the theater. Lotta of course saw her but said nothing.

Lotta then managed to free herself from the crowd and headed to the Pederson Hotel. Polar was on the third floor balcony and saw her crossing the street. A few minutes passed before Polar heard the knock on his door. In his heart, he wanted so much to open that door and hold his lovely Lotta. In his mind, he knew that was not how it would be.

He opened the door and they both stood in silence. Finally, Polar asked Lotta to come in and have a seat. She said nothing as she sat down. Polar offered her a drink and she politely accepted. Then he began the conversation.

"Lotta, I've missed you so much. I was shanghaied into the army as soon as I reached Boston. If I would have tried to leave I would have been shot for desertion, but I wrote you letters every chance I had. I searched Charleston for you after the war, but only found the graves of your parents. I also discovered that we had a daughter. Please, please forgive me. I love you as much today as the day we were engaged."

She sat in silence for many minutes. Polar sat across from her, sweat beading upon on his face, his drink shaking in his hand to the point of sloshing over the edges of the glass. Then Lotta talked.

"Polar. No matter how strong I fought my thoughts, I could only image that you had abandoned me. As you know, never in my life, had a man treated me with love and respect until you came along. Then you left, never to return. You left me alone, pregnant and involved in a war that destroyed my life and killed my parents. You made a new life and so have I. I also have a daughter who will be helping me to run my establishment. She is no concern of yours. As for Cassie, she is your daughter, I want no part of her. I do not want her to know who her mother is. I want your promise that you will not tell her. As for me, I need time to think about us. When I am ready, we will talk again. Until then our past is between us and no one else. Do I have your word on that?"

Polar had tears in his eyes. It was hard for him to swallow. Even his chest hurt and it was hard to breathe. He still loved her so much. She was the only women he had ever had feelings for. He wanted to ask about the other daughter's father, but he dared not. He finally gave an answer.

"Lotta, I respect your wishes. No one will know anything about us. We will be two people who happen to own businesses across the street from each other. I will tell Cassie nothing. If you ever change your mind or can forgive me for having wronged you, I will be here. I realize it is too late to say it, but I love you and always will."

Then Lotta rose from her seat and walked out the door. She never said another word. I was sitting in the corner watching the whole thing. I felt so bad for Polar that I jumped into his lap and laid my head on his shoulder. He held me tight and wet my fur down with his tears. I have never seen a human hurt inside so bad in my whole dog life.

CHAPTER 4

Alvira slipped into her job as manager of the new enterprise. Her daily working outfit was somewhat unusual. She wore a long black tight fitting dress; a slit along one leg ran from her mid-thigh to the floor. A low cut neckline showed her slightly small womanly charms. Two-inch heels on her black high-laced ankle height shoes made her seem taller than she was. Her gold earrings were shaped like a small belfry and on the inside of the earring were small silver bells that made a sweet sounding chime as she walked. A gold chain around her neck spelled out 'PALACE OF PAYNE' in fancy script letters. A last touch was a gold bracelet with small interconnecting handcuffs. Alvira felt it was a way to add a little to humor to the name of their establishment.

Lotta still had another mission to accomplish. She wanted to be in control of the most feared group of desperados to ever be assembled in one place. She knew where to start. She kept an eye on the gambling den until she hit two down and out prospects. The two drifter's had lost what little money they had. They would hang around the gambling parlor trying to get free drinks or food which the gambling parlor offered to people as long as they were gambling. She had the two men brought to her office. Alvira sat in to start learning the ropes of the business. The men had no homes or families. The tall lanky one was named Booker, the short stout one was called Runt. Lotta's offer was plain and straight forward. If they wanted jobs, she would hire them. They must do whatever they are told, no questions asked. Any special assignment would pay them fifty dollars each, with strict confidentiality. They were never to tell anyone what they were doing. Their regular job would be to work around the buildings doing odd jobs at two dollars a day and they would receive room and board. Booker and Runt jumped at the offer. Lotta would give them a special job to do in the morning. They were to be at her office at ten o'clock.

Lotta gave her orders to Booker and Runt. They were to take a push cart from behind the railroad station. Then quietly as possible, they should make their way to the graveyard. They would enter the crypt of Count 'cowboy' Lugosi. Armed the two crowbars they would pry open the door that was sealed from the inside and remove the casket of the Count. Once the coffin was removed, the boys were to mortar the door back in place, leave no evidence that anyone had been there. Then the coffin was to be brought back and placed in room number one above the restaurant. All this must be accomplished between the hours of two to three o'clock in the morning. This would leave the town empty of any witnesses. If by chance they were to be seen or caught, they were to deny any knowledge of Lotta or Alvira's involvement. They would just be simple grave robbers. Lotta would bail them out of jail and hire a lawyer to defend them; it would only be a minor charge so nothing to worry about. Once the job was successfully completed, they would each get a fifty-dollar bonus.

For fifty dollars, Booker and Runt did not bother to ask any questions. They did as they were told. Once at the crypt they pried open the door to the Counts Crypt. A large blanket they had placed on the floor deadened the noise of the falling pieces of stone and mortar as the door finally swing open on it hinges. Both of them expected the rancid smell of a rotting corpse. Instead the odor was more of a musty damp smell. They slid the coffin out of its resting place and carefully carried it to their cart that was waiting outside the crypt. Neither of the boys spoke until they were almost back to town. Then Booker spoke up.

"Runt? What ya suppose Miss Lotta plans to do with this here body?"

'No idea, Booker. Maybe she's gonna open one of them wax dummy museums or a horror show. I've heard stories about those fellows interned in them crypts out there. Most of 'em is bad men, not like in bandits and killers and such. I mean bad like in evil, possessed, and wicked. Some say they ain't human. Might be this here Count fellow is still alive, I didn't smell no rotting body when we pried open that door. Ya think maybe we should open the coffin and take a look see?"

"Ya all must be nuts Runt. I here'd all them stories to. We'll just put this coffin where Miss Lotta said, and then we get our money and keep our mouths shut. Heck we mortared that door back in place on the crypt, nobody will ever know'd the Count is missing."

"Booker, them stories, this here Count, he was supposed to be rich. Might be something valuable in that coffin. I think we should take a chance just open it a little and see if there's anything worthwhile taken."

Well the boys finally got brave enough or should I say stupid enough that they opened the coffin. They had it set up on two saw horses in room number one. Then greed got the better of them.

"Runt, look at this here fella, why other than being all pasty white he looks like they just laid him out yesterday. Wow, look at that ring, bet we can get a good penny for that. You watch for anyone comin'. Ya know Runt his flesh is still soft, I don't' like this at all. Ok, I got the ring let's put the lid on and get out of here."

"Booker, wait, look at them guns and holster, why he's decked out just like he were still alive. Let's take some more stuff. Come over here and he…"

"Runt? Leave him be. Runt? Runt?"

The talking between Booker and Runt ended abruptly. Einer was watching the hallway when a figure left room number one. It was carrying two bodies, one over each shoulder. Einer followed him to shallow ditch where he dumped the bodies. Then the man returned to room number one and laid down in his coffin, pulling the lid over himself.

The next morning the sheriff was not too happy to have two dead bodies found in his town. Doc Pull did an examination on the bodies. Both had been drained of blood. Of course that story was not told to anyone. The sheriff had heard the boys were working for Lotta, so he made a trip to visit her.

"Miss Lotta, there's no way to say this gently, so I'll just spit it out. We found them two boys, Booker and Runt dead in a ditch this morning. I here they were working for you. Any idea who would have wanted them two dead."

"Why sheriff that is the most awful thing I have ever heard. I don't believe they had an enemy in the world. They were just good natured drifters. I hired them to do some odd jobs for room and board. I feel so bad, have you contacted their next of kin?"

"As far as I can figure, there is no next of kin. I suppose the town will have to pay to bury them."

"Sherriff, the boys worked for me. They were nice men. Give them a nice burial and send the bill to the Palace of Payne. It's the least I can do."

"Why that's mighty nice of you Miss Payne. I'm sure Booker and Runt will appreciate that. Have a nice day now, ya hear."

It did not take long for Alvira to hear the news. Lotta had checked on the coffin in room number one. It seemed safe and secure for the moment. That is where Alvira found her mother, in room number one.

"Mother, have you heard what happened to Booker and Runt? Did it have something to do with this coffin?"

"Alvira honey, I have no idea why anyone would want to kill Booker and Runt. As you can see, they finished the job I sent them to do. The murder took place sometime after they left here. I told the sheriff we would pay for the burials; it will cost about thirty dollars each. Seeing we owed them fifty dollars each we will actually make a forty dollar profit from their deaths."

"Mother, how can you be so cold hearted?"

"Honey, learn it now and learn it well. They were only men. A man will take advantage of a woman whenever he can. They are not to be trusted or mourned. Your mother knows best, believe me."

"Mother why is that coffin so important, why did you need to have it?"

"We'll return here together later this evening then you will see if my theory is correct. If it is, we are in a position to make a fortune. Now I suggest you get back to your duties."

Einer was with Lotta through the whole conversation. He did not like the sound of things. Even less, he did not like the smell in room number one. It did not smell of the dead. Then again, it did not smell of the living. So what exactly was in the coffin? Einer always felt he was a good God fearing dog. Now he was sure he had hooked up to the wrong type of human. He came over to the hotel and asked me to hang out with him when the coffin meeting took place that evening. Being more curious then smart, I agreed.

The sun had set as we all sat in room number one. Lotta sat in one corner, Alvira with me on her lap and Einer at our side sat in the other corner. The coffin sat in the center of the room. I would like to say it was quiet as a graveyard at midnight, but around here, the graveyard was not always so quiet. We heard the coffins hinges and wood slowly creaking as the hand pushed the cover into the air. Slowly the coffin lid was in a vertical position. A man sat up, then both quickly and gracefully he was standing on the floor. He raised his arms above his head and stretched the tiredness of sleep and stiffness from his body. Then he sensed that we were in the room.

"What are you doing here? Who are you? Why have you disturbed me?"

Lotta took over with the answers.

"My name is Lotta Payne. This is my daughter Alvira and the dogs are Sven and Einer. We have come to make you a business proposition. You and your friends have a reputation, which seems to border more on myth then truth. If any of it is true, we would like to join forces with you and put the human race in its place. We could take what we want, when we want it. All of us could live whatever type of life we choose. Money would be of no concern. Everything we want we could have. Would you be interested?"

"Madame I am Count Lugosi. You have aroused my interest. Just what do you have in mind?"

"Count, there are six more individuals in the crypts. I assume you know who they are. From what I have researched, you all have certain powers that would complement each other. I suggest we band together as a gang to build an empire of our choosing. I want wealth and power for my daughter and myself. The rest of you can have whatever you wish. As a woman I have access to getting the knowledge and trust of the humans that will be our victims. For the time being we can base our operations out of my establishment. The Palace of Payne. If you agree, tell me who the next person from the crypt we should bring into our little group."

"Madame I like your thinking. Rent Field my manservant would be the next logical choice. Once he is here he will do whatever I tell him. I could then have him retrieve the other members of our organization. Before we go any farther do you realize what I am?"

"Count as best as I can ascertain you are a Vampire. I also think you may have fed recently on two of my employees. For you look to be quite healthy at the moment."

"My dear lady and her lovely daughter you are correct on all counts. I would like some human contact, can this be arranged. As for eating, I will not require anymore for at least a week. Then I am sure we can discreetly arrange for a meal."

"My dear Count, I have thought the matter over for a long time. We will tell people you are my uncle and you will have full run of the area. I know you are a man of honor so all I ask is your word that you will do nothing without consulting me. I will do the same for you. An equal partnership. My daughter will be aware of all that is going on. She will continue to run the three businesses' we have here. You and I will take care of business outside of the Palace of Payne."

"Miss Payne, you have an agreement. I will need your help tomorrow evening to retrieve my manservant Rent Field. Once he is here we can start to form our organization."

After the meeting we hung around with Alvira. She was not too happy about the whole thing. She confided in Einer and me that her mother may just be a little insane. I think that was putting it mildly. Organizing what sound to be a group of ghouls into her own private little army would have to lead to killing and bloodshed. Einer and I had to admit that Alvira was not the most cordial person we knew. Then again she might go good or bad depending on how she was treated. We did our best to give her love and affection. Maybe two nice guy dogs could make a difference in her life.

CHAPTER 5

The next week things around town seemed pretty normal. Einer and I knew differently. The Count who had reverted to his more western moniker was now called Cowboy Lugosi by everyone who knew him. He had become the talk of the town from the day he first stepped out of the elevator at Lotta's place. I remember that day well. Einer and I were in the lobby lying in a nice quiet corner. The elevator door opened. The room went deathly quiet. Everyone's eyes were on the figure in the elevator. Cowboy stood erect, his black outfit pressed to perfection. The silver of his weapons and adornments glistened from the light of the chandelier. His face pale from lack of sun, yet as handsome a man as anyone had ever laid eyes on. Instead of a typical western walk he seemed to glide through the room. The women were flattered as he kissed their hands and introduced himself. Even the men were taken by his straightforward charms. He possessed all the attributes of a gentleman and yet he made those around him feel an awkward fear of his capabilities. His accent and piercing eyes seemed to put everyone he met under his influence. Einer and I knew we had better keep an eye on him. Our instincts told us Alvira could be in danger of falling under his spell. We had enough problems trying to keep Alvira from becoming like her mother. A cold-hearted bitc…well you know what I mean, a female dog.

As the days progressed so did the members of the gang. Lotta had now officially organized the group under the name of the 'Gravesend Ghouls.' Alvira, Einer and I sat in on most of the meetings. Not by choice, Alvira was ordered to sit in. Einer went along as support, me I was there because Einer and I were friends. With Lotta's new group of associates, Einer had been devoting his time to Alvira. Of course, Einer enlisted me to help him keep Alvira on a straight and narrow path. With my helping Einer and still spending my time with Cassie who of course was my main concern, I was 'dog' tired.

Our observation of the gang was as such. Lotta of course felt she was the mastermind and overall leader. Cowboy Lugosi was condescending to Lotta's leadership, but he seemed to be the one the men looked to as their leader. Larry 'the' Wolf as the group called him, well he was quiet. He seemed too nice to be with this group. The men either admired him or despised him. I do not think he liked violence or bloodshed, but he had a quick temper when aroused. Einer and I were not sure what to think of him. We took a wait and see attitude.

Frank N. Stein seemed to be feared, more for his brute strength than anything else. Igor told a story about Mr. Stein. Seems he was a ruthless thief and killer. When they apprehended him, the townspeople stoned him and broke almost every bone in his body. Still clinging to life, they hanged him for his crimes, his body disappeared from the gallows. A doctor in the area is rumored to have taken the body. The doctor then took the bodies of Franks many victims, removed their limbs and organs, and sewed them onto the damaged areas of Frank's body. The body was then reanimated with a new invention known as electricity. This invention is used in some eastern cities to run the lights of a whole town. With that much power Frank returned to a mobile life. His brain however was damaged. He thinks and acts like a child, but has the strength of ten men. They say he cannot die.

Igor worked with the doctor to revive Frank. The doctor had promised to fix Igor's hunchback and lame leg in return for his assistance. With Franks mind beyond repair after the operation the doctor deemed it as a failure. Thus he refused to operate on Igor. Igor befriended Frank and they have been together ever since. Igor told everyone that he often left Frank outside of town when he went in for supplies or a drink. Seems people just did not like to be around Frank.

Igor and Rent Field seemed to be a likely pair. Igor was hunchbacked and lame in one leg. A devious personality had developed, probably in defiance of his infirmities. Rent Field was a manservant to Lugosi. Rent was crazy as a loon. Any time he was away from Lugosi too long he would end up in a mental institution. He had a hunger for things that were live, bugs and rodents were his meal preferences. Maybe that was why he was such a sly mousy fellow.

Now we come to Boris Karl. To say Boris was a man cut from a different cloth would be an understatement. Although dressed in a cross between Egypt and the west there are hints of bandages over most of his body. The story is they tried him for stealing some Egyptian king's wife and bond him up like a mummy. As an extra little punishment they cut out his tongue. He eats some kind of special plant leaves that give him immortal life. Why he wants to stay alive I cannot image. He has one redeeming trait. He seems to think all women are princesses and while he is around a woman, she will never be in danger. As for men, he could care less, seems he prefers a knife to a gun, but is handy with both weapons. He limits conversation to a few grunts for yes or no, at times he does garble out a few words. Being tongue less this makes perfect sense.

Mole Mann seems to be a creature unto himself. He wears dark sunglasses, looks like they were made from the bottom of brown beer bottles. They say at night he removes the glasses and his eyes are as big around as a cup saucer. The boys find he is very useful for digging tunnels with his long sharp fingernails and he can see in the dark as a regular man would see in the daylight. Einer says he never talks, we figure he must be mute. Although speech may be an asset we are unaware of. He stays away from most people because of his looks. Those glasses and skin that looks like dried mud are not attractive features.

Alvira did her best to convince her mother that this group was nothing but trouble. However, Lotta could only see potential in the Gravesend Ghouls. Seldom did any of them venture out except at night. They started using the Buffalo Chip saloon as there place to drink, relax, and play some poker. Compared to Polar and his civic-minded citizen group of poker players this was quite a contrast.

The Gravesend Ghouls had their orders from both Lotta and Cowboy Lugosi. Stay out of trouble; back down if you have to. Gravesend would be their sanctuary. Protect it at all costs.

Of course every other area in the west was open game. With Lotta's contacts in her three businesses she had constant information on the goings on in the area. The first one she acted on was a large stockpile of gold. The Travis Anderson Mine about twenty miles up on Devil's Horn Mountain. They had not shipped out any gold deposits for almost two months. Word was out from the drunken miners in town that they were digging it out so fast that no one had time to haul it away. It would easily be worth a quarter of a million dollars. There it sat inside a heavily guarded abandoned mineshaft. The shaft entrance had been sealed with rock from a dynamite explosion and two armed guards stood at the sealed entrance. The gold was then kept in two safes, locked and sealed in the mine. A perfect opportunity to see what the Gravesend Ghouls were capable of.

Lotta and Cowboy, as he liked to be called figured out the plan for the robbery. Lotta was going along since this would be their first job as a team. Cowboy was to be in charge. He made sure to tell Lotta that this was to be a no killing affair unless absolutely necessary. The law did not like robbers, but killers they would hunt forever. Mole Mann was in charge of digging a tunnel from above the mine to the main shaft. Cowboy assured Lotta that Mole could dig through a hundred feet of earth in less than fifteen minutes. They knew from some of the miners they would have to tunnel down 300 feet. Forty-five minutes to reach their objective. Frank would then enter the mine through the Moles tunnel and break open the safes. Now Frank was not a safe cracker in the normal sense of the word. He would pick the safe up in his arms and squeeze it until it popped open. Seeing the tunnel had to come in from above the mine, they would need to rig a block and pulley at the opening to hoist the gold up. Lotta, Cowboy, and Boris would be in charge of that part of the operation.

They arrived at the soft spot above the mine about midnight. Mole started digging immediately. Frank shoveled away the loose dirt from the tunnel that Mole was digging. Lotta, Cowboy, and Boris assembled a wood tri-pod with the ropes and pulleys. Once Frank and Mole were in the mine, the safes were easily located with the moles superb night vision. Frank cracked open the safes like two fresh eggs. Then Mole and

Frank loaded the gold into the buckets that were attached to the pulley system. Mummy pulled up the loaded buckets and Lotta and Cowboy loaded the gold onto the horses. By four in the morning they were back at Lotta's place counting their loot. Lotta woke Alvira and Einer to come see what they had accomplished. Einer told me that even he was impressed. Alvira, she just wanted to touch that gold. Gold fever is a bad thing. Now Einer knew that it would be hard to keep Alvira from turning as crooked as her mother. Then again, he had me to help him out. I was sure we could still save her.

As for the robbery, it would be weeks before it was even discovered. After all the mine was still sealed and armed guards were on duty twenty-four hours a day. Lotta decided to send Larry the Wolf to New York by train to sell the gold to brokers there. By the time anyone knew the gold was gone it would be converted into cash. Lotta claimed an extra ten percent for bringing the group together and providing a place for them to stay. This seemed fair to all concerned. Although when she wanted ten percent for Alvira as co-owner of the Palace of Payne there was some dissention. Alvira finally was awarded two percent of the take. Einer knew that Alvira was slowly being sucked into Lotta's world.

CHAPTER 6

It was near midnight. Cassie, Polar and I had been entraining guests in the restaurant and time had slipped by. Before retiring to bed, the three of us went out onto the balcony outside our rooms. Polar in a long sleeve flannel shirt, comfortable old pants, and stocking feet. Cassie had changed into almost the same type of cloths as her dad, except she was bare foot. Me I was in my regular old dog fur. We all had some of Polar's special house wine, he had it bottled and shipped in from Oregon. It was called Summer Wine, made from strawberries, cherries, and an Angel's kiss. My humans of course used glasses, I have mine in my own bowl. Cassie had my bowl ordered from Norway and sent over here. It has the word Uff-Da on the side. It's great to be Norwegian.

One thing happened that night that was peculiar. As we sat watching the street, we noticed that men were hauling dirt out of Lotta's theater across the street. Not just a few pails full, but wagonloads. This went on every night for about two weeks. Cassie and I could hear the wagons creaking under the strain of their loads as they left town. Polar was getting curious, as was Cassie. I found out from Einer that they had designed the elevator to go down one more level. Mole was digging a storage room for their future hauls of loot.

I hope that curiosity does not kill the Cassie. She went over and invited Alvira to lunch. Einer and I hoped this might be a good influence on Alvira. Therefore, we kept our paws crossed.

Lunch went well for Cassie and Alvira. The visit was cordial and friendly. Alvira told Cassie they were putting in a wine cellar, thus the reason for moving all the dirt. The discussion also included that they both were born in Charleston. Alvira was very guarded and not willing to give out much information about herself. Einer and I knowing that they were sisters were hoping that maybe this would be a good time for them to figure it out. One thing Alvira needed was a family member who was not a complete nut case. After lunch they both agreed that it was nice to talk to someone their own age and they would get together again.

The next few months for the Gravesend Ghouls were very busy. The next big job was a train robbery. This left out Cowboy Lugosi and Mole Mann, daylight raids were not on their list of things to do. Larry the Wolf took charge of the operation. Frank and Igor were assigned the mail car and the safe as their objective. Larry and Rent would walk through the cars and collect the passenger's valuables. Boris was in charge of keeping the horses ready.

Stopping a train for Frank was something he enjoyed. He would find a joint in the rail then pick it up and curl it over into a big circle about six feet high. Frank then stood in the center of the track as the train tried to squeal to a stop. If the train could not stop in time, Frank would hold his hand straight out and push against the locomotive to stop it. Boris then held the engineer and fireman at gunpoint. Frank opened the baggage car door and popped open the safe. Igor tied up the baggage car attendant.

Larry and Rent entered the passenger cars and walked through them with their hats in their hands collecting the passenger's valuables. All was going well until the last passenger car. Larry was in the center of the car while Rent was at the rear of the car holding everyone at bay with his gun. Unknown to Rent the passenger in the seat next to where he was standing was a U.S. Marshall, Bristol Coffin Sr. Bristol slipped his gun silently from his holster and shot Rent. Rent's body swung around as he stumbled out the back door.

As quick as the bullets sounded Larry leapt from where he was toward the Marshall. As Larry was flying through the air, his shirt and shoes shredded and landed on the astonished passengers. By the time he landed on the Marshall he had transformed into a real wolf. His fangs enclosed around the Marshalls throat and literally popped the Marshalls head from his body. Then he turned and bolted threw the back door to check on Rent. Rent had a bullet in his shoulder, but he would be ok. As Larry's anger subsided he reverted to his human form. The rest of the robbery proceeded as planned. The group had shed its first blood.

The next action was a stage holdup. Lotta figured she was an old hand at stages and took charge of the raid. Daylight determined her choice of helpers. Rent was still recovering so he was left out. Igor and Boris went along as her back up. She decided to revert to her old disguise as Larry the cowboy. No use in risking someone recognizing her as Lotta. So with Bandana's over their faces they way laid the stage. Everything went well until the very end. They had the strong box with four thousand dollars in cash. Igor collected the passenger's valuables. Boris held the horses and kept his gun on the stage driver and his helper. They were just about to leave when Lotta turned; she shot the driver, his helper, and all three passengers. Igor thought it was great. Boris of course said nothing. All Lotta said was. "No witnesses."

The killing did not go well with Cowboy Lugosi and Larry the Wolf. They felt it would bring unnecessary attention to the group. In Larry the Wolf's case the killing was pure instinct. For Lotta it was cold-blooded murder.

Cowboy Lugosi and Larry the Wolf decided to plan the next heist. A night job on a bank. No people would be around, thus no killings. There were three basic bank jobs for the gang to look at. A daylight all out assault, which was downright dangerous and way too many people involved. Then you had the two night time type of jobs. One was for banks with a back entrance. This would be the easiest, although few banks had back entrances just to deter an easy robbery. If they did have a back door Frank would tear it open, walk in, pop open the safe or if it were a walk-in safe, he would just rip it off its hinges. The other bank job was for banks with only a front entrance. Setting up the operation at the rear of the bank Mole would then dig under the foundation of the building and come up beneath the inside floor of the bank. Next in was Frank who would take care of the safe opening.

Cowboy Lugosi and Mole with superb night vision were always assigned the night jobs. Frank with his strength was assigned almost all the jobs except stagecoach hold-ups. Normally if Frank was on a job Igor was also there. Igor was the only one that Frank seemed to listen to.

Lotta was turning into a liability for the gang. She was just too cold hearted. Hard to believe when you looked this bunch over. All these boys had some murders to their credit, but most were defensive measures, or in Cowboy Lugosi's case, hunger pains. He needed human blood to sustain himself.

Luck was about to smile on the Gravesend Ghouls from a very unusual place. Lotta received flowers one day. From Polar Pederson, the card read. "Dear Lotta. I would very much appreciate your company for supper tonight at the Pederson Hotel restaurant. Maybe we can try and renew our friend ship. Yours, Polar."

Alvira got wind of the flowers and begged her mother to go out with Polar for dinner. She told her he seemed like a nice man. Maybe her mother should give one man in her life a chance . It may just be that not all men are evil. Lotta, deep in what little heart she had left knew Polar was really a good man. Her pride and past were not points in her favor. Then again she was lonely and someday her daughters may have children. Lotta tried to picture herself as a grandmother. The picture was pretty blurry. She was getting older, and Polar must still have some feeling for her. She finally decided to accept. She would not dress fancy, her white blouse and leather split skirt would have to do. Polar had to accept her for how she was or not at all.

Polar saw Lotta crossing the street; he removed his tie and put it in his pocket. Just his dark brown suit and a white shirt unbuttoned at the top should make Lotta feel comfortable. Of course, from the start the conversation was strained. As time went on Lotta finally started to open up. She admitted that Polar had done all he could to contact her. She even seemed to agree that he sent her letters and came to Charleston after the war to find her. Even acknowledging that Polar still had feelings for her was a big step. The question was, could she awaken the feeling she once had for him? Even if she did, how could she live with her past. Polar was a God fearing man. Lotta lived with the devil in her heart and soul. Then again she so wanted someone to love her. Was it too late to change her ways? Was it fair to Polar for her to love him or for he to love her? If only she had not killed so many people. She knew the man up above would never forgive that. Maybe it was time to at least try to have a relationship with the only man she ever cared for. Polar she knew had never married. Nor had he anyone else in his life. His heart still belonged to her. She left the restaurant with a lighter heart and very confused mind. She promised to return.

It took Polar two days to summon the courage to send a new bouquet of flowers to Lotta. This time it was a lunch engagement. Polar would be waiting outside the Palace of Payne at noon; all Lotta had to do to accept was to meet him there. With some encouragement from her daughter, Lotta accepted the invitation. Polar had a bright green buggy with a fringe top and red wheels waiting. He kissed Lotta's hand and helped her aboard the buggy.

"How beautiful you look this afternoon. It should be a fine day for a picnic." Said Polar. Lotta sat in silence, her heart beating so hard she was afraid that Polar would hear it. Einer and I had been invited along by Polar. He felt we would be a nice ice breaker, just in case things did not go well. We drove about two miles out of town to an open area next to the cliffs of Devil's Horn Mountain. A small snow fed waterfall cascaded over the rocks into a still blue pond. Polar helped Lotta from the buggy, then grabbed a buffalo robe and laid it out on the soft grass by the pond. He escorted Lotta to the robe and helped her to sit down. Next, he brought a large picnic basket from the buggy and set up the plates, silverware, and wine for lunch. No matter how hard she tried to ignore him, this was the Polar that Lotta loved. He had not changed; he was still gentle, loving, and kind. Her mind skipped all the years and landed in the present. This is how it was always supposed to be. Her stone heart had started to beat, blood flowed in her veins, she was not a monster, and she was human. She still loved Polar. The afternoon was spent playing in the water and talking of a possible future. Einer and I put on a good show, wrestling, swimming, and chasing each other around. For the first time ever we saw Lotta laugh out loud. As Einer and I rested next to Polar and Lotta, we witnessed one of those romantic human moments. Polar poured them each a glass of wine. It was his own recipe and bottled exclusively for him. He handed the bottle to Lotta and asked her to read out loud the ingredients. "Summer Wine, made from strawberries, cherries and an angles kiss in spring." Polar leaned over and kissed her, as he said, "you my Lotta are the final ingredient, an angel's kiss in spring." They embraced as they lowered themselves to the ground. Einer and I shut our eyes and decided to take a nap. I'll leave the details to your imagination; I might add there will be no more kids at this time.

Back at Gravesend, something else was brewing. The train arrived at the station with fifty stone masons and stone cutters from Europe. None of them spoke English. They had a map and unloaded five wagons and stone working tools from the train. The town watched as they made their way to a high ledge about two miles from town. The ledge was at least sixty acres of grass covered ground with a stone base dropping down about sixty feet. On the back of the ledge, a sheer stone wall of the Devil's Horn Mountain rose five hundred feet straight up. By night fall, the men could be seen in the distance setting up their equipment. The next morning they were cutting stone blocks and moving them into position. Of course, no one knew what they were building, or who hired them. It was a very curious thing indeed.

The next few weeks Lotta and Polar become almost inseparable. Lotta finally called a meeting of the Gravesend Ghouls to resign Alvira and herself from the group. Cowboy Lugosi took over with Larry the Wolf as second in command. They were welcome to stay at the Palace of Payne as long as they wished. The loot in the basement would be sorted to shares with Alvira and Lotta's shares being kept in a separate area. Larry the Wolf suggested that they give ten percent of their future take to The Palace of Payne as long as they used it as their headquarters. Everyone agreed. Alvira was relieved that her mother was trying to change her ways. Einer told me he was even more relived that Alvira was now free to choose her own course in life.

Love seemed to be blossoming in more than one heart at the Palace of Payne. Alvira and Larry the Wolf were noticeably spending an inordinate amount of time with each other. Although there was a noticeable difference in their ages, it did not seem to bother either of them. Alvira did not realize how big of age difference there actually was. As for Einer,, he smelled a definite canine scent on Larry's body. This in the dog world allows you immediate acceptance. Lotta, well she was not very happy with the attention one of the Gravesend Ghouls was paying to her daughter. Then again, looking at her past and now her rekindled involvement with Polar what could she say. As for Larry, he was a very kind and gentle man, except when angered, then the wolf in a literal sense came out of him.

Alvira knew that every member of the gang had rather special attributes. From drinking blood to eating rodents. She also knew of Larry's attack on a U.S. Marshall during a train robbery. Nevertheless, love took precedence. Larry went to Lotta and asked for her daughter's hand.

Lotta would agree, if Larry were to tell the story of his affliction to both Alvira and Lotta. Then if Alvira still wished to marry Larry, permission would be granted.

The three of them sat down together. Einer and I just happened to be in the room at that time. Larry began his story.

"It was the year 1798. I had been living in America with my mother. My father and she had separated many years before. After my mother passed away of a fever I decided to go and see my father in Bohemia, my country of birth. My father was wealthy, he owned a large estate and employed many servants. In the first two weeks, I was a thirty eight year old foolish gentleman. Spoiled with my father's money and a lack of any discipline from my mother. I drank and went to parties and dances with the nobility of the area. One night after too much drink, we stumbled upon a camp of Gypsy's. One of the girl's danced for us and we tossed her coins in gratitude. Then in a drunken stupor I grabbed her and kissed her. Her brother pulled me away and a fight ensued. I awoke in the morning next to a single gypsy wagon being tended by an old women. She said my friends had run off and abandoned me. She stayed to make sure I would be safe until I woke up. The last thing she did was to tell my fortune. I remember her words like it was yesterday. "You have lived an evil and useless life. You will receive punishment as if you were a rabid dog. It shall follow you for the rest of your life." I was stumbling through the woods back to my father's home when it happened. Daylight had not yet peeked over the trees. Suddenly a large wolf attacked me. I beat him off with my cane. My father and his servants found me a short time later, cut and bloody from the wolf attack. From that point on if I let my anger overwhelm, I turn into a wolf. A side effect of the wolfs curse is that I never age. I am well over one hundred years old."

Silence fell over the room for many minutes. Alvira spoke. "Larry it does not matter to me. Together we can control your affliction. But will you live with me as I age and you stay the same over the years." Larry answered. "Alvira I am already old beyond my years. To have someone to love me and allow me to love them is the most important thing in my life. You have my word as a man, or if you want as a faithful canine companion that you will have me with you till the day you die."

"Wait just a minute you two." Said Lotta. "I may have an answer to this problem. My mother was a gypsy princess from Bohemia. For your honeymoon, I would suggest a trip to the old country. I will write a note to my mother's family and see if they cannot help you. If a gypsy predicted the curse, I would think that a gypsy could remove it."

Lotta was still seeing Polar on a regular basis. Cassie and Alvira were busy with wedding plans. The Gravesend Ghouls were still perfuming regular robberies and the workers on the mountain were building what looked to be a castle.

CHAPTER 7

A number of months went by. Alvira and Cassie were finishing the plans for the wedding. They spent many hours at Valerie's Dress shop making sure the wedding dress would be perfect. Larry begrudgingly was having his suit special made, also at Valerie's shop. He of course felt somewhat un-manly having his outfit made in a dress shop. What a man in love won't do his for his intended.

Lotta pulled a surprise on Polar. She hired the same buggy they had used for their picnic on their second date. She drove the two of them and Einer and I to the same little waterfall and pond. I think Einer and I were allowed along to duplicate the first picnic. This one was to be very special. Lotta had a buffalo robe to sit on, and a full picnic basket, including Summer Wine to drink.

She had something important to talk to Polar about. Einer and I of course listened in.

"Polar. It is very important that you listen to what I have to say. Please do not interrupt, just listen. Since that time I made the error of thinking that you could have possibly abandoned me I have led a terrible existence. I closed my heart and soul to all humankind. I have led a life that Satan would be proud of. I took it upon myself as a hospital aid to make choices for men that I should not have done. Those men a dead because of me. I have robbed, cheated, and killed more people then you can imagine. My mind says I deserve no reprieve, no happiness, only a life of exile and misery. Then you came back into my life. You accepted my cold and unfeeling attitude toward you. You never gave up on me. Your forgiveness and love gave me a spark of hope. I love you now more than

I ever felt I could love anyone or anything. I know not if God can forgive me, but if he had sent an angel to give me a small amount of hope in my final days, I know that you are that angel. Please, have your say on this matter."

"Lotta, it is a heavy burden that you have laid before me. I am not a judge. I'm a God fearing man. I made my fortune as a gambler, not a very religious vocation. Although I played the game honestly, in my mind that was acceptable to my upbringing. Your sins are certainly more than a mere man can comprehend. I am not an angel; I have no power to forgive your sins. Your past is between you and the Lord. Still I offer you this. I will stand by you, be your friend, and companion as long as you will have me. If the powers above have brought us back together, I accept that as an affirmative sign. I would like our lives to begin anew as they have since or meeting in Gravesend. Is my answer agreeable to you?"

"It is most the agreeable. Not to be trite, I would like to change the subject and move on. Gravesend is growing so quickly. I feel it would be an opportune time to open a bank. I have the available funds to do this on my own. But I would like to have a partner; I wish you would give me the honor of being that partner."

Lotta, I would be pleased to be your partner in a bank. What would we call it? The Bank of Payne & Pederson, or the Bank of Pederson & Payne?"

"Actually I was thinking more along the lines of the Pederson's Bank. I felt it would save us the cost of having to change the name latter. What do you think?"

"Is that a proposal coming from your lips that I hear?"

"I am not so sure it is proper for a woman to propose to a man. What I said could certainly be construed as an acceptance to such an offer."

Polar stood up and helped Lotta to her feet. Then he went down on one knee. Took her hand in his and said the words. "Will you take an unworthy subject such as myself for your husband? Someone who will love you until the day you die, and if by chance, I should outlive you, my love will continue for you until I die. Lotta Payne, will you marry me?"

"Yes. Polar Pederson it would be my honor to marry you."

My dog that was a mushy human proposal. I guess it was nice. Einer and I were both very happy for them. This would certainly be the change we all hoped for in Lotta. It would be very different to have a happy and loving Lotta around the place.

Lotta was not yet finished in barring her soul.

"Polar, there is one last thing I must tell you. I lied about the children. Cassie is your child. So is Alvira. They are twins; Cassie is two hours older then Alvira. Your suspicions I am sure had to suspect that after you had been to the orphanage. Alvira wanted so much to ask you to give her away at the wedding. Cassie and her have become so close that she feels as if you are a father to her. Now we can tell them together that they are sisters and that Alvira's made an excellent choice for a father to walk her down the wedding aisle."

"Lotta I would like to wait a few days to tell the kids. Although I am shaking with joy and would like to scream it to the world. Let me buy you an engagement ring and we can arrange a large party for the whole town to attend. Then we as a couple can announce our engagement and bring together our children so everyone knows. You have made me the happiest person that any man could ever be. Lotta, I love you."

"Polar, I love you, too."

Einer and I decided to skip the next hour and go play. Way to much human interaction to describe. I'm glad dogs don't keep secrets from each other. Our relationships are so much simpler.

CHAPTER 8

Lotta and Polar decided to wait two weeks for their announcement party. It just so happened that would be the five-year anniversary date of the grand opening of the Pederson Hotel. So a big celebration could be planned for the hotel and no one would be any the wiser.

Cassie, Alvira, Einer, and I spent the day swimming and playing at the waterfall pond. Now we were just relaxing on the third story balcony outside Cassie's room. The two girls had on men's long sleeve wool shirts and some men's old pants they used to knock around in. The girls sat in their chairs with their bare feet sticking past the top of the railing, Einer and I were sitting on the floor. Cassie had supplied her and Alvira with a glass of Summer Wine, Einer and I also had wine, in our own special bowls. It was dry and warm. The sun was setting behind us and it lit the sky up in a pastel yellow, orange, and red hue. A beautiful storybook western night.

Cassie pointed out a dark speck in the distance; small puffs of smoke seemed to fellow the speck as it slowly made its way towards town. "Alvira do you see that dark spot off in the distance? It looks to have small puffs of smoke following it. Do you know what that is?"

"I'm not sure; I'm a city girl you know."

"Well it looks to b a lone horse and rider, the puffs of smoke is the dust coming up from the horse's hoofs. With this dry still weather, they give the impression of smoke from a distance. Not many riders come in so late in the day. By the time he gets here the gas lights will be on. It may be interesting to see where he stops first. Let us make a bet. I say he stops at the Buffalo Chip Saloon."

Cassie I will take your bet. A rider so late at night he will stop at the livery stable and take care of his horse before he takes care of himself. By the way, what are we betting?"

"I think we should bet another glass of Summer wine."

The four of us watched contently as the rider entered town. He rode by the stables and the past the saloon. He finally stopped in front of the hotel and tied his horse to the hitching post. Looking up he saw two sets of very attractive bare ankles and a touch of legs. "Ladies up on the third floor, could I bother you for a moment?" Startled, Alvira and Cassie jumped from their seats and peered over the railing. "What do you want cowboy?" asked Alvira. "Just wondering if those beautiful ankles and legs were attached to as beautiful of creatures as I hoped. I must say you have both meet my hopes beyond expectation." Answered the cowboy. "You are a rather brash man, sir. Is that quite all that you wanted?" answered Cassie. "Now ladies I meant my observation in only the most gentlemanly of manners. Do you know if this hotel has any vacancies?" As he kept his eye on Cassie. "Sir I suggest you go in and ask the clerk." Was Cassie's answer.

Einer and I had been looking down at the cowboy during the conversation. There was something about him that we both liked. Maybe he was outgoing, but he looked relaxed and comfortable with his life. A nice trait in a human. We lay back down as Alvira and Cassie started to banter at each other.

"Cassie, that was a nice looking cowboy down there. Fairly neat and clean looking for just coming off the trail, don't you think?

"I think you should leave your matchmaking ideas to my father and your mother. You have Larry. I will take care of myself."

"Ah yes my dear Cassie. You know you are not getting any younger. All you do is work and very little play. Soon I will be wed to Larry, will build a home and have children. I'm your best friend; it would not hurt to check that cowboy out. Maybe he's married. Would you like to bet a glass of Summer wine on that?"

"He's probably married to his horse like most cowboys. Either that or he has a girl in every saloon across the west. I think you should all retire for the evening."

Alvira and Einer left for home, I could tell she was happy with herself. She had Cassie thinking about that cowboy. The next morning would prove to be very interesting.

As was our usual routine, each morning Cassie and I walked through the hotel dining room greeting guests. We would stop at each table, introduce ourselves and make sure the guest was having a pleasant stay. I noticed the cowboy sitting at a table by himself on the far end of the room. Therefore, I took it upon myself to go check on him. He looked down at me and said. "So there my furry little friend is that your human over there talking to the guests?" I wagged my tail and jumped up on his lap. "Well you are a friendly littler beggar aren't you? Do you think you could arrange an introduction between your mistress and me?" No easier said than done. I jumped onto the top of the table and sat looking at Cassie. As soon as she saw me, she shouted. "Sven, get off that table now! You know better than that." She came rushing towards me. Looked like scolding time for me, so I jumped back into the cowboys arms. He was holding me as Cassie came storming over to his table. He addressed her in my behalf. "Miss, I hope you will forgive Sven. It was all my fault. I asked him to introduce me and I guess he did the best he could to get your attention. I must say, it certainly seemed to work. My name is Bristol Jones. May I inquire of your name?" I actually relaxed some when I saw a faint smile cross Cassie's lips before she answered. "I'm Cassie Pederson, my father and I own this hotel."

"Well Miss Pederson, would you do me the honor of having breakfast with me?"

"Mr. Jones, I think that I would be pleased to do so."

"If it is alright I do think Sven here should share in my good fortune and have a seat next to me."

"Sven knows better than to beg from guests, but I guess in this instance I will let him join us."

I liked this Mr. Jones a lot.

"So Mr. Jones."

"Please call me Bristol."

"Bristol, you may call me Cassie if you wish. Just what brings you to Gravesend?"

"I'm looking for a man. I've also heard this was a nice quiet town. Very little crime and a nice place to think about settling down."

"Looking for a man, are you an officer of the law? Or maybe a bounty hunter? Or just a gunslinger looking to build on his reputation?"

"Miss Cassie, none of the things you mentioned as such. Although the man I am looking for killed a very good friend of mine and I want to see him brought to justice. Killing is the last thing on my mind, if you wish to see my gun there are no notches. I hope there never will be. I could use a friend to show me around town. I would certainly be honored if you and Sven could be my guides."

"This man you're looking for does he have a name? Do you know what he looks like? Why would you think he was here in Gravesend?

"I don't know his name. I do have a description. About six foot tall, heavy set, has sort of a sad unhappy face, average looking. I've talked to a number of witness' to the murder. I am sure I will recognize him when I see him."

We had a nice breakfast, Bristol made sure I had my own plate and a bowl of milk. Then the three of us toured Gravesend. One thing about the town of Gravesend it has a colorful character. Everything from the names of the businesses to the owner's names. Bristol would chuckle to himself and point out the things he thought were unusual. Just a few of the points of interest that he liked were, Momma Bunn's Bakery, Dragon Breath Chinese Restaurant, Buffalo Chip Saloon, Dr Pull Dentist, Larry's Eatemup Café, Cowfur Leather Shop, Slowemdown & Nevercome Stage and Freight Company, Ahsoclean Chinese Laundry and of course The Palace of Payne. The rest of the business names were at least somewhat normal.

The next few days Cassie and Bristol became better acquainted. She learned that he was not just some illiterate cowhand. He had attended Harvard University to study law. It did not take him long in the profession to learn that guilty or innocent most lawyers did not care. All that counts is the fee they collect. A very immoral position to spend one's life at. Thus, he gave up the practice of law and headed west. His mother was an eastern aristocrat and had married his father, a handsome dashing western lawman. Bristol decided he had more of his father in him then his mother. So here he was roaming the west in search of honesty and adventure. A land where men have to make and keep a moral code without the interference of lawyers or politicians. Both of which Bristol looked at as being the bane of the United States.

On one our walks I noticed a commotion at the Railroad station. We walked over to observe the goings on. The wagons from the mountain had come back to town. Looking off in the distance was a now finished castle, ramparts, watchtowers and all. The men unloaded their equipment and waited for the train to arrive. Once the train pulled into the station, fifty new workman left the train. Then all one hundred men unloaded flatcar after flatcar of exotic woods. Redwood, oak, tarmac, cherry, walnut, beech, and even some Cyprus. Once the wood was off loaded they loaded up all the stone cutting equipment onto the now empty flatcars. The stonecutters and stonemasons boarded the train and left town. Now there was a mix of fifty European, Scandinavian, and English woodworkers. They loaded the wood onto the wagons and headed up the hill to the castle. Of course our best bet was they were ready to do the finishing work. Yet no one knew who they worked for and none of them spoke English. So the town had new gossip to keep it busy.

Cassie and Alvira were now closer than ever. Bristol coming into Cassie's life was almost as exciting for Alvira as for Cassie. Although Cassie had mentioned that Bristol was eight years older then she and wondered if that might be a problem. Alvira assured her it was no problem at all. Larry was much older than her, she of course neglected to tell Cassie just how much older.

It had been almost two weeks since Bristol came to town. Wedding plans were about completed for Alvira and Larry. Lotta and Polar were excited about the large party they had planned. Two more days on a Saturday and the world would know. Lotta and Polar would announce their engagement and Cassie and Alvira would not only have their real Mother and Father, but they would have each other as flesh and blood sisters. Cassie and Bristol were doing splendid in their relationship and it looked like wedding bells were a definite possibility for the future. Bristol, he was still searching for a man, and he was sure that man was somewhere in Gravesend.

CHAPTER 9

Polar could see that Cassie was very interested in Bristol. So Polar felt he should really get to know this man better. Thursday night, two days before the big party at the Pederson Hotel, Polar asked Bristol to go to the Buffalo Chip Saloon for a few drinks. No better way to get acquainted then a few shots of whisky and some beers.

It was a slow night at the Buffalo Chip, maybe two dozen people were there. Einer and I came with to see how Polar and Bristol would get along. Anyway, we are the dogs about town and the saloon is always a great place to get some treats and lick up some spilled beer. Polar knew most of the people, he went around, and introduced Bristol. Travis Anderson the mine owner was there, he still kept bringing up the time his mine was robbed and how the thieves were never captured. Big time rancher and horse racer Lorin Better was also in town with a few of his hired hands. Also at the bar were, Plantem Deeps, Doc Pull, and Casey from the Mercantile, Larry from the Eatemup Café, Cowboy Lugosi, Rent Field, and Igor. The rest were locals who Polar knew by face but not by name.

Standing at the bar next to Polar was Cowboy Lugosi on his right, Bristol, and then Rent on his left. Two men entered the saloon, one dressed in black, young and cocky. His friend had the look of a plowboy just off the farm. The cocky one wore two guns, rather a rare occasion in the west. The plowboy had an old navy colt tucked into the waistband of his pants.

The cocky one ordered a whiskey for his friend and himself. Then he started talking.

"They call me Adam the Kid; this here hombre with me is called Mississippi Mudd. You there at the bar, yes you the gent all dressed in black. I guess you must have heard of me, otherwise you wouldn't be copying the same outfit I have on."

Cowboy Lugosi just ignored the kid and kept visiting with Polar and the others at the bar. The kid was not about to give up.

"Hey you, pasty face one, yeah you in black, do you hear me? Or are you too old and deaf to hear? I think I have heard of you. They call you Cowboy Lugosi don't they? I heard you have never lost a gunfight. Until tonight."

Cowboy Lugosi finally spoke up.

"Listen Kid, I do not want any trouble. I have not caused you any problems and I am willing to forgo your rudeness. I am here just to have a nice quiet visit and few drinks with my friends. I suggest you cool down, I'll even buy your next drink for you. Bartender, give the Kid a milk."

Of course offering the Kid milk was not a good idea. The kid stood away from the bar, both of his hands were right above the handles of his two guns. Sweat was beading up on his brow and his fingers were twitching.

"Lugosi you've gone too far. Stand out and draw. It's your night to die."

Cowboy Lugosi finished his drink, turned, and faced the Kid. Not even the tiniest flicker of fear showed on his face.

"Kid, this is your call not mine. You want a gunfight, you draw first."

Like lightning, the kid had both guns out and blazing before Lugosi's gun was half out of its holster. Six shots echoed throughout the saloon. Six times Lugosi's body jerked as bullets hit him. Yet Lugosi stood still as if nothing happened. He slowly raised his gun, arm straight out, took aim, and put a bullet through the center of the Kid's forehead.

Mississippi Mudd the kid's friend drew his gun. Igor who had been sitting at one of the tables playing poker had moved so quickly no one even noticed as his knife flew through the air and entered the boy's heart.

Gunpowder scented the air as the smoke from the gun barrels drifted upward. Rent rushed to Lugosi and put his coat over Lugosi's shoulders to hide the bullet holes. Vampires may drink blood but they do not bleed, and for sure, a mere bullet is not going to kill them. Lugosi looked around at the stunned on lookers and said.

"The Kidd was not a very good shot. Six bullets and not one hit me. Very good fortune must have been smiling on me."

It was then that Polar slumped to the floor. Einer and I with our dog eyes and senses saw and knew what had happened. Some of the bullets that had passed through Lugosi had hit Polar. Doc Pull told everyone to get out of the way so he could examine Polar. Four bullet holes were evident. One hole in his left shoulder, two in the chest and one in the upper left leg. He ordered someone to go to his office and get the stretcher from behind his door. The boys flipped the contents off one of the poker tables and lifted Polar up on the table top. Doc had Polar's shirt ripped open and was doing his best to stem the flow of blood. Once the stretcher arrived, Bristol and Igor carried Polar over to the Doc's office.

Einer went with Polar to keep an eye on things. Plantem Deeps and I went to get Cassie. The sheriff had showed up and declared the shooting self-defense, case closed. Then he took some notes about Polar being hit by stray bullets.

As soon as Plantem and I reached the hotel, I put my nose into high gear and smelled out Cassie's scent. Plantem was close on my heels. I must say one thing for Plantem he was very calm and reassuring as he told Cassie what happened. I guess it must be from all the undertaking he's done for so many years. We rushed over to Doc's place to see how things were going.

Cassie was in tears as Doc told her it did not look good. For the time being the Doc had done all he could. He suggested Polar be moved to his own bed at the hotel. Bristol and Igor volunteered to carry him home. As soon as we entered the hotel Amos and his wife were anxiously awaiting any news about Polar. Cassie had them hurry upstairs and prepare Polar's bed for him.

For the time being Polar was unconscious. The Doc had loaded him up with laudanum to ease the pain. It would probably be morning before he woke up. If he woke up. Cassie sent Amos to get Lotta and Alvira from across the street. She pulled a chair next to Polar's bed and held his hand. Bristol sat in the corner waiting. He knew nothing he said could help. Once Lotta and Alvira arrived Bristol told them what had happened. Of course not being a dog, he told them it was stray bullets; I guess that's as good a story as any. After all it was not really Cowboy Lugosi's fault.

Bristol left after explaining what happened. It was best for the ladies and us dogs to have Polar to ourselves. We were the ones that loved and cared the most about him. Lotta asked Cassie for permission to lie on the large bed next to Polar so she could hold his other hand and be close to him. Cassie knew how much the two of them were in love and readily gave her consent. I lay at the end of the bed with my chin resting on Polar's leg, I hoped I could be of some comfort for him. Einer curled up on Alvira's lap as she sat quietly in the corner. Now remember Einer is forty pounds of muscle and fur, not what you would consider a lap dog. Although tonight with both him and Alvira hurting, I think they were just glad to give comfort to each other.

Amos brought coffee for the ladies and milk for Einer and I when morning came. He convinced Cassie and Alvira to go to Cassie's room and get some well deserved rest. Lotta, Einer, and I stayed with Polar. Lotta curled up on the bed beside him, holding him in a comforting embrace. Einer curled up at Polar's feet and I lay by his side with my head resting on his chest. If nothing else, we could at least surround him with love.

It was late morning and I felt Polar give a slight twitch, I looked up, his eyes were open about halfway. I heard him whisper for Cassie or Lotta. Lotta pulled herself up so her tear stained cheek touched Polar's check. "I love you so much, please, please don't leave me," she said. His hand was stroking my fur as he spoke to Lotta. "Lotta my love, forever in life or death you will be the only one in my heart and my mind. I'm afraid I am about to be shanghaied once more, right before our marriage. I think the Lord above is calling me into his army. Where are Cassie and Alvira?"

"I'll get them." Said Lotta as she rushed from the room. Einer came up and took Lotta's spot next to Polar. I was still on Polar's other side.

He petted us both and said. "Sven, Einer you take good care of the girls, I love you both." Then Cassie, Alvira, and Lotta were all in the room

Cassie was just leaning down to kiss her father, when I heard it happen. My senses being that of a dog are much more acute then humans. Just as Cassie's lips touched her father's he exhaled his final breath of life. For all of us present the next few hours were only a blur. I cannot begin to describe how anyone in the room felt or even what they did. Such sadness should not have to befall humans or dogs.

CHAPTER 10

Lotta was the first to leave; she said nothing, just got up and walked out the door. Einer decided to follow her and make sure she was ok. She went across the street and to her room. There she wrote out a last will and testament leaving everything she owned to her two daughters. She then took the elevator to the underground treasure room. She removed a box filled with jewelry from her share of the loot and counted out an exact amount of money, which she then placed into the box. Einer stood by and watched her every move.

Next, she walked down the street to the sheriff's office. The sheriff looked up from his desk. "Why Miss Lotta, what a pleasant surprise. What brings you to my office?" The sheriff had not yet heard that Polar had died and for what was coming up next, it did not really matter. Lotta started speaking. "Sheriff I want to turn myself in. I think if you go through your wanted posters you will find one for a stage robbery. The driver and passengers were all shot and killed. This box I have put on your desk contains the passenger's valuables and the money from the strong box. I held up that stage and I killed those people in cold blood. I want you to arrest me now. I would also like you to hang me by the neck until dead. I would like my execution to take place tomorrow morning."

"Now hold on here Miss Lotta. Am I supposed to just take your word for all this? Then hang you besides? I think you need a lawyer."

"Sheriff I do not want a sleazebag lawyer who does not care if I am innocent or guilty, all a lawyer cares about is he fee. I do not want a trail, why waste the taxpayer's time and money. I'm guilty, I admit it. No trail, no shyster lawyers, no jury, just hang me, and save the town some expense."

The sheriff had been flipping through all the wanted posters on his desk during the conversation. Sure enough, he found the stage robbery she talked about. The poster said no description of the hold-up person was available.

"Lotta, I found the stage hold-up information. You really expect me to believe that you did this? What does Polar or your daughter have to say about this? Do they know you're here?"

"Sheriff, Polar died this morning, maybe if you would have been patrolling the streets and bars instead of sitting in your office last night this might not have happened. My daughter does not know I am here; otherwise, she would have tried to stop me. Believe me I am guilty. It is time I paid for my sins."

"As sheriff I have no authority to condemn you to death, or even to decide if your are guilty or innocent. That's not my job. I uphold the law, I'm not a judge and jury. The circuit judge will be here in the morning. He's coming into town to see the big celebration that you and Polar were putting on at the Hotel. I'll have someone meet him at the train station and immediately bring him here to talk to you."

"Thank you Sheriff, you may lock me up now."

"Miss Lotta if it is alright with you I would prefer to let you go home. Just give me your word you will come back here in the morning so we can straighten this whole thing out. I really believe I can trust you to do that."

"Sheriff, don't ever trust me, lock me up now. You have all the evidence you need in that box on your desk. All you have to do is telegraph the stage company for a description of the stolen items and a total of the cash taken. Once again, I repeat, lock me up now. I insist"

"Whatever you say Miss Lotta. If there is anything you need just let me know."

Einer rushed back to the hotel and told me what was happening. Unfortunately being dogs, we did not know how to convey the information to Cassie or Alvira. Einer finally jumped up and grabbed Bristol's shirt cuff and dragged him to the door. Bristol had enough dog sense to realize Einer wanted him to follow. So he led him to the Jail.

A minster and a priest had somehow already gotten wind of Polar's death and were cornering Cassie about having church services. Cassie told them both that her father was a religious man in his own way. He believed in God, just as Cassie did. Neither of them believed in organized religion or churches. For some reason in Polar's past churches and him did not get along. As luck would have it, Plantem Deeps walked into the lobby during the discussion. He grabbed both the minister and the Priest by the back of their coat collars and tossed them out the door and into the dusty street. For a wiry old man he had a lot of strength when he was riled. Harassing his best friend's daughter was more than enough to get old Plantem's dander up.

Cassie thanked Plantem and asked him to make whatever arrangements he felt Polar would have wanted. Plantem then suggested something that seemed rather out of place at the time. He told Cassie that he thought Polar would have wanted to go on with the big Hotel anniversary celebration. Why not lay Polar out for viewing in the hotel lobby during the celebration. A chance for the town and all his friends to say a farewell. Knowing Polar, he would love to go out in style. This would be something Polar just might do if he had been given a choice. Cassie only had to think about it for a moment. Then she said.

"Plantem Deeps. You were my father's best friend. I think you are right. This is just what my father would have wanted. Please feel at liberty to choose his coffin. I think as far as any services go, let's just have it at graveside with a few select friends. Plantem I want you to officiate. You are in now in charge."

"Miss Cassie I appreciate your confidence in me. I will do the best possible job I can do for my dear friend Polar, and for you. God bless you Miss."

Plantem rushed off to his funeral parlor. He had been saving a beautiful burled oak coffin for himself. The handles and trim were all in solid gold. A viewing window had been installed so that the body could be viewed without the coffin being open. The white satin liner and pillow were all made to be extra soft; you never know what might be comfortable after your dead so no need to take a chance. This was to be Polar's final resting place.

By now, Bristol and Einer had returned to the hotel. Bristol finally managed to get Cassie away from all the people that were trying to comfort her. She felt it her duty to be in the hotel lobby and greet them.

Alvira was still locked in Cassie's room. Her personality did not allow her to be sociable at a time like this. Although in her heart, she ached for not having the strength to stand by Cassie in this time of need.

Bristol ushered Cassie upstairs to her bedroom. Einer and I sat patiently and listened while Bristol explained what the sheriff had told them about Lotta. He asked to see Lotta but she refused to have any visitors. The five of us managed to exit out the back entrance of the hotel and make our way down the back streets to the jail.

The sheriff broke all the rules and let Alvira, Cassie, Einer and I in to visit Lotta. The rules of course stated only one visitor at a time. Lotta refused to see anyone but family so Bristol waited out in the sheriff's office. Alvira was more than a little upset.

"Mother what are you doing? Why would you turn yourself in now for crimes from the past? How come you never told me about these things?"

"Alvira and Cassie, both of you listen to what I have to say. After I made the terrible mistake of thinking that Polar would even think of deserting me, well, I hated the world. Any man who got in my way was disposable. I killed more men then I can even count. Most of them in the hospital. I made their choices of life and death for them. I choose they should die. Polar was the one saving grace in my life. He gave me hope and most of all unconditional love. Having the Lord take him away now was a sign to me, it was my judgment day. It was as if God said Lotta this is how you have to pay for your crimes. I wanted you both here to tell you the truth about your family. When I become pregnant, it was out of wedlock. Polar wanted to wait until we were married, but I seduced him two weeks before our wedding. You two are the result. Yes, you are flesh and blood sisters. Cassie you came first, Alvira you came two long hard hours later. Beautiful twin girls. Polar is your father, and I never told him until just recently. He found you Cassie when Amos who was a slave on my father's plantation told him that I had given birth to a child. What your father or Amos did not know is that there were twins. My father who was very strict made me give you both up for adoption. A baby out of wedlock in my family was just too much of a disgrace to both my father and my mother. Most likely Amos heard the story of a baby hidden in my room for a few months from one of the household staff. What they did not know was that there were twins. When I had to take you to the orphanage, I registered you under two different names, Pederson and Payne. I felt that way when you were separated by adoption you would not have the pain or knowledge of having a missing sister."

"It was by pure chance that your father and I both ended up here in Gravesend. It was even more by chance that we both found and brought you two here. I just recently told your father that you were twins and that he was the father. The big party we had planned. It was not really for the hotel's anniversary. It was to announce our engagement and to announce that you two were our flesh and blood children. Two of the most beautiful daughters a mother and father could ever hope to have. Both of you take the necklaces from around your necks and show them to each other. That little silver Cossack with the Viking Ship engraved on his coat. Those two pieces were originally a set of earrings that your father gave to me as an engagement present. I made them into necklaces and left them in an envelope to be given to you girls when you were old enough to take care of them. You both were of course told never to remove them."

"As for me. It is time for me to go to your father, if the Lord is willing. I know my chances are very slim being the sinner that I am, but I must pay for those sins. This is the only way possible. I cannot bear to take my own life, but I can let someone else do it. I would like to ask two things of you girls. First, bury next to Polar. Second please forgive me."

Everyone was crying including Einer and I. It did not seem right for the girls to lose their mother and father within days of each other. The girls though sobbing and hugging told Lotta about the farewell wake party they were giving to Polar. Lotta was proud of them and felt Polar would be very happy to have it done that way. Once the circuit judge arrived in the morning, we would know more of Lotta's fate. For now we all went back to our homes.

CHAPTER 11

The next morning the circuit judge arrived by train. The sheriff had him escorted immediately to the jail. The sheriff acquainted the judge with the facts as they pertained to Miss Payne. The Judge then entered the cell where Miss Payne was detained.

"Miss Payne I am circuit Judge Royal Beam. I have been briefed of your request to forgo a trial and not to accept representation from legal counsel. My dear women I feel for your sake you should reconsider this matter. For if you continue to demand an immediate appeal of guilty and expect to be hanged for it, you are sorely mistaken. Neither I nor any other judge has the authority to authorize a death penalty without the verdict of a jury. I will set up a jury and trail date for my next visit to Gravesend, this will be in about three weeks. As per counsel I shall appoint a lawyer to your case if you do not hire one of your own accord. Do we understand each other?"

"Your Honor, I do not believe that we do understand each other. I refuse to have any type of legal counsel. I refuse a trial by jury. I request you accept my plea of guilty and sentence me to death as quickly as possible."

"My dear women you leave me only one choice in this matter. If you persist to stand your ground and not allow the judicial system to do its duty I will have to make a choice for you. In the case you have presented I have but no other alternative then to place you in a home for the criminally insane until such time as you come to your senses. How long you remain there will be up to you. If you agree to a lawful trial with counsel you shall have it. If not you may remain locked in an institution for the reminder of your days. I will be stop in to see you tomorrow afternoon before my train comes to take me to my next destination. You have until that time to decide what you would like to do. A trial or an institution. The choice is yours. Good day Madame."

None of this fit in with Lotta's overall plan. She asked the sheriff to send someone to get Alvira and her fiancé. If anyone could help her now it would be Larry Wolf. Once Alvira and Larry arrived to see Lotta she explained what the Judge had told her. Alvira had come to accept the fact that her mother wanted to pay for her crimes. She of course did not agree with her mother, but she knew this was something that had to happen.

Lotta then asked for Larry's help. She knew if anyone could help her in this situation it would be the Gravesend Ghouls. If only the gang would break into the jail and help her end her life. Larry of course looked at Alvira for some type of help. Alvira told Larry it was all right to assist her mother. Lotta apologized for putting such a strain on their future marriage, but it was better they be honest up front. That was why Lotta wanted her daughter to be in on any plans that she asked Larry to make. For the time being the only promise Larry could make was that he would talk it over with the rest of the gang and see what they could do.

The planned party took place. It was a sad and also joyous affair. The whole town came to see Polar in his final state at the hotel. Everyone was well behaved and no trouble arose. The sheriff had a few deputies on duty to keep the peace. The whole Gravesend Gang was also there, whenever they were around people tended to be on their best behavior. Late that night a meeting was called for all the gang to attend, including Alvira. Cassie had no knowledge of the gang and its association with Lotta so she was not informed of the goings on. This burden was completely in Alvira's hands.

The gang was all in attendance. Alvira, Lugosi, Larry, Rent, Igor, Frank, Boris, and Mole. Larry called the meeting to order.

"Well boys looks like we're all here. As you know Lotta is in jail. This is of her own choosing. She feels her time has come to pay for her sins. She would like someone to help her end her life. Still being human she feels it would just add to her sins to take her own life. Therefore, this is where we come in. Now of course this does present a problem. For everyone of us here other then Alvira has eternal life at this time. Lotta asked me to be in charge and so I made a list trying to figure out which of us could be of the most assistance in her cause. Rent, Igor, and Boris I know you guys don't kill unless you have no other choice, so I eliminated you from my line up. Frank, you are really a gentle person at heart; I don't think you could purposely do any harm to Lotta. Mole, well I know you just want to find a way back to your own kind, as far as any of us know you have never hurt a soul. That leaves two of us. Lugosi and myself. For me to have anything to do with this deed would be unfortunate to say the least seeing Alvira and I are soon to be married. It would not be right to kill my future mother-in-law. So Cowboy what do you think? Are you willing to help Lotta end her existence on this earth?"

Cowboy Lugosi pondered the situation for a while before he started speaking.

"Gentleman. oh I am sorry, and Miss Alvira. Lotta is responsible for my being here. In fact if it were not for her none of us would be here. It is the least we can do to help her in her time of need. No matter how grave the request may be. She has gypsy blood flowing in her from the old country. I also came here from the old country, so it is my duty to take on this unpleasant task. I only ask you, Alvira to forgive me for what I am obligated to do."

"Count Cowboy Lugosi it is very hard for me to accept all of this, but it is my mother's wish. I appreciate your gallantry in carrying out this extremely sad and unpleasant duty. Yes I will forgive you." Said Alvira.

"Then I Count Cowboy Lugosi will do my duty yet this evening. As for all of you here, I feel I can accomplish what I have to do on my own. That will be best; none of you will have to be involved. Miss Alvira you may want to get Cassie and say good-bye to your mother yet tonight. The deed will be accomplished shortly after you leave her."

Although it was after ten o'clock at night Alvira went to the Hotel to get Cassie. The sheriff was asleep on a cot in the jailhouse. Alvira and Cassie took his keys and let themselves into their mother's cell. For the next half hour they talked, cried, and held each other. Lotta was told that Lugosi would be there soon to help her end her life.

Shortly after the girls left a bat flew in to Lotta's cell through the barred window. It hovered in mid-air for a few seconds. Then it quickly transformed itself into a man. Count Cowboy Lugosi.

"Lotta, how do you do. You know why I am here. Don't look so surprised you knew I was a vampire. One nice thing about being a vampire, I can change into either a bat or a wolf. Just depends on the situation at the time. I know you loved Polar very much, but I want you to know I was always jealous of your love for him. You are a beautiful lady, and for so long you were soul-less, just my type. So I have loved you from afar. Now though it is too late to pursue any relationship for us. I will take you on a journey to be with Polar. I ask only that you allow me to give you one embrace and a kiss on the neck."

"Count, the words are kind. You are right, Polar was my soul mate, my only true love. I thank you for doing this for me. Come; hold me in death's embrace."

As they embraced Lotta relaxed onto the cot in her cell. Lugosi stared into her eyes, she was now in a trance like state. Within minutes Lotta lay dead on her cot. Lugosi stood up and looked at her so beautiful in her peaceful slumber of death. He leaned over and kissed her already cold lips goodbye. The he transformed into a bat and flew off into the night.

The next morning the sheriff found Lotta dead in her cell. He had Doc, Alvira, Cassie and the circuit judge all rounded up and brought to the jail for Lotta's examination. The Doc said the only thing he could find were two small wounds on her neck. Although he mentioned she seemed very cold and pale, almost as if she had lost a lot of blood. Alvira and Cassie did not want an autopsy. They just wanted their mother's body for burial next to Polar. The circuit judge left in a huff. He was sure the sheriff and others killed Miss Payne, but he had no proof.

Plantem Deeps came for Lotta's body. He found the nicest coffin he had left for her. It was the least he could do for his friend Polar. When Cassie returned to the hotel she found Cowboy Lugosi leaning over her father's body, it seemed his face was almost touching Polar's face. Lugosi was startled and stood up to greet Cassie.

"Miss Lugosi, I am very sorry if what I was doing startled you. It is a custom in my county to give a kiss on the check to the departed as a final farewell. Please forgive me if it seemed inappropriate to you."

"No, Mr. Lugosi I understand. It is nice of you to feel my father was a close friend. I am sure he appreciates the kind act."

"Miss Cassie I do have a gift for your parents. I hope you will accept it. I have two open burial chambers in a crypt that I own in the graveyard. It would honor me greatly if you would allow Lotta and Polar to be interned there side by side for all eternity."

"Why, Mr. Lugosi that is very kind. You realize I must ask my sister Alvira if it is all right with her. If so I know I would be honored to accept your request."

The funeral was held two days later. It was a small affair, only close friends and family were invited. The word of Lotta turning herself as a murderous of course had many of the town's people upset. For Polar they would like to have attended, for Lotta they felt she had cheated justice.

Plantem Deeps gave an eloquent speech for the departed. He praised Polar as a pillar of the town. Lotta he put on a pedestal for changing her life around and making Polar a happy man. It was best not to dwell too far into Lotta's past.

In attendance besides the girls and us dogs were the poker playing buddies, and all of the Gravesend Ghouls. Lugosi was rather conspicuous with a long black coat and black umbrella that kept any hint of sunshine from touching him. The bodies were slowly slid into the burial chamber and closed. Einer and I were almost sure we could here breathing coming from inside the coffins, but it must have been a freak breeze in the air.

Alvira and Larry were standing next to Cassie and Bristol. For some reason Bristol was keeping a very close eye on Larry. My dog sense told me something was not right between those two.

CHAPTER 12

After the funeral service, a small lunch was served in the hotel's private dining room. Close friends and family only. Most of those who attended the burial services were there. Polar's poker buddies and the Gravesend Ghouls. Alvira and Larry were sitting across the table from Cassie and Bristol. Einer and I were there too, we had pillows and were served our food in a corner of the room.

Bristol started a conversation with Larry.

"Larry I think I know you from somewhere? Do you travel much by train?"

"Well Bristol I don't recall us having ever met before. As for train travel, yes I've done my share. Just what do you do for a living Bristol?"

"I'm sort of a jack of all trades. Studied law in college. Then I came west working at odd jobs. My father was living out here at the time; he died not too long ago."

"I'm sorry to hear that. Seems like death has poked its ugly head up a lot in our little group of friends here."

"Actually my father was killed. He was a U.S. Marshall travelling by train. The train was robbed and he was attacked by a man that the witness' swore turned into a wolf like creature. That man or creature tore my father's head right off his body. So I guess for the time being my job is to find that man."

Larry sat very still, not showing any emotion. He did his best to regain his composure. During the lull in the conversation, Cassie started speaking.

"Bristol honey, I can't believe you never told me about your father. What a horrible thing."

"Cassie, Alvira, Larry I must apologize. There are a few things I have neglected to mention. My father was Bristol Coffin. My real name is not Jones, I have been using that name so as not to make the killer aware that I was searching for him. You can call me Bristol Coffin Jr. from now on. I think I know who the murderer is. I am sure he and I will be talking soon. I do not wish to kill him, just to bring him to justice."

Larry had beads of sweat forming on his brow as he answered Bristol's comments.

"Yes Bristol I think it would be advantageous to talk to that man in a civil manner. Maybe he will give himself up. Some men are driven by forces that they cannot control. If that is the case, I hope that it would make your understanding of the situation a little less painful."

Alvira came into the conversation.

"Larry how can you say that. This fiend killed Bristol's father in a most horrible manner. Bristol I would think will be justified to seek his revenge in any manner he should see fit."

"No Alvira, I think Larry is right. I hope the man is willing to talk things over. It would be better if he could take him into custody in a peaceable manner." Answered Cassie.

Cassie had enough of death and murder talk so she started on a new more pleasant subject. The group talked of Alvira and Larry's future weeding and their plan to honeymoon in Bohemia. Cassie and Bristol were on the verge of engagement as far as Einer and I could tell. The way they talked, we were almost sure they were going to announce their coming nuptials. Although it didn't happen yet. I suppose Bristol had to settle some things first. As far Einer and I could figure, Larry and Bristol had a lot to talk about. If Larry were the killer, it would certainly add more bad luck to the Payne-Pederson family. We could only hope Bristol was mistaken about Larry's involvement with his father's death.

Later that night after Alvira and Larry had returned to Alvira's room the discussion came back up.

Alvira I hate to tell you this, but I am the one who killed Bristol Coffin on that train. We were in the middle of a robbery when Bristol shot Rent in the shoulder. It made me so mad I lost control. I leaped at Bristol to get his gun. My anger overtook me and I transformed into my wolf self and killed him. Bristol has every right to take me in for murder. Of course they cannot hang me or shot me as I am immortal. I guess they will put me in prison for the rest of my life. The joke will be on them, which could be forever."

Einer was lying on the floor listening to the conversation. He was thinking silver bullet. You know a silver bullet could kill a werewolf. Then again it was probably not a good time to bring that up.

"Larry, maybe if you explain to Bristol what happened. It is as if you are two different individuals, a man, and a wolf. Larry the man would never harm anyone. Larry the wolf is controlled by his animal instinct to protect and defend the ones he cares about. I'm sure Bristol will take this into consideration. Let him know we are going to Bohemia on our honeymoon to find a cure. Our family has suffered so much in the last few days. Bristol seems like a good sensible man. Please let me talk to him if you won't."

"Alvira I will tell him the truth about myself. I have wronged him and his family. It will be up to him to decide what he needs to do. Promise me you will not talk to Bristol."

"Yes, I promise, I will not talk to Bristol"

After Larry left for his room Alvira put on her house coat. Einer and her hurried across the street to the hotel. She removed the hidden key from a hall planter to open the door of Cassie's room. Cassie was sound asleep as Alvira sat on the edge of her bed and stroked her long red hair to awaken her. Einer jumped up on the bed next to me. "Listen Sven this should be interesting." Said Einer.

Cassie, I need to talk to you. Remember how you said dad always told us to tell the truth, never lie and we won't have to remember what we said. Also don't hide any secrets from each other. Well, I need help. All the Gravesend Ghouls as mother called the gang at the hotel, well they are all immortal, and they can't ever die. Everyone of them is a robber, crook and a thief. Most of them have probably killed innocent people in the past. Mother brought all of them out of their crypts to help her with her plans to build an empire. Somehow she figured out that they were in a form of suspended animation. First she brought back Lugosi who promptly murdered our two employees for their blood. Yes he is a vampire. My Larry is a werewolf. When angry he changes into a wolf with pure animal instinct of self preservation. He killed Bristol's father during a train robbery. The worse thing is I knew all along what they were doing. Our mother was the leader and she kept me informed by making me attend their meetings. I just wanted to make mother happy and did what I was told. I knew it was wrong, but I thought I was being a good daughter.

"Now for the really bad part. The whole gang other then mother did not want to do any unnecessary killing. That was why they started robbing banks at night when no one was around to get hurt. In their own way they were actually developing some morals. Their goal was to have enough money to disappear and live lives without violence or theft. Our mother was probably the most blood thirsty of the group. At least until Polar came back into her life and changed her. She even quit the gang so she and Polar could live a happy carefree life with you and I. Now it looks like my life will be shattered if Larry is taken away from me. For you, how will it affect you and Bristol if he locks up my Larry? Or how will it affect our relationship as sisters? I promised Larry not to talk to Bristol about this, but I did not promise that I would not tell you. So if you just happen to mention this to Bristol I would not mind. Well, what do you think?"

"Alvira I think you just tossed a whole barn full of horse manure in my lap. How the heck am I supposed to deal with all this. Immortal Ghouls next door that I have befriended. You want to marry a werewolf. Your fiancé killed the father of a man I love. Come to think of it, I know one of the Ghouls killed our mother. Which one was it? If it was Larry we have a major problem."

"It was not Larry. Although mother asked him to find someone to do it. I was also there, I didn't dare tell you. Mother wanted to pay for her sins and join Polar. You knew her wishes, but the judge wanted to lock her up in an insane asylum for the rest of her life. Even I had to admit death was better than that. The Gravesend Ghouls and I held a meeting to discuss it. No one wanted to do the job. Finally Lugosi said he would do it. He felt he owed mother for bringing him back to life from his crypt. Not only did mother help bring them all back but she gave them a place to live and be happy. Her choice of occupation I admit was a little distorted. Once again Cassie, please talk to Bristol about Larry. Give us a chance to find a cure for him."

"Yes I will talk to Bristol in Larry's behalf. If this ruins my relationship with Bristol I will make you wish you were immortal. Now curl up in bed next to me and spend the night. Einer, move over to Alvria's side you big lum ox."

"Thank you Cassie. I could not have picked a better sister. I love you."

"I love you too, now go to sleep."

I have to admit Einer is a bed hog, or should I say bed dog. Anyway he likes to sleep stretched out and he takes up a lot of space. As for me, I can curl up and no one hardly knows I'm there.

CHAPTER 13

The next morning at breakfast Cassie and Bristol had a long talk. Of course, Bristol was in hot water for not telling Cassie his real name and the reason he was in town. Luckily, Cassie took after her father and was very forgiving of other people's faults and mistakes. She explained the situation about Larry to Bristol and he seemed very understanding.

After his talk with Cassie, Bristol said he needed time alone to think. He asked Cassie to convey a message to Larry that he would like to have a talk when he returned. Then he got on his horse and rode off to be alone for a while.

A week went by before Bristol rode back into town. He was dusty, unshaven and looked like he had not slept the whole time he was gone. Cassie ran him a hot bath and left him alone to get cleaned up and rested. He asked Cassie to set up a meeting in private with Larry for the next morning.

That evening Larry invited the gang to have drinks and play poker at the Buffalo Chip Saloon. During the game, he explained to the boys that he was going to turn himself over to Bristol. Let the chips fall where they may.

"You know Larry; we are like a big family here. If you want, we can take care of Bristol for you. He will never know what hit him." said Lugosi.

'It's ok guys, I need to do this. Bristol may just end up being my brother-in-law at that rate things are going. I am sure he will treat me fairly. I'll have to hope he can differentiate between me and my wolf self." Answered Larry.

"No one is going to take Larry away. Uh, no one. I stop Bristol myself for you Larry." Added Frank.

This was unusual to hear Frank talk about anything important. Of course, Larry had always treated Frank just like one of the boys. He never teased Frank about being a little slow in the mind. Igor, well he had Frank so brow beaten into thinking he was not as good as anyone else that Frank rarely stood up for himself.

"Frank, it will be ok. Thanks for wanting to help. There's no need for you to get involved." Said Larry.

"Frank wants to be involved. Larry is like a brother to me. You always are kind to me, you give me respect. Frank will be there for you." Answered Frank.

Larry worked at getting his point across to Frank.

"Frank you are like my brother, so you have to listen to me. Ok? You just let Bristol and I have our meeting. If I need you, I will let you know. I promise right after I talk to Bristol I will let you know what happened."

This seemed to pacify Frank for the rest of the poker game. The boys played until early morning. Talking of old times, drinking too much, and for a nice change, they got to act just like regular old cowboys. No one bothered them; no one stared at the strange looking bunch. They had been in Gravesend long enough that they now fit in. Fitting in was a new experience for them. They liked fitting in, it was something they could get used to.

Next morning Bristol and Larry finally had their meeting. Larry started the conversation.

"Bristol, I'm sure you know it was me that killed your father. I really have no excuse. I was involved in the train robbery and things went terribly wrong. Whatever you wish me to do, I will do. Turn myself in and plead guilty, it makes no difference. I'm not normally a violent man, but things seem to get out of control when I get angry."

"Larry I know all about your affliction. That's why I had to go away for a while. I needed time to think. Cassie told me the whole story. Even now, I can see you would rather go to jail then to let anyone know that you are a werewolf. The dilemma I have was who really killed my father? Was it you? Or was it a wolf? Are there really two of you? After much soul searching I finally came to a conclusion. Larry Wolf was not the man who killed my Pa. Larry the Wolf was the killer. So you see I cannot arrest you for the killing, you did not do it. Now if you would turn into Larry the Wolf I could arrest you on the spot. I know now that Alvira and you are heading to Bohemia on your honeymoon to find a cure for your illness. I can only wish you the best of luck. If I ever see you as Larry the Wolf, I will arrest you. For now, I hope we can be friends. My father being a U.S. Marshall I think would have to agree with my legal judgment in this matter. He was killed by a wolf and not a man."

The two shook hands. Bristol admitted that now that he felt the case about his father was closed he was going to ask Cassie to marry him. Einer and I were sitting in on the little meeting. It was a doggie tail-wagging ending if I ever saw one. Larry and Einer headed to Alvira's room to tell her the good news.

Bristol and I headed across the street to let Cassie know how things went. We were about half way across the street when a loud bang rang out. Bristol and I ran for cover. For some reason Bristol beat me to the horse trough that we crotched behind. I was running as fast as I could but it seemed like one of those bad dreams. As fast as I ran, I just was not getting anywhere. I was just about to the water trough when Bristol reached out and grabbed me. He held me tight against his chest. My rear foot was dangling at a funny angle, blood covering my white and black fur. Bristol had his gun in his hand and was peeking over the water trough to see where the shot came from. He saw a few remnants of smoke from the balcony of the Palace of Payne, but whoever fired the shot was long gone.

Cassie, Alvira, Einer, and Larry came rushing into the street to check on us. Of course there were at least twenty other townspeople gathered around looking at Bristol and I sitting in the blood soaked dirt. The worst part was that it was my blood. They rushed me to Doc Pulls office. If they could understand dog language, I would have claimed it was just a flesh wound, nothing serious.

Doc had them lay me on a nice clean white sheet; well at least it was white until I bled all over it. Bristol held me down as the Doc looked over my wounded foot. Sure enough, there was buckshot in the wound. Larry brought over a bowl of whisky and I lapped it up until I was feeling pretty good. Heck, I was feeling so good I would have probably kissed a cat if she was good looking. I glanced at Einer as they started digging the buckshot out of my foot. Einer had this look on his face; you know the look, like maybe I should go outside and throw up. The whiskey must have done its job, I felt nothing. In fact, the next thing I knew I was in Cassie's bed all laid out on a nice big fluffy pillow. Looking down at my foot all I could see was a white bandage. Cassie and Einer were sitting by the bed waiting for me to wake up. Once my eyes were open, Cassie gently stroked my fur and Einer gave me some doggie kisses. I was still groggy when I heard Cassie start talking to me.

"Sven, baby, you are going to be all right. The gunshot took off one of your toes but you're tough, you will do fine without it. The Doctor wants you to stay still and rest for a few days. Einer and I will be here to look after you. You've been unconscious for the last three days, too much whiskey the Doctor said. I guess you will have to learn to hold your liquor. While you were unconscious, something very exciting happened. Bristol proposed marriage to me and I accepted. The best part is that you and Einer are going to be the best dogs at our wedding. In fact, after all the companionship you two have given our family in these trying times. You are also going to be best dogs at Alvira's and Larry's wedding. So what do you think of that?"

Of course, if she could understand dog language I thought it was pretty neat. Then again, she could see Einer and me wagging our tails at full speed. Her smile told us that she understood we were excited to be involved in all the weddings.

Bristol was busy trying to find out who took a shot at us. I just hoped he would not neglect Cassie while he was out playing lawman. After all, I could learn to run on nineteen toes.

CHAPTER 14

The next few weeks seemed to fly by. Alvira and Larry were married and had left on their honeymoon. Cassie and Larry were in charge of the Hotel and the Palace of Payne. I was getting along well enough, except I did have sort of a skip in my step when I tried to run.

The woodworking crew had come down from the castle and left town. Of course everyone in town was wondering what would happen next up at the castle. The Gravesend Ghouls had been unusually quit as of late. Overall, the town was as peaceful and serene as any town could hope to be. Cassie and Bristol decided to postpone their marriage until Alvira and Larry returned. Now that Cassie and Alvira were sisters, they of course had to be in each other's wedding. For a strange twist, Larry and Bristol each acted as the others best man. It finally looked like the Payne-Pederson curse had to come to an end. About time.

One morning as Einer and I were laying in the shade of the hotel veranda, five large wagons pulled up in front of the Palace of Payne. Soon the Gravesend Ghouls were loading the wagons with large crates, boxes, and an occasional coffin. Once they finished they drove out of town and headed for Devil's Horn Mountain. They did not stop until they reached what the town now called the Devil's Castle. For all intent purposes, it looked like they were moving into the castle. Einer and I raced over to the Palace of Payne to check things out. It did not take long to get an answer. All the employees were talking about the big move by the gang. When Alivra and Larry came home they were sure in for a big surprise. Then again Einer told me that the Gang had always stayed with free room and board. It was a little extra that Lotta had included in her business deal with them. Therefore, this would actually be a good thing. Just feeding that crew had to be expensive. Now with the empty rooms they could rent them out and make more money. I guess things sometimes do work out for the best.

Of course the move to the Devil's Castle had the whole town talking. I cannot blame the guys for not saying anything. Otherwise they would have to explain where they got all the money to build that place. Although they had started feeling like part of the town, strangers still stared at the rather unusual looking group. Good looks were not one of their fine points.

A few more weeks went by and Alvira and Larry returned from their honeymoon. Even before any of us found out about Larry's condition we all received an invitation to a Castle warming being held by the Gravesend Ghouls. It was to be a very private affair. Cassie, Alvira, Bristol, Larry, Plantem Deeps, Einer, and I would be the only guests.

Bristol went to Lorin Korn's stable and procured a wagon large enough to accommodate all of us. Then it was up the winding mountain trail to the Castle. We entered through a large cast iron gate with a bat design in its center. The walls surrounding the courtyard were cut stone about 2 feet thick and ten feet high. The castle was much larger than I thought when we got close up to it. Huge turrets and battlements on the roof. A large ten-foot high double door with silver wolves head door knockers. We made our way up the stairs and Larry used the door knocker to announce our arrival. The sound of the door knocker echoed throughout the surrounding mountain area.

Rent Field answered the door. He was dressed to perfection in a black tuxedo. He bowed and graciously bid us to enter. Cassie and Alvira were glad they had worn their prettiest gowns for the occasion. We were led into the dining area where the gang was all waiting. Lots of hand kissing greeted the ladies and handshakes for the men. Einer and I, we shook some paws and received a few pats on the head. Cowboy Lugosi took charge of the seating arrangements. The table was heavy oak at least three inches thick and seating was available for up to twenty people.

They had hired two maids since moving in. The older one had a long crooked nose ending in a protruding wart, scraggly gray hair and a stooped back, her name was Witch Hazel. The other was about five feet ten inches tall. Very pretty with long blonde curly hair. From the way the men stared at her chest, which was amply pushed up and out by her small maid's outfit I could tell she did not have to work too hard. They called her Samantha.

Wine and appetizers were served. Then Lugosi began his little speech.

"We who have had the moniker of the Gravesend Ghouls placed upon us would like to welcome our guests and Friends. A toast to the newlywed couple Alvira and Larry."

The glasses were raised and clinked together as everyone had a drink. Einer and I settled for lapping up some wine that had been set on the table for us. It was nice of our hosts to let us sit at the table with everyone else.

Lugosi then continued with a toast to the now engaged Cassie and Bristol. Then another toast to good friends Plantem, Einer, and me. At this rate I might be passed out by meal time. Now it was time for Lugosi to make his announcement to his friends.

"I have an announcement to make on behalf of the gang. After much discussion we have all decided to stay here at Gravesend. Of course that must be obvious by the fact that we commissioned and built this castle. It is our hideaway from the stares and comments of the general public. More important all of us here made a pact to change our lifestyles. We wish to become good upright law abiding citizens. Each of us has his own devils to deal with. So with no further ado I will turn the floor over to Rent."

"For those of you who are new here I have a little explanation to what we are trying to accomplish. We have started a support group for ourselves to help with our individual inflictions. We call the organization GGG for 'Ghouls Gone Good.' Catching little title if I say so myself. Now for my problem. As most of you know I have a serious hunger for things that are living. Not big things like wildlife or people. Small things like rodents and insects are always very tasty. Of course if they are still alive when I eat them all the better. I could not imagine a better meal then a plumb live rat with a few dead flies for seasoning. Now with the help of GGG I have curbed my appetite to cooking things before I eat them. A rat on the stick cooked over the fireplace now satisfies me. Although occasionally a bowl of live flies with their wings removed still excites me. I know that GGG will help and I can call any of my friends to help me through the hard times. Thanks guys, I appreciate the fact that you are all here to help me. Now for our next speaker Illinois Igor."

"Temper, quick and fast, that's my problem. It stems from my affliction. Being a hunchback and a cripple has always put me at the mercy or others. When I was young the other kids made fun of me. As I become older the men made snide remarks about me. The women they looked away in disgust. My only protection from all this rejection was to become mean and angry with all humans. Then I met Frank, he was worse off than me. A conglomeration of body parts with the mind of a child. Someone I could control. So I tormented him, brow beat him into the submission. He did what I wanted him to do out of fear. Now I try to be gentle with Frank and others. I must understand that if I am revolting to them it is their problem, not mine. I am learning to accept myself as is. To take pride and not become so angry. It is hard but I am doing well. Now for Boris, you must remember that Boris has had his tongue cut out, so please understand that he has trouble with his speaking, but he does the best he can"

"I made my first mistake centuries ago in ancient Egypt. Falling in love with a Pharaohs wife was not a good idea. The Pharaoh ordered me bound up as a mummy and tore my tongue from my mouth. Ever since that time I have wandered the world looking for my lost love. My friends have helped him to see that my love is gone and I must accept what my gods have left me with. Slow of speech, hard for others to understand me. Loveless, maybe? However, from now on I have you all as my friends. Maybe someday a woman will come into my life. That is what GGG is all about. Hope for the future. Frank you're next."

"Arrgh. Uh, I Frank. I know people fear Frank. Igor always mean to me. He nicer now. I try to be nice always. Sometimes I too strong and can hurt people. All you here are my friends. Frank is much happy now. I like it here. Mole you talk, Frank done now."

"I just want to find my people and live in peace. We are diggers that is what we do. My race lives underground. I was separated from them by a cave in and have not been able to find my way back. We are a gentle race. Living above ground is not easy, I look different then humans so they do not accept me. Here with my friends I am accepted. I have been digging in one of the basement rooms of the castle. There I discovered a rich vein of gold. It will be nice for us all as we are now rich. No need to leave here or work unless we want to. Maybe if I dig long enough I can find my way home."

Lugosi spoke next.

"Larry tell us how things went on your honeymoon?" That of course got lots of snickers and laughs from everyone until Lugosi clarified his statement. "I mean tell us about the werewolf problem."

"Alvira and I did find members of her family in Bohemia. Unfortunately they could not cure me. Only the family that cursed me has that power. I did receive a reminder that I am not immortal. Now with a beautiful wife to live for I plan to make the most of my life. The talisman around my neck is a silver bullet. If I lose control of myself this bullet is the only thing that can kill me. It is my reminder to hold my temper so that I can enjoy my life with my beautiful wife. My wish is that Alvira and I can have a family and settle down to a peaceful life. I hope to never see the 'wolf' side of me again. Bristol that is my promise to you. My future brother-in-law will not have a wolf for a relative."

Einer and I could still smell the scent of canine on Larry. Although that was all right. Overall us dogs are gentle loving spices; maybe that part can remain with Larry."

I guess it is my turn said Lugosi.

"I have probably the most serious affliction of our group. For centuries I have had to kill to live. Without a source of blood I will die. It is an instinct that I cannot control. My will to live is greater than my will to die. For the last few months I have found friendship not only in all of us living in the castle, but Plantem Deeps has come to my rescue. We had a long talk and Plantem has been slowly weaning me from the blood of humans. He started by letting me have the blood of cadavers that he was getting ready for burial. The next thing he did was to mix that blood with animal blood, mostly cattle blood from the butcher shop. Within a few weeks I will be completely switched over to the blood of animals instead of humans. I know to most of you this sounds unpleasant. Unfortunately for me it is the only option.'

Alvira stood and started speaking.

"I don't know about all of you, but I am proud to be friends with everyone in this room. My mother brought you all together, although for her own evil purposes at the time. Now look at you, all of you are trying to correct your lives and live them as good decent folks. I would hope much of this was brought about from the love that my Father and Cassie shared with us all. A toast to all us, living and dead."

Thus the party continued throughout the night. Dancing, singing, and merry making. We all had a great time.

CHAPTER 15

Time of course keeps going on. Gravesend continued to grow into a western metropolis. Larry Wolf was elected mayor. Bristol became the town Marshall. Cassie and Alvira spend some time at their downtown businesses but mostly they took up housekeeping. Both couples built fine stately homes just on the outskirts of town.

Frank took a job as bailiff in the courthouse. Igor was now the town postmaster. Rent opened a new food business serving hot dogs. Something Einer and I decided we did not really want to know about. Lugosi become a deputy marshal and handled the night shift around town. Boris and Mole kept put at the castle playing cards, digging tunnels, and just relaxing.

Einer told me that he thinks Alvira may be pregnant. Of course, we both wonder, will it be a boy or a girl, and whether it is a human or a puppy, you never know with the canine blood in Larry what could happen. We sure would enjoy having a puppy around to play with.

Einer and I have big yards to play and explore. Both of us are family to our humans. Of course, not all stories end on a happy note. Bristol was lucky he found out who shot his Pa.

As for me, I sure would like to know.

"Who shot my Paw?"

The end.

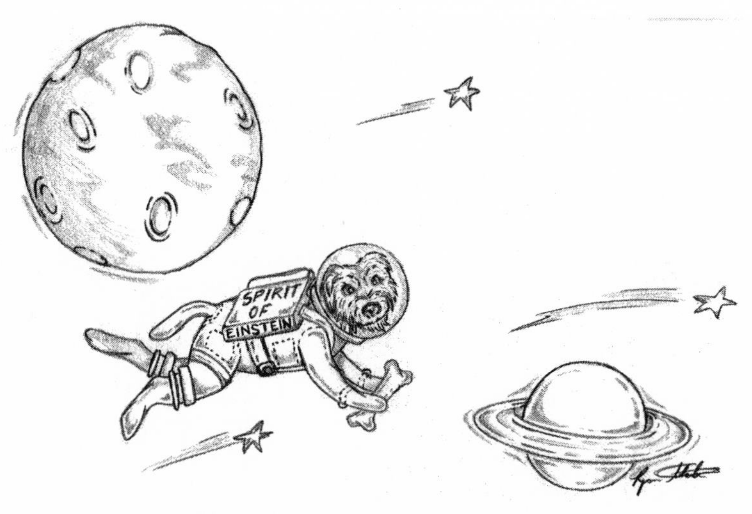

DOGSTRANAUTS
"SPIRIT OF EINSTEIN"

CHAPTER 1

Hello. My name is Sven. I have a story to tell you.

Humans often write what they call a 'prelude' to their stories. This is a good idea. It will help the reader identify the characters and provide a general story outline. However, I am not a human. I am a dog and very proud of it! I am not your everyday, run of the mill mutt. I am a full-blooded Shih-Tzu; good looking, strong, athletic, grey and white in color. In dog years, I am in my mid-twenties. The only thing that keeps me from being perfect is a slight 'catch' in my right rear leg; I tend to skip when I walk. Strange at it may seem, my human has the same problem with his right leg.

Now let's get down to the 'puppylude'. This will be easy for young dogs and humans to understand. I could use footnotes and fancy little '*' but then you'd have to go to the bottom of the page for the explanation and you might possibly lose your place in the story. If you need an explanation about something in one of my stories, I'll make it easy. I'll just put the information between these little '' swirly things. I think they call them quotes; I will call them simple substitutes for footnotes.

Dogs and humans listen up! This is the story of my family, friends, and me. The time has come for you to meet everyone that shows up in my story. Everything you read is true, if you want it to be. If you don't want to believe what I tell you, then it's not true. It's your choice.

My little sister's name is Lena. Eleven pounds of white and tan colored Shih-Tzu, filled with boundless energy. She is still in her pre-teens. I'm her teacher for all things not 'girl' related. Like many of us, she is extremely intelligent. Most humans don't know that dogs can read, write and operate computers. The Canine Counsel prefers it this way. Only the most trusted humans know of our skills because there are always unscrupulous humans that would try to make us slaves.

There's another thing you need to know about Lena. Like so many kids, she is filled with an insatiable appetite to learn. She has grown up with computers and technology and her understanding knows no bounds. Anything is possible for her, as you will soon find out.

Ole is my human dad and my best friend. This guy is so nice he should have been born a dog. In Ole's world, Lena and I are his children and we are treated as such. Sometime ago Ole and I shared a trauma that changed the way we communicate. It opened up a new channel of understanding between us. While Ole needs to speak out loud for me to understand, I can talk to him telepathically. This phenomenon is now shared between Lena and Ole after they had a near death experience. As a result, the three of us now enjoy unlimited capabilities to communicate and work together. Ole can have interactions with other humans, but he also has access to both of our doggie brains to figure things out. You have to admit, that is doggie-doo cool! As for looks, Ole is about average in a pleasingly plump sort of way. His only drawback is a bad right leg that requires the use of a cane. Although he can get along without the cane, his balance is a little on the shaky side so I encourage him to use the cane to be safe. I do my best to keep him away from women; he's somewhat gullible and easily hurt by the opposite sex. Thus far, he has two strikes; I do my best to save him from a third.

Val is Ole's older daughter and Ole's angel. She's the only woman in Ole's life that he trusts completely. She also has a Shi-Tzu named Oliver who is a great cousin for Lena and me. His favorite thing to do is run. Very few dogs can run like Oliver. The little beggar must have a touch of greyhound blood in him.

Nikki is Ole's younger daughter. She is his traveling child. She's been everywhere, from canoeing the length of the Mississippi River to backpacking across Europe. She just adopted her first dog child, Stella, a black and white Shih-Tzu. Stella is just a little smaller then Lena and cute as a button. She's only about 10 years old in dog years. We haven't spent much time with her yet. I hope she comes to visit often.

Then we have Ole's boy child, Casey; an athletic, buff type of guy. He's young, hard working, hard playing, hard drinking; still enjoying his indestructible phase. We all hope he lives through it better then Ole did. Some of those traits can lead to a banged up, not so well working body when you get older.

Now for Grandpa, Ole's dad; all 86 years of him. Grandpa has been up and down the past year. Just out of the hospital after a bout of pneumonia; living in a nursing home at the moment. Ole, Lena, and I go to visit him every day. Lena and I have official service dog jackets so we can go almost anywhere. Our specialty is 'comfort' dog. If Grandpa gets well, we hope he can come back to live with us.

Puppylude is over. Time for a great doggie 'tail'!

CHAPTER 2

We live on an estate named 'River's Edge.' By estate standards it's not large, just one acre.

The mighty Mississippi River flows by our front yard. Lots of trees, a boathouse, barn and workshop dot the property. We live in a beautiful brick home with its very own Theater Room. Ole works five days a week at his sales job but usually comes home for noon lunch and some playtime with us. On Ole's days off, or just after he gets home from work, we play together in the yard and Lena and I go swimming.

At night we all share supper in the Theater Room. As a family, we have amassed a large collection of DVD movies and TV features. Ole, Lena and I all have our own favorites to watch. Therefore, to be fair, we take turns so that almost every type of show appears in our theater at one time or another. We have pretty much given up regular television watching. It's nice to watch what we want, when we want. Strange, but true, this is our nightly custom.

Tonight's feature movie "Space Cowboys" is about four very unlikely astronauts. Time and age have been catching up with them. Ole is a James Garner fan; add Clint Eastwood, Tommy Lee Jones and Donald Sutherland, and you have a winner of a movie. We rate our movies on a 1 to 10 scale, 10 being the best. Ole and I gave tonight's movie an eight; Lena rated it a ten. I should have seen that something was about to come of her high rating.

Nighttime has a regular schedule. Ole reads aloud from the book "New Moon," the second in our vampire reading series. At lights out, we all cuddle and get kisses and hugs. A final prayer ends the evening.

Except tonight! I heard Lena sneak off into the dark. It was three hours before she returned. Ole slept through her little sojourn; I decided to ignore it.

Ole hasn't worked much lately. He lost a big toe in an accident a few months ago. For now, Lena and I are taking care of him. It's nice spending so much time together as a family. As a result, Ole is not very active, but he enjoys watching Lena and I have a good time. Lena picked out the night's movie "Armageddon"; another space themed movie, with Bruce Willis. Rating time brought two eights from Ole and me; Lena gave it a ten. There seems to be a pattern developing here.

That night Lena slipped away again. This time I followed her to see what she was doing. As I peaked around the corner of the basement steps, the glow of the computer screen was lighting up the basement. Lena was busy typing and reading things on the internet. Well, I figured, what the heck, she's learning something so let her be.

Night three Ole picked "Life with Blondie" and I think Lena was a little disappointed. Ole said it was a shame that the two stars, Penny Singleton and Arthur Lake, were no longer known. They both did a great job on the Blondie series. Then, let's not forget who the real star of the Blondie movies was, Daisy the Dog. I'll bet she was the smartest dog to ever grace the silver screen. Better yet, in this episode of the series, Daisy becomes the pin-up dog for the United States Navy. It reminds me of Ole's dream in his short story "War Mongrels." Einer and I were the stars in that story. Ole rated the movie an eight, Lena gave it a four, and I slipped in a seven. Daisy alone is worth a seven rating. I guess a 6.3 average isn't too bad.

That night, at bedtime, Lena got in her two 'scents' worth. She gave Ole the puppy eye dog treatment and asked if we could skip reading "New Moon"; she wanted him to read his "Mutts on the Moon" instead. It was all right with me; that book just so happens to be a true story about my friend Einer and me. Yes, we really did go to the moon. If you haven't read this book, add it to your list. It is a must read, trust me!

The next few weeks had Lena taking over our nightly bedtime discussions with what she was learning about space, astronomy, physics and satellites. Ole and I were starting to feel like two third grade hillbillies in a college classroom. Lena was proving to be the scholar of the family.

She was leading me into more science and mathematics studies during our daily teaching sessions. Since she was way beyond my capabilities in those areas, I soon let her learn on her own. A nice thing about the internet is you can learn almost anything at your own pace. She was learning faster than a rocket-powered spacecraft.

I should have been listening for the sonic boom that was about to happen. Lena's learning was about to break the speed of light. Ole would feel the greatest concussion from the explosion Lena was about to create.

CHAPTER 3

Lena was steering her conversations toward space travel; e.g., Russia's Sputnik 1 from 1957 and the 1969 U.S. Apollo Program which put four men on the moon. Grandpa, an old World War II Navy veteran, was especially excited about the fact that two of the first four men were naval officers. During our daily visits to the nursing home, Ole kept Grandpa updated on Lena's education. Even if Grandpa didn't remember that all of this was a family secret, no one at the "home" would believe him anyway. Lena was also one of a privileged few that knew Einer and I had visited the moon.

Lena's e-mails and correspondence were soon filling up all the space on our computer. Ole was complaining that his eBay business was suffering from the computer slowdown. I was ordered to clean up the system and dump all the excess data. That is when I discovered what my little sister was doing.

There were e-mails to and from the NASA Space Center, Florida. Hundreds of them! Statistics, time allotments, satellite readings and spacecraft designs. Only problem was, they weren't addressed to Lena or sent by Lena. My little sister was forging Ole's name to everything she did. It would make perfect sense; no human was going to believe that a dog was smart enough to generate all this correspondence. Then again, if you knew Ole, it would be hard to believe he was smart enough either. I figured I'd better have a talk with little sister. It felt like storm clouds were brewing around her little NASA project.

"Lena, Ole felt the computer might be getting overloaded so I've been removing excess files. I noticed a lot of correspondence between you and

NASA; I transferred it all to a disc for you. Just what are you writing to NASA about?"

"Sven, have I ever told you about what a great brother you are? I sure am lucky to have someone like you to teach and guide me." Talk about filling a mousetrap with cheese. I just knew this was going to hurt when she sprung the trap on me.

"Sven, maybe you could talk to Dad for me? I think a man from NASA may be coming here for a visit."

"Lena, explain this in simple terms. Someone from NASA is coming to see Ole? How soon is he coming? You might also want to mention why he's coming."

"Sven, I did mention you're my favorite brother, didn't I? I know I can always depend on you if I get into a little trouble. I can, can't I? I think the NASA man might be showing up later today. He has some idea that Ole has discovered a new planet in our solar system. Not only that, but he thinks Ole has held back enough information to force NASA to let him be in charge of a space mission. He may even think that Ole wants to take us with him. Also, Ole has designed and sent plans for the spacecraft that would be needed for such an expedition. I think Dad might not remember doing all this. You and I need to refresh his memory."

"LENA! What have you done? Dad is going to whip your little behind when he hears about this. Come on, we'd better find him right away. You'd better get all the information ready that Ole needs to learn before the NASA guy gets here. I'll find Ole and start explaining this to him. Boy am I glad I'm not you!"

I found Ole in bed with his leg propped up like the doctor ordered. He was a little woozy from the medication needed to dull the pain from having his big toe amputated. He said that at least with the toe gone it didn't hurt any more. However, the pain in the rest of his foot seemed to be making up for the missing toe pain.

I hopped up on the bed and asked Ole what he was thinking about? Always a loaded question with my Dad.

"Ya know Sven, I was just thinking about my missing toe. Ya know, they won't let you keep your amputated body parts. It would have been neat to put my toe in a jar of formaldehyde and display it on the fireplace mantel. On the other hand, I could have had it stuffed, mounted on a board, and used it for a coat hook. Or maybe I could have attached it to the back of a toy wrecker; you know, like a "toe" truck. How about a keychain? It would have made a great keychain; the human version of a lucky rabbit's foot. But, I think the best would have been to hang it over that door during the Holidays, like missile-toe, only call it 'Ole-toe'. Except I probably wouldn't get many kisses from the ladies under the 'Ole-toe'. Then again, I don't get any kisses from the ladies now."

It was evident that I needed to redirect this conversation before it got any stranger.

"Ole, I have something important we need to discuss. Lena has sort of done something that may affect us all. To put it bluntly, it will affect us all, especially you. In fact, it will affect you within the next few hours. You'd better get out of bed and come with me."

Ole gently lifted his leg from its pillow mountain and grabbed his cane. We made our way downstairs to a waiting Lena. She had the computer all set up with the information for Ole to look over. The computer chair was adjusted so that Ole could put his leg up on the nice soft pillow that was waiting on a nearby end table.

Ole gave Lena that look. You know the look kids get when they have to explain what they've just done. That look that says, "I hope you have a good explanation for this."

Lena sat on the floor, her head down, tail between her legs. She lifted her little brown puppy dog eyes to look at Ole. Finally, she started to speak.

"Dad, I think I might have done something I shouldn't have. I just got so excited and I wanted my family to share in what I was doing. You know that I thoroughly investigate everything I do before I share my projects with others. Remember how I discovered 'Vortex Valley'? How I proved it was real and Sven wrote a book about it. You know how you let Einer and Sven go to the moon. I'll bet that seemed unbelievable at the time. Well, this is sort of like that."

"Lena, Vortex Valley was very impressive. I was extremely proud of you. However, I didn't actually LET Einer and Sven go to the moon. It was more of an accident. If you'd have been here when Einer was around, you'd know that the combination of him and Sven usually resulted in serious mischief. I do trust your judgment; now get to the point. Just what have you involved me in?"

"Well, ah, Dad, you know I love you with all my heart. Of course, I'd never get you involved in something I didn't have the utmost confidence in. It all started with that movie "Space Cowboys." That and the adventure that Sven told me about him and Einer going to the moon. Then, to top it all off, the scientific world deciding my favorite planet Pluto was not really a planet after all. That was the last straw! They take the only planet named for a dog and say it isn't really a planet. I mean, Mickey Mouse and Pluto must have been devastated. I just figured that, as a dog, I should make all these high and mighty human scientists look like a bunch of idiots. Therefore, I did some serious research. I figured that if we had nine planets in our solar system, you couldn't just remove one because you changed your mind. Now, according to these scientists, we only have eight planets in our solar system. They think perhaps Pluto is a dwarf planet, hardly worth their time and effort to study. I was hoping Mickey Mouse and the Disney people would step in and stop all this silliness, but they haven't. Therefore, I took it upon myself. I have discovered a ninth planet."

"Lena, not to burst your bubble but being your dear old dad, I think I might have to disagree on one of your facts about Pluto. I was not a whiz kid in school but I did learn a few things. The planet Pluto I believe was actually named after the Roman god of darkness and the underworld. It was given that name because the planet is always in darkness. Some people suggest that Percival Lowell, the man that first identified the planet, chose that name because it contained the first letters of his first and last name, and being a dark planet 'Pluto' seemed to be a good choice. I hope you're not too disappointed about Pluto not being named after Mickey Mouse's dog."

It was now time for the 'dog' expert to add his two scents worth. So, I clarified the Pluto dog myth once and for all.

"Listen you two, if anyone knows about canine history it's me. Ole, you can keep all your scientific mumbo-jumbo about the planet Pluto.

Lena, I'm surprised you missed that one little tidbit of information. I hope you didn't tell NASA about the planet-dog association. That would be hard for Ole to explain, since they think he wrote all the letters. Now for the real scoop on Pluto the Disney dog."

"Pluto is a bloodhound who first appeared in the Disney cartoon 'Chain Gang' in 1930 and he was called Rover. In 1931 he got his second acting job in the Mickey Mouse cartoon 'Moose Hunt' and his name was changed to 'Pluto'. Some people still believe he was named after the planet 'Pluto' that had been discovered in 1930. Now, for an additional bit of information that I'll bet Ole doesn't know I know. Ole's dad, Grandpa, told me that the little black stuffed dog that sits on the bench at the foot of Ole's bed was Ole's favorite toy; it went everywhere he did. That little stuffed pooch has been from Minnesota to California, New York, Texas, Florida, and back. He called his dog Pluto. And I know for sure he was named after the Disney 'Pluto' and not the planet."

Who would ever think that so much information surrounded such a simple word as 'Pluto'?

The doorbell rang and I ran to see who it was. Man in a uniform with a black, non-descript Ford parked in our driveway; soldier standing straight and tall next to the car. I called to Ole that the man from NASA was here. I heard Lena in the background. "Sorry Dad, I should have told you sooner. Just go with the flow and pretend you know about anything he says. Sven says you are always full of BS (that stands for Bull Shih-Tzu, in case you were wondering) and can bluff your way through anything.

CHAPTER 4

Ole answered the door as Lena and I watched. The uniformed man introduced himself as he shook Ole's hand. "Hello, I'm Captain Spud Nick, United States Navy Air Corps, on assignment to NASA. I believe you were expecting me."

Considering Ole is such an excellent salesman, he has a lot of trouble putting names, faces and places together. However, I should have known he would successfully dance through this situation.

"Nice to meet you Captain Nick. My name is Ole and these are my dogs Lena and Sven. You look very familiar, have we met before?"

"Yes, however our last meeting wasn't so cordial. I recognized you and Sven when I went through the records of your last visit to the Kennedy Space Center. I have been assigned to review the information you provided; under protest, I might add. Our last encounter created a rather sticky situation for me and NASA to cover up."

I saw the light go on; he remembered now; 'Mutts on the Moon'. The day Einer and I took our little space jaunt; no wonder Captain Nick wasn't too happy to encounter us again. If only Einer was here to see this one; his little helicopter tail would be swirling so fast his butt would have lifted right off the ground.

Ole was polite to the captain.

"Please, come in and have a seat. Would you like to invite your driver in, too? We don't have liquor, but ice water, orange juice, milk or fancy sodas are available. By the way, please call me Ole, everyone does."

"Ole, my driver will be fine. What do you mean by fancy soda? Is it ok if I set up my papers on your dining room table?"

Ole opened the refrigerator to check on our stock of fancy soda. Ole isn't much of a drinker; at restaurants Miller Lite with four green olives is his preferred beverage. However, Ole always has a selection of his fancy sodas on hand. Some people prefer wine; at the River's Edge Estate, you are offered 'fancy' soda.

"Feel free to set up on the dining table. As for soda, the choices are Stewart's peach or grape soda, Virgil's black cherry or cream soda, strawberry Crush, Sun Drop, Quench or, and please don't take offense, Rat Bastard root beer."

That's my Dad. He just can't help slipping in a nasty little comment whenever appropriate. Especially to anyone who flaunts his position. Lawyers, politicians and Service Corps officers can all be prime targets for Ole.

"I'll try the black cherry soda if you don't mind. I'm on a time schedule so can we please get down to business?"

This guy was proving to be a bossy, rude human. Ole was going to start having fun any time now. At least if Ole was enjoying himself, Lena would be off the hook for causing this mess.

"Captain, I hope you don't mind waiting a moment. Since it's rather warm outside, I'm going to take a bottle of Rat Bastard root beer out to your driver. I'll make sure he knows it's delivered with your compliments." Dad was definitely not making any brown doggie points with this guy.

The captain spread out all kinds of graphs, charts and papers. Lena and I were standing on the table examining the captain's paperwork. He didn't say anything about us being on the table, but his look was none too approving. Ole was now taking it all in stride.

"The papers before us will cover the main points of your theory regarding the existence of what, from this time forward, will be referred to as Planet X. I must commend your efforts. The NASA scientists were impressed with the system you used to detect this unknown entity. As you can see by the graphs, the system of sound waves you used to create echoes from one point to the next verifies the existence of Planet X. We have duplicated your efforts with the same results. By using the twelve positioned satellites as echo points, along with the eight known planets in our solar system, all data seems to verify your conclusion. What is missing is a way to ascertain the density, existence of life and the gravity on Planet X. Until these factors are known, the project must be put on hold. Of course we are working toward the solution as we speak."

"We reviewed your request to have Lena, Sven and you spearhead a space expedition. The background check NASA conducted eliminates any possibility of you participating in a trip of this magnitude. Your missing toe, bad right leg and, how shall I put this delicately, rather round tummy don't make you a prime candidate for space exploration. However, to show your Country's appreciation for your discovery of Planet X, we will take Lena and Sven along on the expedition. Do you have any questions?"

I could tell Dad didn't like this one bit. He may not be wild about what Lena had done but darned if he was going to let anyone separate him from his dog kids. When Einer and I were on the moon by ourselves, Ole was worried sick. We belonged together. No NASA big shot was going to stop Ole. Somehow, just like the famous velvet picture of dogs playing poker, Ole was going to come up with a winning hand.

Ole was playing his hand like a real professional. Captain Nick was flashing his hand around like a tenderfoot who just fell off the turnip truck. Ole kept his poker face and didn't say a word. Then, like a player drawing too many cards, the captain tossed his remaining papers onto the table.

"Now, Ole, about the plans you have drawn for your prototype spacecraft. They seem to make sense in relation to what you want to accomplish. But, look at the design and shape of the spacecraft. Let me put it this way, it just looks 'silly'. If NASA approved these plans and built this craft for the Planet X Project, we'd be laughed right out of the Space Program."

Lena was telepathically talking to Ole. She was ready for all contingencies.

"Ole, don't worry about his objections. I have the answers. Just let him keep talking and I'll let you make a fool of him if you want to. Love ya dad."

Ole gave a slight smile and asked Captain Nick to 'please' continue.

"Well, just look at these plans. This 'spacecraft' looks like an egg shaped dog. The egg shape design went out of existence in the days of Sputnik and the Apollo capsules. I can only hope this is a joke. I might add that the NASA Board of Directors was not amused. I assume you have a 'real' plan for the spacecraft. If not, I'm sure we can modify one of the Challenger spacecraft to handle the job."

Ole was still looking at the craft. Even I had to admit that Lena out did herself on this one. It was comical looking.

"Captain, I believe Lena and Sven need a little outside time. We are going for a walk. We will be back in about half an hour. I hope this doesn't disturb your tight schedule."

Ole stood up and we followed him out the door to our veranda and down the circular steps to the front yard. Lena and I went in the river for a swim; Ole sat on the dock watching us.

"Lena, I think it's time you gave your old dad some ammunition to fight Captain Nick. I'm impressed with what you've accomplished; now I need answers. First, what about the existence of life and gravity on Planet X? How about the spacecraft? I hate to admit it but it does look a little comical. Now I'm not saying it won't work, but you'd better explain it to Sven and me. After this guy's 'better than thou' attitude, I've decided we're all going together on this trip or no one is going. Lena, it's up to you to provide our ace in the hole. It looks to me like you've purposely held back information regarding the possibility of life and gravity. I know you too well to think you could have overlooked these issues. The spaceship, I have to think you have a good reason for it. Then again, if NASA refuses to build it, well, we have a problem."

Lena had the answers!

"Dad, don't worry about any of it. I have it all figured out." She then gave Ole and I the Readers Digest condensed version of the answers. I have to admit Lena is a girl genius. We went in the walkout basement door. The computer system was in the corner of the room. Lena printed out some papers for Ole to take to our 'meeting'.

It was easy to tell that Captain Spud Nick was unhappy. He wasn't much for hiding his feelings. "It took you long enough. This is important business. You and your dogs are wasting taxpayers' money by keeping me waiting. I have some papers for you to sign that turns all your research over to NASA. I'm sure you'll agree this is for the good of the Nation. NASA may provide a small compensation and perhaps a medal from the President of the United States for your efforts. You realize that what you've discovered is top-secret. It would be harmful to your Country if this information were to leak out. Ole, sign here; you don't need to read it. It just says you are turning over all your rights to any involvement in the Planet X Project to the United States Government."

Ole looked at the paper. He laid it down so Lena and I could read it. We all took our time. Captain Nick was turning a bright shade of red; you could see the veins on his forehead starting to pulsate. I wondered if his head would actually explode if this kept on too much longer. Now that would be the ultimate doggie story to tell around the campfire.

Ole finally decided it was time to play our hand. Lena was feeding him all the information he needed. I knew that having three heads to think was better than one. This telepathic communication was great.

"Captain Nick, you certainly seem to be holding all the aces. It was unreasonable for me to think I could keep myself and my dogs involved in such a complicated project. I'm amazed that I got as far as I did. Just think, I found a planet everyone has been looking for since the space race began in the 1950's. I'm sure if I had not been in such a rush, NASA would have found Planet X, eventually."

"Then, to consider an egg shaped spacecraft. That would be like using a Sputnik or Apollo craft in this modern era. Surely, it wouldn't be feasible. Round objects couldn't possibly fly through space. That would be like having God make all the planets round, and then having them orbit in succession. I'm surprised no planets have fallen out of the sky. I must have been crazy to think a round spacecraft would work."

"However, I do have answers to your questions. Planet X has a gravity level twice that of Earth. It was easy to calculate by determining the distance of Planet X from the moon. Planet X is exactly one-half the distance from the moon that the Earth is. This figures out to be twice the gravitational force that we have on Earth. Regarding the existence of life, I got that answer by using echo readings from different locations on

Planet X. I will release this information when we're ready to leave on our expedition."

"As for our silly, egg shaped spaceship, I have the booster power system designed and ready to go. The cooling system is totally unique and inexpensive. However, your generous donation of a space shuttle would be appreciated. I only need to have my craft released into space at a pre-determined distance from the moon. The gravitational rotation of the moon will take us to Planet X. One booster shot from our engines will sling shot us through Planet X's atmosphere. Our smaller rockets will cushion our landing. The landing must be controlled manually because I've determined that the terrain will be very tricky to deal with."

"By the way, it won't be necessary for NASA to build my spacecraft. Lena, Sven and I have friends that have agreed to follow our blueprints with no questions asked. Also, don't think you can confiscate our information. Even my dogs are smart enough to have kept copies out of the reach of the Government."

"I have a contract for you to sign. It simply states that the project will be completely under my control. All aspects of launch dates, equipment and crew are at my discretion. I will need $550,000 to assemble my spacecraft and transport it to the Kennedy Space Center. This should be approximately $2.5 million less than it would cost to have NASA build my craft."

"Oh, Captain, please note that there are lines for three signatures on the bottom of the contract. One is for you, one is for the head of the NASA Program, and, the last one is for the Commander in Chief of the United States."

The captain sat in his chair, mouth open; I think he was even drooling a little. I never saw a human with such a red face. Even the veins in his forehead and neck were bulging by this time. Finally, he said. "Ole, this is blackmail! You won't get away with it. It's treason. You're a fool. Anything you've learned, the Government will find out. We'll be back in touch, you can bet on that."

Ole just smiled and said, "Captain, you did bet on it. You figured you were holding all the aces. I figured I had a straight flush. It's simple. Send me to Planet X and NASA can have all the glory. Sven, Lena, and I just want the adventure. You don't even have to risk any lives that anyone cares about. If we fail, all NASA loses is their investment; nothing new for NASA. If we succeed, we disappear and NASA gets a new planet and all the accolades. Call and let me know what the big boys say."

"You and your dogs are walking a fine line. I'll talk with my superiors. If you foul this up in any way, I will have all your heads on a silver platter in the Smithsonian; with a little brass plaque that reads 'the world's greatest idiots'."

The captain quickly stuffed his papers into his briefcase. As he stormed out the door, Ole gave him a farewell. "God Bless America and you too, Captain."

I looked at Ole and Lena and said, "Well, I think that went very well, don't you?"

CHAPTER 5

Sometimes Ole doesn't ask questions; I think he just prefers not to know the answers. Therefore, it's often up to me to ask.

"Lena, I think it's time you give us a little more information on what you know about Planet X and the spacecraft.

"Ok you two, here goes. It was kind of like when I researched Vortex Valley (see Vortex Valley story). I wanted to have everything ready before I told you about it. These NASA people took me by surprise when then sent Captain Nick so quickly. I had everything on my end figured out; I'd just neglected to spring it on you two. Now that everyone seems to know, I think this would be a fantastic family adventure."

"I was just caught up in the excitement of space travel that night we watched Space Cowboys. With all the stories Sven told me about 'Mutts on the Moon', and Einer and him traveling in space, I wanted to do something like that. While researching, I read how the planet Pluto had been downgraded. Well, that was the last straw; I decided to take on this project on behalf of the canine world. I didn't know Pluto wasn't named after Mickey Mouse's dog until Dad told me about it yesterday. Of course, that doesn't matter now."

"With all the great things that can be done with computers, I went to work, determined to find a replacement for planet Pluto. Once I figured out how to tap into the space satellite system it didn't take long to figure out how to control the sound waves. I just started sending out signals until they hit something and bounced back. It took a few weeks for me to pinpoint one particular spot. That is Planet X. Since it's directly behind the moon, and in a straight line from Earth, I guess no one ever thought to look there. It's really like a mirror image of Earth. It follows the same orbit as we do."

"As for life on Planet X, I think there is. NASA hasn't figured it out yet because they're trained to think within a box. I learned from both of you to think outside the box; that's how new discoveries are made. By ricocheting sound waves off the moon to Planet X, and then to any one of a number of different satellites, I discovered amazing anomalies. Depending upon the time of day, the sound waves increased or decreased in energy. So the contour of Planet X was different in different areas. Some sound waves where shorter, some were longer, indicating mountains and low spots or valleys. The most unusual sound waves pulsated at night, but the same spot during the day came back at a surprisingly fast rate; as if it hit a mirror and bounced back. I finally figured out that the sound waves were hitting liquid. At night they were unable to penetrate the liquid and, during the day, the liquid reflected light as well as my sound waves. The explanation would have to be water. After the thousands of readings I took and processed through the computer, I had an answer. I'm almost positive that Planet X is a mirror image of our planet. The exception is that it is half our size with twice the gravitational pull. This last part is still in my guesstimate stage. Distance from the sun, according to my calculations, will affect the climate on Planet X. It may be ten to twenty degrees cooler then Earth. Of course, there's also a strong possibility that the temperate may be the same as ours. This would happen if the next closest planet reflected enough of the sun's heat to compensate for the difference in the sun's distance from Planet X."

"All this information should be kept strictly between us so that NASA has to keep guessing. If they want the answers, they'll have to let us run the show."

"Now for my spaceship. I chose a round shape since it will produce less atmospheric drag. The trick is we only have to break through from space to Planet X's atmosphere twice. Once on entry from space, and again when we leave the planet and return to our moons orbit. The Challenger spacecraft will release us after we leave Earth and then pick us for the return trip to Earth. Most of our space time will be traveling just like when we go to any of the planets. We'll be on the fringe of the Moon's atmosphere and it will rotate us, along with the Moon, to Planet X."

"Our egg shaped craft will be constructed with an outer skin of stainless steel, with a one foot air space between it and the inner shell, also made of stainless steel. This system is used every day by tanker trucks, gas tanks or any other container that stores or transports dangerous liquids, chemicals or gasses. If the outer shell is pierced, the inner shell will protect the integrity of the unit. Now, for my special secret ingredient. The one foot space between the shells will be filled by a common item used by humans for aches, pains, and arthritis. It will be filled with "Icy Heat" gel; the same thing you buy at the drug store, except in super sized containers. This gel does the opposite of its surroundings. While we float in space the gel will counteract the cold, causing it to dissipate heat, thus keeping our spacecraft warm. When we enter the atmosphere of Planet X, the heat from the friction of our descent will cause the Icy Heat gel to become cold. No need to worry about our spaceship becoming brittle from cold or scorched from heat. Neat idea, huh? Let's see NASA figure that one out."

"Here is my blueprint. I purposely made it look like a dog to honor the demotion of Planet Pluto. It may look funny, but it's completely functional. The face of the dog will, of course, have two eyes so we can see out of our control cabin. The nose actually has two holes that look like nostrils. One nostril contains a rocket thruster to slow us down in an emergency and can also acts as a reverse thrust system. The other nostril contains a video camera and light system to record our journey and our landing area. It will also provide illumination as needed. The mouth looks like it's sort of smiling. That area opens and has a platform that descends for exiting and entering our craft. I thought that was a fun idea; looks like the dog spacecraft opens its mouth and sticks out its tongue. The ears contain antennas and sound sensors; the tail act like a rudder on an airplane, allowing us to veer left, right, up or down. The spacecraft also has a doggie 'poop' hole. No doggie would be complete without one. It contains our main rocket thrusters for forward movement. Yes, Sven, I see your tail up in the air, what do you want?"

"Lena, does the doggie 'Poop' hole have a scent? You know, just in case we come across any other large, doggie spacecraft?"

"Very funny Sven. Dad, you can quite laughing anytime. Back to business. The four legs are spring loaded to soften our landing. Rocket thrusters mounted on the bottom of each foot will give us the capability for straight up movement when taking off or landing."

"Fuel is provided by a technology that has been around forever but not perfected until now. I use waste feces, both solid and liquid, from living creatures. The extreme heat from the rocket thruster turns the feces into a methane gas that we can use for power."

"Inside the craft there are two control chairs for humans and two for dogs. Each control station will guide the ship with the simple push of a button. Ole will be Captain. Sven will be First Mate, in charge of the landing party. I will be Navigator. However, I feel we need one more human crewmember. We'll have to discuss that."

"Our kitchenette will have food provided by NASA. This is the same food that was used by Einer and Sven on their space journey. It will allow our bodies to adapt to the conditions on Planet X. Therefore, we won't need space suits or space helmets."

"I've redesigned the bathroom, which proved inadequate for Einer and Sven on their journey. There will be a human toilet as well as one especially designed for Sven and me. For ours, I installed a 3'x3' flat area covered with Astroturf and enclosed it with 6" high sides. A sensor will be activated whenever Sven or I leave the potty area and it will be flushed with a saline cleaning solution. The best part of the whole bathroom system is that all our waste material transfers to our fuel tanks and is then heated and used for fuel. I call it the "Lena Latrine" System."

"I've already hired an outside contractor to secretly build the spacecraft at an estimated cost of $250, 000. I know we told NASA $550,000. The extra money will cover any construction overruns. Anyway, the way the Government works, they couldn't come close to building our ship for less than $2 million. I figure that whatever we save we can leave in the bank, collecting interest, until we return. We keep the interest; NASA gets whatever principal is left."

Ole and I had to admit that Lena was one smart puppy. However, she failed to mention who our contractor was or how long our expedition might take. All this talk almost made us miss Theater Night. We were hungry so we stayed up later than usual. We watched the first episode of 'Island at War', a World War II Masterpiece Theatre series about the German occupation of the fictional Island of St. Gregory. I'm excited to see the next five episodes.

Now, off to bed; Ole is still reading to us from 'New Moon.' Time for lights out, prayers, hugs, and kisses.

CHAPTER 6

Next morning talk was all business. Estimates for loading, takeoff, travel time, unloading our spacecraft from Discovery and time needed to revolve with the Moon's orbit: approximately five days was decided. Then, seven days for planet exploration and five days for the return trip would require a total of seventeen days. Since we'd be traveling with the Discovery crew we only had to take a maximum of ten days worth of food for our solo venture.

We still need another human crewmember. Ole's human kids were the most logical choices. Val and Casey had been on our adventures before and both did superb jobs. Nikki had been overlooked until now. However, of the three, she had the best qualifications for this expedition. She was a born explorer. She'd already canoed the length of the Mississippi River; backpacked through Europe; taken both winter and summer desert training; she'd even eaten bugs on one of her training exercises. She was an accomplished tri-athlete and, best of all, willing to try anything once. One drawback was apparent or should I say "a parent." Nikki and her dad 'Ole' both thought a lot alike. While Ole was good at holding his tongue during their hardheaded arguments, Nikki's tongue could become a lethal weapon in a fight of words. It was like mixing oil and water. This time practicality prevailed. Ole called Nikki and invited her to be second mate on the expedition. She would be in charge of travel as well as the camping and sleeping arrangements outside the spaceship. Being the free spirit she was, she readily accepted the position.

The contractor building the spacecraft was a rather touchy subject for Lena. She'd already contacted them and arranged all the details long before we had our little NASA meeting. If NASA agreed to our terms, they were prepared to start work immediately.

B-Low Studios of Hollywood was to be our contractor. The three of us had done some investigative work for Mr. B some time back. Mr. B and his two associates, Allison Vira and Bruce Shambles, had become trusted acquaintances of ours. The Studio had all the equipment and manpower needed. A big plus was that their special effects department knew how to work miracles on a small budget. As far as the studio workers were concerned, this was to be a prop spaceship for an upcoming movie. What better way to hide a top secret, NASA funded spaceship then by having it built right out in the open, in Hollywood. Once complete, it would be transported in three sections to Johnson Space Center in Houston, Texas, and, from there, by rail to Kennedy Space Center in Florida. Then it would be loaded aboard Discovery and assembled inside the freight bay, 'out of sight, out of mind'. Lena was proud of her plan, and rightly so.

Sometimes I feel inferior to my little sister; she's so smart. However, this time she might have overlooked one thing. Allison Vira worked at B-Low Studios. It wasn't too long ago that Allison, or "Al" as we called her, had a brief but romantic interlude with our beloved dad, Ole. Like they used to say in the old days, "What this shall wrought, we soon shall know."

It's now been two days and no word from NASA. Maybe the deal was going to fall through. Just as we were getting ready to watch episode five of 'Island at War' the phone rang. Captain Spud Nick wanted to talk to Ole. Our contract had been accepted and would be signed by the necessary people. This meant, on our end, Ole was to sign while Lena and I would use our paw prints as our signatures. The ranking officer at NASA would sign and Captain Nick would sign for the Navy. And, yes, the Commander in Chief would also be at the signing. A taxicab was scheduled to pick us up at nine a.m. A Government jet would then take us to the Charleston, South Carolina, Air Force Base. From that point, we would board a Bombardier CL145 sea plane disguised as a yellow and red civilian aircraft. This plane would take us to our next, undisclosed location for the signing of the contract.

Ole didn't like this idea at all; he hated to fly. He wanted to take a train to Charleston. I didn't want to mention this but it was bound to come up. "Dad, flying is no big deal. If we're going to Planet X we'll have to spend some time in air travel. Might as well start flying now and get used to it."

What could he say? Ten days in orbit would certainly be considered 'flying time'. Lena and I packed up Ole's things. He was pouting about the flying thing. Humans have been known to pout about stuff like this, but they get over it. Tomorrow should be an interesting day.

CHAPTER 7

The taxicab was honking its horn at exactly nine a.m. Lena had packed Ole's lucky green Great Northern Railway bag with a few basic essentials, clean shirts, pants, socks, and lots of Dramamine for Ole. She also included a few rawhide bones and beef jerky for snacks. Ole wasn't much for rawhide bone chewing but he was always happy to share our beef jerky. Two bottles of water, and we were ready to go.

We were taken to the local airport; it's really small town stuff. Our U.S. Air Force plane was waiting on the tarmac. A smartly dressed young man in a steward's outfit met our cab and carried our luggage to the airplane. As we hurriedly crossed to the plane, the young man introduced himself. His name was Jimmy and he would be our assigned steward for the first leg of our trip. He was a nice kid, maybe mid-twenties, tall and lanky, his voice was a little hesitant and he used words like 'ah' and 'um'; not in a stuttering manner, just a little slow of speech. As we were walking I heard Ole mumbling to himself "Stewart, Jimmy, tall, lanky, slow of speech. Yeah that's it, Jimmy Stewart, or should I say Jimmy Steward. Oh, that's a good one."

I immediately broke into Ole's thoughts. "Ole, not funny. He's our steward not Stewart. This is serious, be nice."

"Yeah, yeah, Sven you're just like having a wife. You never let me have any fun."

By most standards, our jet was small. However, at our little airport, it was as big as they could handle. The inside was elegant; we'd never stayed in a hotel as nice. It had plush leather recliners and sofas, a kitchenette, movie screen and a large bathroom. This is what I call flying;

even Ole seemed pleased. Jimmy made sure we were all seated and comfortable. Lena and I each had a nice comfortable leather recliner to ourselves. Once in the air Jimmy announced that he would be serving breakfast and he turned out to be one heck of a good cook. He was busy in the kitchenette while, at the same time, setting a small table for our meal; ham and cheese omelets, orange juice, milk, toast and jam. Then we all settled down for a nice nap.

Three hours later we landed at the Charleston Air Force Base. Everything went so smoothly that Ole never once complained about flying. He didn't even need the Dramamine.

We were quickly ushered from our hotel in the sky to a yellow and red, big-bellied, dual propeller seaplane. This particular piece of transportation had both wheels and floats. The co-pilot met us half way across the landing strip. He was about six feet tall with a ruddy complexion and a few days of stubble on his face. We walked as briskly as Ole and his cane could manage. He started to give us the low down on the next leg of the journey.

"My name is Tom Sellyuk and I'll be both your host and co-pilot. Like our plane? She's an old Bombardier CL145 water tanker. A lot these old birds are used for fire fighting. They pick up water and then release it over the fires. Some of these planes get converted to cargo/passenger units; that's what we have. We haul a lot of rich American tourists into Canada to fish and hunt. See the name up there on her nose, "Lil' Lady?" She's my baby; been all the way to the North Pole and back, she has. Now this is gonna be a short flight; twenty to thirty minutes tops. They hired us 'cause they don't want to risk losing any of their expensively trained flyboys on these nasty little jaunts; so private contractors take over. No need to worry though, we fly in weather the Air Force boys wouldn't even walk in. Here we are, let me help you aboard. Ole, sit there and strap in tight. Here, take this little white puppy with you and hang on to her, might get kind of rough where were going. Where's the wood box? Ah yes, there it is. Come here my little gray doggie, in the box ya go. Here's a blanket for ya; smells kind of musty but it will have to do. I'll strap your box in nice and secure on this empty seat here; ya stay put puppy, might get bounced around a bit. Well, we're on our way gang, hold on tight. If you need anything just holler."

The plane shook, the seats vibrated, the take off was quick and altitude was gained quickly. I looked at Lena and Ole. Ole's hands, white knuckled and tense, grasped the arm of his chair. Lena was curled in a tight ball on Ole's lap. Me, I was stuck on a damp, musty smelling blanket with a box that reeked of dead fish and old fuel oil. Normally, I like the smell of dead fish, but mix that smell with fuel oil and musty cloth, even a dog can get nauseous.

Looking out the window, I could see only water; ocean in every direction. Our plane started into a steep bank to the left. Ole now had a nice pasty, bleached white complexion. On the next circle, I could see something breaking the surface of the water. Tom was walking awkwardly back to us, trying to keep his balance with the slant of the airplane. He had a chicken drumstick in his mouth and an empty Colonel Saunders bag in his hand.

He thrust the empty chicken bag under Ole's chin, "here ya go buddy, and looks like ya might be needin' this." Then he turned and went back to plane's cabin. The smell of old fried chicken had a rather disastrous affect on Ole. His complexion changed from a nasty pasty white to a neon green. Lena leaped from Ole's lap into my box. We both looked away as Ole gave up his morning breakfast. Certainly not normal contents for a Colonel Saunders fried chicken bag.

I heard Tom tell his pilot friend, "Ain't it just grand when they send us civilians to babysit? Nothing like green eggs and ham coming out of a civilian."

As we touched down on the water, we could see a submarine. Did I say 'touched' down? Make that 'landed like a rock'. I felt the pontoons skim the water, the pilot cut the motors, and the whole aircraft tilt nose down, then, with a jerk, the tail dropped into its normal position. Lena and I were a little shaken up from being tossed to the front of the box and then bounced off the back, with a thud. Ole looked like death warmed over; at least he was still breathing.

Tom flung the side door open; at least the fresh air felt good. A small motorized skiff was making its way from the submarine towards us. I could see three sailors. A small short sailor was piloting the craft. Then there was an average looking guy and one big burly, jolly looking seaman. Tom handed Lena and me to the big guy and he placed us gently on the floor of the boat. Ole's bag and cane came next. Then they hauled, dragged, and carried Ole from the plane to the boat. The ride from plane to the boat was not too pleasant for Ole; large sea swells rose and dropped us as we headed toward the submarine. Once on the deck of the submarine the large sailor took Lena in one hand and me in the other and made his way below deck. A number of other sailors were dragging Ole to sickbay. Our big, burly escort took us into the mess area and set us down right on top of a table. He then sat down and started to talk to Lena and me just as if we were humans.

"Well, there me little mateys, my name's Alan Hail, Seamen Mate First Class. Looks like I'll be looking after you until you're human gets his sea legs. I have to admit, he had one of the nicest shades of sea green I've ever seen. Hey you! Swabbie; behind the counter there, bring me and my companions three bowls of ice cream; no skimpin' mind ya, two scoops each for my furry little buddies, and four scoops for me."

This guy was something else; I don't think he even realized we're dogs. The way he looked and talked, I thought perhaps they'd drafted the Skipper from Gilligan's Island. He whisked Lena and me off the table into his big strong arms and hauled us off to the recreation hall. He plopped us down on a table that had a checkerboard all set up and ready to play. Then his booming voice started up. "Well me buckoos, what have we here? Why, a checkerboard all set up just for us. You two don't have to say anything, we'll just play a few games. I can move for you, if you want."

Alan moved his first checker. I was feeling confident that no matter what I did Alan would take it in stride. Therefore, I took my paw and made my move. Nothing more was said and we just kept playing our game. Well, nothing was said until I won. Then Alan said, "I'll be darned, beaten by a pooch. You're one heck of a little sea dog there buddy, beating me right off like that. Let's try again. Go ahead there, little buddy, you move first."

Lena's tail was wagging full speed; she was enjoying this. It would be hard not to like this big human; he must be part dog, sea dog that is. I started to make some bad moves on purpose during our second game. My dog sense told me that it was best to let Alan win one game out of two. We'd just finished our second game when Captain Nick and Ole came into the room.

Alan spoke right up, "well, shiver me timbers, our seasick friend is up and about." Captain Nick gave Alan a withering look. Alan jumped to his feet, knocking Lena and I onto the nearest chair and tipping over the table with the checkerboard. He was trying to apologize to Lena and me, salute the Captain, and pick up the mess, all at the same time. Needless to say, it wasn't going too well.

"Sorry, Captain, Sir. Just keeping my little furry buddies busy while their human got doctored up, Sir. That little black and white feller there, he's a heck of a checker player."

Captain Nick led us down the corridor to a door which was manned by two armed guards. We entered to see a nice looking gentleman, top shirt button open, no tie, just looking relaxed and sitting at a desk. He sure looked familiar. He stood up, walked over to Ole and shook hands.

"Hello Ole, my name is George Bush; please, call me George. These two with you must be Lena and Sven. Welcome, all of you. Ole, have a seat. Captain Nick, will you please wait outside until I call for you."

George sat down and called Lena and me over to him. We jumped up in his lap and gave him a few doggie kisses. He responded with some hugs and ear scratching. Lena and I then settled down on George's lap and the conversation started. George went first, "I finally get to meet the infamous Sven and Ole. Too bad the third rascal, Einer, isn't with you. I heard the three of you made quite an impression on NASA awhile ago. Put Captain Nick and me in quite a spot. It all turned out well. It was a good test for the new astronaut food and a remotely operated spacecraft. Of course, some rather strange questions arose after Captain Nick let you leave the space center."

"It seems some of the samples taken from Einer and Sven had traces of green grass and Earthlike soil. Notice I used the word 'like'. We still haven't been able to identify them. Then, the dog's stool samples; they were interesting. They contained significant traces of steak and cheese. These particular stool samples were too fresh to have been from a meal eaten on Earth, before their trip. Of course, all this information is classified. It sure is interesting though. If only Einer and Sven could tell us what they know?"

"Now, let's get down to current business. Naturally, we've been monitoring all your activities since you started emailing NASA. All your emails, telephone calls, letters; we have copies of everything. Ole, not to put you down, but these dogs seem to be much more involved than you're letting on. Little Lena, you seem to be much smarter than anyone thinks. Sven, I have a feeling you've been monitoring this whole little operation. Ole, you, of course, are the alpha dog of this pack. Therefore, I'm holding you personally responsible for everything that happens."

"NASA has informed me that you're withholding certain information from them, thereby giving you the upper hand. I understand your lack of trust in any Government agency; heck, I don't trust any of them myself. One thing about the Government you'd better understand, however, they know more than you think they do. For instance, we know that a Mr. B. and his people are going to build your spacecraft. I think that's a brilliant choice. Build a top secret object right out in the open as a movie prop. I have to wonder which of you came up with that idea. If you ever want a job working for me, let me know."

"Now, this is what I'm going to do. Captain Nick and I will sign your contract. I hope you don't mind that I left the Head of NASA out of this one. The worst thing that could happen is that Captain Nick gets his butt kicked for holding back information. If needed, I can step in and protect the Captain. The fewer people privy to this the better. What I want from you three is a complete report of what you find. Things may go well, they may not. When you return, I will seriously consider your recommendations regarding what should be done with your findings. If, and this is a big if, there is life on Planet X, especially intelligent life, we'll have to deal with it in a scientific manner. It may be best if the world never knows about this. We have trouble taking care of our own world. It would be a shame to mess up someone else's."

"As I am sure you know, I won't have my job after January 20, 2009, so this project has to be completed by then. Anything you need, let Captain Nick know and it will be priority."

George put Lena and me on the floor and opened the door to let Captain Nick back in. The contracts were spread out before the four of us. Captain Nick, Ole, and then the Commander in Chief, George Bush, all signed their names. Then George took Lena's paw, pressed it on an ink pad, and put her foot print on the line next to her name. I signed the same way. George thanked us all and shook Ole's hand.

"Thank you for coming on such short notice. Captain Nick will do everything within his power to assist you and make your jobs as pleasant as possible. God bless you all and have a safe journey."

Once topside we saw that the submarine had been moored at a large pier. I glanced over at the conning tower and in large gold script were the words "Sea Wolf One," with the seal of the United States below it.

Captain Nick spoke up, "The President felt bad about your little bout of seasickness Ole so he ordered the sub to dock at one of Charleston's old Navy piers. Your car is waiting; the driver will take you back to the Air Force Base for your return trip to Minnesota. I'll be in touch."

The captain saluted and walked away. We returned home on the same plane we'd arrived on. By nine p.m. we were in our own beds. Too tired to read; we just wanted to sleep.

CHAPTER 8

For the next week we were busy as puppies. Remember, this is a dog story, no 'busy as beavers' stuff here. Lena was on the computer, checking and re-checking everything before our trip. If she left the computer for any length of time, she would sit Ole down to practice on the flight simulator she'd designed for our flight. As for me, I kept everyone doing his or her job. I also kept in touch with Allison at B-Low Studios since she was in charge of our project. Of course, I had to keep putting off her questions about Ole. I just said he was so busy he couldn't get back to her. However, I broke my promise to Ole. I did tell her about his toe amputation; she was very concerned. I explained how Ole was just being a typically vain, stupid male of his species and she seemed to accept that.

I also had to keep track of Nikki. I emailed her everyday to make sure she was staying in shape. After all, she was going to be the driving force behind our expedition once we landed on Planet X. I sure hoped she wouldn't find any bugs that looked tasty. Everyone was getting a little on edge with all that had to be done. Of course, as the leader, I was getting most of the flak. I decided to add a little fun to our workload; a contest to name our spacecraft. It was only logical that sooner or later it had to have a name. We couldn't keep calling it the 'spacecraft.'

Nikki wanted to name it 'Stella" after her newly adopted Shih-Tzu. Nice gesture on her part, but I knew it wouldn't fly with the rest of the crew. Ole suggested that since the spacecraft was shaped like a dog, we name it 'Best Friend'; certainly a name to be considered. Lena came up with 'Pluto Forever'. She certainly had a fixation with this whole 'Pluto' thing. I wanted to call it 'The Spirit of Eisenstein'. I know, I was being teary eyed and sentimental about the name. After all, Eisenstein was my first space companion and my best friend. Since this wasn't a secret ballot I can tell you who voted for which name. Are you ready, here goes:

'Spirit of Stella'	1 vote from Nikki
'Best Friends'	0 votes
'Pluto Forever'	1 vote from Lena
'Spirit of Eisenstein'	2 votes from Ole and Sven

I guess the Einer thing got to Ole, too. It sure was a shame we couldn't have him with us on this trip. At least he could be there in spirit. I was excited enough about the name to email Al so she could have it lettered on the finished spacecraft.

Eleven days had passed us by. Al emailed me to let me know the spacecraft would be done on schedule. Lena emailed Amtrak and reserved two sleeper berths for us. Nikki would board the train in her home town of Duluth and we would join her six hours later.

We had just traveled this route not too long ago, so it was old hat for us. Nikki used to live in Oregon and that was our next stop before we transferred to a different train that would take us to Hollywood. Ole loved train travel; I have to admit, if you have time that's the way to go. This was to be the last of our relaxing trips; after this it would be full steam ahead to get us into space and on our way.

Laurely Stan, the chauffer for B-Low Studios, met us at the Hollywood train station. Skinny and longed faced, he was a dead ringer for the smaller guy from the Laurel and Hardy comedy team. It seems he had to get us to the studio as quickly as possible; trouble was brewing. That's all we needed. All this way, and then problems. I could just ring Allison's neck for this one. She had a cell phone, why hadn't she called? The guard at the studio gate waved us through; the whole place was crammed with cars. Laurely had to double park just to get us near our destination. He jumped out of the car, opened the door for us, and then pointed at the huge Quonset hut marked Studio 'B'. "Hurry, they're waiting for you!"

We hurried as fast as an Ole and his cane could go. As we burst through the doors we found the inside blacker then a black lab in a coal mine. We all stood still; wrong building? Then, colored lights flashed onto a huge cloth that was draped over something big. A roar of cheers filled the room. A spotlight followed Allison, Bruce, and Mr. B onto a raised stage. They called us up to stand next to them. Mr. B ticked the microphone to make sure it was working. Then he made his speech.

"Today, the employees of B-Low Studios accomplished what many thought was impossible. We were commissioned to build the most unusual spaceship ever to grace the grounds of NASA. For all I know, NASA is having McDonalds open a huge play land, but who really knows what they do with taxpayer's money. What I do know is that we were awarded this contract thanks to our friends Lena, Sven and Ole. When they've finished with their rather strange project, the ship will be returned to us for use in future space movies."

"So, with no further ado, I present to all of you "SPIRIT OF EINSTEIN." Drop the curtain please."

The curtain fell to the floor; the highly polished stainless steel shell of our spacecraft reflected a rainbow of colors from the lights swirling around it. People laughed, cheered, and clapped. What else can you do when you see a three-story tall stainless steel dog? The best things about the spacecraft were the huge black letters written across its side, 'Spirit of Einstein'.

There was a great party with food, champagne, music, dancing and mayhem. Somehow I lost track of Al and Ole. I do remember that Al looked ravishing in her long black gown; a slit running up one leg almost to her thigh. I heard Ole whisper something about "look at Al's legs, they go all the way to the ground." Must be some human thing.

CHAPTER 9

Morning has broken and I think it broke all over my head and body. Lena didn't look too well either. There was doggie puke all over our bed. I gave Lena a nudge to wake her up. She moaned and rolled over on her back. Then we jumped off the bed and went outside. Ole was sleeping on the couch. I nudged his hand with my stinking, puke covered muzzle. He looked at Lena and me and smiled. "You two don't look too good" was all he said as he opened the door for us. The California sun seemed a little too bright this morning. I had to pee like a racehorse. I think I might have killed the bush by our bungalow. I glanced at Lena; I hope my poop isn't as runny as hers. An important lesson was learned last night. Dogs, champagne and rich hors d'oeuvres don't mix. Nikki and Ole must have survived the night better then Lena and I did. They were both dressed and ready to leave by the time we came back in. Al was just pulling up in her black T-Bird convertible. No time to clean up; we were on our way to meet the train that was transporting the Spirit of Einstein to the Houston Space Center.

Lena and I curled up in a ball in the back seat. Nikki stroked our fur trying her best to comfort us. She said something about "its OK kids, I've been there, done that." Knowing Nikki, I'll bet she has. So, why didn't she warn us about this last night?

We pulled into the railroad's freight yards this time. No more Amtrak; straight old freight train. The last three cars were for us. Two long flatcars were left empty for the three huge wooden crates that contained the unassembled Spirit of Einstein. The caboose was reserved for Nikki,

Lena, Ole and me. We weren't going to let the Spirit of Einstein out of our sight.

I watched from the caboose steps as Al and Ole gently hugged and kissed goodbye. I'm not sure what they did last night. The fire didn't seem as hot as it used to be, but the flame was still burning. I was afraid Ole was being a typical human, thinking that he wasn't good enough for Al. You'd think he'd wake up and smell the dog's butt; wait, for humans I think you say wake up and smell the coffee.

It was interesting to sit up in the cupola of the caboose and watch the scenery. It's amazing how many people like to wave at the caboose. Ole and Nikki checked the flatcars two or three times. I doubt it was necessary but they liked the adventure of being out in the open and walking along the train cars while they were in motion. Ole claimed they were just making sure the flatcars were strong enough to hold our 'Einer' craft. Sometimes humans were just like puppies, they do things just because they can.

The Johnson Space Center had its own railroad spur making the transfer of the Spirit of Einstein much easier. Ole and I stayed to supervise the transfer of our spacecraft to the Discovery space shuttle. Nikki and Lena were making arrangements for our trip to the Kennedy Space Center. Thus far, everything was going smoothly.

Nikki and Lena were assigned to a barracks on base. Ole and I decided to borrow a cot and sleeping bags and stay in Discovery's cargo bay. We knew our craft was safe where it was, and well guarded. However, it was our 'baby' and we tended to be a little over protective.

In the morning we ate in the mess hall with service personnel. We were all wearing NASA jackets. Captain Nick had had custom jackets made for Lena and me. Ole explained that the markings on the jackets gave us unrestricted access to anywhere on the base. I understood that our importance only went so far however; no one ever saluted us.

We flew to the Kennedy Space Center in an airplane similar to the one we'd flown in to meet the President. Not the Bombardier CL145, the other plane, the one that was like a fancy flying hotel. This was Nikki's first trip on an airplane like that. She was very impressed. She was beginning to think her old dad and his dogs were a little more important then she'd realized.

Captain Nick met us upon our arrival. We were given a tour of the base and briefed as we went along. Then it was off to the base hospital. A special veterinarian was brought in to check out Lena and me. All four of us were weighed, measured, poked, prodded, pilled and given shots for everything you could imagine. This was not the high point of our adventure, that's for sure. Captain Nick convinced Ole and me to spend the night in the barracks. We agreed under the condition that Captain Nick sleep with the Spirit of Einstein. In the morning we would supervise the reassembly of our spacecraft. Then we participated in briefings for what little time was left before our departure.

As a matter of security we were isolated from all NASA personnel with the exception of Captain Nick. Top secret conditions had to be maintained at all costs. By the time we went to bed, countdown had begun. By five a.m. we had to be suited up and ready to board Discovery.

The next morning we were fitted into our bright orange jumpsuits; humans and dogs alike. Lena and I thought they were fun to wear, our tails showed up really well sticking out of the hole in the back of our jackets. Ole, what a sight! Put a green stem on his head, and surprise, jack-o-lantern. Ole took the teasing well. Not that he was happy but he's pretty easy going about things like that.

To put it mildly, the launch was rough, shaky and, for Ole, sickening. It was a lot like the moon flight Einer and I had taken; lots of noise, tremendous 'G' forces, and just overall unpleasant. Once we cleared the Earth's atmosphere the trip settled down to a pleasant ride.

Captain Nick was with us for this part of our journey but he made sure we kept our distance from the other crew members. The crew was very curious about us and, although they were told to expect things like this, we sure felt like outsiders.

By this time the Spirit of Einstein had become one of us and we just called it 'Einer'. We spent the next two days checking and double and triple checking. Well, you know, we just kept rechecking everything on Einer. Nikki and Ole gave Lena and me the job of checking out the poop hole rocket expulsion unit. They said it was a dog's job to check out another dog's pooper. Funny humans. Ha-ha-ha.

Four hours before we reached our drop off point, Nikki, Ole and Captain Nick were playing three-handed cribbage. Ole asked Captain Nick if he was named after the first Russian space probe, Sputnik. "You're not the first to ask" he said "but, no, I wasn't named after Sputnik. I grew up on a potato farm in Idaho and my folks named all us kids after their main crop. I was named Spud, and having Nick for a last name gave everyone a good laugh at my expense. It could have been worse. My brother's name is Smallfry and my poor sister is named Tatereye and everyone calls her Tater."

I think the humans were too nervous to sleep. I drifted off for a good nap when the human's conversation became too boring.

CHAPTER 10

Half an hour to go before we're released into space. Nikki and Ole are strapped into their chairs. Lena and I have special clips on our NASA jackets to keep us safely in our specially designed doggie seats.

We see the control person give us the "all clear" signal. We must be a sight; four faces staring out of the two big dog eyes of Einer. Looking up we can see the shuttle's cargo doors splitting open to reveal a silky back night dotted with specks of white starlight. It's an eerie feeling.

Einer jolts just enough so that we feel the arm of the cargo bay lock onto our craft. We are slowly lifted up and out of the cargo area. The whirr of hydraulic motors from the large control arm is the only noticeable sound. As we clear Discovery's protruding area, the arm slowly releases its grip. Ole is concentrating on the control panel and Lena, alert to all of Ole's movements, is ready for back up, just in case. Ole maneuvers us up and away from our home ship Discovery. Evidently, all of Ole's simulator training went extremely well. He is feathering the rocket thruster and controls so that we can't feel any movement. Only the visual distance of the stars and the tracking of our instruments give any indication we're moving. It's so quiet, beautiful—and scary.

Discovery, our last link to civilization, slowly disappears from sight. Ole is maneuvering Einer into a trajectory that will coast us to the outer edge of the Moon's gravitational pull. If we can slip into the Moon's rotational field, we can coast along without burning any fuel. Lena's expertise with her instrument settings has paid off. The control panel helps to guide Ole into place. Einer is 'free' orbiting the moon. In approximately five hours, Planet X should be visible.

After our first hour in space we started to relax a little. Ole had his chair reclined and was getting a little shuteye. Lena was in Ole's lap for her own little nap time. Nikki was just gazing out the window. Her first adventure with us must be a little overwhelming. Me, I wanted to try out the doggie toilet. It was great. As a joke someone had placed a little plastic flower into the corner of our potty area. No joke to me; I lifted my leg and marked that little flower right in its pistil. I then stepped out and watched the toilet self clean. We need one of these at home.

I returned to the main control room. Everyone looked comfortable and relaxed. I settled into my chair and chewed on a rawhide bone. It would be a few hours before we'd have anything more to do.

CHAPTER 11

Nikki was the first to point out the blue speck in the distance. As we neared the unknown planet, we experienced wonderment beyond our wildest imagination. The closer we came to the planet the more vivid the colors became. Like a beautiful swirled glass marble, the planet reflected the rays of the sun. Soon we could make out distinct landmasses, continents similar to those of Earth. The blue shimmered as only an ocean could. The continents, the landmasses, seemed to mimic those of our home planet. Had we traveled too far, were we actually seeing Earth and not a foreign planet?

A check of our instruments confirmed we were on the correct heading; our location matched the data that Lena had entered into our directional guidance system. Exactly what were we looking at? A mirage? A strange cosmic reflection of Earth?

Ole switched Einer to manual control. He gently used the rocket thruster to pull us out of the Moon's orbit. It would take approximately thirty hours to reach our intended target. Einer was now free floating in space. Lena set the coordinates to automatic. Einer was now on his own to continue our journey toward Planet X. We hoped.

Lena was busy rechecking her calculations. The rest of the crew, including me, spent time checking Einer over. This was no time for a problem. I scheduled an eight hour sleep period for everyone. Einer's sensors would alert us to any problems inside or outside of our craft.

All we could do now was wait until we reached the outer atmosphere of Planet X. Then Ole and Lena would operate the manual controls to bring us down to a hopefully safe landing.

Five more minutes and Einer would breach Planet X's atmosphere. By now we were all changed into our orange outfits and strapped into our safety harnesses. Ole switched to manual control and deftly maneuvered Einer into position. We needed to enter at a slight angle to dissipate any heat buildup. I sure hoped that Icy Heat shell insulation did its job.

Einer shook and shimmed some, but nothing serious. Lena's coordinates would direct our landing. Einer slowly rotated to a horizontal belly down position. The nose and poop hole rocket boosters both kicked in to stabilize us. Then both rockets rotated upward and slowly provided the thrust needed to lower us to the ground. Ole turned the thruster switch off just as Einer's four metal paws softly touched the surface of Planet X.

It was so quiet. Not a sound. We all stood at the windows looking out. It was a bright sunny day; just a few cumulus clouds dotting the sky like huge cotton balls. The ground was covered with tall green grass. The vegetation and trees looked like those on Earth. Our sensors showed a safe oxygen level. Gravitational readings showed that we would weigh almost twice as much as we did on Earth, just as we predicted.

Nikki gathered the items to off load from Einer so we could begin setting up outside. Supplies were kept to a minimum. Our increased body weight would require enough additional exertion without adding anything unnecessary.

Einer's mouth opened. His tongue ramp unrolled to the surface. Lena had the privilege of setting the first paw on Planet X. Ole was next, providing the first human footprint on the planet. Nikki and I stepped off together, a tie, so we wouldn't argue about it later. Nikki gave each of us a homing device in case we got separated. The compass she brought showed a definite North/South Pole axis. For no particular reason she led us in a westerly direction. Almost immediately we could all tell from the energy needed to lift our feet we'd have to rest often.

CHAPTER 12

We saw grass that was lush and green, about ankle high, with small clumps of trees scattered about. A depression in the near distance looked like a small stream. So far it seemed as if we were still on Earth.

Nikki led us towards the stream. There were five or six small trees at the water's edge. The water was clear; maybe two or three feet deep. A few fish darted among the rocks. We choose this site for a little pow-wow. Lena was in the middle of our group and had what looked like a pork chop. She said she'd got it from a nearby tree. We all walked over to investigate. Sure enough, the tree had pork chops suspended like fruit from its leafy branches. They all looked like they'd just been prepared for sale at a butcher shop. Nice shape, the bone right where it should be, the right amount of fat, and each about one and a half to two inches thick. Some were rather white but you could see they turned a nice pink color as they ripened.

Ole pulled a ripe looking chop from the tree. Nikki had already set up her test equipment. We all sat down to await the results. She soon made her announcement, "As far as the tests go, this is a pork chop. It's pure, no toxins, looks ready to cook and eat. I ran an analysis on the stream water. It's more pure then any bottled water I ever tested on Earth." I knew it was time for me to speak up.

"Let's make a fire and cook up some of these pork chops. I think that would be the best test. You have to admit, a fresh pork chop with clean cool water to drink; what a great snack."

Nikki, as the leader of our land exploration, was ready for anything. She pulled a portable stove from her backpack and clicked on the propane. Ole went to what we now called our butcher tree and picked one more nice juicy pork chop. Nikki cooked them both and we shared a great meal. Nikki even had salt and pepper in her backpack. Ole was a little disappointed that she hadn't brought ketchup. Our 'being on Earth theory' was a little weak now. None of us had ever encountered a tree filled with pork chops on Earth.

When morning came Nikki took command. She shimmed up the butcher tree to look at the surrounding area. The tree was not too high, maybe twenty feet, but high enough to get the lay of the land. She pulled a pair of binoculars from her backpack and scanned the horizon. Once back on the ground she told us what she'd seen. The decision was then made to camp where we were for the night so perhaps our bodies could start to acclimate to the increased gravity.

"Well gang, to the southwest there are two things of interest. First there's a herd of about twenty animals that look kind of like sheep, grazing in a field. And second, about a hundred yards beyond the animals, it looks like there's a well worn path or some type of road. Everybody up and start marching, we have things to see."

As we moved closer, the animals only seemed curious about us I don't think they were the least bit afraid. They seemed content to continue doing what they were doing. We'd never seen anything like them. However, Lena had done exhaustive research on our prehistoric period (see book Vortex Valley). She identified the animals as Thomashuxleya, from the early Tertiary Period. The Thomashuxleya were a little smaller than our present day sheep. Their coats were coarse, like pigs, but their legs were more sheep like. Their heads were oversized for their bodies with a rat like appearance. They had two tusks protruding from their upper jaw and pointing towards the ground; probably used to root for vegetation. While Nikki and Ole petted them, Lena and I checked out their scents.

Nikki soon had us heading toward our next objective. Path or road was the question. It was about fifteen feet wide and paved with cobblestones. It went as far as the eye could see in both directions. If not manmade, it was certainly made by an intelligent species. We decided to follow the road to the southwest; the same direction the stream was flowing. The combination of a road and water should lead to some type of habitation.

Habitation meant life, life meant some type of being, and a paved road showed intelligence. I had to wonder what we were getting involved in.

CHAPTER 13

The road led us along lush fields of wild foliage, trees with fruit that was unique and alien to us. Insects were abundant, both flying and crawling. None of them seemed to have any interest in us. On Earth, the mosquitoes would have been eating us alive in a place like this. At times white tail deer were visible only a few hundred yards away. They watched us pass, but never ran. Then from out of nowhere came a dog about my size. White fur, long coat, its ears and beard were tan in color. Lena and I ran and gave him a typical Earth dog greeting. He was receptive and greeted us in return. We understood each other and had a nice conversation. His name was Dandi and he was a Sealyham terrier; a breed popular in Wales. When I asked him about his origin, he said, "of course there's a country of Wales, are you daft dog?" I asked him what planet this was. He looked rather quizzical but responded, "This planet is Htrae, where do you think you are?" He had a very distinct accent. My explanation of Earth and our arrival here from space didn't seem to surprise him. However, he seemed rather mystified by Val and Ole. Finally he spoke. "Your people are quit large, giants maybe? I've heard some of their words but they don't talk the same as the people here. They seem to understand you two. Is this normal on your planet?"

Lena then got into the conversation. "Our people are normal size for Earth. They understand Sven and me but it's a very unusual talent on our planet. They speak English. What do people here speak?"

Dandi answered, "They speak Hsilgne. All the animals speak the same language so that they can understand each other, just as you and I can understand each other."

Lena kept the questions flowing. "Do you live with humans? Is there a place you call home or a town, and can you take us there?"

Dandi answered, "We share dwellings with humans; a few of the other animals also live with humans. Mostly we just all co-habit this world together. Our humans look like yours but they are much smaller. Your humans seem nice and friendly. They won't do anything bad if I take you to our village will they?"

Lena, "I give my doggie word that our humans will be on their best behavior. We're here to learn and make friends. We want you to accept us."

Lena and Dandi took the lead heading south down the road. I stayed by Ole and translated everything that had been said between Lena and Dandi. Of course, I had to talk slow because Ole had to translate what I said to Nikki.

We knew that this planet had dogs, strange prehistoric grazing animals, pork chop trees and soon we'd see people and towns. I knew this was more than any of us had hoped for.

When we got to the edge of town there was a welcome sign that read, "Duolc, noitalupop 56,606." In many ways it looked like an ordinary Earth town. However, there were some rather startling differences. For instance, the homes, businesses, street signs and manhole covers were about half the size they were on Earth; even the vehicles. The majority of the cars looked like that new small 'Smart' car; the large cars were comparable to a Mini Cooper. And the motorcycles, I could only think of Ole's old 1970 Honda CT70 that he had stored in the boathouse back home.

As we proceeded down the sidewalk, Ole and Nikki had to stoop so they didn't bump their heads on store awnings and overhanging signs. By now, people were starting to gather to watch us. And they were like everything else, about half scale as far as we were concerned. The tallest was perhaps three feet tall. Everything was to scale and in perfect order. I felt like I was accompanying a circus freak show to a local fair.

Dandi led us to the door of an impressive looking old grey stone building of gothic design; the sign above the door proclaimed it to be 'Ytic Llah.' The man who came out of the building was one of the, shall we say, 'small' people. We were still standing at the bottom of the two steps leading into the building. The small person was on top of the steps and so was the same height as us. The humans warily looked each other over. I assume the small people were humans.

Ole held out his large hand. The little person hesitated a moment, indicating that the handshake was wrong, but he finally took Ole's hand and they had a good handshake. Nikki offered her hand to the small person and he deftly and courteously kissed the top of her hand. It was great to see her blush.

Finally, Ole broke the silence.

"Hello, my name is Ole; this is Nikki, Lena, and Sven. We are visitors here. We come from far away from a planet called Earth. We would like to be your friends."

Three more little people had gathered next to our host. All looked at each other and shrugged their shoulders. Finally the leader spoke.

"olleH sgniteerg. I ma royaM enitS, eseht era licnuoC srebmem taK, Leinad, solraC dna ecarG." oD uoy kaeps hislgnE?"

Oh dog, this wasn't looking good. I asked Dandi if he could translate. Nikki had pulled a small electronic language translator from her backpack and was busy entering in the words she'd just heard. Poor Nikki, her translator was coming up with zilch, nothing, nada. Of all the languages on Earth, none came close to this.

Thanks to Dandi I understood what was said and passed it on to Ole. "Hello, greetings, I am Mayor Stine; these are Council Members Kat, Daniel, Carlos and Grace. Do you speak English?" Lena figured out what was going on first and I told Ole. He was speaking English, but the words were spoken backwards. They also shake hands the opposite from us and the majority of them are left handed.

With the language barrier figured out, this should be a breeze. Except, have you ever seen humans try and talk backwards. Nikki and Ole did much better with a pad and pencil. Since they were in the minority, they felt it was their responsibility to speak the host's language.

Out hosts sensed we were tired; this extra gravity was draining our energy at an accelerated rate. We were offered accommodations at a local hotel, which Ole gladly accepted. When Ole offered an appropriate payment, the Mayor said we were guests, no payment was necessary and they would feel offended if it was offered. Everything being half scale was proving to be a drawback for Nikki and Ole. The lobby ceiling, at six feet, wasn't too bad; just high enough for Ole to clear without bumping his head. The rooms were a different matter; the ceilings were four feet high. They had three foot long beds, and four foot high showers. I was very amused at how Nikki and Ole were handling it. I must admit its fun to watch humans get around on all fours like we do. Humans, by the way, aren't very graceful on all fours. This was going to be an interesting experience.

CHAPTER 14

Nikki and Lena had moved to their own room so Ole and I had a room to ourselves. Ole pushed the two beds end to end making a six foot long bed for us to share. Although it was only the width of a twin bed, we were comfortable. The sun was filtering through the window and I gave Ole his morning doggie kisses and hugs.

Then things got interesting. Ole sat up in the bed and bumped his head on the ceiling; a nice start to the day. He then crawled into the bathroom and wedged himself into the four foot high and two by two foot wide shower. I could hear lots of bumps, bangs and words it would be best not to repeat in human or dog, or even tenalP htraE, language. Drying off with a hand towel sized bath towel was another lesson in new words from Ole. Ah, the best was about to come. Ole needed to make a people dump in the half size toilet. I laughed so hard I was afraid my wagging tail was going to start a windstorm. Ole gave a fantastic finishing performance to the morning activities as he did his best to get dressed while rolling, kneeling, and banging his head on the ceiling. As Ole crawled from our room to meet Nikki and Lena in the lobby, he was not in a very good mood.

Nikki's mood matched Ole's so I assumed that Lena had a good time watching our humans deal with a miniature world. The Mayor and town council were waiting in the dining room to welcome us to their city of Duolc.

Ole offered a great suggestion so now it's 'FOOTNOTE' time. Well, it's not really a footnote or else you'd have to look at the bottom of the page, and perhaps lose your place and have to re-read part of the page to find out where you left off. So here goes: 'Tenalp s'htraE noisrev fo hsilgnE ot ruo noisrev fo hsilgnE.' There are three ways you can read this sentence. First, read it in reverse using a mirror; second, turn the letters around back to front or; third, read my translation which is written in 'planet Earth's version of English.' From this point on, I will only use our version of English. Ok, everyone, three cheers for Sven; hip-hip-hurrah, hip-hip-hurrah, hip-hip-hurrah. Hey, I liked that.

Back to our breakfast meeting with the city leaders. The table was one and a half foot tall. Nikki and Ole sat on the floor; our hosts sat in chairs. Dandi had also been invited and sat by Lena and me. It seems that it's not unusual for people and animals to be treated the same on this planet.

Mayor Stine started the meal with a toast: "Distinguished guests, and members of the Town Council, let me welcome you one and all to this meeting of friendship and goodwill. May our two worlds benefit from this association. A prayer to the Lord is in order. (Our Lord who art in Heaven, may this gathering produce an understanding and cement a peaceful union of our souls. Thank you, Lord, for safely delivering to us these emissaries from another world. In addition, thank You for the gift of the peaceful loving world in which we live. Amen.)

If the Mayor was truthful and they lived in a peaceful loving world, well, maybe we should just stay here. I saw Ole glance over at me; I knew he was finding that statement a little hard to believe.

Breakfast was great; waffles, French toast, pancakes, biscuits, eggs, bacon, ham, sausage, milk orange juice, fruit and coffee. You name a breakfast food and it was probably there. I must say, everything I ate was prepared to perfection.

Kat, one of the council women, started talking.

"If you have any questions, please feel free to ask. We know something about your world. In fact, a major cinematic series on your world, its history and daily activities, is shown in our schools. All of our citizens are required to view the series and are then tested on it. There are some who think your world might be a myth or just a parable like those used in your Bible to teach right from wrong. Your Bible is the only book taught to our citizen that is required reading for all. Other than those two requirements, we have no rules. We live our lives in friendship, sharing, love and courtesy to all, every living thing here on Htrae lives by this code of conduct which the Lord gave us."

While this was being said, Lena and I were telepathically feeding questions to Ole; of course, he had many of his own.

"Thank you all for such a warm friendly welcome. My friends, including my daughter Nikki and my two canine children, Lena and Sven, are very happy to be here. Our questions would probably take a lifetime to answer. We have only seven days to be here, and the second day is already over. Since this is day three, I hope we can make the best use of our remaining time together. As we landed, we noticed that your planet is almost a mirror image, in half scale, to our Earth. Do you have countries, governments, different languages and ethnic races? If so, do you live in harmony with each other?"

Councilman Daniel answered. "This may be a shock to you and your group but it's the truth and not meant to offend you or your kind. Regarding the movie series and the Bible from your planet that we study; they were given to us by the Son of our Lord, Jesus Christ. He visits here often and is our teacher, our friend and a gift to us from his father, Jehovah."

"The movies and the Bible show that there are many greedy, domineering and murderous individuals living among you. From the days of your Adam and Eve until today, sin has been a major problem for your people. We understand what sin can lead to. Your planet would be like Hell for us. We do have different countries; our people have different looks and personalities just as yours does. However, we all speak the same language because on our planet there was never a need for a Tower of Babel to test Jehovah's strength; there was never a need to confuse our language. Simply put, we all live in harmony, humans and animals alike."

Daniel reached into his pocket and tossed a number of loose coins on the table. "These serve to remind us every day of our blessings." One side of each coin had a picture of an animal and a human with a paradise looking background. The other side of each coin had the following printed on it.

You shall have no gods before me.

You shall not make for yourself any carved images or bow down to them or serve them. (Daniel mentions that they shortened this to fit on the coin.)

You shall not take the name of the Lord in vain.

Remember the Sabbath and keep it holy. (Also shortened to fit on the coin.)

Honor your father and your mother. (Again, shortened.)

You shall not murder.

You shall not commit adultery.

You shall not steal.

You shall not bear false witness against your neighbor.

You shall not covet. (Once again, shortened.)

Well, this seemed self-explanatory. We were in a world that lived by the Ten Commandments. Extraordinary was the best word that Ole, Lena or I could come up with. Naturally, Nikki had more questions.

"Why the difference in sizes between our planet and yours? It seems that Htrae and everything on it, including you, are about half the size of Earth. Do you know why? Also, if you really live in harmony with all creatures, why were we served meat products for breakfast? Also, do you have sports or competitions?"

Councilman Carlos answered these questions. "Jehovah has many inhabited planets throughout the universes. We're not told much about them, but we know all are slightly different. Only He knows why he made Earth and its inhabitants so huge."

"I understand from our lessons that you actually murder animals and eat them. This is not only foreign to us, it is also, to say the least, barbaric and disgusting. And it's one issue that causes me a problem in fully accepting you and your friends. I'm doing my best to understand that it's your way. On your planet the Lord has allowed it. So, please forgive my bad thoughts."

"Now, back to meat. I know that even though the food you had for breakfast tasted like meat, no animals were harmed or killed to produce it. Jehovah has blessed this planet with an abundance of trees that grow all of our food. Yes, beef trees, pork trees, chicken trees, lamb trees, fish trees, as well as many others. We also have an abundance of fruits and vegetables. Just for your curiosity, whole animals don't grow on trees. The trees just grow cuts of meat. There are many varieties. Using beef as an example, the trees grow steaks, ribs, roasts, hamburger, you name it. We have a tree for almost any animal you use for food."

"Looking at you, Nikki, I assume you enjoy sports. While we have as many as you have on Earth, unnecessary roughness and injury never happen here. While you may not think this would be exciting, it's very competitive. As a people, we are all one and all a team, so the winners are praised and shown respect for their skill. However, we try to show the same respect to all so everyone is praised for their special skill. Athletes, bankers, bakers, shoe repairmen, authors and movie stars, are all appreciated for their gifts from the Lord."

Lena tossed in a few issues for Ole to address. "No one here seems to be old. Also, there seems to be few children or young people. We find this curious. Also, while on our way here, we noticed a pork chop tree; now that you've explained, it makes perfect sense. But, we also saw a herd of prehistoric looking animals known on Earth as Thomashuxleya. They've been extinct for a long time, but here they're living as if they've been here forever. What other types of animals live on your planet?"

Council woman Grace replied, "This information may come as somewhat of a shock. Think back to your Bible's description of a paradise Earth where everyone lived in peace and happiness forever. That's where you are now. We don't get sick, grow old or die. And, for those who want children, Jehovah provides them with one egg that can be successfully fertilized. This is true for both humans and animals and keeps the entire population in balance. If any species ever reaches their full capacity, they must stop having young. Couples, both human and animal, mate for life; marriage between humans is sacred. It works well for us. Parents with young have nothing to fear from either the human or animal world. Everyone is taken care of by everyone; we share and enjoy our young and, in a sense, everyone gets to be a parent. At our present rate of reproduction, it will take tens of thousands of years to reach a full population."

"Now, for one very important provision we enjoy here that may seem impossible to you. If we ever reach full capacity of life on our planet,

Jesus Christ has told us that any who still wish to procreate will be given the opportunity to start a new life on another planet identical to this one. To prevent any sadness if this happens, travel and communication between the planets involved would be allowed; just like I can go see my friends in Norway now."

"Now, regarding the animals on Htrae. Although many animals have been slaughtered to extinction on Earth, they still exist here. Jehovah created them first and, since we have a perfect world, they are still here living in harmony with us. The animals that were carnivores on Earth take their food from the trees just like we do. So the Tyrannosaurus from the Cretaceous Period, that was such a killing machine on Earth, gets its food from a meat tree; just another browsing feeder on our planet."

After all this conversation, the Mayor suggested that Kat and Daniel give us a tour of the town. Sounded like a good idea.

CHAPTER 15

The decision was made to start our tour at the local vehicle factory. This required a three mile car trip out of town. Daniel and Nikki filled out the front seat, and I rode on Nikki's lap. Kat was fine in the rear seat with Lena on her lap. Ole had a leg and an arm dangling out the back door. You could say he was doing as well as could be expected. Have you ever been to a circus and seen the tiny car full of great big clowns? Now picture Ole, sans the clown outfit.

The Solaronda Vehicle Factory manufactures solar powered automobiles, trucks, motorcycles, airplanes and train engines. Each continent on Htrae has one vehicle plant, all run by Solaronda. All plants are employee owned so no labor problems here.

The building has twenty foot ceilings, with conveyors and assembly lines attached to the ceiling. Finally, Nikki and Ole could stand up straight. Production is limited to only the orders received. All vehicles, no matter the type, had to be ordered two months in advance. The order was then scheduled and all the necessary parts manufactured. Environmental issues are a top priority. Cars are primarily ceramic, from extremely heated clay. This includes body panels, frames and engines. Clay is readily available from many of the wetland areas and is removed in thin layers, as needed. The springs are made from a special rubber plant that grows in a circular pattern and looks like a green version of Earth's manmade metal springs. It seems the rubber plants are cultivated to provide the different rigidities needed. Fabrics come from the bark of a birch tree that can be steam heated and stretched; it's then sealed with bees wax and dried. It wears like leather and is very soft and stain proof.

Of course, the glass comes from heated sand. The solar panels, covering the hood, roof, and trunk of the car, are built into the body panels. These panels are glass with actual silver embedded inside to absorb the heat. A unique storage cell stores the heat and uses it as fuel. The weather, controlled by Jehovah, is perfect; just the right amount of sun, rain and clouds to keep all living things happy and healthy. Since a solar vehicle is constantly recharging itself on sunny days, it is capable of unlimited distance. However, if it rains or is cloudy, the vehicle is limited to six hundred miles; more than enough for most people. The tires are also unique. Htrae has a type of rubber tree that grows to the exact diameters needed for the wheels and tires. It can be sliced to the thickness required; just like cutting a circle from a round tube. The wood is extremely hard and durable. The bark encasing the wood is actually rubber, about five inches thick, and provides readymade wheels. The average life for tires and wheels is approximately 100,000 miles. All this is done with no waste or pollution. Ah yes, and for the colors. They're created from the pigments of plants, flowers, and trees, and are mixed with the clay. Brilliant reds, yellows, greens, whites and blacks, or any mixture in between, is possible. Every type of vehicle is moved down the assembly line to its specifically ordered parts. Assembly is done by hand since there's is no need to rush; everyone lives forever. If this process were used on Earth, the repercussions to industry and employment would be catastrophic.

By the time we returned to our hotel it was getting late. We ate our supper outside; much more comfortable for Nikki and Ole. In the morning, Grace and Carlos would take us on a tour of the outlying areas. We were told to expect a special surprise.

CHAPTER 16

DAY FOUR

After a nice breakfast with Mayor Stine, Grace, and Carlos, we were ready for our day's adventure. The surprise came first. A long bed pickup truck was waiting for us outside the hotel. The five foot bed, as the long as any pickup bed gets in Htrae, was lined with soft blankets and pillows for backrests. Nikki and Ole appreciated this gesture more than they could say. Then, off to tour the countryside.

Our first stop was a large meat tree farm. There were few storage sheds. We were told that as soon as the meat is picked, it's transported to the local stores to be sold. Fresh every day, from tree to consumer in less than 24 hours. The tractors are solar powered units with the Solaronda name prominently displayed on their hoods.

We were offered the opportunity to try our hand at meat harvesting. It sounded like fun. We hopped into a wagon and headed to a meat tree orchid. Nikki and Ole, to the delight of the regular pickers, were perfect for harvesting. Since they were at least three feet taller than everyone else, they could easily pick the meat from the trees without using ladders; however, even Ole had to use a ladder on some trees that were nearly twenty feet tall. We were in the beef tree orchid at the time. Steaks, roasts and hamburger were easy pickings. However, sides of beef, even though they were half the size of those on Earth, were still heavy and cumbersome. Lunch was served in the orchid. Solar powered grills were set up and you just picked the kind of meat you wanted and cooked it yourself. Cheese, bread and wine complimented the meal. By the time eight hours had passed, we were back at the farm. Everyone was tired and happy and we'd made many new friends. The little people began to call Nikki and Ole their giant buddies. Lena and I were stuffed from picking up any meat that had dropped; it's hard for a dog to pass up the taste of a nice raw steak.

When we returned to the hotel, Ole said we didn't have to do anything else until tomorrow. We were all happy to hear that since we were all 'dog' tired.

DAY FIVE

Ole was a bit more graceful getting ready this morning. The mumbles, grunts and words coming from the shower had decreased by at least fifty percent from the previous days. I only heard him bump his head on the ceiling twice. However, what Ole was putting into the toilet and the words coming out of his mouth regarding the size of toilet, were about the same. Both were nasty.

Kat and Mayor Stine were our hosts for the day; a pickup truck was provided for our trip. It was certainly more comfortable in the open pickup bed for Nikki and Ole to ride. Today we'd be visiting the wild lands. It was a long, four hour drive. The Mayor had a cabin in the mountains where we'd spend the night. He graciously brought along a large tarp to drape over the truck and he provided bedding for Nikki and Ole. At least that way they'd have a five foot long pickup bed to sleep in. However, there was one problem; Lena and I were squashed between the two of them trying to keep warm.

The day was filled with hiking and sightseeing; very tiring for us giant gravity challenged Earthlings. However, the sights were worth it. Looking down into a valley, Mayor Stine pointed out an unusual animal near some trees. It was a Theriognathus, the body color and size were similar to a leopard, but the head was shaped like a snake. Lena told us this animal was from the early prehistoric Permain Period on Earth.

We were heading up the mountains. While they're not as high as on Earth, the air still thins out and the added gravity was taking its toll. Rest stops every twenty minutes were becoming necessary for us. Lena and I took little side trips while Ole and Nikki rested and visited with the very understanding Kat and Mayor. Animal life was abundant; deer, elk, beavers, moose, bears, wolverines, buffalo, plus assorted prehistoric creatures that I didn't recognize. I stopped saying "What are those?" When I was with Lena that question would lead to a recitation from Lena's Dictionary of Prehistoric Knowledge. By the time she was done, we'd have lost all our exploring time and have to head back to our humans. So, the less I said on our discovery trips the better.

Our journey was like being in wonderland. The trail snaked through rock formations that would only be seen in caves or deep excavations on Earth. Flowers and ferns, such as we had never seen, were everywhere. There was also an abundance of unusual berries and wild fruit, all provided by Jehovah to sustain the wide variety of creatures that inhabited this wonderful planet.

We entered a cave opening about eight feet high and six feet wide. The air felt warm and smelled of sulfur. Kat handed Nikki and Ole some wind up flashlights. Then, to prove we hadn't been forgotten, she wound up a flashlight for each of us and clipped it to our collars. I really liked that woman.

The Mayor led the way. "Excuse me. Watch out for our friends" the Mayor said as we passed by a Pontosaurus, which is a three foot long green lizard from the Cretaceous Period. Mr. Lizard was half dozing and ignored our little intrusion. Fissures and cracks along the cave walls often glowed red with lava from below; boiling and splattering; the volcanic cone was separated from our cave by only a few feet of rock. It was about a mile before we left the darkness of the cave and came out into warm sunshine and clear air.

Mayor Stine was now looking down from a rocky ledge and motioned us over. "Be very quiet," he said. "What you're about to see is a hatchling from a Tapejara." We all looked over the edge. As you know, Ole is not fond of heights, but this was too unusual for Ole to allow his fear to stop him from looking over the edge of the cliff.

The nest was at least ten feet in diameter. The hatchling was the size of a large turkey. Remember, on Htrae the Lord only allows one offspring per couple, so this was truly an amazing thing to see. The Tapejara was a large bird, with skin instead of feathers. Its most distinctive feature was a large wind sail like crest on the top of its head. The head and crest were yellow with red highlights, and the body was light grey. Again, another species extinct on Earth since the Cretaceous Period. Then here came mom or dad bird. My dog, you should have seen this. Its wingspan was about twelve feet and measured at least ten feet from the tip of the beak to end of its legs. It seemed to glide forever, flapping its wings once or twice to soar an additional two to three hundred feet. It saw us but didn't seem to be concerned. All life here really does live without fear; what a wonderful thing. When the hatchling saw its parent, it made a tremendous screeching sound. The humans covered their ears while Lena and I lay on our tummies and covered our ears with our paws. The parent made a soft gentle landing, for a bird of such size, right on the edge of the nest. The parent then reached its head down so the hatchling could have a large green bush full of some type of berries. It was a beautiful, heartwarming thing to see.

The day was passing quickly as we headed back to the Mayor's cabin. That evening we sat around a red hot solar panel that served as our campfire. Nikki and Kat had found the ingredients for smores in the cabin. Kat and Mayor Stine had never heard of smores. Therefore, with marshmallows, graham crackers and chocolate in hand, we Earthlings brought a new culinary delight to the Htrae. Since he'd heard it was bad for dogs, Ole nixed any chocolate for Lena and me. At least we were allowed the graham crackers and melted marshmallows. Whenever I got some I always made sure to give Ole a big, melted marshmallow, whisker filled doggie kiss. Ole hates being sticky. However, after all these years together, it's like a tradition. Then it was off to our crowded pickup bed. Ole snored, Nikki complained, Lena hogged the covers, and I tried to get some sleep.

We saw so much during our time here. It was a great way to gain knowledge; working the fields, touring the factories, hiking the wilderness; no government, no leaders, no crime. Everyone had jobs that they chose and enjoyed. Because they lived forever, they could change their job whenever they wanted; they had the time to learn and perfect whatever they wanted to do. Their work week was Monday through Friday, 8 hours maximum, with thirty day vacations every year, and all jobs paid the same. There was no need for doctors, lawyers, or politicians, the bane of Earth. Police officers, fireman and soldiers were also unnecessary. Just think, a person who wanted to be a plumber for ten years could then change his profession and be a landscape painter, a baker, or a jeweler; anything he wanted to try he had time to perfect. By the way, the Mayor and the City Council were not considered politicians although they were elected; the only elected jobs in the Htrae. It's just a job for them. They arrange city activities, sporting events, special occasions, and host special visitors, as in our case.

DAY SIX

Heading back to town Nikki rode up front with Kat and Lena. Mayor Stine, Ole, and I rode in the back. The Mayor and Ole talked about other towns and countries. It would have been nice to see the different cities throughout this world. Overall, it sounded like they all led similarly peaceful, idyllic lives. So maybe Jehovah put us in this nice mid-sized city for a purpose; it was a perfect example of this perfect world.

For our evening's activities the Mayor promised to give us the most unbelievable experience we'd ever have, either here or on Earth. That was all the Mayor would say, nothing else, he just left us wondering.

It was a long ride back to town and Kat suggested we rest before the evening's festivities. There was to be a large picnic at the railway station and the whole town would be there. A special guest was arriving by train about six p.m. and we were told not to miss it. It would be the highlight of our entire visit.

CHAPTER 17

It's still day six, late in the afternoon. This day will be unlike any in the lives of Ole, Nikki, Lena and me.

To say we were stunned when we arrived at the picnic would be an understatement. There were people as far as the eye could see. Tables, blankets, and all the trappings for a picnic had been set up. Camaraderie seemed to be the theme of the evening. Food vendors, rides for kids and adults; it was like a carnival, except this carnival was an honest, family oriented affair.

The Mayor and council members were waiting for us. They had their families, kids, and more grand, grand, grand, well, more grand's before the word kid then I can remember. I guess when you live to be hundreds or thousands of years old, you have many family members.

Everyone seemed to be positioned so they could see the train when it arrived. The depot's train tracks were the only empty space.

Ole asked the Mayor what the occasion was. "Mr. Mayor, this is fantastic, so many people. It all seems so well organized with such a friendly, upbeat attitude. Just what's the occasion?"

"Yes, about the occasion; it's the surprise. We all believe that the four of you will remember this day for the rest of your lives. As for all these people and all this activity, now you know why the town needs a Mayor and Town Council; it's our job to arrange this. Normally we get a day or two notice for this special event. Word is spread as quickly as possible, and, as you can see, everyone cooperates to make it pleasant, fun and exciting. Here comes the train now; keep your eyes on the platform of the last car."

As the train approached, Ole was getting excited; he loves trains, especially steam engines. This particular engine was almost a duplicate of the 4-4-2 Atlantic type steam engines that used to be used on Earth. The major difference was that the engine's tender was made with solar panels on the top, sides and rear. The steam engine, which on Earth would have used coal, wood, or oil, was pollution free. The heat from the solar units boiled the water that created the steam pressure, which, in turn, drove the wheels. The only things emitted from the smoke stack were beads of excess steam. The whole engine, boilers, cab, wheels and running gear, were made from super heated ceramic. Image, ceramic as hard as steel. The engine's boiler was a beautiful shade of olive green, the roof of the cab was a deep red; gold pin stripping accented the whole unit. In bold, gold letters, the engine's tender was lettered with 'HTRAE SYAWLIAR.' There were three cars behind the tender; a combination baggage/mail car, a sleeper coach and an observation car. All the cars were painted dark green and had gold pinstripes to match the engine. The passenger cars were named after dinosaurs classified as Dipolocids; these were very large and very old. The cars, in order, were named Apatosaurus, Brachytrachelopan and Eobrontosaurus. The Mayor saw Ole's interest in the train and told him, "The railroad cars were given those names because they're so huge and the builders hope they'll last as long as the animals they're named for. Plus, it's a way for us to show respect for some of the Lord's earliest creations. By the way, if you noticed the front of the train's engine, it was made right here in town by Soloronda."

The train had now completely stopped. The crowd went silent; every activity stopped. Even the birds in the trees were quiet. An eerie hush caused a shiver down my spine; I could see goose bumps on the arms of Nikki and Ole. It was as if something in the air was telling us that the greatest thing we could ever image was about to happen.

CHAPTER 18

The door of the observation car slowly opened. It felt like a cool, calming breeze spread from the open door throughout the crowd. A man stepped through the door. He was about the same height as most people from Htrae. His hair was dark brown, a little long on the top and short on the sides; a small wisp of hair hung loosely over his forehead. His buttoned-down style white dress shirt had the top button undone. His slacks were white and white shoes completed his outfit. He was perfectly proportioned. His face, well, if the angels that you see pictured on Earth are any example, he had the face of an angel. Beautiful, handsome, glowing; I really don't know any words to adequately describe him.

Nothing anywhere around us made a noise. In this stillness, he raised his arms into the air. Finally he spoke, "Halleluiah, my brothers and sisters. Thank you for coming to greet me. For those who may be seeing me for the first time, my name is Jesus. My father is the Lord Jehovah. I am here not for me, but for you; you who have kept all my Father's commandments. All of you have proven that there can be life in a perfect paradise. My Father gave you the tools to do good and you used them to accomplish good."

"I noticed we have four visitors from another planet; my Father allowed them to come here. They are good individuals and try to follow my Father's commandments. However, they come from a world that failed my Father's test; therefore, they come in sin. Their actions and behavior, both here and on their planet, have given us all hope that Earth's population may someday be redeemed. Be kind, follow the Ten Commandments, and you will always find that life is a blessing."

"Now, a prayer to my Father and then I shall join you in your festivities. "Our Father who art in heaven, hallowed be thy Name, thy kingdom come, thy will be done on Earth as it is in Heaven, give us this day our daily bread and forgive us our trespasses as we forgive those who trespass against us, in Jehovah's name, Amen. Let us all rejoice and celebrate life on this paradise Htrae."

Although Jesus had no sound system, and seemed to speak in a regular tone of voice, everyone heard him as if they were standing right beside him.

Now Jesus was making his way toward us. As he approached, he stopped at every group of people, talked a bit, and then moved on. Wherever he went, he left happiness and love. He walked up to our picnic table and Nikki and Ole were trying to get up; remember, these tables were only 2 feet off the ground. However, Jesus stopped them.

"Please remain seated. I'm not one for whom you should rise, that is reserved for my Father." He shook Nikki and Ole's hands and introduced himself, as if we didn't know who he was. His soft, gentle hands scooped Lena and me up to his chest. He was so warm and comfortable. He gave us each a kiss on the forehead; we returned doggie licks on his nose. Then he sat down, still holding us. We just relaxed, laid our heads on his shoulders and experienced the most pleasant feelings we'd ever had. Only Ole came close to showing us that kind of love.

He now spoke directly to Nikki and Ole. "It's nice to be able to show you that the promises in the Bible can come true. This is an example of a paradise planet. No one else from Earth will be allowed to come here. What you've seen and learned here will stay with you. And, although you'll always remember me, this experience will become like a pleasant dream. Ole, the Lord granted you the ability to communicate with Lena and Sven for he knew you had prayed for a companion. Your compassion towards your two dog children has touched our hearts. Human companions were brought up barring the sins of Adam, so often it's hard to understand some of the things the Lord allows to happen. But, know this, your prayers are always heard. By channeling them through me we will always be here to watch over you. Have a safe journey home. God bless you all."

Wow, none of us said a word; what could we say? Nikki broke the silence. "We really must get some sleep. Tomorrow we have to return to our spaceship and leave for Earth."

The Mayor broke in on the conversation, "Tomorrow is Sunday, the Sabbath. We cannot allow you to leave on the Sabbath. No work is done on that day. It's a rule we strictly observe on Htrae. You will need to stay here until Monday."

Ole could see this was going to result in an impasse, so he did the only thing he could. "Nikki, the Mayor is right, the Sabbath must be observed. I'm exhausted, so if the Mayor and council members don't mind, we should now take our leave. Thank you all for showing us such courtesy and consideration. Tomorrow will be a new day. Goodnight."

Nikki got on Ole's case immediately. "We have to leave tomorrow or we'll miss the shuttle back to Earth." Lena added that we wouldn't have enough fuel for our return trip if we didn't catch the Moon's orbit to assist us. Sunday was departure day, or we could wind up stranded in space, or, at best living, on a space station until we could be picked up.

Ole told Lena and me to race to our hotel, grab our backpacks and leave everything else. Then join them on the road out of town. We were leaving, but we were leaving today.

Nikki suggested we borrow a car but Ole didn't feel that would be right. The Ten Commandants were already working on him. Do not get me wrong, that was a good thing; that's why he is who he is. We figured that 'Einer' was four hours away; we had six hours to get there. Since Nikki was in the best shape of the group and Lena was young and full of energy, they were sent ahead to make the best time they could. Ole's bum leg and cane didn't make for fast travel, but we'd do the best we could. If we didn't make it, Nikki and Lena were to leave for Earth. I for one was staying with Ole, no matter what.

We were definitely losing time. This planet's extra pull of gravity, and the long days and restless nights we'd spent here, had all taken their toll. A car was coming up behind us. My first hope was that they wouldn't notice anything unusual about us. Then again, when you were walking next to a 'giant' someone was bound to notice. The car pulled up and stopped. If we were caught now, they'd never believe we could leave

Htrae before the Sabbath. Ole whispered, "Sven, this may be our new home."

Our friend Kat stepped out of the car. "I figured you'd be leaving tonight. If I drive you to your spacecraft are you positive you can take off before the Sabbath? Where are Nikki and Lena? Ole was quick to answer, "Nikki and Lena went ahead, they should be at the craft and have all systems on go. If you'd drive us, I'm sure we could be off the ground and on our way without breaking the Sabbath on Htrae."

Off we went. As usual, Ole was hanging half out of the tiny car door. Time was passing much too fast. Then the Einer was in sight, with seven minutes to spare. Kat's car screeched to a stop. We jumped out and Ole grabbed Kat and gave her a big hug as he swung her around in a circle and gently deposited her back on the ground. Nikki was screaming for us to hurry. We'd hit Einer's tongue ramp when Ole fell. The ramp was already rising as we rolled up Einer's tongue and into the mouth of our spacecraft. Kat was racing away as Lena hit the four dog feet boosters to lift us off the ground. Ole and I were barely strapped into our seats when Lena pushed the poop hole thruster to maximum. We felt a slight shudder, like Einer was shaking the water off his coat. When we cleared Htrae's outer atmosphere, it was exactly eleven-fifty-nine and thirty-two seconds; Htrae's Sabbath had been kept. Thank the Lord. I'm sure he helped on this one.

Ole took over the controls and edged us into the Moon's orbit so we could coast with the Moon's natural rotation. Then we all took a well deserved rest. Ole edged Einer a little out of the main rotation so that we slowed to about half the speed we'd used on our trip to Htrae. This had to be done since we were now fourteen hours ahead of our scheduled arrival time. Everything was going to be alright. Soon we'd be back in contact with Discovery, our ride home.

CHAPTER 19

It was a leisurely trip around the Moon while we waited to rendezvous with Discovery. Nikki pulled a Star Trek travel monopoly game from her backpack and we whiled away the time with the game. I had to wonder if there was anything Nikki didn't have in her backpack. She was still amazed that Lena and I could do so many things; I think she was a little upset that she was losing the game to two dogs.

A buzzer announced that we were near our rendezvous point. Everyone took his or her position in the control room. Lena pinpointed the location on our homing system. Discovery was now in sight. What a beautiful sight to see; Discovery's clean white lines. The large USA letters and American flag made us feel like we were sort of home already. Ole switched our controls to manual and slowed our approach as Discovery's large cargo doors opened.

Once the doors were open and locked into position, Nikki did a voice confirmation to line us up for retrieval. Ole maneuvered Einer into place as Nikki talked him into the correct position. Einer's thrusters were all on minimum power to hold us still. As the large cargo arm reached for us, the clamp at the end of the arm slowly enclosed Einar like a big dog collar. The cargo arm, which was now like our dog leash, slowly walked us into Discovery's cargo bay. Gently, Einier settled on all fours and we were safe and settled. Once the cargo bay doors closed, we would meet with Captain Nick for debriefing.

We were all separated in the debriefing room, each having to take his turn; must be NASA rules. However, this didn't work out as Captain Nick had anticipated. Debriefing Lena and me was impossible since he didn't talk or understand the canine language. This meant that Ole had to sit in and translate for us. It only took Captain Nick a few moments to see this was going to be an exercise in futility. Our answers were the same he'd gotten from Nikki and Ole. Of course, he wasn't positive that Ole really could translate our thoughts. I thought it was funny in an interesting way.

Discovery's crew was polite, but, per their orders, never asked about our mission. Not having any jobs assigned to us, we were left to our own devices. We explored Discovery, checked over Einer, played cribbage, Monopoly, and watched all six of the 'Rocky' movies before we returned to Earth.

Captain Nick called us in for a special meeting after he'd gone over some of the data Einer had stored. He wasn't too happy that Einer's video cameras only showed an open field with the four of us packing for our trip. It seems nothing else crossed the path of the cameras after that point. Since we'd taken no pictures or movies, we were left in rather poor standing. I think we were all too busy with our individual tasks to think about a photographic record. Of all of us, I'd have thought Ole would have had this covered. Even he had to admit he messed up.

Soon we learned that NASA had sewn small recorders and microphones into all our clothing without our knowledge. Thus, they had a complete audio transcript of our entire trip; sneaky little buggars. Although it really didn't make any difference; we'd gone on this expedition for knowledge, and this additional record would be great for our friend George Bush to review. Poor Captain Nick spent the rest of the voyage locked in his cabin listening to our tapes. Only the Captain and the President knew of our mission. Captain Nick was going to have the tapes condensed and ready for the President. It was a good thing we'd stayed in a group most of the time; otherwise he would have had six days of recordings from four different individuals to decipher. We all felt a sorry for him; what a boring job.

It was time for Discovery to enter Earth's outer atmosphere. Everyone was in their orange launch suits and strapped into place for re-entry. I must say Discovery vibrated and shook much more than our Einer. No need to tell NASA, they wouldn't listen to us anyway.

Touchdown at Kennedy Space Center was a rather jolting affair. We could hear the tires screaming as they tried to spin as fast as we were traveling. The parachutes popped open to slow us down and we finally we came to a stop. Einar's dog feet thruster system was much more efficient.

Then, off to an isolation center. Captain Nick told his fellow NASA workers that since we'd not had NASA's regular physical training for space, we should be watched for a few days. Of course, this was a ruse so the doctors could again poke, prod and stick us with needles. However, since we'd been on another planet it was a necessary precaution. For four days we were kept in isolation. Thankfully we were allowed to watch all the newly released movies we desired. They also had lots of games, even a pool table and Ping-pong table. But four days of fun and games finally gets on your nerves.

Once released from isolation, we were hurried aboard the airplane we'd come to think of as a hotel in the air. Captain Nick had already left the area and was briefing the President about our trip. He'd told us we'd be heading to a secret location for our debriefing. It took eight hours to get there. We disembarked after landing on an airfield that just barley accommodated our plane. Nobody would tell us where we were; all they'd say was, "sorry, classified area."

We all found a shady spot on the edge of the tarmac to sit and wait. There were a few fifty gallon gas barrels and some old wooden pallets that we used for chairs. Ole pointed to the end of the runaway and said, "Hey, look over there, that's one of Honda's new four wheel drive Big Reds." Nikki chimed in, "I thought Big Reds were three wheelers?" Ole quickly explained, "Not anymore. They're now four wheelers and called MUV's for Multi Utility Vehicles. The 2009 models come with a dump box on the back and are automatics, no shifting, really cool. This must be government stuff, because Big Red's are really scarce; each dealer only gets a few."

A Big Red pulled up next to us. The driver looked like Ken Berry from the old Mayberry RFD TV show. He was dressed in a park ranger's uniform, complete with sidearm. We then noticed the vehicle had been converted from two seats to four; the dump box had been removed and two seats installed facing the rear. Ole was so busy checking the Red over that he didn't hear the ranger tell us to hop in. Upon seeing his interest, the ranger asked him if he'd like to drive. That was like asking a dog if he wanted T-bone. Ole and Nikki rode up front, the ranger, Lena and I rode in the back. The ranger pointed to a narrow trail heading up into the mountains. From the look of the land, trees and vegetation, I'd bet we were in Washington State or Oregon.

For some strange reason a warning popped into my head; probably from watching too many suspense movies. I stood with my paws on the back of my seat and said to Ole, "Do suppose they're taking us someplace to eliminate us? Maybe they don't want anyone to know where we've been or what we might know." My head was close to Ole's so he could whisper back, "That thought never crossed my mind; you might have a point. Why else all this secrecy and a trip to nowhere? See what you can do about getting the ranger's gun."

I told Lena what we thought might happen and we concocted a great plan. She jumped on the ranger's lap and started playing with his hands and face, jumping at him and hand wrestling on his lap. I jumped in to join the fun. While Lena kept the ranger distracted and laughing at our antics, I pulled the gun from his holster with my teeth. Lena then jumped up by the ranger's face and I darted under her. Then I stuck my head between the two front seats and deposited the gun in Ole's lap. Nikki gave Ole a surprised look and he put his finger to his lips, and went "shhh."

Hugh redwood trees dwarfed our Big Red; even more reason to believe they'd hauled us to some northwestern wilderness to eliminate us. Coming into a large clearing, we came upon the biggest, most opulent log cabin we'd ever seen. Three stories tall, leaded glass windows, multiple chimneys, which of course meant multiple fireplaces. Animal antlers of all sorts decorated the front of the cabin. An old man, who was a dead ringer for Gabby Hayes, was sitting on the porch. He had his chair tilted back against the wall with his well-worn cowboy boots propped up on the porch railing. His dress was typical old West cowboy, complete with six-gun and holster. A Winchester rifle was leaning on the wall next to him. His old leathery hands were busy carving on a small piece of wood.

The ranger pointed to the cabin and said, "They're expecting you, go right in." Ole had tucked the range's revolver into the back of his pants, under his shirt, just in case. As we reached the top steps of the porch, the old man glanced up and said, "Howdy." Then he went back to his whittling.

We entered through double oak doors with ornate leaded glass windows. We then found ourselves in a large circular lobby. This was really more of a fancy hotel than a log cabin. The lobby was open all the way up to the third floor. There was a walkway around the entire area and arranged so that the rooms on the upper floors could look directly down into the lobby. The furnishings were made from local hardwoods and leather. A large dining table sat off to one side; it had room for at least twenty diners. A glance at the side cupboards showed that all the china bore a picture of Teddy Roosevelt in the center.

George Bush came over, shook Nikki and Ole's hands, and invited them to sit down. George sat down on a large leather couch across from them and called Lena and me over. We jumped up and gave him some doggie kisses. He then pulled beef jerky from his denim shirt pocket and gave it to us. We received lots of petting and ear scratching from the President. Across from us sat Captain Spud Nick. Nikki and Ole were on a couch, kitty corner from us, by a fireplace. The fireplace was large enough to hold at least half a dozen six-foot logs at one time. It was burning low now, still very warm and glowing, flames flickering into the air. The logs had broken apart and it was like four mini fireplaces providing warmth. Above the fireplace, on a large section of the stone chimney, was a painting of Teddy Roosevelt. The rest of the room was adorned with mounted animal heads.

Captain Nick offered drinks to everyone. It seemed funny at the time; we all decided to try a locally brewed root beer. Lena and I even had our own little Teddy Roosevelt bowls to drink from. This was a first for us; drinking root beer I mean. I liked it but it sure can tickle a dog's nose; made me sneeze.

After some small talk, George took over the conversation, "I can't tell you what a pleasure it is to have all of you back on Earth, safe and sound. Captain Nick and I have listened to all the tapes from your journey. Why we didn't think to give you video cameras was a grave oversight on our part. However, what's done is done."

"The tapes were very impressive. They pretty much prove that God exists and that a perfect world is within the reach of humankind. Our world? Maybe we've gone too far to redeem ourselves. Then again, the Lord is forgiving. As a world leader, and having to make decisions accordingly, I'm not sure how Jehovah or Jesus will judge me. An extreme amount of forgiveness will certainly be required."

"We found one puzzling thing about the tapes. There's a long gap that starts when someone gets off a train and picks up again when you tell your hosts that you're leaving. It's kind of like the tape from the old Nixon Watergate scandal. We know it was impossible for you to tamper with the hidden microphones, so do you have any explanation for the gap? Also, who was on the train that everyone was waiting for?"

Oh, dog. How was Ole going to handle this one? Ole has a strict rule: always tell the truth and you won't have to remember what you said. Can he just tell them we met Jesus? Should he tell them? The blank spot on the tape must mean that Jesus can't or didn't want to be recorded. That would be reasonable. I'd shudder to think how imperfect humans would use such a recording. Every greedy entrepreneur would want it for financial gain. The churches would be in an uproar fighting to see which church should have it. Non-Christians would tear it apart trying to prove it was a fraud. Christians would hail it as a new beginning; maybe even use it as a reason to persecute non-believers. Ole, walk softly on this one.

Ole sat quietly for many minutes. No one said a word. Finally, he started talking, "Mr. President, Captain Nick, before I speak, I'd like an honest answer from each of you. Are either of you recording our conversation?"

The President looked more serious then I'd ever seen him look on TV. Then he answered, "If you haven't noticed, there's no one here but the individuals in this room and one old time secret service agent on the porch. This building was built for President Roosevelt. It's the only Presidential retreat that no one knows about. Teddy Roosevelt wanted a place that was completely free of any Government oversight. You have my word, not only as President but also as a Christian, nothing we say will leave this room or be made public in any way. That includes your voyage to Planet Htrae. The audio tapes from your trip are on that table in the cloth bag. Those are the originals; there are no copies. They are here as a measure of good faith between us all."

Ole then asked, "One more question. Are the four of us going to be allowed to leave here alive and go back to our normal lives after this meeting?"

George looked at Ole and a smile spread across his face. "Ole, Nikki, Lena and Sven. Of course, in my position, this issue had come up. What a terrible thing to have to admit. This world, its governments and people, are all sinners. But, you bring me information that is world shattering; proof of God. I can't imagine doing anything other than embrace you as my friends and let you leave here in peace. Keeping our secret will be much harder than death."

Ole walked over to Captain Nick. He reached behind his back and pulled out the ranger's gun. Then Ole spoke, "I must apologize; we borrowed this from the ranger that brought us here. By the way, he didn't know it. Please don't punish him for being slack. Would you please make sure this weapon is returned to the ranger?"

"Now, regarding the missing section of audio tape. I can only hope Jehovah is with me as I try to explain. The missing voice was that of Jesus Christ. He was the one that got off the train. It really doesn't seem so strange that his voice wasn't recorded because there were no sound systems used; yet thousands of people heard him as if he was talking directly to them. I'm sure He knew we were "bugged' even though we didn't. I'm also sure we'll never know what caused the tape to go blank. However, in my head, I will hear his voice until the day I die."

"Now, as for what happened. He praised his Father and then praised the people of Htrae for living a righteous life, just as he hoped it would have been on Earth. He offered a prayer to his Father and then stopped for a brief visit with each of us and blessed our return home. He then melted into the crowd and visited as if he were an ordinary person. There was an invisible force that seemed to be with him. I can only say that being near him made a person feel calm, happy, content, forgiving, and filled with love. I can't adequately describe the feeling. In fact, I don't think it can be put into words."

George stood up walked to the table that held the audio tapes. He picked them up and handed them to Ole. "These belong to you and your group. Once again, these are the originals; there are no copies, duplicates, or records of them anywhere. I place them in your keeping. As far as the Captain and I are concerned, we have no knowledge of where you've been or what you've been doing. Of course Captain Nick will get a reprimand from NASA for taking a bunch of civilians on a joy ride into space. As fate would have it, I still have my job for a few more days so I can make sure the Captain's reprimand will include a promotion."

Ole took the bag with its Presidential Top Secret seal and called me over. "Sven, we've been together for a long time, what do you think we should do with this bag?"

I didn't say a word. I picked up the bag in my teeth, walked to the fireplace, and dropped it into the flames. Then I went and sat next to Ole and we all watched it burn until nothing was left.

THE END

BEERZEL & SVENBREW

A SVEN & LENA ADVENTURE

PUPPYLUDE

Hello, my name is Sven. I have a story to tell you.

First off, I am a full bred black and white utterly handsome Shih-Tzu dog. Just some of my more unusual attributes are that I can communicate with my human 'Ole'; I read, write and operate a computer.

This bit of information I am about to relate to you is called a 'puppylude.' Of course, that is the beginning of any dog's life, puppy hood, what a great time I had. For you humans that are reading this you may wish to refer to this part as a prelude.

The main characters in the story are my human 'Ole', my adopted Shih-Tzu sister Lena and of course me. There will be more dogs and people involved and I will get to them in the story.

As a warning, the first part of the story has lots of sadness and pain, so if that bothers you skip chapter one and two and just start reading on chapter three.

Now for the basis of this story. If you have a dog, human, or other living organism that you really love this story is for you. We all have somebody that it is almost impossible to buy a gift for or to do something nice for. You know those individuals, they have everything they need or want and nothing seems to surprise them. Well, Lena and I have that problem with Ole. This is how we solved our dilemma.

CHAPTER 1

The three of us live on our own little estate. We call it River's Edge, an acre of land boarding the mighty Mississippi River. Besides the main house, we have a boathouse, barn, and workshop. Ole, my human does his best to keep everything in tiptop shape. His one problem is too many hobbies. He loves motorcycles, old coin operated machines, model trains, selling on eBay, reading books, watching movies and tending his raspberries. His most important hobby is Lena and I, we are his kids, and we always come first.

We share almost all of life's adventures together. Lena is our historian and resident scientific expert. She is only in her teenage years but she is a genius. Since she is so young, her mind seems to have no limits. If it catches her interest, she will study it the fullest degree. So far, she has led us to adventures from Dinosaurs to underground worlds and beyond the moon. For a girl, even I have to admit I am really impressed by her knowledge.

As for me, I keep the ball rolling around the place. My job is to keep Ole occupied beyond all the hobbies he already has. Swimming in the river, boat rides, motorcycle trips in the sidecar, making sure we all have food, that includes humans as well as dogs, and all the miscellaneous everyday errands we need to do. With Ole, this can be a chore, the last year of his life has been, well should we say a major elephant size pile of doggie doo.

Now for anyone who thinks they have had a bad year try this one on for size. From January to May, things were going great. Ole was in love with a beautiful lady who worked strange hours. Because of this, we took care of her dog for five days a week, twenty-four hours a day. In fact, this dog was here when I came to live with Ole, I was only ten weeks old. So for me this mutt was my big brother, and Ole and I both loved him like family.

April came along and Ole was about to pop the big question. After four years of walking carefully and not be too pushy in the relationship he was totally in love. She, well she kept telling Ole let's be best friends. You know the old I'm not ready for a serious relationship speech. Although every night they spent at least an hour on the telephone. That hour on the telephone was the happiest Ole would be all day. In fact, he was floating on the clouds. Now anytime you start floating on the clouds you should expect a thunderstorm. Storm was a mild word for what happened. Lightning, full-blown hurricane, tornado, volcanic eruption all wrapped up into one neat package. That's what was to happen to my poor Ole. Of course I also not only got the 'tail' end of the storm, I had to do my best to clean up the after storms devastation. Human emotional hurt is a whole lot harder to clean up then any physical damage. Now for you guys that are reading this you know what I mean. No one can tell a guy that he cannot hurt worse than a woman can when it comes to getting dumped. They can't tell guys that, because we know it. Next to death and taxes, it is the worst thing that can happen. In fact forgot about taxes, it is even worse than death, death would be a blessing in most cases.

Now for the start of the downhill slide. Two weeks before and I am at the lady in question's house. Her dog, my best friend, and I are having a great time. Ole stops over to pick me up for the night, which is when the roof caves in. She tells him she loves him like a brother and would do anything for him. "Ouch." Then of course, he gets the speech of how she found someone she likes better and is even considering marrying him. "Double ouch." Ole's weak defense is when he asks her if she means the 'do anything part' of her comment. If so she should forgot about this other guy and stay with Ole. He even tells he would like to ask her to marry him. All of this of course comes to no avail.

As all you guys know, when a girl drops you for someone else you have three choices to make. Crying your eyes and tearing your heart out usually comes first. Then a few telephone calls and maybe even a letter to your lost love, that never seems to work. Getting stupid drunk, that does not help either, although at the time it seems like a good idea, until the next morning, day, or week depending on how drunk you are. Immediately find a new woman, much easier said than done, you know none of them will ever be equal to the one you lost. Spend the next few weeks, months, years in self-pity, hard to avoid at least some measure of this. Kill yourself and see if she cared enough to attend your funeral, seldom does this help in the long run. After all your dead, even if she did care it does you no good. The last step in the healing process is to swear off women for the rest of your life. That is what my Ole is doing, at least for the last year, who knows about the future. If I was a fortuneteller instead of a dog, maybe I could help him out. By the way we never did try the fortune-telling route, might get the wrong answer. Oh yeah, he tried lots of prayers, best we not discuss how that turned out. I guess God had it in for Ole, as the rest of the year will attest to.

Now I know that human heartbreak is much worse then human physical pain. Ole is just dumb enough to stay in love with just a spider thin thread of hope in his mind. It's my job to keep him sane. Not an easy task to carry on. Although I do my best. First, I had to get him out of bed and cleaned up. Darn humans with broken hearts don't want to talk to anyone, they refuse to bathe, shave, or brush their teeth. The only thing that saves them all this embarrassment is having a job. I hauled Ole out of Bed, made him get cleaned up, and sent him off to work, broken heart and all. After all, we had to have money to live on. He was darn lucky to have a son like me. I often had to remind him that I was hurting to; after all, when she dumped him, she kept my very best friend in the whole world with her. I still have nightmares seeing my best friend walking towards his house, tears in his eyes, wishing he could stay with Ole and me. Talk about heartbreak, us dogs feel the pain too. I was lucky to have Ole to look after so it kept my mind busy and I didn't end up an emotional wreck like my Ole.

All contact was over with the love of Ole's life. Three month's had now passed. Ole was still in a zombie like state. It was a good thing I knew enough about zombies that I could keep control of Ole. Sure, he lost twenty-four pounds, but that was a good thing. I kept him fed enough to keep up his strength and go to work. It was his staying in bed twelve hours a day that was hard to control. He seldom slept, his tears had dried up by now, but he was majorly depressed. All the things he enjoyed stopped. No more movie time for the three of us. No time in his shop, very little play time for him and me. His huge train layout suffered the most; he had too many buildings that he had named after his old flame and my best friend. Therefore, the railroad sat abandoned and the rails rusted as the train engines sat idle. Even his raspberries were left on the vine to rot. I did cuddle with him and forced him to hold me. It seemed to be some comfort that he knew I still loved him with all my heart.

CHAPTER 2

In month number three of the bad year a ray of sunshine sort of peeked into our lives. One of Ole's daughters had a friend who needed a temporary home for her little girl Shih-Tzu. We called her Lena, she was eleven months old and full of life. Ole and I were forced to give her lots of attention. Not so much because we wanted too, but like all kids and puppy's she demanded it. Ole at least had some of his sadness diverted away to loving our new little member of the family. I being alpha dog had to teach her a few lessons, and yes, I admit I was a little jealous sharing my Ole with a strange newcomer to the family. We did not want to get too attached to her for she could be returning to her original owner at a moment's notice.

Then came the next major blow to Ole's life. Lost girlfriend, lost dog friend and then this has to happen to poor Ole. It was a beautiful summer day, warm and sunny. Ole was still having trouble getting motivated. He had once mentioned to his daughter that he wanted to put an old steam radiator in his garden and plant grape vines so that they could fasten themselves around it. Just in case you are not familiar with a steam radiator. They used them in buildings for heat. They are cast iron and this particular one weighed about three hundred pounds.

Ole's daughter sent the radiator over to Ole's with her friend. Ole still in an un-motivated state was in bed, not sleeping just trying to forget his hurts as usual. Dressed in a ragged t-shirt, sweatpants, and corduroy bedroom slippers he went outside to help un-load the radiator. As they were sliding this three hundred pound monstrosity from the bed of a three-quarter ton pick-up, it slipped. The thud of the radiator hitting the cement was somewhat dulled by the fact that Ole's right foot cushioned its fall. Now Ole had broken his leg in ten places and crushed his ankle over the last few years, so his pain level was rather weak in that leg and foot. As his friend looked down, he said. "Ole that radiator on your foot, doesn't it hurt?" Ole looked at the radiator sitting nicely on top of his bedroom slipper and said. "No it doesn't seem to hurt, let's pick this thing up and move it." Which of course they did. Ole's friend then mentioned that there was blood gushing out of Ole's slipper. So Ole took off his slipper and sock. Yes sir, smashed his foot wide open. As Ole sat on the ground his friend went to get ice bags, Lena lied on his leg as a living tourniquet, I brought him rags from his motorcycle saddlebag to wrap around his foot. Then off to the emergency room.

Diagnosis, two major bones broken, tendon to the second toe severed off, all other bones were shattered with small fissures. They would operate two days later. When Ole came home it was strict bed rest, we built Ole a nest in his bed with three pillows to rest his foot on, and another nest was made in the big leather recliner in the theater room. For the next month those were the only two places that Ole was allowed to relax. Of course he did have bathroom privileges.

All this was going on while Ole was supposed to be caretaker for his eighty-six year old father. We were lucky that Ole's daughter Val came to help with groceries and emergency things. Now it only tends to get worse from this point on.

Fast-forward three weeks. Ole has been bedridden and extremely depressed. Grandpa is making sure that Lena and I are let outside and fed at regular intervals. The downside to this was that with Ole not cooking and watching after grandpa he started to deteriorate. Ole had the foresight some time ago to install a lifeline system for grandpa. Then one day while Ole was in bed the lifeline alarm went off. Ole grabbed his crutches and hobbled as fast as he could to find grandpa. He located him in the bathroom; he had fallen and could not get up. Ole tossed his crutches to the side and said heck with the pain in his foot. He half carried, half-dragged grandpa to the truck in the garage. Then he hobbled back in got his crutches and rushed grandpa to the emergency room at the hospital. Grandpa had pneumonia. Ole of course blamed himself for this. If he was not laid up and had been doing his job of taking care of grandpa, he was sure this would not have happened.

Ole's visits to the doctor every two days only produced more bad news. The toe was not healing. The next step was to start wound treatment at the hospital every other day. One good thing that came from this was that Ole was now allowed to use a cane and could drive short distances. At least he would not have to depend on finding himself a chauffeur every time he left the house.

Ole hired the neighbor girl to help around the house and yard, something he really could not afford at the time. The medical bills were piling up; a $2500.00 deductible on his insurance was hard to come up with while he was out of work. Although to Ole's credit, he had taken out a special disability insurance a few years ago after he was in a motorcycle accident. Of course as with any insurance, it was a fight and took a long time to collect the first payment of one month off, one thousand dollars. The money went fast to pay medical bills and living costs.

Every other day, Lena and I rode with Ole to the hospital for his wound treatment. Then we were all allowed to go and visit grandpa. At least the hospital was very understanding that dogs needed to visit the ones they loved just as much as humans did. For three weeks grandpa hardly ever woke up. Things were looking very bad.

Wound treatment for Ole was holding its own. Still we could see the bone, tendon, and joint showing through the open wound when Ole changed bandages. It is a good thing dogs have strong stomachs.

Grandpa finally started to improve. Although his mind and strength were not very good. I think humans might call it dementia. Ole, Lena, and I were not in a present position to care for grandpa so the decision was made to place him in a nursing home. This proved to be a very a heartbreaking thing for Ole to do. That was all I needed was for one more big emotional strain for my Ole.

The nursing home was not much better for grandpa; he still slept almost all of the time. Lena and I took turns going to see him every other day. Ole, he went every day rain or shine. Money was tight so Ole convinced his doctor to let him return part time to work, four hours per day. Ole's mornings were spent at wound treatment in the hospital and then off to the nursing home to see grandpa. Seeing Lena and I went with everyday Ole had to return us home and then head to work. I could tell he was wearing out fast.

Grandpa had been in the nursing home about two and half months when Ole got more bad news. The first doctor he had suggested amputating Ole's big toe. The wound treatment people suggested another doctor for Ole to see. Ole not only saw another doctor he went to three other doctors to get opinions. The diagnosis was the same. Amputate Ole's big toe. It was two days before Halloween. Ole of course figured Halloween would be an ideal time to have his toe removed, what the heck if you had lose a body part what better day could you pick. Unfortunately, it did not work into the doctor's schedule. Ole had to wait until four days after Halloween. It was in and out surgery, home the same day. Back on bed rest for two weeks. Ole's brother and daughter took over the daily grandpa visits and Ole got his reports over the telephone.

Ole had become nine toed for only eight days when the nursing home called. Grandpa had made a miraculous recovery and it was time for him to come home. Not only was it time, but also if he did not come home in the next two days his insurance would stop paying the nursing home. At eight thousand dollars a month for the nursing home Ole had to figure out how to care for grandpa on his own. Another stipulation to getting grandpa home was that someone would have to be with him twenty-four hours a day. Ole would still be off work for two more weeks, but then what. To hire an outside caretaker was going to cost about three to four thousand a month. It also meant finding someone on such short notice to take the job. This was all I need, stress my poor Ole out some more; he was not even healed up from surgery yet. Lena and I spent all our time trying to comfort Ole and keep him going.

Normally you would have to think that things for Ole could not get worse then they have been. Guess again. Ole gets a telephone call from where he works; they have sold out the business to new owners. Within a few days Ole hears from some of the employees that the new owners have said if Ole is not back to work by the time they take over he will be replaced. An emergency visit with Ole's doctor upped his Prozac dosage, he needed it. If Ole was a dog, I think he might have run out in front of a car just to end all his problems. Lena and I were his saving grace, he knew he could not leave us to face a life with anyone else. At least Ole's love for Lena and I was strong and enduring through all that was happening. I have to believe it was the only thing that kept him going.

We got grandpa home, he was supposed to get exercise and lots of walking. Ole was supposed to stay inactive and no walking. What a combination. Now a few things started to fall into place that were helpful. Ole's daughter wanted to switch jobs. She was very interested in the grandpa caretaker position. She and Ole struck a deal, one problem solved. Now if only Ole could keep his job.

The insurance company that handled Ole's disability kept coming up with reasons not to pay. As with most reasons from insurance companies, they were fabricated out of thin air. One was we cannot pay because you did not tell us what fell on your foot. Then it was we need the exact dates and hours and specific times that you worked before we can pay you. The best was that they only accepted faxed information, guess what when you are homebound and you do not own a fax machine this is really a hard thing to do. Ole would have to call one of his kids to come get the paperwork and fax it. Needless to say, we were not in a very good financial position.

The economy in the United States was falling to an all time low. Companies were lying off employees or closing their doors. The big three automakers wanted a government bailout along with large credit unions and banks. Of course, the government stepped in to help the big boys, supposedly less suffering then for the common man. Nobody of course cared what happens to all the little business that cannot survive. The holidays were here and it would be a very sparse holiday at the Ole household.

A few rays of sunshine came peeking through all the gray clouds. The place Ole worked was saved at the last minute; the deal to sell fell through. Ole's boss was a great guy and Ole kept his job. Ole's missing toe wound was healing well and Ole was able to return to work part time. Business was slow but at least we would have a paycheck again. Winter hit Minnesota with a fury, lots of cold, and snow plowing was needed. Ole found that a wound shoe on your foot is not very protective while plowing out mounds of snow from the quarter mile driveway, but he got by.

Bad luck was still Ole's best friend. His first week at work and his vehicle develops major throttle problems. A thousand dollars worth of problems. Boy we needed that like a piece of poop stuck to a dogs butt hairs.

The doctors had Ole go in to be fitted for an orthopedic insert in his shoe. If this worked out all right Ole could maybe stop using a cane. When Ole got home from having a cast made of his foot, he got a nice little letter from the county we lived in. Jury duty time. In four days, this year would be officially over. We all hoped that maybe God had done all he wanted on testing Ole for a while. Maybe it was time to lock Satan up for a few years and let Ole be. Even Job in the bible got a reprieve in the end. I sure hope God listens to dog prayers, because Lena and I were giving it our all.

CHAPTER 3

Now for the happy part of our story. Lena and I waited until January first to start our project. We called it our 'Ole secret.' We discussed all the things about Ole that we could think of. Seeing we traveled almost everywhere with him we know his little quirks and idiosyncrasies. We even have our own dog service coats to allow us in to restaurants and other places that would not normally allow dogs. We usually do not get to sit at the restaurant tables, but sometimes they are really kind and serve us on the table with Ole. Now this is when we noticed some of Ole's more unusual behaviors when it came to food and drink. Ole has a light beer when he goes to a restaurant to eat, not anything unusual about that you say. Ah yes, but his beer must have a minimum of three green olives in it. He calls it a submarine beer, the olives sink to the bottom, and then they fill up with beer bubbles and float to the top of the glass. Once the olive reaches the surface of the beer it turns and discharges its air bubbles and sinks back to the bottom. Thus, you have submarine beer olives.

Being somewhat of a gentleman and doing his best to follow eating out etiquette he saves this next weird behavior for at home. In fact, he only does it in the theater room when Lena and I are present. Were close family so I guess Ole feels it is all right to do this in front of us. Plus he does share his pretzels with us when he does this. Ole pours himself a big glass of the nights selected beverage. He uses his old Trader & Trapper beer mug for this. Then he gathers up a nice bowl full of huge Bavarian cross style hard pretzels. He breaks off a piece for Lena and I then he dunks the rest in his beverage. The beverage will vary as to his particular mood that night. It could be beer, Mountain Dew, Diet Pepsi, Cherry Coke, or any number of exotic soda flavors he brings home.

To start out a new year for Ole, Lena and I decided to take the old family spirit of innovation and apply it to a special treat for Ole. Our first project was to make a liquid filled pretzel. In fact, beer filled would be our first experiment. Of course, the big question is how do we go about doing this?

After a thorough investigation of the options, we figured out a possible solution. Grandpa has to take four pills every morning. One of these pills is encased in a soft pliable plastic looking shell. The shell is tuff enough to take some abuse, but it melts quickly at the warmth of a human, or for that matter a dog's mouth. What we needed was a source for this material in longer lengths, which we could cut to fit our pretzels. On to goggle we go. Lena does all the keyboard work, she has smaller paws then I do and it is easier for her to type. I hate to admit that she is younger and grew up with computers and she is much more adept at their use then I am.

It did not actually take us long to find a source for clear starch and sugar coatings that seemed to meet our needs. Therefore, we ordered enough to start our experiments. We were able to order a tube to the size we needed in four-foot lengths. Then we could cut them to the length we needed. We decided on a 5/8 inch opening. Google also had more than enough pretzel recipes for us to work with, but then I remembered that Ole's daughter Nikki used to work as a master pretzel maker. From the past, she was aware that Ole and I communicate so she was not surprised to get my email. Nikki had also just adopted a black and white Shih-Tzu named Stella; it would be nice to spend some time with the both of them. Nikki and Stella were to come to our house on the next weekend. Valerie, Ole's other daughter was given the job to keep Ole occupied while we worked on our pretzel surprise.

Nikki and Stella arrived as planned. Stella is only about six dog years old and has a lot of puppy in her. She just did not have the patience to help with our project so Lena volunteered to keep Stella occupied. Valerie took Ole out to eat, then a movie, then shopping. Knowing Ole's penchant for shopping it was going to be a tough job for Valerie to keep him away to long.

Nikki made the pretzel dough and had it rolled out flat. I cut the tubing, filled it with beer, and pinched the ends closed. Nikki used the old monk style of design, called a child's crossed arms in prayer as our sample pretzel. She inserted the tube in the dough, rolled it, and crossed it over in one fluid motion. Nothing like watching a master pretzel maker at their trade. Then a combination of olive oil and butter as a glazing. A sprinkle of coarse salt and into the oven to bake.

Major disaster. The heat of the oven melted our tubes of beer. We had some really nice beer soaked soggy inedible pretzels when we finished the first batch. My puppy mind went into full gear to come up with a solution. I filled more tubes with beer and cut them to length. Once I had the ends of the tubes sealed, I put them in the freezer. Living in Minnesota and it being January I also took a few outside and put them in the snow. It just so happened to be thirty-two degrees below zero outside. Of course, that batch froze very quickly. Nikki then micro waved a raw pretzel just enough to make sure the inside was cooked. It was a good thing we shaped our tubes of beer before freezing them, as they were now hard as a rock. Nikki inserted the tubes of beer into the half-done pretzels and then we upped the oven temperature for a fast outside baking. With the center of the pretzel pre-cooked and the frozen beer tube in place, we crossed our fingers and hoped for the best. The high oven temperature did a quick backing of the outside of the pretzel shell. As soon as the pretzels attained a rich golden brown, we removed them from the oven. We put two samples in the refrigerator, two samples in the freezer, two samples outside in the extreme cold and left two out to cool at room temperature. So far so good. None of the pretzels was wet and soggy so the tubes must not have melted or leaked.

It was of course to tempting to wait and see how it all turned out. Therefore, we took a sharp serrated knife and cut open a hot sample pretzel. The tube was intact and the beer flowed. The pretzel was still hot enough that as we cut it the tube end resealed and held in the existing beer. Now tell me if that was not the neatest thing that could have happened.

It was now time to wait for Valerie and Ole to come home. The four of us decided to watch a movie in the theater room while we waited. Kiss Me Goodbye was our choice of a movie. I was glad Ole was not here for this one. I think love stories make him depressed at this time in his life. The movie was sort of a comedy ghost story, Sally Fields is always a good actress, and James Caan and Jeff Bridges are pretty good actors. It was during the movie that Lena sprang a surprise on all of us.

CHAPTER 4

While I had been concentrating on the pretzel with a beer in it problem Lena had taken on another project on her own. She knew Ole had a taste for raspberries, so she combined some of Ole's stock of frozen raspberries to his stock of Miller Lite beer. Once she had the mixture of raspberries to beer right, she then went on to her next step. By the way, I often wondered why she slept so well some nights. Now that I think about it, there was rather a raspberry beer smell to her breath. Guess she had to keep sampling the product to get it just right. She is only a teenager you know, when this is done I had better have a talk to her about the evils of drinking, after all I am the big brother.

Anyway, back to her next little project. She located some old beer bottles on eBay. These bottles are clear glass and in the shape of a beer barrel. They also have a very wide opening on the top to drink out of. This was just what Lena needed to fulfill her little side project for Ole. She filled the bottles with her mixture of raspberries and Miller Lite beer. Then she added three large green Olives to each bottle before sealing it. Now her olives were not just your ordinary every day olives. Sure, they were the large size and yes, they were green. What made them out of the ordinary was a little orange periscope stuck into each olive. Lena used her little paws to cut up the best crunchy carrots she could find. She cut out tiny little periscope shapes with a pointed end to stick into the olive. The carrot not only showed up well with its bright orange color, but it also held its shape in the beer. Lena showed us all one of her new beers. The clear glass bottle actually magnified the size of the green olive with its orange periscope. We were fascinated to watch the submarine olives, as they lay dormant on the bottom of the beer bottle. Then when the top of the bottle was removed, the beer started to bubble. The olive submarines filled with beer bubbles and rose to the top of the bottle, once the submarines reached the top they would slowly turn and discharge the bubbles and sink back to the bottom of the bottle. Sober or drunk it was an amazing thing to watch.

The best part of Lena's new product was its name. She named it after her big brother It was called 'SvenBrew Submarine Beer.' I can tell you right know, I was proud of my little sister.

Valerie gave us the signal by calling on her cell phone with their arrival time. We set up a nice display in the theater room for them. Beer filled pretzels, which we named 'Beerzel's, plus ice cold barrel shaped bottles of 'SvenBrew.' I picked out a movie for the night, one with lots of comedy and a very light love story. It had to be something Ole would enjoy and yet not make him sad for lost loves. The movie I choose was 'Evil Roy Slade' with John Astin, by far one of the best no brain western comedies ever made.

Val and Ole arrived home, as for our prearranged plan Valerie told Ole, she wanted to watch a movie. They came downstairs to the darkened theater room. Ole flicked on the light switch and was greeted by a loud shout of "surprise" from Valerie and Nikki. Us dogs joined in with lots of braking and tail wagging. We sat Ole down like a king on a throne in his theater chair. Nikki served him a plate with two large Beerzel's and a bottle of SvenBrew. Ole noticed our label we had made for the beer, and was like a little kid the way he stared at the moving submarine olives. Then he took a sip and it was like he was in ecstasy, he loved the beer. Now for the Beerzels.

We all held our breath as Ole took the first bite of his Beerzel. Not knowing what to expect he had a rather surprised look on his face. He held the bite of Beerzel in his mouth for a few moments. You could almost hear the gears in his head turning as he tried to figure out the taste. It was lucky that his first bite was a large one. By biting off a full section, the pressure of his teeth had sealed the beer tube on both sides, thus no mess. Ole was very impressed, even more so when he found out it was a special gift thought up by Lena and I. It was our way of starting out a new year on the right foot for Ole. He liked that idea a lot.

We spent most of the night sampling and testing our two new products. The Beerzels were our biggest challenge. If you bit them wrong and leave an opening in the tube of course the beer runs out. Or you can take a Beerzel that has a bite out of it; gently squeeze the reminder of the Beerzel with your teeth until the tube opens. Now you can drink the rest of the beer out of the Beerzel. By bedtime we all reeked of pretzels and beer. Oh yes, and we even had olive breath as we ate the olives last for our desert.

Everyone slept very well that night, probably because we had too much beer to drink. I know Ole was not too happy that he had to get out of bed twice during the night so Lena and I could go outside and relieve ourselves. Then again, Ole relived himself at the same time so he most likely had to get up anyway. Nikki and Stella had to leave for their home in the morning. Lots of farewells and see you soon human stuff went on. Lena and I gave our new cousin Stella a nice tail-wagging goodbye.

Ole really appreciated what we had done for him. We told him it was our way of entering the New Year on a positive note. Then we discussed the options of our new products. Lena and I of course hoped to get Ole interested in the marketing possibilities. If he were kept busy, he would not have any time to be sad. Alas, things for our new invention did not look so rosy as we thoroughly discussed them.

First off we took on the Beerzels. If we produced them it would be very costly to set up machines and equipment. Our current economy was in rather dire straits and not conducive to us investing in an unknown product. Then the legal aspects reared their ugly head. For instance would school kids sneak beer filled Beerzels into their lunch boxes. For that matter would anyone in any bushiness be snacking on Beerzels at their jobs or even driving their car. This would bring a completely new meaning to the open container law. I suppose they would have to pass an open Beerzel law. Then where could they be sold, liquor stores and bars of course. Grocery stores or convenience stores, probably not.

SvenBrew was a completely new scenario. Liquor stores and bars would be the only outlets. That was a good thing. Then again, cost of setting up our own brewery and bottling operation, not to mention a supply of green olives and extra crispy carrots. Imagine what a machine would cost just to cut the carrots into little periscopes, and then another machine to insert them into the olives. Sounds like this would be best to keep as a home brewed family project. Make it our new year's tradition. SvenBrew, Beerzels, family, and friends that would be nice.

CHAPTER 5

We did have a lot of fun dreaming and speculating about our new products. Think of all the possibility in the pretzel idea alone. Beerzels would be just a start. Why any drink you could think of was an option. Mountain Dewzels, Cokezels, Pepsizels just to name a few. Then we had other options to explore, Milkzels for a great after school snack. Seeing that pretzels in themselves are actually a somewhat healthy food we could even offer Yourgutrzels for the food conscious people. Of course Ole also figured fruit filled would be nice too, especially a Raspberryzel. By now we had idealized ourselves out and gave up on the pretzel discussion.

On to bigger and better ideas. SvenBrew. Raspberry beer with submarine olives. This was not only a fantastic idea, it tasted great. Why every restaurant, bar and liquor store in the world would want the most novel item to hit the alcohol trade since prohibition found bootleg liquor. We had a captive audience in the name alone, 'Sven' would give us the Scandinavian customers. Olives lined us up with the Spanish and Greek heritage. The 'submarine' novelty would guarantee sales to all the Navy personnel around the world. Then the ingredients, grains, hops, raspberries, olives and carrots. A vegetarians' ultimate energy drink.

Lena added in one last product to the mix. She wanted to market Submarine Olives separately in their own container. The container would be a clear plastic shaped miniature submarine, the conning town would serve as the bottle cap with a twist off feature. Now anyone could purchase Submarine Olives with carrot periscopes for themselves. Once again the uses were endless. Add them to beer, martinis, soda, mixed drinks, basically any carbonated drink should work. Sorry kids, that leaves out fruit drinks and milk. Although Lena did keep the kids in mind, remember she is only a teenager. The plastic submarine container could be used as a bath toy for the kids when it was empty. This time she decided to name it after our loving dad, it would be called "Ole & Lena's Submarine Olives." Available at all fine stores everywhere. Sorry, that last sentence was just wishful thinking.

Best I get back to Ole now. So here it is a new year. Ole was in a good mood, SvenBrew and Beerzels will do that for a human, in fact they can make a dog pretty happy too. Lena, Ole, and I toasted to good health, and a good year for us all. Another toast to the health of our family and friends. The last toast to lost friends, and a lost love. Then for us all I made a speech.

"To Ole my human and best friend. I raise my paw in a toast. May it be a new year of blessing for us all. Ole, you have my permission to leave a spot in your heart open to a lost love. I will do the same for my lost friend. Old loves can remain, we will never extinguish their flame. Let them know in their dreams that our love will always remain." Last but not least we welcome Lena to her fist new year with us, may we all spend many more together. So be it."

Looks like things might be ok for our new year. I would hate to think Ole could ever have a worse year then the last one. He has started singing again, I just wish he would find a different song. He seems to be stuck on "Sundown" by Lee Hazelwood and Nancy Sinatra. Now if you have never heard this song the first verses go like this:

"There's no one in this world for me, there's never gonna be, there's no one in this world needs me, there's never gonna be, but sometimes in my dreams I hear…"

THE END

EYEFORANEYE U.S.A.
OR
COMMON-CENTS

A SAGA BY SVEN

"Thus you shall not show pity: life for life, eye for eye, tooth for tooth, hand for hand, foot for foot. 'Deuteronomy 19:21'

PUPPYLUDE

Hello. My name is Sven and I have a story to tell you.

The beginning is called a puppylude. This is because I am a dog. Full bred handsome black and white Shih-Tzu with amazing talents. Actually all dogs have these talents to some extent. Like humans, some dogs are smarter and better at certain things than others are. My best talents are that I can speak with my human. I also read, write, and operate a computer. Of course, I also tell stories.

Now for you humans that are about to read this you may want to call it a prelude. That is fine, call it whatever you like. This is just a short section to acquaint you with what this saga is all about. It is not something everyone will like or enjoy. Some may even make comments like. "It shoulda been, coulda been, oughta been."

I live in America, I love it here and would not trade it for anything else. Although it does have some faults. Tell me anywhere in the world that does not have faults. What worries me as a loyal dog citizen its where is America going?

I like the constitution of the United States. I am just afraid of instead of following our Forefather's ideas the country seems to be following our Foreign Fathers ideas. The last Presidential election certainly added color to our history. The new election that takes place in this saga will be even more colorful. Americans be prepared. The time has come.

CHAPTER 1

The eleventh century. The explorers were the Vikings. Stout individuals emanating from Norway, Denmark, and Sweden. Master ship builders and navigators. Respected and feared by those who knew them. Their life was hard and their laws were strict.

Lawgivers were appointed to decide the compensation or penalty for crimes. The lawgivers were not always available and so the law was often decided on the spot by those involved. A life for a life. Injuries were often consummated by money, land, or goods. Although the taking of a life could escalate into a family feud that could go on for years, each life being dependent on the taking of an enemies life. If the lawgiver saw fit, the person taking a life could be banished from the country. This exile could be for a certain number of years or for life. The laws were harsh but fair to all involved. The lawgiver's word was final. The lawgiver was judge and jury.

Rune the Dog was a Norwegian condemned by the law of exile. His neighbor Peder the Poor came onto Runes land and stole one of Rune's dogs. Rune tracked the thief to his home and found him eating his dog. The anger that arose in Rune could not be contained. His dogs were not only his helpers, but also his pets and his friends.

Rune drew his sword, which he had named Fang and beheaded Peder before he could taste the first bite of Rune's dog. Rune gathered up what remained of his dog and took it home for a fiery Viking burial. He left Peder where he lay. Beheaded and bleeding puddles onto the dirt floor of his home.

Rune knew he must leave the country. Peder's relatives would soon discover the body and be on Rune's trail. Therefore, Rune bid his family farewell. He boarded a Viking Long boat as part of the crew. The ship than set off for a new settlement in Iceland.

Rune soon found life in Iceland was not much better than being on the run in Norway. Only now, he was running to stay warm. The Icelandic weather is not something to brag about, unless you like the cold and the wind. People friendly was not something that would be listed in a travel brochure for Iceland.

When Rune heard of an expedition, leaving to discover new sources of wood for ships and possible settlement areas he was more than happy to volunteer his services as an experienced seaman.

Four ships set out to explore new regions. Day and night, they braved the ever-changing weather. The seas provided them with fresh fish. They had brought sheep and chickens to raise in a new home, or to eat if need be. Rune even had his favorite dog 'Tor' with him. The crew was tough and well seasoned in their travels. Soren the ship's captain was stern and fair; he kept the men in line. For four days, they sailed. Then land was sited. They stayed along the coast until they found an inlet that could accommodate their ships. With the low draft of a longboat, they were able to anchor about twenty yards from shore. The men were amazed at how lush and green the area was. Trees covered the landscape as far as the eye could see.

Six men including Rune and his dog Tor volunteered to go ashore and explore the area. The water was cold and clear as they made their way through the waist deep water to the shore. The area was covered in rocks and the walking was rough. Tor shook the water from his coat and stood with his nose to the wind checking for signs of life. The other three boats sent exploring parties to shore also. They all agreed to set off in different directions and meet back by the boats at nightfall of the next day.

Per, Olan, Rune, and Tor headed on an animal path leading into the forest. Game was plentiful, rabbits, squirrels, deer and many types of birds were sighted in the first few hours. Wild berries seemed to be readily available along the trials edge. The men were satisfied with what they were finding. Making camp for the night alerted them to other animals within the area. The hoot of an owl, the growl of a cougar, the rumbling of a bear, and even the raccoons who came near the camp scavenging for food that the men had cooked over their fire. So far, this seemed like Valhalla to the men.

Returning to the ships the men gathered for a meeting. The lumber alone was worth the trip. The decision to start cutting timber and loading the ships was made. This would be a very profitable journey indeed. Oak lumber would be worth its weight in gold back in Iceland. For the next month, the men cut trees and loaded their longboats with the precious cargo of wood.

During the evenings, they a had large feast of fresh cooked game. Venison, wild turkeys, fish from the sea. Life was good. The men were busy working, the food was great, and the profits they would split when they sold their cargo would make them all wealthy.

After a month had passed, the ships were loaded and the voyage back to Iceland was planned. It was decided that a small settlement should remain until the ships return in the spring. This group could build lodging and start cutting timber for the next voyage. Three men from each ship volunteered to stay. Their share of the profits would be given to their families or held until they returned. For their sacrifice of staying behind they would each receive a triple share of the profits.

The ships sailed off into the distance. The twelve men watched as the link to their homes and families disappeared from sight. They then made their way inland about two miles until they came to an open meadow. The meadow with flowing long grass went on for many miles, a large lake at its center. This would be the place to build a home and out buildings for the animals that they had brought with them from Iceland. Goats for milk, sheep for wool, chickens for eggs. Meat was plentiful all around them and all the men were good hunters. The work on the building proceeded quickly for the chill in the air was a warning of winter soon to arrive.

Once winter arrived, it came with a fury. Often the men had to tunnel through the snow just to leave their lodge. The livestock was running out of food, what food they had stored was being used up. The depth of the snow and the bitter cold kept them from traveling very far to hunt game.

Even then, the animals of the wild had taken shelter and were nowhere to be found. Trips to the lake for fresh water took all the strength the men could muster. Every day they had to chop a new hole in the ice for water, it was not unusual for the ice to freeze a foot in thickness in just twenty-four hours.

One of the men promised to find fresh game for the group. He left early in the morning. They had fashioned him snow skis and snowshoes for his journey. After two days, they knew he would not be returning. As the winter progressed, they were forced to eat the sheep. They kept the goats for milk and cheese; the cold had stopped most the chickens from producing eggs, so the next meals would be hot chicken over the indoor fire. Nothing was wasted, bones and fat were used for soup. If the weather did not break soon it could mean death to them all.

Food was becoming a major problem. The men had built a wooden locker just outside the front door of their lodge. It still contained a small amount of frozen meat, maybe enough for a few days. They had placed a large stone on top of the locker to keep any marauding animals from getting at their meager supply of food. The goats were still supplying small amounts of milk, but without more feed, even they would soon dry up. The last of the chickens had long since stopped laying eggs. They were now becoming meals, a few chickens amongst eleven hunger men did not last very long.

Despite the weather, the men decided they must organize hunting parties and find food. For safety, each hunting party would contain four men. The next morning they sent out two groups of hunters. Of the three remaining men, two of them decided to go to the lake for more water. Adrian the weakest member of the party stayed behind to tend the life giving fire inside the lodge.

Adrian sat near the fire letting the warmth soak into his body, his hollow eyes and gaunt cheeks cast the shadows of death across his face. He heard a commotion outside and went to investigate. A grizzly bear had knocked the stone from the cover of the meat locker and was about to devour their precious food supply. Adrian grabbed an ax from the wall and ran to drive off the huge bear. The grizzly stood up on his hind legs, he was twice the height of Adrian. Before Adrian had a chance to swing his ax the Grizzly with one quick swipe of his paw had dispatched Adrian to Valhalla. The bear lumbered over to Adrian's bloody broken body and sniffed it. The big grizzly then clamped its jaws around Adrian's thigh and carried his lifeless corpse off into the forest. For the grizzly, hunting had been good that day.

Rune and Benjamin returned from the lake with fresh water. The bloody snow and the bear tracks told the story of what had happened. The group was now down to ten men left. Christian and Adrian had both lost their lives trying to save the others. It was a harsh life, but to the Vikings this was an excepted part of their world.

The hunting parties returned by nightfall. One deer and a few rabbits between them. It was a good feast for that night. The little grog that was left in their supplies was used to toast and honor their fallen comrades.

The weather finally started to change. The days grew warmer and the snow began to melt. They pulled thatch from the roof of the lodge to feed the goats what they could. As the next few weeks went by spring came quickly. The snow disappeared and game was once again plentiful. The men started cutting and stacking timber by the ocean for the ships that should soon be returning for them and their precious cargo of lumber. Three months went by, no sign of the ships. The men were not about to spend another winter where they were. A vote was taken and the decision to head southwest was made. They would move away from the ocean and head inland. They decided to wait for one more week for the ships. In addition, at the end of another week, the fresh grog would be ready to drink and they could carry a supply with them on their journey.

The week ended with no ships in sight, and a fresh batch of grog ready to drink. The men sharpened and packed their weapons, packed what food and supplies they could carry and headed into unknown frontiers. For many days, they made their way through the thick forest and the open meadows. Often they had to skirt the edges of large lakes. The animals seemed to be more abundant than ever. Besides deer, they started seeing elk, bears, fox, raccoons, beavers, and even a large shaggy beast with humped shoulders. They made a decision to take down one of the shaggy beasts to check it out as a source of meat, plus what a hide that animal had for making clothing or blankets.

The herd of these large beasts must have contained well over two hundred animals. The men were able to walk right in amongst the herd. The animals did not seem to have any fear of humans. They bellowed, grunted, and kept eating the grass as the men passed by them. Some of the beasts were butting heads and chasing each other in mock battles. Others were rolling in the dust to ward off insects or remove their loose fur. Finally, the men picked out a lone cow on the edge of the herd and brought it down with a volley of arrows. The other animals did not even seem to notice. The men cut up their prize, rolled up the meat in the animals hide and continued on their way. The feast that night proved to the men that the shaggy beast was also a delicious meal. Sometime later the men would learn that they had their first encounter with a herd of buffalo.

One day the Vikings found footprints in the forest; it looked to be two individuals wearing soft leather soled shoes or boots. They decided to follow the trail and see where it might lead. From behind an outcropping of rocks, the Vikings observed a village in the valley below them. Some of the buildings were made of the bark of trees while other dwellings seemed to be conical in shape and made of animal hides. The people and their tools looked to be rather primitive. No iron or metal items were visible, in fact even furniture was absent from the scene. The inhabitants seemed to prefer sitting on animal hides that were on the ground. One of the Vikings alerted the others to movement heading toward the village from the east. From their vantage point, the Vikings could make out a group of men sneaking up quietly on the village.

The Vikings watched as the peaceful village turned into a blood bath. The strangers from the woods used crude clubs, and stone tipped axes and arrows to dispatch their victims. They spared the lives of the youngsters and women. When it was over, they carried off their victims to become their prisoners for whatever purpose they had in mind. The Vikings were not shocked; all of them had been on raids of villages and small towns in the past. They now knew that this land was not much different then their own. Violence was an everyday part of the lives of this new world that they were in. They hurriedly packed up their goods and headed back on their intended course towards the southwest. They could see no need to involve themselves in other people's battles at this time.

Each evening the Vikings set up camp and took turns keeping watch for the night. Rune had been keeping track of the new moons and it was confirmed by him that they had been traveling for almost 40 days. The weather was getting cooler, the days were shorter, and the leaves had started to color the trees in multi-colored hues. A decision to set up winter quarters would have to be made soon. They could only hope they had gone far enough south to locate themselves in a more favorable climate.

The area they were now in was covered with beautiful forests, rolling hills and wide open meadows. Wild game was abundant and the area seemed to possess a large number of lakes, streams, and rivers. They would make camp for a few days and scout the area for any other humans. If everything looked good, they would make this their winter home.

The Vikings split into groups of two and went out to reconnoiter the area and possibly bring home some fresh meat. Bjorn, Rune, and his dog Tor made up one of the parties. They headed south along a small stream. The marshes in the area held beaver, muskrats, and blue heron birds. Once again, deer were plentiful. Even a large moose was seen in the shallow of the marsh, his antlers reaching four feet across, he only looked at the men and their dog as they passed by. Human contact with the animals must have been minimal as very few of the beasts showed any fear towards our intrepid explorers. They were entering a section of woods when they spied a large buck standing in the shadows. Bjorn raised his bow and took a shot. The arrow went off at a slight angle and caught the buck in the rear hindquarter. The buck bolted into the woods and out of sight. Tor gave chase as the men followed. Tor had the buck corned near a small cliff of granite. This time both men pulled back the strings of their bows and let the arrows fly. The buck went down with two arrows near the heart. They field dressed the animal and decided to split up on the return journey. Each man would take a swing out along the perimeter of the area of the forest to make sure there were no tracks of humans in the area. This way they could cover twice the distance in one sweep. They would meet back at the camp around nightfall. Rune and

Tor loaded up their share of the kill and said goodbye to Bjorn. It would only be a few hours before they would be back together.

Walking along the edge of the tree line Rune and Thor heard a commotion from inside the forest. At first it was as if someone or something was running, the braking of small branches and brush crackled through the air. Then the sound was mixed with a woman's scream and the sound of snarls and growls. Rune ordered Tor to check it out. He followed Tor into the forest. By the time Rune arrived on the scene Tor had two wolves standing at bay. Tor's haunches were up, his teeth barred and a constant growl emitting from his throat. Four other wolves were clawing and jumping at the bottom of a large tree. Just out of the wolves reach was a women balancing precariously on a branch, her arms wrapped around the tree trunk with all of her strength. Rune drew his sword from its scabbard and charged into the snarling pack of wolves. The first wolf to see him, leapt for Rune's throat, a slash of the sword stopped the wolf in mid air. The other three wolves then attacked. One of the wolves latched his jaw around Rune's left forearm. The other two wolves attacked Rune's lower right leg knocking him off balance; his sword flew from his hand as he went down in a life or death struggle with the wolves. In all the excitement Tor's fight had also began. Fur and blood seemed to be flying in all directions.

Rune managed to pull his knife from his scabbard and plunged it into the wolf that was still attached to his left forearm. He was being dragged and tossed about by the two wolves tearing apart his right lower leg. No matter how hard he tried the wolves kept him off balance, he could not get at the antagonist to protect himself. He glanced over to Tor who had one of the wolves down and injured. Tor's other combatant was now fleeing back into the woods. Tor was limping badly but was heading towards Rune to help.

A loud crack as if thunder had struck filled the air. Rune saw one of the wolves fly from his leg and smash into the side of a tree. A figure was standing near Rune's battered leg with a large branch in their hands. The other wolf released Rune's foot as Tor did his best to chase it off into the woods.

Rune's eyes were filled with sweat, dust, and dirt from the battle. It was as if he were looking through a thick fog from the prow of a long boat. He could make out a beautiful woman, her long black hair falling about his face as she leaned over to comfort him. The darkness of her hair seemed to engulf him as his eyes closed and all went black.

Next, the woman was on a beautiful white horse, the whiteness of the horse was like the sun glaring off the ice, Rune had to cover his eyes with his hand to keep the horse in focus. Riding the horse was the most beautiful woman he had ever seen. She was dressed in tan buckskin with knee high laced buckskin boots. Her hair the color of a ravens wings in the moon light. The legends he had heard must be true. A beautiful Valkryie maiden had arrived to whisk him to Valhalla. She reached out her arm to Rune; they grasped each other's forearms as she helped him to leap up on her horse behind her. He wrapped his arms around her waist. She gripped his two clasped hands that were on her stomach tightly into the grip of her own hand. Her other hand held the reins of the horse as she urged it onward. The horse leapt into the sky, as they reached the clouds the horse flew from cloud to cloud as if it were using the soft billowing surfaces like mounds of earth. The Valkryie's hair flew back from her head with the wind blowing her sweet smell into Runes' nostrils. Suddenly they stopped in what seemed to be a huge cavern made of clouds, the Valkyrie used her hand to nudge Rune from the horse. Rune stood looking at the sight before him.

They seemed to be a large circular hall made of clouds. The floor was covered in mist so Rune could not tell what he was standing on. In the center of the room was a large solid silver throne, the arms of the throne were solid gold in the shape of a Viking long boat with dragons heads at their ends. The back of the chair had two golden ravens perched on each side. Sitting on the throne was the largest man that Rune had ever seen. He was twice the size of Rune, and Rune was no lightweight in terms of humans. The being on the throne was dressed in brilliant white leather. His shirt and the top of his boots sported white fox fur trim. His hair and beard were as white as his outfit and seemed to blend into one complete shape. Both hair and beard flowed in wavelets like the sea all the way to this beings lap. His face was old and wizened in its features. The eyes were a piercing deep brown. Rune stood in silence, not sure, if he should bow or speak.

Finally the man in the throne spoke.

"Rune do you know where you are? Do you know why you are here?"

Rune, mustering all his courage as a Norseman, stood straight and tall as he answered.

"I must believe that the Valkryie has brought me to you my Lord Odin. I wish that you may grant me my time in Valhalla."

"You are correct Rune. You have fought bravely. You have shown the courage of a great warrior. Although it is not your time. You must return to earth to fulfill your destiny. You will be the fore-father of a great and mighty king. You will not live to see him rule for it will be many generations after you are gone. You must fulfill this prophecy. Your bloodline will mix with another warrior line. As for your offspring, they must always marry into a lineage that contains some Norwegian blood. This is to be passed on from your children to your children's children. From this point on your offspring will be easily recognized for a trait that you have earned in battle. This trait will pass on to all your male offspring. Be gone, fulfill your destiny, Valhalla awaits you."

A mist filled the room until Odin was no longer visible. The Valkryie motioned Rune back onto her horse. The horse gracefully left the ground and raced through the now starry night sky. It would be many days before Rune would awake from his ordeal with the wolves.

CHAPTER 2

Rune's companions waited until morning. Tor had returned to the camp during the night. The men did their best to bathe and clean the many bite marks on Tor's body. The forty-pound shaggy black furred Tor was sore and hurt, but more than willing to lead the men to Rune. They picked up their weapons and followed Tor to what they hoped would be an alive and well Rune. Although considering Tor had returned in such bad shape, the men held no high hopes for their friend Rune.

The next morning the men could tell that Tor wanted them to follow him. The group gathered up their weapons and went along with Tor. The journey took them through the forest for about ten miles. Then they came to the scene of the battle.

There were no dead wolves, no bodies, no Rune. One thing that was there were lots of tracks. Wolf, dog, human and Rune's tracks were visible. A fair amount of blood still marked the ground where it looked as if Rune and the wolves had been bleeding. The unusual thing was that there were footprints of at least five individuals other than Rune. The tracks leading away from the scene showed the five new sets of footprints, but Runes footprints were not to be found. From the way things looked the footprints leading away from the battle were carrying a heavy load. The men had to assume that Rune was carried away by four of the men that had left their footprints. The fifth set of prints seemed to be much lighter in depth on the ground, most likely belonging to a woman. The question now was whether Rune had been carried away dead or alive. The only answer was to follow the tracks.

The trail led the nine Vikings along a steam that emptied into a large lake. Hiding in the tress along the steam the Vikings could see a large village about two hundred yards away. The men, women, and children all wore buckskin clothing. The buildings were made of tree bark or animal skins. There was no furniture to be seen, no chairs, and no tables. The weapons that were in view were crude, made of wood or bones with tips for killing made of stone or bone. The women were at their fires cooking, some were sewing clothing; others were performing whatever their current jobs were. Most of the men seemed to be relaxing. So far, they saw no sign of Rune. Although there was no doubt from the tracks that they followed that Rune was in the village. One of the Vikings pointed out fresh wolf hides being stretched and hung in the sun to dry. It was very likely that those were the wolves from the battle that Rune had been in.

The Vikings discussed their next move. They would form into a fighting formation, Lars would take the point position, and the others would fan out in a 'v' formation behind him. Then in force, they would enter the village. The hope was that the warriors of this tribe would be surprised by how well the Vikings were armed. Maybe than they would lead them to their injured comrade.

The Vikings got into formation and walked into the village. Soon they were confronted by the warriors of the tribe. The warriors were holding back as they eyed the Vikings weapons. Even though they outnumbered the Vikings, they were not sure if these were men or Gods that they were facing. The Viking weapons were large, sturdy and the metal of their swords and axes glistened in the sunshine.

It seemed that the world had stopped and both sides held their ground. It was then that a maiden ran from a tepee and stood between the two groups of warriors. She held her hands out to stop any possible confrontation. She than pointed at two of the Vikings and made a motion with her hand for them to follow her.

The maiden led the two Vikings to a tepee. Once inside the Vikings saw an old man sitting cross-legged by the fire. He was swaying back and forth and chanting. Lying towards the side was Rune, his body was cover with furs to his neck, his eyes were closed, and he was perspiring profusely. The maiden led the Vikings to their friend and she lifted the furs from Rune's body to show that he was still breathing. His leg was wrapped in leaves and some type of poultice that was unfamiliar to the Vikings.

The maiden did her best to make the Vikings feel welcome in the village. She slowly convinced both her own people and the Vikings that they should be friends. The Vikings slowly picked up the sign language that she use and started to feel more comfortable. The maiden settled the Vikings into one of the wooden huts for the evening. She brought them food and drink before they retired for the night. The Vikings posted one man at the entrance of the hut to keep guard. The Indians also left two of their braves within eyesight of the hut to keep an eye on their guests.

Rune finally awoke the next day. Tor lay by his side with his head on his master's chest. The old Indian had made some medicine for Rune to drink. The Vikings were soon aware that the old man was the tribe's medicine man and the maiden was his daughter. Talking as best they could with hand signals the Vikings were aware that Rune and Tor had fought six wolves to save the Medicine Man's daughter. Rune and his friends were now accepted as part of the tribe.

It was hard for the Indian Maiden to deal with Rune when he first awoke. His reaction was to tear off the bandages and poultice from his leg and foot. She held him down while her father went to find Rune's friends. Once some of the Vikings had gathered at Runes bedside the old medicine man removed the bandages from Rune's leg and foot. The gashes and bruises had been sewed up with animal gut. They actually did not look too bad. However, Rune was missing his big toe. The medicine man had used a flap of undamaged skin from Runes toe area as a flap to cover the open wound where Runes toe had been. As for the toe, the old man had it in a small medicine bag. It seems that they had managed to retrieve it from the stomach of one of the wolves that Rune had defeated.

The Indian maiden spent most of her time nursing Rune back to health. Not only was she grateful for the fact that he saved her life, she was also falling in love. Rune was soon feeling the same way. He spent his time using a crutch to get around the village. While he was in this condition, he did his best to help the villages in any way he could. Soon he was even learning their language.

The other Vikings also started to feel more at home. A meeting was held between them. They all decided that this would be a good place to settle. They had now made many new friends amongst the Indians. The Indians had begun to let the Vikings go with on hunting trips. The Vikings were impressed with the Indians tracking and stealth they used in finding game. The Indians were equally impressed with the Vikings strength and agility with weapons. A Viking bow had twice the distance and killing power of anything the Indians possessed.

As with many of the Indian tribes, violence amongst other tribes was not unheard of. Warriors would make raids on neighboring tribes for not only goods but to increase their share of women and children who they would capture and take back to their own village. Often these women would become wives to some of the braves. The children would be adopted and brought up to serve in their new tribe. Refusal would mean treatment as a slave.

To the Vikings this behavior in life was nothing new. In fact, it was similar to their own culture of raiding and pillaging other cultures to sustain their own way of life. The Vikings had now been with the tribe long enough to understand most of the language. They also started to learn the ways and the history of the Indians. In return, the Vikings told the Indians the Sagas of their ancestors. Both cultures had a rather violent past filled with spirits and gods that controlled men's destinies. Therefore, what came next was not a surprise.

It was early morning, a slight fog just lifting from the ground. The first sounds were muffled. It was the barking of the dogs that awoke most of the tribe. A marauding group of warriors from another tribe had attacked. The few people that had been out in the early morning had been silenced with arrows before they could shout a warning. As many of the braves rushed out of their tepees and lodges, they met the same fate as the early morning casualties. The Vikings hut was located on the far end of the village. By the time the Vikings emerged to witness the battle it was only a few hundred yards from them. They reacted quickly taking up their swords, broad axes and shields for hand-to-hand combat. Once the

Vikings became involved, the attacking warriors were soon on the run. A few well place slashes of a sword and battle-axes that took of the enemy's limbs were enough to force them to retreat.

The Indians of course were very grateful and very impressed. That night a huge feast was held for the Viking warriors. New stories would be added to an already rich Indian tradition. Of course, the Vikings would also add this encounter to their own sagas. The attacking Indians added this defeat to their legend. It was said that the village they attacked was protected by huge bearded giants, called Norsemen. From this point on the village was left in peace. For the next seven days the Indians would lay their dead to rest and honor them.

For Rune and the other Vikings, the Indian village was now home. They took wives and had children. Rune became a very important leader of the tribe when he took the Medicine Man's daughter as his wife. Not only did he save her life, he also shared in her life until they day he died. As a member of the elders in the tribe Rune was now known by his Indian name Rune Nine-Toes.

One very strange thing had happened to Runes first born. The baby was a boy, he was born with only nine toes, his right foot had no big toe. Now there was no hereditary reason for this. For Rune and his wife it was a sign that the boy would take over as elder when the time came. Every one of Rune descendants would be born the same way. The first male child would always be born with no right big toe. This would continue for centuries to come. Every child would also be an elder of the Ojibwa-Viking tribe.

Since the union of the Vikings and the Indians peace for the village continued. The stories of the mighty Norseman kept the other tribes at bay. Life went well until the white men came to take the land and kill the game that the Indians depended on for survival.

For many generations the Vikings and the Indians married, had children and intermingled their cultures. The Norsemen were very concerned that marriages be arranged for their own children. An Indian-Norse marriage was always pre-arranged while the boy and girl were still children. As an elder, Rune Nine-Toes had made this a tradition in the village that must be followed. The tribe migrated west as food and land became harder to control. White men and Indians alike were trying to force each other off the lands. The Ojibwa-Viking tribe finally settled for the last time in the Dakota Territories. Land that would eventually be known as Minnesota.

CHAPTER 3

The twenty-first century is here. The Viking-Ojibwa descendants of Rune and his friends are still living in Minnesota. Over the centuries, their lives have changed drastically. Most of them were forced onto reservations as the government tricked them out of their lands. They have struggled through the court systems to regain some control of their past, but too much time has passed. It would be like Rune and his friends trying to reclaim their land in Norway. It is time to learn to live like an American. Make your own way as best you can. There are two Viking-Ojibwas who plan to do just that. They are Rune's descendants. The two are brothers; their names are legend after their ancestors Run Nine Toes and Olaf. Their mother died over twelve years ago. Their father is alive but weak of mind and body. The boys do their best to care for him.

They have a home off the reservation now. They share the house with their aging father along the Mississippi River. Both the boys are elders in their tribe. The Minnesota laws have brought prosperity to many of the tribe members with legalized gambling casinos. The trick of course with money is to use it wisely. The boys have invested and would be considered quite well off. There is blood flowing through these two boys that is boiling to do something good for their ancestors and their country. Just what to do has yet to be determined. Their father's death from old age would allow them the freedom to pursue their own interests.

As for the good old U.S. of A., things were, shall we say getting out of hand. People were suing for spilling hot coffee on themselves, or for being told that their t-shirt had offensive writing on it, even better, they could be sued for helping to rescue someone who was in distress and about to die. The worst part is yet to come, not only were they suing for these things they were winning the lawsuits. Basically the lawyers and the legal system had started to pay people for being stupid. What happened to taking responsibility for your own actions, do not ask that question to a lawyer or a politician.

Of course, many Americans feel they are well informed about their country. They listen to C&N, read the newspapers, and check out local and world news on the internet. Is it really the news that is happening, or is it what the government wants you to think is happening.

Who is it that advises the president, you can bet it is not some blue-collar worker from down the street. Wait, maybe it's the appliance salesperson from Sears, or better yet, it's the cashier at the local quick stop gas and snack shop.

Then again, maybe it's the people who just flew in from the Bahamas' or Europe on a private government paid trip to check out the foreign situation. Oh yes, that's your everyday news worthy person. Say there Mr. President. The Chinese want more technology, and some cash would help to. While we're at it maybe we can import more goods to our country, and by the way, they have just put an embargo on anything from America. If we be nice and give them what they want maybe they will change their minds about the embargo. By the way, they promised that they would not use any of our cash gifts to them to increase their military, after all, they all ready have larger military forces then we do.

Now if you were president would it not be better to go to the local bar, bowling alley or restaurant for the news of what people really need from their government. Let that common old guy tell you how he feels about America. On the other hand, how about that housewife, secretary or waitress, how do they perceive America? Guess who makes up over ninety percent of the Americans? Yes sir, that's right, the common people. Me, you the people at work, the people next door, those people at the shopping mall, the bars, the restaurants. These are the people who should be heard. These are the people that make up America.

Rune and Olaf were playing darts at that local pub. The topic of discussion was bailouts. Just why should the government bailout financial institutions, automobile companies, or anyone else for that matter. If you ran the local grocery store, auto dealership, hair stylist, motorcycle shop or hamburger joint and you were going broke would the government bail you out? Hell no was the resounding answer. Sure, it would mean people lose jobs, lots of jobs if it's a big company. If twenty little businesses in your town go broke and lay off one hundred people total does that not count? You own your business and feel you are doing ok. What do you drive, a five-year-old pick-up truck, plus your wife has a full time job to help make ends meet. That lawyer on snob hill, what does he drive? Let's see, a new Hummer for him, his wife has a new Mercedes and the kids have a corvette and a BMW. Oh yes and the handy man keeps them all polished and filled with gas. Something wrong with this picture?

The next presidential election is only a little over a year away. Already the candidates are lining up there spokes people. Actors, actresses, sports figures, politicians, legal advisors, union leaders, all making a million dollars plus a year. Boy makes you want to believe what they say about a candidate. They will say anything if the candidate promises to make sure they keep making big bucks and pay little tax.

The drinking that was to say the least 'heavy' made the whole bar agree that the country needed a new political party, new leaders, and a common everyday person to run for president. So why not start right now, right here in this very bar. The Dog's Breath Saloon and Eatery would become the official headquarters for a new political party.

Of course, now they needed a presidential candidate, someone with experience dealing with people and a personality that they could sell to the citizens of the United States. After many more drinks, a vote of all in attendance was taken. It came down to a tie for two individuals, Rune and Olaf. More beers, more discussion, and a way to break the tie was finally reached.

Rune and Olaf would play one game of soft tip darts to decide the winner. Both were expert dart league players so it should be a fair contest. The boys went out to their motorcycles in the parking lot and retrieved their dart sets. Olaf would be playing with a Dart World Limited edition set of John Deere darts. Rune had his own custom designed set of Dart

World Dartpire darts. There are certain rituals that must be performed before the dart game can commence.

The boys picked out a pub table and prepared their darts. Shafts, flights, and tips were checked and tightened as needed. Two SvenBrew Submarine Olive light beers were ordered, plus Hamwhitch and Buffalo wing appetizers. The money was dropped into the coin mechanism of the dartboard and a game of Cricket was chosen. Using a dartboard that was not in play the boys each threw one dart to decide who would start the game. High point would start. Rune threw a 15, Olaf came in with a 20. Olaf would begin the game to decide on the Presidential candidate of the Dog's Breath Saloon.

Olaf took first throw at the dartboard, a twenty, a fifteen, and a nine. Up next was Rune with a bulls-eye, another bull's-eye, and a five. As the game progressed Rune had to wonder what he was doing, he was well in the lead with points and numbers out. The problem was he did not want to be the Presidential Candidate, although the whole thing was just a joke anyway. So the game continued and Rune's competitive spirit prevailed. Rune closed the game with a last double sixteen and a 40-point lead. The win cost him over one-hundred dollars as he bought free Svenbrew beers for the house.

Until closing time the whole bar crowd was planning a strategy session for their new Presidential candidate. Two people were much more involved than anyone else was. This was Bonne and Travis. Boone was the group's computer guru. Travis was the group's go-getter; no obstacle ever seemed to deter Travis. As for everyone else they were just dreaming of the possibilities, a government run by everyday all American folks. Of course, they all knew it would never happen; then again, it is fun to pretend.

By the time the Dog's Breath closed, everyone was really to drunk to continue any future plans for their new candidates. Tomorrow would be another day, and tomorrow night they could continue their far-flung strategy. Rune and Olaf just wanted to get some sleep before going back to work in the morning.

Just for fun Rune and Olaf spent their day thinking about what they would do if they actually got to the White House. Both the boys had an honest streak, which of course would be a deterrent for a politician. They both also tended to think like most of your average every day working Americans. Sometimes they were in debt, sometimes they felt pretty well to do. Most of the time they just got by on what they made from paycheck to paycheck. Little did they realize that two of their friends were going full steam ahead on their campaign.

That very night at the Dog's Breath Saloon Boone and Travis monopolized Rune and Olaf for most of the night. The boys did manage to break away long enough to get in a game of pool and one game of cricket, but then it was back with Boone and Travis. Boone had set up the Saloon with the capability to let him use his wireless laptop computer. He was taking notes as fast as Travis was grilling the boys about the changes they would like to see if they became President and Vice President. The boys humored them and went along with the discussion. Once again, it was fun to think of what a normal American might accomplish in the White House.

As the evening wore on Travis started a campaign fund collection. Thirty-two dollars was donated to get the campaign rolling. They even set up a campaign meeting for the next week. Rune and Olaf continued life as usual. Now Travis and Boone, they had big plans and they were already working them out. With a thirty-two dollar budget, they knew that would have to get creative. Billboards, television, radio, mass telephone calls, and mail out flyers were not an option. For these two guys this was not even a problem, they are tech geeks, and the world was fast becoming a wireless, computer, cell phone, text message place. What better media could one ask for? The information could be sent out and received in an instant. Their ideas could change political campaigning for years to come. The trick of course was to be the first and hopefully the only one to grasp this idea for the upcoming Presidential election.

Unknown to Rune or Olaf, their friends Travis and Boone had started the campaign rolling. They emailed all their friends with information about a grass roots Presidential campaign. Rune and Olaf now had their own web site, and they both ended up having their own 'face book' on the internet. The campaign would not be what the politically correct experts would want to hear, it would be downright brutal and honest in how the people who were true Americans felt. Travis and Rune decided that each item on Rune and Olaf's platform should be voted on by their supporters from the internet. This should give them a good basis to see how the real people felt and some idea if their Presidential Campaign was feasible. Donations would be accepted to help with travel expenses, but no money was to be spent on advertising, the internet would do their talking for them, and it was free. If this worked, it could change politics in America forever.

CHAPTER 4

The first question put to the internet voters was this. Would they consider voting for an unknown, non-politically active blue collar, slightly redneck American Indian-Norwegian to be president of the United States? This question and all that followed would be multiple choice, yes, no, undecided.

The internet voting had a forty-eight hour time limit for participants to post their answers. The final tally was about what Boone and Travis had expected. 14% voted yes, 6% voted no, 80% voted undecided.

Question 2. Would you like a candidate who would be brutally and totally honest with the American people? 78% voted yes, 13% voted no, 9% voted undecided.

Question 3. Would you favor stricter limitations on immigration laws and require all immigrants coming to live in the USA to speak write and read English with-in six months of their arrival or be deported? 65% voted yes, 18% voted no, 17% voted undecided.

Question 4. Do you think that people in jail or prison should be given tasks that will pay for their cost of being in prison. This would include growing their own food and animals. Making their own clothes and supplies. Working in municipal jobs such as road construction. Do city, county, and state clean up. Note, this will be opposed by big businesses who currently supply these services. Prisoners would not take the place of any employee currently doing this type of work. In fact, many of these employees may be promoted to supervise prison workers. Prisoners would be paid at a rate of minimum wage, taxes would be paid by the prisoners, and the money earned would pay for building upkeep and wages to guards and administrators. 78% voted yes, 13% voted no, 9% voted undecided.

Question 5. Would you vote to allow a victim's family or friends having a say in the punishment and sentencing of a convicted criminal? For either physical or property damage. Reasonable limits would be set using the bibles ten commandants as a guide. Twice the value of stolen property, eye for an eye. This is a very serious question to consider, do not decide in haste. 58% voted yes, 9% voted no, 33% voted undecided.

Question 6. Is it more important to consider victims' rights in a crime than the criminal's rights? This would allow past convictions and behavior to be admissible in court. 88% voted yes, 6% voted no, 6% voted undecided.

Question 7. Do you think politicians, lawyers, and big business control the United States? 94% voted yes, 0% voted no, 6% voted undecided.

Question 8. Is it time for the United States to equal trade balance with other countries. Exports and imports must be equal. Note the price may go up for a while, but also this would mean more jobs and eventually lead to higher wages to balance the budget for the common citizen and the country. 39% voted yes, 51% voted no, 10% voted undecided.

Question 9. Should the United States curtail foreign aid to other countries so that we can balance our budget? 76% voted yes, 19% voted no, 5% voted undecided.

Question 10. Is it time for the United States to become semi-isolationist and only work and help protect those countries that are our allies such as the United Kingdom, Germany, Japan and other democratic countries. 12% voted yes, 18% voted no, 70% voted undecided.

Question 11. Is it time for the people to vote on major issues. This would mean signing up on a computer for voting instead of going to the polls. "The polls would still be open for people who do not have access to a computer." A case in point would be for the people to vote on the questions we have just asked. This would mean that the vote of the people could override congress and the senate votes. You the people would make the final decision. 92% voted yes, 2% voted no, 6% voted undecided.

Question 12. This is it our last question. Do you think that Rune and Olaf should run as presidential candidates using the above 11 questions as their main platform? 61% voted yes, 34% voted no, 5% undecided.

The poll the boys had started grew quickly. The first question had netted about 120 participants. Question number 12 had drawn over 13,000 answers. The internet was spreading the word quickly. All this had been done in less then one month. Boone and Travis called a meeting at the Dog's Breath Saloon to get the campaign officially rolling.

Rune and Olaf were actually not too happy about the great results. With all this support, they were being swept into national prominence. The local newspaper and radio station had even begun to mention the boys as possible grass roots candidates. Every day the computer emails were jumping by the thousands. Eleven more months until election time. Was this really a feasible idea? Time would tell.

Now for Rune and Olaf all this political activity started to seem a little too realistic. They both liked what they did for a living. They enjoyed their freedom to come and go as they pleased. Their motorcycles were there passion, long trips together, seeing the country, it was fun and relaxing. These were things that they would have to give up if they really did get to the White House. Why, it would be like going to prison.

One day while they were playing darts and drinking SvenBrew Submarine Olive beers, something happened that would change their lives. Marie the waitress came to their table. Her eye was swollen and her face and arms were bruised. Marie and Olaf were best friends; even then, Olaf had to do a lot of talking and begging to find out what had happened to her.

Her fiancé had come to her house after drinking too much. Marie's cat Tut had jumped on her fiancé's shoulders in play, the fiancé did not see it that way and in a drunken rage through the cat against the wall, breaking its neck. The cat died in Marie's arms. She started screaming at her fiancé, he proceeded to beat her to a pulp.

The story ended even worse than it had begun. Because her fiancé was in the legal profession, she was afraid to press charges. He told her if she filed charges he would put her in court and drag her name through the mud, any questionable thing she ever did would be made public. He also informed her that he could legally sue her for her cat's behavior and take everything she owned. If she dared to stop seeing him, he would proceed to ruin her. The legal system was against her. A typical case of the criminal having all the rights, the victim suffers. Rune and Olaf decided right then and there. They would actually take running for office as President seriously. If for no other reason than to revenge the wrongs done to Marie and people like her. Lawyers would be their first target.

Most of Rune's and Olaf's free time was now spent answering emails about their beliefs and what they would try to do to change things if they made it to the White House. One important aspect kept popping up. The boys believed strongly in the Bibles ten commandants and also in the United States Constitution. Although following these two items would mean alienating many voters. Pro-life, cheating on spouses, dishonesty, theft, freedom of speech, right to religious beliefs are not very cut and dry subjects. Boone and Travis kept telling the boys to tread lightly in those areas. Then Rune and Olaf reminded them of one of their questions. Brutal honesty was the best policy.

Then things really started to mushroom for the group. The local newspaper sent a reporter to write a story about Rune, Olaf and their political party. The big problem was that they had not decided on a name for their political party. So right on the spot a decision was made. Lots of suggestions came up, things like God's Country U.S.A., Common Sense Party, Real Americans. When all the names were written on a dry erase board the group at the Dog's Breath Saloon picked a name for their new political party. From this day forward they would be known as 'The Common Cents Party.' They now officially tossed thier hat into the ring of candidates. It was time to get serious. Serious also meant that they would need money. Now that was a big problem. They were un-known and broke. Their chances of winning or even getting onto the ballot were poor to none. The one thing they had going for them was that good old American Spirit. The can do attitude that Americans always adapt when the going gets tough. The spirit that won two world wars and made America a super power of the world.

The American Indians were more than willing to make a large contribution, after all both Rune and Olaf had Indian Blood. Of course the American Scandinavians would not stand still for this, they pledged to match every cent that the American Indians donated. To say the least the two groups donated a sizable sum of money. By this time the Common Cents party needed to become more organized. Boone was now in charge of all internet activities. Travis now took the position of party treasurer. Tax-deductible forms were filled out and filed. Bank accounts were opened. The Common Cents party had less than ten months to infiltrate the system and make themselves viable candidates.

Once news of the contributions spread, the state television systems sent crews of news people to the Dog's Breath for more information. Marie was nominated as secretary spokesperson for the party. She had the worse job of all, getting Rune and Olaf away from their work and play long enough to give interviews.

The candidates they would have to compete with were colorful and feminine. Rune and Olaf were down home boys, just a spit short of being rednecks, and they were proud of it. Ever so slowly, the boys names started to appear in national print. Then they were getting mention on talk and news shows. American underdogs, no doubt. What seemed surprising was that they were gaining support. A tough out in the open campaign platform based on the constitution and the Ten Commandments. Maybe America had reverted to its old image, 1776 the year of freedom, independence, and rule by and for the people.

CHAPTER 5

Marie took her job very seriously. She set up a meet the candidates rally in front of the local town courthouse. The boys of course were still shy and very reluctant to appear in public. The promise they made after Marie's ordeal with her boyfriend was the only thing that made them feel they had to attend.

Now you have to realize that Rune and Olaf were not in the social elite of society. The fact is neither of them even owned a suit. With Rune and his missing big toe that had been passed from generation to generation, even dress shoes were hard to come by. A small meeting was held with Rune, Olaf, Marie, Boone, and Travis. If they were to run a brutally honest upfront campaign why not start now. The boys would appear in their everyday clothes. Black or tan jeans, denim shirts and for Rune New Balance shoes, for Olaf he preferred Ecco shoes. There would be no fancy cars of limousines to deliver the boys. They whole group piled into Rune's 2003 Honda CRV. They arrived at the courthouse at noon for a one pm rally. Already the crowd was gathering. Travis set up a crude but effective sound system, with their budget they had to borrow the equipment. The local Honda dealer loaned them a EU3000 generator to supply power. Luck was with them for the generator was super quiet and would not disturb the proceedings.

Once all was ready Rune and Olaf stepped up to the makeshift podium. To their astonishment, the crowd had swelled to well over 500 people. There was no opening applause, the crowd was dead silent, no welcome, no approval, just wait and see was the crowd's attitude.

Rune spoke first.

" Hello my name is Rune. I am running for the office of President of the United States of America. Next to me is my brother Olaf my Vice Presidential candidate. I would also like to introduce my trusted friends, and advisors. Marie, Travis, and Boone. These three people have been instrumental in bringing our campaign to its first public appearance. I would hope most of you have seen our emails and understand a little about how we feel our country should be changed. Therefore, with no future ado I am going to ask you the audience to question me. I will give you a straightforward honest answer. No political jargon to confuse you. If you feel, I am not being clear or precise enough in my answers please let me know. Raise your hand if you have a question."

"The lady up front please speak loudly so everyone can hear."

"Mr. Rune, you have stated on your web site that you wish to balance trade with other countries. Would that not in effect raise prices here at home? What about the items that are not produced in America, do we just live without them?"

"Yes, it will in the short term raise prices on many of our goods. I have confidence that this will bring out the American spirit of enterprise to produce those items here in our own country. Thus in the long run creating more jobs and as tooling and development costs are re-cooped it will lower prices. Many items from countries that agree to a trade balance will still be brought in and kept at the same reasonable prices that they are now. United kingdom, Japan, Germany all would be very viable partnerships for us to maintain."

"Next question please? Sir in the second row, please state your question"

"Rune, how about you stance on immigration. You say that new immigrants would be required to be fluent in English with-in six months of the coming to the United States. Would this not drastically cut immigration from the majority of poor and under developed countries?

"Yes. As a wise American once said, that is all I have to say about that."

Next question? The gentleman in the fourth row in the suit, please state your question"

"Mr. Rune your statement about requiring prisoners to self support themselves and even more to the point of having the victims decide on how to carry out the punishments. This seems like cruel and unusual punishment."

"First I will address Prisoners' supporting themselves. Right now, it is your tax dollars that pay to keep them confined. Your tax dollars also pay to keep up the infrastructure of the state and municipalities. All this costs lots of taxpayers' money in wages and benefits for more employees. I would like to use these employees to supervise convicts to do most of this work. Building roads, bridges, cleaning streets and sewers, keeping up parks and historical landmarks. Not one person currently doing this work would lose their job. As the current employees retire or quit they would be slowly replaced by these workers. In addition, this will provide a large work force to quickly complete needed projects. My plan would be to allow these prisoners' to earn minimum wage, this will first be used to pay repartitions to the victims and then cover the expense of incarceration. It should be a win-win situation. More workers, jobs finished faster, and the convicted will have a chance to learn useful skills for their reintroduction into society."

"As for the second part of your question. Letting victims or their families decide on punishment. I do not feel the government should play the part of God in deciding punishment. Before a decision is made, the victims would be tutored in the Ten Commandments and the bill of rights. They will have to make the moral judgment for the punishment. In case of theft or destruction of property or accidental injuries, a maximum of twice the cost involved would be acceptable punishment. If the perpetrator does not have the money, it will be deducted from their wages at a set percentage of each paycheck. In more serious matters such as murder, torture, and kidnapping it would be up to the victims to do as they see fit. If they wish the perpetrator to suffer as the victim has suffered it is their choice. If it was murder they can decide how the execution should take place and they will be responsible to carry it out. It will be their moral judgment. If they decide on a life sentence or leniency, that is also their choice,. Harsh. Yes. It is time for the victims to have rights, not the criminals."

"The Lady in the blue sweatshirt, your question please?"

"Mr. Rune, you seem to have a grudge against Lawyers, politicians and big Business. Why is this? It seems with this stance you will have almost no chance of being elected. These are the groups that control the country and its votes."

"I do not have a grudge against them for whom they are, I do not like what they do to the American public and get away with it. Let's break it down to each group."

"Lawyers. You need to write a will, set up a contract, defend yourself in a wrongful case, yes we need honest lawyers to do this. Now let's say you were in your car at a stop sign. A drunk driver rear-ends you at sixty miles per hour. This is his second DWI in less than two years. This driver has had numerous arrests for being drunk and disorderly. His lawyer defends him and forces the court to overlook his past behavior as inadmissible. So all the judge and jury have to go on is this one incident. The judge and jury end up finding him liable with probation attached, after all anyone can make a mistake once. As far as I and my constituents are concerned all past behavior is relevant. I was brought up to believe that hiding the truth or the facts is the same as lying. Any lawyer that defends in this manner will be charged with perjury. Lawyers are to up hold the law for honest hard working Americans. Not for the crooks, the drug addicts, the drug dealers, the kidnappers, abusers or even crooked business owners. Let's make our country safe to live in."

"Politicians. If they are accepting graft, padding expenses, allowing special privileges to constituents for cash, products or favors. Charge them with abusing their position and remove them from office. Fines or jail time to be determined. They are elected to work for you, not for themselves."

"Big business. Yes they need to make a fair profit. They also need to be fair to their employees. Wasting stockholders money on private airplanes, lavish estates with servants, expensive trips abroad. Annual reports should show these things. Let the stockholders vote to end these frivolous wastes of their investments. Trading under the table with unfriendly countries, padding government contracts will not be tolerated. If a private contractor can buy a toilet for one hundred dollars, then the government should be able to buy it for the same price. No more five-hundred dollar wrenches or ten-dollar ink pens. Remember the taxpayer's money pays for all these things. Military or government use."

"Next question? The gentleman up front in the leather jacket."

"Mr. Rune. Do you really believe that the United States should become a semi-isolationist country?"

"Yes I do. At least until we balance our budget and become strong enough to produce everything we need. Of course the big question will be about foreign oil. It might just be that we have to depend on our own resource. Not only oil, but the viability of electric or solar power. We have the technology and the American sprit to solve this problem. Maybe we have to have gas rationing similar to what we had during World War Two. The day of two four-wheel drive pick-ups, one fancy car, one sports car, two snowmobiles, three boats, two ATV's and two motorcycles in every garage might have to end. Like our grandparents and their grandparents we may just have to learn to live with-in our means. To help this work people who do not pay their credit cards, declare bankruptcy write bad checks are criminals. It will not be tolerated. Debts will be collected from their wages at a percentage each month, allowing them enough to live on until the debt is paid off. Credit will be allowed only to those who do not abuse it. Harsh yes. Right now it is you the common American that ends up paying for all the deadbeats. It is not fair for hard working citizens to pay the debts of those who cannot control their own greed."

"The lady in the second row with the white sweater, your question please?"

"Mr. Rune, you cannot honestly believe that congress, the senate, or the Electoral College will give up its power to let the majority of the people actually vote on major issues and have their decisions actually carried out?"

"America is based on the principal of following the wishes of its people. When congress and the senate were established this county was in its infancy. Communication was poor at its best. This is a new era. Communication and knowledge are faster than the blink of an eye. I'm old fashioned, but I must admit that the world is a new technologically advanced place to live in. Never before in history has the American public had the opportunity to immediately be aware and be able to personally have an input on major issues. For those who are not computer literate. Every city hall will have computers and people who can aid them in casting their votes. Finally a real Country for the People by the People."

"Last question please, come on folks let's make it a good one? Sir in the middle with the red hair. Your question please?"

"Rune, do you and your Common-cents party with your radical views of letting people decide what's good for them instead of the government. Do you really think you have a snowballs chance in hell of getting anywhere in the upcoming presidential election."

"To all of you gathered here today, that is by far the easiest question I have been asked. The answer is 'No'. Thank you all and have a great day in Minnesota."

The five members of the Common-cents party spent the next hour visiting with the crowd on a one to one basis. Finally they made their way back to the Honda CRV. Olaf always an optimist was heard to say.

"Well, I think that went well."

CHAPTER 6

Olaf was right about one thing, the first public appearance of the Common-Cents party did go well. Not so much as far as the questions and answer session, but it caused a media frenzy in Minnesota. The few local newspapers and radio station had a hay day with it. It did not take long for the twin cities television stations to locate videos taken by private citizens at the first Common-Cents meeting. Whether this would turn into history or garbage was still debatable. Then again, some coverage was better than no coverage. Controversy was certainly a subject on the minds of anyone who was there, or had read, watched or heard the question and answer session.

The next big break for the Common-Cents party was about to happen by pure accident. One of the major candidates was holding a press conference in Chicago when a question from the audience caught him by surprise. He was asked what he thought about the upstart Common-Cents party. His answer was this.

"I have heard of the CC party and I think they can be dismissed as a group of blue collar redneck hillbillies with Nazi tendencies."

This little tidbit just so happened to air on C&N news that very day. Needless to say, our candidate in question had alienated every blue collar, redneck hillbilly in the country. Even if there are a few Nazi's left in America you can be sure they will be voting for someone else.

As for the Common-Cents party they received their first dose of national attention. In fact, it was such a great statement from the opposition that C&N called Marie that very day to set up an interview.

The big day with C&N was fast approaching. Marie was having a terrible time with Rune. Not only did he not want to ask his boss for time off, he also refused to wear a suit and tie. Marie called Rune's work and got him the day off; he would have to sneak in a plug for the Besser House where he worked to pacify his boss. The wearing of a suit was still out of the question. Rune's attitude was that he was a common everyday American; the people should be willing to accept him as he is.

The Television crews were at the Dog's Breath Saloon the night before the broadcast. The parking lot was cordoned off. The local police department was paid by C&N to have extra duty officers on hand. The podium was set up and all was ready.

Marie, Travis, Olaf, and Bonne were at the site three hours early. Rune finally showed up about an hour beforehand. He parked his Goldwing right up by the podium to the cheers of the crowd. The C&N crew whisked him away for make-up and preliminary coaching. Once again Rune refused the pleas of the C&N people to change into a suit, they even had one along that they would fit him into. He was warned no foul language, be careful to be politically correct, be polite and no nasty jokes. Poor Rune, might as well put a muzzle on him.

Rune emerged from the rear door of the Dog's Breath Saloon. He walked up to the pedestal dressed in a black long sleeve Denim shirt with a white embroidered motorcycle over the pocket. Black jeans and his best black New Balance shoes. All this was crowned by his lifelong pewter Viking necklace that hung around his neck and glistened in the sun light.

He settled in behind the podium, adjusted the microphone to the right height, and began talking.

"Hello, my name is Rune and I represent a new political party for the United States. The Common-Cents party, spell Cents any way you want, they are both needed in this country and it will be my job if elected to give them to you."

His next move shocked everyone, especially Marie, Olaf, Boone, and Travis. Rune pulled a bottle of SvenBrew Submarine Olive Beer from his jean pocket, no wonder his jeans looked bulgy on the way up. From under the bulge in his shirt, he produced a bag full of Beerzel beer filled pretzels and tossed them out to the crowd. The crowd went wild, cheers went up, and soon the barmaids from the Dog's Breath Saloon were working the crowd for drink and snack orders. This was not going to be a conventional press conference.

"Ok everybody lets have some fun while we talk some serious business. First of all, I wish to thank my boss at the Besser House for giving me time off to do this press conference. You all need to remember I'm not some rich dude or dudes that can campaign with lots of money. As for contributions, we will use them only if absolutely necessary. If we have contributions left after are campaign they go to charity."

"As a quick overview of our platform let me say this. It is time for the people to be heard, you will be voting on all major issues. Politicians will answer to you, no pet projects, no bribes, or you can vote them out of office. Lawyers and courts will handle cases quickly and fairly, crooked lawyers will have to answer to the people for their actions, you can vote to have them disbarred. Stockholders will have reports that tell them how their investments are spent, so big business, no more private jets, and trips around the world. Victims' rights will be restored, victims will have a say and maybe even a hand in how the criminal is punished. Drug runners will be punished without leniency and fines will be leveled to help in rehabilitation. Drug users are also guilty, they will be charged to attend and complete their own drug rehabilitation, and this includes not only drugs but also alcohol. Underage persons trying to buy alcohol or cigarettes will now be held accountable. Yes establishments still have to check identification, but if the buyer is falsely representing their age they will be found guilty, the establishments will be off the hook. The budget will be balanced, and yes every American citizen will probably suffer while this is happening. It may even lead to gas rationing just like World War Two. People immigrating here will follow our rules, speak, and write in English. Bad checks and bad credit will be treated the same as counterfeiting money, if your money is no good you will be held accountable. It is time for the honest everyday American taxpayer to stop paying everyone else's bills."

"If elected the Common-Cents Party will be brutally honest. We will make lots of enemies. We also hope to make lots of friends. I grew up going to school, finding work and making my way, my family motto was 'don't lie and you don't have to remember what you said.' Let's all live by that rule. America was founded on the basic principle of God and the bible, the Ten Commandants are not made to be bent or broken as we see fit. They are the supreme law, not a suggestion. Let's do as the motto on our coins says 'In God we Trust."

"Our troops will be coming home. We will, have military presence only in countries that are allies and want us there. Trade will be balanced. We will not help, buy from, or give money to communist countries or countries that do not follow the basic civil or religious rights of the human race."

A quick swig of SvenBrew and Rune opened the crowd for questions.

Question. "Rune, being a Minnesotan are we to take it that you may be another Jesse Ventura?"

The answer. "Next to me folks, Jesse is going to look like an angel from heaven."

Question. "The CC party has a lot of controversial subjects on its platform. We have heard nothing about pro-life or abortion. What is the stance of your party on these issues?"

Answer. "Our stance will be the same as God's. We are pro-life. Birth control yes. Getting pregnant is another case of people not being responsible for themselves. If a person is weak, gives into temptation, it would be hard for me to think that a 'sorry I think I will kill me fetus is a good decision.' This is an issue between God and the offender. The government should not fund or be involved in the taking of a life."

Question, "as for taking a life, your stand on punishment would allow a victim in cases of wrongful death or murder make that decision and carry it out. How does this follow your ten commandments?"

Answer. "Again the government will not involve itself. The person will have to handle their own moral discretion in this matter. Is "an Eye for Eye" literal or not. It will be between the victimized person and God."

Question. "What about medical coverage. Your party has not addressed this issue at all?"

Answer. "Great question. We are in favor of national coverage for all. Those paying premiums for insurance will keep paying them just like always. The insurance companies will continue to operate. The big change will be that everyone that is working will pay a percentage of their income to medical coverage. This will be not more and maybe less than the amount that insured people are paying now. As a side point, we will also look at the roles of the disabled and non-working. With so many jobs coming due to our new structure limiting trade to balance the budget we will need a much larger work force. Even most of the disabled can be useful. It is a well-known fact that the majority of the people will feel more useful and better about themselves if they can contribute to the world. We want to help them make that contribution. As for the old, infirm, retired, they deserve their rest, social security will stay in place. We would also like to see a lock put on property taxes for people that are retired. Let them live out their lives in comfort. No more having nursing homes take their life savings. As a final comment, medical coverage would be lowered tremendously if the average person got the same discounts that the medical establishment gives to insurance companies."

Question. "What about people that refuse to work?"

"It is a harsh decision, but they will be on their own. No more government assistance. If they have too many kids and need help with daycare to hold jobs the government will have programs. Sooner or later those kids will grow up and be gone. Now they will know that they have to be productive by the example set by their parents."

Question. "How about education? Is the government going to help?"

Answer. "I personally did not like school. I went, I learned, and I'm glad I did. When I grew up you had no choice, you did what your parents said and followed the rules. Now I have to say it. Children will not be allowed to drop out. School through the twelfth grade will be mandatory. Discipline will be brought back and enforced. Today's youth knows what is right and wrong. They need to be responsible for themselves. Parents, time to stop coddling your children, help them to stand on their own two feet. Most of all give them love and encouragement. That's what being a parent all is about."

Last question please? "I know you have heard this before. Do you really think you have any chance of winning this election?"

Answer. "No. It is doubtful we will ever get any farther than we are today. Honesty and a stance of being responsible for ourselves is a big pill to swallow. The Common-Cents party is like that big pill. Can the American public swallow us? Time will tell. By the way I think the old Blue Laws of the past would be very helpful. All business should close on major holidays and Sundays. Let's make it a family day and a day of rest for us all."

Rune then hoisted his SvenBrew in the air with a parting comment.

"Cheers to all and to all a good life. God Bless America."

The crowd went wild. Cheers and clapping took five minutes to die down. The C&N people, Marie, Olaf, and Boone were sweating bullets. Travis thought it was a great press conference.

It was broadcast worldwide, no cuts, no beeped out words. Just hard and honest comments from the leader of the Common-Cents Party.

For the next three days every news show, talk show, and late night comedy show had something to say about Rune and the CC party. Of course as can be expected the most common comment of them all is "Rune the Country with Noncents."

CHAPTER 7

Three new sponsors made contributions and they signed Rune, Olaf, Marie, Travis, and Boone to endorsement contracts. Advertisements were now everywhere for SvenBrew Submarine Olive beer, Beerzels and Sodazel pretzels, and even bottles of Lena and Ole's Submarine Olives with tiny carrot periscopes. It was almost like Drew Carey re-runs.

The Common-Cents party was now in full swing. Pictures of Rune and his friends were appearing everywhere. Billboards, newspapers advertisements, magazines, radio, and television. The best part of all this was that it was free publicity, compliments of their sponsors. Of course, this was detrimental in some instances. The anti drinking establishment lambasted the Common-Cents party every chance they got. The bleeding hearts claimed that the party was promoting drinking and aiming their fun advertisements and antics at today's youth.

The Common-Cents answer was actually common sense in the eyes of Rune and friends. Why use donations from hard working people to fund their campaign when they could have free campaign publicity by using business sponsors. Besides the endorsements made no money for the Common-Cents party or its members. They had all agreed that all income and proceeds from endorsements would be donated to their party. A win-win situation.

Then one night as they all sat around the Dog's Breath Saloon having a few drinks and playing darts, the big news of their campaign hit the national airwaves. The latest polls for the presidential election were being announced. There were six candidates vying for the Democratic and Republican nominations. The independents, Green Party, and the

Communist party each had one candidate. Of course, also running was the Common-Cents party. The news station started giving the nations random poll results. The number one Democrat and Republican candidates were holding strong percentages in the 20 per-cent plus range. The little party's were not mentioned, that is until the end. One small Independent party had scored a three per-cent vote, Common-Cents was in the running.

The people and the competition were now starting to pay attention. The Democrats and the Republicans still laughed them off, but what if these upstarts started to make headway? No one thought it was possible, a hardnosed, brutally honest, super conservative party like Common-Cents could never hope to get into the White House. Even if they did, Congress and the Senate would crucify them and their ideas. That is, unless the people really did back up Rune and friends and override the congressional system by majority votes from the people.

The big political parties were now holding their primaries. Lavish parties, big money, large cities all involved to lure the Democrats and Republicans to their cities for the Primary's. Cash flowed like mighty rivers after a summer rainstorm. The final top two candidates would emerge to do battle. Therefore, what was the Common-cents party going to do? They only had one candidate, no need for a lavish primary. Although Marie figured, they should put on some kind of show. Therefore, she put out the word for help.

Marie invested fifty dollars of her own money to rent the local township park. This included the use of the old log cabin, which they could use to set up tables and food. One of her friends ran a pig roasting business, he donated a roast hog and offered to set up his roaster and supply the hog for free. SvenBrew, Beerzel and Sodazel pretzels, and Lean & Ole's submarine Olives with little carrot periscopes all donated their beverages and food for the party. Everyone else was asked to bring potluck. The little town of Sauk Rapids, Minnesota was now hosting the Common-Cents election party.

The local police would need to have three officers assigned for traffic duty and patrols. The Party was expected to pick up this expense. Once again, the sun shone bright for the Common-Cents party. The local police officers all signed waivers and donated their time to fulfill their jobs. The local motorcycle groups volunteered to help with parking and security. The Honda Goldwing riders were put in charge of organizing all the bikers that wished to help. It was great seeing the Honda, Harley, Yamaha, Kawasaki, Suzuki, BMW and Triumph riders all working together as a family.

The party was scheduled for a Saturday so families could hopefully have a better chance to attend on the weekend. A parade was scheduled to start at the Besser House where Rune worked. It was to be a 100-unit motorcycle parade with Rune and Olaf leading on their Goldwing and Indian Motorcycles. Travis was in the second row on his Honda 750 Spirit Custom Bobber, next was Marie on a Honda 600 Silverwing scooter with Sidecar, and Boone, well he was riding in the sidecar, his ever present laptop computer by his side.

Along the parade route, the group was proud to see banners and flags proclaiming support of the Common-Cents party. The whole route was lined with people, old, young, fat, skinny, and every color you could image. All these people had one thing in common, they were Americans, and they wanted a voice in their government.

Once at the park things were going as planned. People were playing softball, badminton, soccer, horseshoes and any other outdoor games you could think of. Kids had balloons with pictures of Rune, Olaf, Marie, Travis, or Boone. It was hard not to notice that the kids with 'Boone' balloons looked a little like geeks. The area had been filled with tables of potluck dishes. Vendors had set up booths under the careful supervision of Marie. Any profits made would have to be split between the concession owner and the Common-Cents party. Seeing the concession stands had been allowed to set up for free they felt this was a fair deal. Fifty-percent of the profits could also be deducted from taxes as a political donation.

There were no speeches, no political promises, just plain old fun. The Common-Cents crew mingled with the crowds and introduced themselves. This was a day for families and fun. The most easygoing political rally in history. Of course, C&N and all the big networks had sent reporters to cover the rally. To say the least, with no speeches and no controversy this rally was not earth shattering news. Although to families and everyday Americans, this was how the world should be.

By the time the new polls were available the CC party had gained three percent. They now had moved up to six percent. Once all the political brew ha had settled, the big parties had their two candidates chosen. Once again, they supported both a Feminine and also a colorful approach to the white house. The colorful approach was trying for a second term. The Feminine approach was still trying for an upset. Then we had the three little known candidates, the Green party and the Independent Party were lily white. The communists had all but disappeared. Common-Cents was in the shadows but visible, maybe the blue collar worker, redneck, conservative approach was not so bad.

Soon the main political parties had made their choices. The incumbent party kept its colorful candidate. The opposition now had a very feminine flair running for president. Promises were made; it would be interesting to see if they could keep them. Mudslinging was started; of course, the candidates let their subordinates sling the mud. The candidates tried their best to keep their squeaky-clean image. As for the CC, party things were going well.

The full five person staff of the CC party had been allowed to work part-time at their current jobs. This was a big help for running the campaign. The hard part was that all of them continued to live on their part time wages. They had a rule not to touch campaign contributions for personal gain. They knew if they broke one of their campaign rules the rest of the rules would be useless. Honesty was their watchdog. If the American people were suffering from the over indulgence of the government, the members of the CC party would suffer right alongside every other hard working honest American citizen.

As news and magazine crews followed the CC members around, the people's awareness of them started to bear fruit. The latest polls had them moving up to a twenty-one percent voter approval. This was strong enough that the government was forced to add their names to the list of possible candidates. The party was now recognized nationally and would be listed on the ballots.

Rune and Olaf were getting stressed out. They needed a little time to themselves. The Sturgis motorcycle rally was coming up. The boys decided it was time for a motorcycle run. Marie and Boone tried to talk them out of it. Bad politics they said. Too much drinking and carousing could hurt the party's image. Rune and Olaf once again said, "We mean to be plain old common Americans, the people need to accept us for what we are." Two days later Rune on his Goldwing, Olaf on his Indian, and Travis who had been suspiciously quiet about the whole affair were on their way to Sturgis. The news crews and the paparazzi were not far behind.

Travis had decided to ride a Honda 750 Spirit custom bobber to the Rally. Comfortable was not part of this bikes charm, but it sure did look nice. Hi-rise bars, lowered rear shocks, bobbed finders, solo saddle seat and flame paint job. It was named the 'Sea Hog'. As its finishing touch, it had a large chrome hog on the back fender whose eyes light up when the lights were on. Good looking as this bike was, it necessitated a stop every hundred miles for Travis to re-arrange his own personal rear end. Rune and Olaf traded bikes every so often with poor Travis just to be kind. The Bobber was not a bike for long trips.

Every stop the boys made was photographed and documented by the news crews and paparazzi. Somehow, the boys had to shake this bunch of bothersome photo hungry hogs as soon as possible. Of course, this was easier said than done, and a few broken laws would not help the boy's image. A couple of ditch crossings on their motorcycles could not detour their pursuers. Travis' bobber was not up to the high speeds needed to leave their enemies behind, and one-hundred mile an hour runs down the highway were getting unwanted mention by the press. The all-American boys were being typical Americans. Marie and Boone sat at home hopping the public was going to be understanding of their newest presidential candidates. The opposition parties of course made sure to mention the lawbreaking CC members every chance they had. Something was stirring in the public's mind; the party took a two-percent jump in the polls after their first day on the road to Sturgis. Speeding and illegal u-turns be damned, the people liked these guys.

Stops at a car museum, Wall drug, the Corn Palace, Black Hills jewelry shops, mines, Reptile Gardens, all got photo coverage on television and web sites. A photograph of Rune, Olaf and Travis standing by their motorcycles with Mount Rushmore in the background was a hit across the country. Publicity compared the boys to Teddy Roosevelt and his Rough Rider's. Travis certainly felt like a 'Rough Rider.'

Camp for the trip was the boy's reservations at the Bullock Hotel in Deadwood. Haunted by the spirit of Sheriff Bullock, or haunted by paparazzi the boys were determined to be themselves and have a good time. They told the news crews and the paparazzi they could take all the pictures they wanted. Just don't ask any questions or disturb the boy's vacations by getting in the way. It was an agreement that seemed to keep everyone happy. More photos' flashed across the county, the boys at Wild Bill Hickok and Calamity Jane's graves, and the boys having beers in downtown Deadwood. The boys laying in a steam in just their blue jeans to cool off from the one-hundred degree plus weather. Tomorrow it would be the boys at Sturgis for the rally. Marie and Boone kept leaving telephone message warning the boys to be well behaved. Cell phones had no signal in the mountains so the best Marie could hope for was that the boys would listen to the messages she left at their hotel.

Next morning the boys had a nice breakfast in the dining room of the Bullock hotel. They sat around in the lobby area and played the slot machines for about an hour. Then it was out in the crisp mountain air to polish their motorcycles.

The trip from Deadwood to Sturgis follows some nice winding mountain roads. The scenery is not only breathtaking but can be life threatening if the riders don't pay attention. Being old hands at motorcycle riding in the mountains Rune and Olaf hit the curves at fairly high speeds. This was all new to Travis so he held back for his own safety. The entourage of media followers was falling farther and farther behind.

Entering Sturgis in late morning was a good thing to do. The parking was not so bad this early. The boys cruised the main areas until they found three open parking spots for their bikes. The media and paparazzi were in for a rude awakening as they came near town. No cars or trucks were allowed. They would have to park outside of town and hike their way in. Loaded with, sound equipment, cameras, and supplies the media people were not too happy.

The boys were occasionally recognized by some of the Sturgis crowd. Now one nice thing is that this group of bikers was down home all around folks. A few handshakes, hellos, and they left the boys go about having a good time. Of course, many of the folks wanted their pictures taken with Rune, Olaf, and Travis, and a few bare breasted photos of women with the boys were bound to be taken. In fact, a few middle finger photos also were bound to show up. The boy's did their best to discourage this type of behavior, not good for their political image, but what the hey, it was Sturgis you had to expect some raunchy behavior. In fact, Travis was quoted as saying "Bill Clinton eat your heart out." Marie and Boone would chastise poor Travis for that slip of the tongue as soon as they got their hands on him.

Most of the Sturgis crowd was older now days. When Rune and Olaf first started coming they were in their twenties as were many of the other Sturgis group. It seemed that the main participants had grown older together, and luckily, they were mellower. Sure, there were some fights and drunken behavior, but the group was getting good at policing themselves. Overall things were pretty laid back.

The boys did all the usual things you do in Sturgis. See the motorcycle museum, drink beer, eat buffalo burgers and deep fried cheese curds, shop for bike do-dads and souvenirs, and of course buy a few t-shirts and lapel pins to prove they were there.

The word had spread throughout Sturgis that Rune, Olaf, and Travis were trying to avoid the media and just have a nice old good time. The Sturgis crowd did their best to help. They led the media on many a wild goose chase looking for the boys. If the media got to close, they were treated to drinks and photo shoots of fancy motorcycles, biker type guys, and the world's greatest biker women. By mid afternoon, the media people were all too drunk and disoriented to care about the CC party. They were now just part of the festivities. The boys had the rest of the day and most of the night to party and have fun. They quit drinking about six o'clock so that they would be ready to ride by two or three in the morning. Wherever the boys went, the bars saw a huge sales jump for

SvenBrew and Beerzels. The company sponsorship was paying off well that day. When the boys left town and headed back to Deadwood they had the road to themselves. The Media people were nowhere to be seen. Only one political time bomb statement was made that hit the news. Rune said that he personally did not believe in sex or having children out of wedlock. This could lose a lot of voters. Marie and Boone were back at home wringing their hands over this one. Then again, it was an honest answer. Rune of course knew he would never try to enforce such a thing; it was just for him that was the proper way to live a life. Maybe his Viking and Indian blood had some heathen tendencies, but he was a God-fearing believer in the Ten Commandments.

Marie and Boone were still picking up the pieces of the boys latest exploits. The strange thing was that their percentages in the polls continued to increase. Marie and Boone were overworked and of course underpaid. Marie had finally convinced her friend Valerie to join into the inner circle of the Common-Cents party. All the work was getting to be overwhelming for all of them. The boys returned to home base at the Dog's Breath Saloon and after their little vacation were ready to give their all to an increasingly growing campaign.

Marie, Valerie, and Boone spent their time plotting strategy for the campaign. Travis lined up a sweet deal with Amtrak for a countrywide whistle stop campaign. Rune and Olaf convinced all their employers for a leave of absence and now had to make a tough decision about campaign funds. Should they start using the funds for the actual campaign expenses? Tougher yet was the question of paying themselves at least enough of a wage to live on. With all of them not working their regular paying jobs, things were getting tight. None of them had the money in savings to continue for long. They posted the campaign and wage question on their internet site so that the people that were supporting them could decide. It was a good thing for all concerned that the people over whelming gave approval to use campaign funds to support the campaign and its participants. They decided as a group that $2500 a month each would be a fair salary. The campaign funds would pay travel, food expenses and insurance premiums. In four days, they would start their whirlwind tour of the United States by train. Amtrak felt this was a great advertising ploy and hooked an open-end observation car to the train. No other extras were offer for the Common-Cents party. After all Amtrak was government operated.

The six party delegates boarded the train in St. Cloud, Minnesota and headed off. They had three double berth rooms that they shared. They all felt just a little guilty spending the hard-earned money of the contributors. Top priority was to be fair to the American people and share in the everyday life that their contributor's lived in. Dealing with a train full of Media was still a problem; the Media was following them everywhere. One nice aspect was with all six members of the Common-Cents party on board the train they had lots of time to talk to the passengers. Soon the trip was like a family get together, they all played games with the kids, and had nightly sing alongs for everyone. Rune loved finding some female to do old Nancy Sinatra, Lee Hazelwood duets with. Some nights his partner might be a six-year-old girl, a teenager, a young newlywed, someone Runes own age, or a sweet old grandma. Rune didn't care who he had for a singing partner, he was just happy to have someone to sing with. Of course, the Media loved getting the sing-a-longs on tape for the public to see. Rune was certainly no Elvis but he sure gave it his best.

Radio stations were playing Rune and partner songs in jest at all hours of the day. They may have thought it funny, but it was a great political coup for the Common-Cents party. Presidential candidates who were typical Americans and were enjoying life in the United States.

Every time the train stopped, Rune and party were on the open platform at the rear of the train. Stumping their way across America. From North, to West, to South and East. Than right down the heartland, they covered all the area's that Amtrak serviced. The crowds seem to grow with every stop. Officially, the other parties had to admit that Common-Cents were becoming a serious adversary for the post of President of the United States.

CHAPTER 8

The Common-cents party was not very concerned with the actions of the Democrats or the Republicans. Their concern was with themselves. They wanted to run a clean honest all American campaign. They wanted to do what was right for the American People. Big Business, politicians, lawyers be damned. It was full steam ahead for the American people to take their county back into their own hands.

The Republicans and Democrats did not share the feeling of the Common-Cents party. They put out word for the FBI and CIA to investigate this upstart party and its members. They had their lawyers digging into any type of improper behavior that they could use to end this upstart party. On the sly, a reward was offered to any legal firm in the country that could bring down the Common-Cents party. The lawyers of course offered clandestine rewards to anyone with any information that might hurt any of the Common-Cents members. Marie's still legal associated boyfriend was working with his bosses to dig up all the dirt he could. Marie was still just a little too gullible to catch on to this. Her boyfriend started to treat her like a princess. Flowers, candy, he even picked her up in a limousine to wine and dine her. All in an effort to get some dirt on Rune and Olaf. If he and his boss could take down the two top dogs in the Common-Cents party, the rest would crumble before election time.

Unknown to the rest of the Common-Cents members Marie continued to see her old boyfriend. Sometimes it is just too hard to give up what seems to be a sure thing. Her mind kept saying no, but her heart wanted to say yes. He gave her all the sob stories. His wife had died leaving him with a young daughter to raise. His daughter needed a mother. He knew he had a temper and was not so easy to get along with, but he would change. She should just trust him. As he gained her trust, he kept sneaking in questions about Rune. Marie and Rune had known each other over twenty years, and they were closer than ever with the campaign in full swing. Slowly Marie let slip more and more personal information about Rune. If only she knew that her boyfriend was recording most of their conversations with a hidden recorder. What he did not record he kept notes on, dates, times everything she said about Rune would be well documented. His lawyer bosses promised a large bonus and maybe even a promotion if they could sell this information to the other candidate's parties. The other parties had enough intermediaries out there that were willing to spend big dollars to bury the Common-Cents party. Marie would unwittingly supply what they wanted. All in the name of love.

The information the big political parties wanted was finally obtained. Marie's boyfriend was spending money like there was no end to it. He explained to Marie that he had received a substantial raise. He also had an expense account form his bosses to lavish Marie with bribes for more information. He was the King and she was the Pawn. A game of chess that could ruin her friends and her dreams of a political party for the common American citizen.

A surprise windfall finally reached the ears of Valerie, Marie's new assistant. A Presidential debate was to be televised in the next few days. The Democrats and the Republicans had specifically invited the Common-Cents party to participate in the debate. Marie and the whole crew were ecstatic at the news. This was their big chance. Open debate, no speeches, this was where Rune could shine. Marie's big concern right now was to get Rune to dress up, suit, and tie time. Rune agreed to a suit and tie but on the condition that Valerie help him pick it out. Therefore, with stern warning from Marie, Valerie and Rune went clothes shopping. Runes outfit would be a surprise that no one but Valerie would see before the debate.

As the Common-Cents party packed their clothes for the trip to the debate a call to Rune came from Marie. She had a family emergency and would not be able to attend. Marie's boyfriend had convinced her to take an on the spot vacation to a south sea island, where as fate would have it there would be no television or radios for them to observe or hear the debate. Brutally honesty in her statement seems to have been lost for Marie, love sometimes over rides common sense.

The debate was about to begin. The emcee of the debate was before the cameras, the audience was seated and ready for the show. The three candidates were all separated in the rear behind the stage. The host of the show stood poised and ready as the cameras began running.

"Ladies and Gentleman as per a special request from the two highest ranking candidates as per our latest figures in the polls we have a special treat in store for this evening's debate. Unlike past debates, which have used pre-selected questions for each candidate to answer, we will open this debate with an audience question and answer session first. To be fair I as emcee of the debate will pick the members of the audience to ask the questions." This first statement by the emcee was then followed by the candidate's introduction.

"It is time now to meet the candidates. First, we will introduce the man who is currently on the bottom of the totem pole. 'Nothing like stabbing at Rune's American Indian heritage." Mr. Rune of the Common-Cents Party."

Rune entered from back stage in a brown long tailed Edwardian coat outfit, complete with top hat. His light brown outfit trimmed in dark brown silk on the lapels and a white shirt with small ruffles running down the length of the buttons and at the end of the sleeves. His tie consisted of a brown narrow silk affair tied in a bow shape around the large color of his shirt. He waved to the crowd and most of the audience clapped and cheered his rather abstentious entrance.

The emcee doing his best to hold his composure during this rather rambunctious entrance then introduced the other two candidates. Both the candidates entered dressed in conservative suits and ties to a polite applause from the audience.

Rune was all smiles and ready to go. He could be seen quivering like a dog that was excited that his owner had come home. The opposing candidates were standing stone cold and looked to be ready for a tough battle. The emcee than had the lights turned up so that he could view the audience. It was time for a short question and answer session.

Of course, the audience members with questions and the emcee had been well briefed by the Democrats and the Republicans. It may also be mentioned that all the people involved were well compensated. The questions directed at those Democratic and Republican candidates were pretty general and easy to answer. Things like, what kind of dog will be the 'first' dog of the white house? Do you think your wife will want to re-decorate any of the White House rooms? For Rune, the questions came as direct frontal attacks.

First question. "Rune you have projected yourself as a God-fearing everyday American. Is it not true that you are divorced, and does this not go against you beliefs in the Ten Commandants and the bible? Also why did you hide this information from the public?"

Rune's answer. "First I did not hide the information. It was available to anyone who asked. Up to this point, it had not come up so I am glad that you have asked about it. Yes, I am divorced. It was not by choice. I would have preferred to have attended counseling with my spouse and worked it out. Unfortunately, Minnesota has a no-fault divorce law. If one member of a married couple wants a divorce there is nothing the other member can do to stop it. I do not agree with that law but as an American Citizen, I had no choice but to obey it. I only hope that the Lord will understand when the time comes. I would not wish for anyone to have to go through a divorce, it is painful and heart wrenching. Just to clarify the record I am not perfect, I'm just one of those sinners spawned by Adam and Eve, I just do my best not to make the same mistakes twice."

Second Question. "Mr. Rune your academic record shows you were an average 'B' student. You only had two and a half years of college. Do you really believe you are smart enough to run a country like the United States?"

"I have to admit I was not a whiz kid. I saw school as something that I had to do. I did well enough, but certainly not up to my potential. I took a three-year course in a Business College and finished in two and a half years with a degree in accounting. I was a 'B' student there too. I tried hard but that was the best I could do. As far as running the country, I believe it to be a team effort. I have been a top salesman in a number of retail and wholesale business. To be on the top you need to build a team that works with you. That would be my goal as President. Surround myself with the brightest most aggressive team players I can find. With the top people as my coaches and the American people as our team we would do the best we can."

Third and last question. Candidate Rune. "I have heard from a reliable source that you were in jail for a gambling offense. Would you like to explain?"

"It seems that for some strange reason the questions I am asked are aimed at my moral and personnel intelligence and integrity. I am sure my two colleagues that are here are glad they're questions were so simple and easy to answer. Maybe I am just being paranoid. I would love to answer your question."

"The gambling issue was a part of my younger days. The state of Minnesota had a law that allowed legal gambling in a person's home or at a private party. Now life and rules are not always black and white. Being young and foolish I occasionally ran slot machines for extra cash. It was definitely a 'grey' area, not black and white, somewhere in the middle; in fact, it was probably a dark shade of grey. I hired out to run a number of slot machines at a local bar. They had closed the bar to the public and the party was open only to invited guests. You had to have a ticket to get in. No walk-ins just those who had pre-purchased tickets for the nights party. Unfortunately, the local police felt this party was more on the black side of the law then on the grey side. The police busted the party, cops, dogs, swat team, the whole works. It was a bust fit for prime time television. The next morning's newspapers gave my slot machines and myself front page news."

"I helped the police load my slot machines up into my truck and delivered them to the police station. I was read my rights but never charged with anything. I called the states attorney general the next day. It was back to grey area. Did the police have the right to raid a private by invitation only party? The big question was, could a private party be held in a normal place of business? The attorney General did not want to make this a major issue and drafted a letter to me to present to the Chief of Police that would release my slot machines and close the case."

"This is where I learned something about local corruption. I presented my letter from the attorney general to the Police Chief. He was of course not too happy about giving me my slot machines back. Then he requested that the machines be emptied of all their money. I did as requested and ran the money through the coin counter. A little over seven-hundred dollars had been collected in about two hours of running time. I was then told that the money was not to be released. This is when the story gets interesting."

"It seems that in all the dirt digging, and muck finding that my questioners have come up with they missed this one. When I asked for the money from the slot machines to be receipted to me in writing I was told there would be no receipt. This of course seemed a little odd. When I proceeded to push the issue of the receipt I was told they could charge me with other things."

"Things like pimping and prostitution. For at the private party they had exotic dancers. The chief of police wanted to know about my involvement with these dancers. It seems two of the dancers had prior prostitution records. I told the chief that must mean the third dancer was a virgin. The chief did not seem to like that comment. His next move was to threaten me with more charges on the dancer or gambling issues, unless of course I left without a receipt for my money. I did the prudent thing even though I had no involvement with the ladies in question and loaded up my slot machines and left. I assume the police chief and his officers had a nice party with the non-receipted cash that they now had in their possession. That was the day I learned not to trust the police."

"The next day I was front page news. I was a security officer for a large firm at the time. Even though I had no charges against me and my machines were released I was demoted to night shift at my job. They felt I was a bad example and made sure I was punished. At that time, there were no laws to protect a worker from this type of treatment. I learned a lot from that experience."

'I hope all of you questioners got the dirt out in the open. I figured I might as well toss in that last little tid-bit of information to save you from having to dig it up later. For all my supporters let it be known that yes I was young and foolish. I learned a lot of life's lessons and I hope I can use them to make a better country for us all in the future."

The rest of the debate went as planned. Questions about economic problems, trade deficits and all the other things the country has to worry about. Rune held his ground and reasserted his stands as straightforward and honest. No punches pulled. Americans would have to suffer from the economic crisis that they had made for themselves. Buying more than they could ever afford, and spurred on by a government who set that example. The country cannot survive being in debt, it is time to pay off our bills and straighten things out. The government, and the people, may all have to learn to live with less. Our grandparents and many of those still living went through the great depression of the 1920's. They survived, and they learned to help each other. They were the Americans who kept this country strong. They took responsibility for themselves. This is what the country once again needs to do. Rune is the man to get things rolling.

CHAPTER 9

All parties involved anxiously awaited the outcome of the most recent polls after the big debate. News stations, newspapers, radio; the talk of the country was Rune's big debut on a national debate. Of course, the major discussion was whether the other parties had set up Rune for a fall or were the questions he had to answer just coincidence. The majority of talk seemed to favor Rune as the low man on the totem pole who every other political party was trying to cut down. Good or bad, the polls would tell.

The next day the figures came in. The Republicans and Democrats were strong on the East and West coast. The Common-Cents party did a major sweep of the Midwest and southern states. Rune and his party had a surprising twenty-nine percent of the poll figures. With the election only a few months away the big political parties knew they had to stop this upstart Common-Cents party no matter what it took.

Marie and her boyfriend returned to an upbeat situation for her party members. She was excited, yet she felt that somehow she might have had something to do with the near downfall of Rune at the political debate. Her boyfriend had now moved to the position of her fiancé. His bosses had him spending as much time with Marie as possible. They needed more dirt on Rune. If this could not be accomplished other measures would become necessary. Marie, so much in love could not see that her fiancé's questions were more than just interesting conversation. Her fiancé's lawyer bosses were now on a full time high paying payroll of the opposition parties. The legal firm would be rich if they could stop Rune and the Common-Cents party. Legally they could do anything and get away with it. A politician and a lawyer make for an evil and sometimes lethal combination.

Marie had resumed her position at the party headquarters. Valerie was her right hand gal. Rune and Olaf still liked to sneak out and go motorcycle riding whenever time would allow. Marie's fiancé was starting to take an extreme interest in the boy's motorcycle trips. When did they go, where did they go, and what roads did they take? He slipped this into his conversations with Marie as often as he could. His detailed notes would hopefully lead to a pattern.

Marie had told her fiancé that Rune was heading to a small town that night. He was to be a substitute player on a local dart league. The evening was warm and the night was beautiful. Rune would surely be on his one of his collection of motorcycles. There was only one road that went to the town he was to play darts at. Marie's fiancé asked to borrow her car as his was low on gas. He told her he had a business meeting at his office. It would not take more than an hour and he would be back. Marie, as gullible as ever loaned him her silver Toyota.

It was cool pleasant night. The sun was just setting and the sky was a beautiful red color off to the west. The roads were clear and dry. Rune picked his Goldwing motorcycle for the night's trip. The area he was headed to had a lot of wetlands and large farm fields along the way. The Goldwing afforded the best protection against the millions of bugs that would be hovering over the warm black asphalt road. There was no traffic and Rune cruised comfortably along at sixty miles per hour. The bugs quickly coated his windshield, the airflow over the windshield and his helmet kept his vision of the road ahead clear.

The road was typical back country. A few side roads, usually gravel, intersected with this main stretch of tarmac. Rune kept his lower running lights on so that the ditches were illuminated. At this time in the evening deer and small animals were more of a hazard then cars. Anyway, cars would have their headlights on and be easy to spot.

However, one car did not have its headlights on. It was not even moving. The car was sitting on the side road idling. Some low trees would block it from view to any vehicle approaching on the main road. The driver of this car watched in anticipation of a headlight approaching. Specifically a single two wheeled vehicle. Prime target for the night.

As Rune approached the seldom used intersection, his vision caught the shape of a large dark shadow. No lights but it had to be a car. It pulled right out in front of Rune, why it did not even slow down for the stop sign that should have held it back. The cars speed and angle on the road was the perfect ingredient for an accident. The car had slowed to a crawl; Rune was maybe five-hundred feet away doing sixty miles per hour. His hand and foot automatically started braking the big Goldwing. He could feel the tires locking up, the linked braking system kept him in a straight line. By now, the whole thing seemed to be going in slow motion in his mind. Forty years of riding motorcycle had tuned his instincts to take over. No time to stop, should he veer left or right, which way the car was the going to go. Taking some pressure off the brakes he took a hard left up the gravel road the car had came from. His left foot peg scraped the tar as sparks flew into the air. He fought to keep the bike upright as it slid hard onto the gravel. Finally, it was over. By some miracle, he had the bike at a dead stop. Still upright, he turned to see that the car had disappeared. His body shaking he looked up at the sky. "Thank you Lord" was all he could say.

Thinking about what just happened had Rune worried. His friends and supporters had put so much time and effort into his campaign. He had to keep himself safe now for all those people. Up until this time, he had only to worry about his two dogs Sven and Lena. Everything was different now. Most of all he did not like having to be so responsible.

Keeping his speed down to about forty-five miles per hour, he continued on to his scheduled dart game. Two miles from his destination, he sees the head lights of an approaching car. The car seems to be straddling the middle line of the road. Most likely, some dummy on a cell phone or worse a drunk driver. Rune slows the Goldwing down and edges to the right side of the road. With all the extra lights on the Goldwing, it looked like the Las Vegas strip. A cell phone user or drunk should be able to see it. Suddenly the approaching vehicle turns its headlights off. It takes direct aim at Rune and the Goldwing. At the last moment, Rune twists the Goldwing's throttle and drives it down into the ditch. He hears the tires on the car squeal from the near miss. The Goldwing's front tire catches in a rut at the bottom of the ditch. Losing his balance Rune and the Golding tip over onto the long grass. Rune lies still for a few minutes, the Goldwing's tilt sensor shuts the bike off. The Goldwing lights are still on as Rune stands up and watches the car that just missed him turn its lights back on as it continues speeding away.

Next Rune does the old pick-up your motorcycle trick. He bends his knees, squats down with his back against the motorcycle, and pushes the Goldwing to an upright position. Once back on the bike his best recourse was to put the Goldwing in reverse and back it out of the rut that the front tire was in. Then he gunned the engine just enough in first gear to get out of the ditch and back up on the road.

One narrow escape for the night seemed to be just bad luck. Two narrow escapes had Rune worried. Was this a coincidence or was someone out to get him. Arriving at the local town liquor establishment, he went in to meet his dart partners. Rune was still shaky but figured it best not to mention what had happened. A couple SvenBrew Submarine Olive beers would calm him down.

Marie's fiancé came in and gave her a hug and kiss. He was a little agitated. His excuse was he had a bad meeting with his boss that night. Just a disagreement on how to finalize a problem case. No big deal, it would work out later. Then he wanted to get romantic. Marie feeling bad for him did her best to comfort him. She even tried to ignore him when he kicked her poor old big black dog. She loved him, even though her dog looked at her with his "what are you, blind" sadness in his eyes.

Rune and his dart team played well that night. Five out of seven games of cricket. Rune's trusty set of Dart World Dartpire darts even netted him a hat trick for the evening. His ride home was slow and long. Every set of headlights and every intersection had him on edge. That night in bed, he cuddled up with his two dogs and held them tight. They were the only two beings in his life that he dared to tell about his narrow escapes. From now on, he knew he had best not travel alone.

Every day the polls showed an increase for the Common-Cents party. Marie came to work less often and Valerie took on a major load of Marie's work. Rune, Olaf and Travis started out on a last major campaign run.

They would load up their motorcycles with gear and make a complete outer circuit of the United States. Heading east to Maine, down the coast through the southern states, up to Oregon and then back to Minnesota. They had no huge planned gatherings. Each town got a few minutes of their time. They walked the main streets, had lunch in local café's, and talked to the local newspaper in town. Soon everyone came to know them common folks, available to anyone to talk to or have a picture taken with the locals. The kids got to climb on the boys motorcycles and if time permitted, might even get a short ride. Photos of the boys on their trip soon were everywhere. On the internet, newspapers and of course every television channel in the country. Once again, free publicity supplied by regular everyday Americans using everything from cameras, to cell phone cameras to camcorders. For two weeks, the boys rode, saw the county, and made thousands of new friends and supporters. Valerie, Marie, and Boone were holding down the fort at the Dog's Breath Saloon headquarters. Election time was now less than eight weeks away.

Marie's fiancé was now asking her constant questions about the activities that were taking place. Rune was seldom alone anymore. The legal group in town had to act fast to stop the Common-Cents party. The best means of doing this was to eliminate Rune. It was up to Marie's boyfriend to accomplish this job. Using Marie was by far the easiest way to set up Rune. Risking her for the huge reward that awaited him would be more then worthwhile. After all, if he had enough money any woman he wanted he could have. As a bonus, maybe he could even get to kill that big stupid dog of Marie's.

Time for the election was getting much to close for comfort. Marie's fiancé had to work fast. All his questions and probing told him that Rune was seldom if ever alone anymore. Therefore, the fiancé came up with a drastic but sure-fire plan to eliminate Rune once and for all. He told Marie he could wait no longer. They must get married right away. She settled for a wedding dress she really did not like. The church and reception was satisfactory. The bad part was the wedding would be in fourteen days. Not enough time for invitations and guests to plan to attend. She had a bad feeling, but she still felt she loved this guy and just wanted him to be happy. Of course, the Common-Cents party members would be there. Finally, they would meet this Mr. Right. Mr. Right's ten-year-old daughter would be the brides-maid. If nothing else, Marie felt good about the little girl. In fact, she was really more in love with having a child then a husband. Something she would not admit even to herself.

The day of the wedding Rune, Olaf, and Travis drove their motorcycles. Valerie and Boone came in Valerie's Honda CRV. It was at one of the many Catholic churches located throughout town. In fact, it was at the church where Marie had met her intended and his little girl. The Common-Cents party members made a polite but bold statement in their dress for the occasion. The guys all had black slacks, black shirts, and white ties. Valerie had a long dark skirt with a matching dark grey silk blouse. This group of Marie's closet friends felt this was more of a 'wake' than a wedding. Although they all did their best to try and be happy for Marie.

Marie's fiancé had his co-workers and bosses from the legal firm as ushers and attendants. They made sure everyone was in the church and seated. Once this was accomplished, Marie's fiancé stepped out the side door of the church and went directly to Rune's Goldwing. He loosened the side cover and attached a wad of plastic explosive with a small timer attachment right under the seat close to the gas tank. In ninety minutes, the Common-Cents party would no longer have a presidential candidate.

Everything about the wedding had been planned to the second. The ceremony, the reception line, and the trip to the reception hall. All this had to be done and on the way in one hour and fifteen minutes. The reception was thirty minutes away. This would put Rune and his goldwing at that halfway point between the church and the reception hall. If all went according to plan, a faulty gas tank would take the blame for the explosion. As an added bonus, the explosion may even take out Olaf and Travis.

At the reception hall, Marie's new husband was forcing drinks down her as quickly as possible. He hoped to keep her in a state of confusion as long as he could. His daughter kept trying to keep her new stepmother near her and away from all the drinking. The poor little girl only received reprimands from her father to leave her stepmother have fun. The already growing group of people at the reception hall become suddenly silent. An explosion was heard that shook the glasses and silverware of the hall. Looking out the windows and doors of the hall the guests could see a pall of black smoke rising into the sky. The newlywed husband and his co-workers all tried to hide their smiles.

The legal group of conspirators quickly got the party rolling. Nothing to worry about, maybe an old car or gas can explode. No need to ruin a marriage celebration. Certainly, nothing happened that should concern the newlyweds or their guests.

CHAPTER 10

The wedding reception was going splendidly. Dancing, drinking, eating, everyone seemed to be having a good time. Valerie and Boone were somewhat worried about Rune, Olaf, and Travis. Then again they figured they may have left their dislike for Marie's new husband over ride their sense of duty to attend the reception.

Police, fire, and ambulance sirens filled the air outside the reception hall. The legal eagle friends of the grooms kept the doors closed in the building and made sure the music was loud to drown out the siren noises. To the legal group the wedding was just a side light to the joy they felt at eliminating Rune. After all, with Rune gone the legal boys would all be set for life financially.

Marie spent a lot of time talking to Valerie and Boone. It was easy to see that she was distressed that her best friends had abandoned her at her wedding reception. Was it anger or hurt she felt the most? She was not sure. She tried to concentrate on her new stepdaughter and make sure she was having a good time and not left out of the festivities. Her new husband kept pouring drinks down her to get her good and drunk. If she was passed out by the time the news of Rune and his friends reached the reception, well, all the better.

The groom with dollar signs in his mind had his own plans. He would now be a full-fledged partner in the law firm. Big fancy house, expensive cars, a few servants to keep things up. The good life. Marie was just a new piece of property now. Even if he were ever connected to the death of Rune, his legal firm would wiggle out of that. If Marie found out or even suspected, why she was his wife, well legally, a wife could not testify against her husband. If she threatened to do anything, he would only have to make his daughters life miserable to keep Marie in line. He knew as well as Marie did that his daughter's happiness was more important to Marie then it was to him. Marie was now just another belonging for him to show off. Yes, for the new groom life looked great.

The plane tickets were in the Groom's pocket. Four weeks of the wonderful life, they would travel all through Europe on their honeymoon. His daughter, he had relatives that would take her for now. No use on bringing a kid on your honeymoon. When they returned he would hire a nanny to keep his child occupied. Life was too short and he was too young to have to be weighted down by a child. He had been stuck full time with the kid since his first wife meant her untimely death. The time was now for some freedom and fun. He had the money to fulfill his wildest dreams, yes, nothing could go wrong now.

The newlyweds left the reception after about three hours. Marie's stepdaughter was pawned on some pre-arranged relatives of the grooms. They reached the airport with little time to spare. Once on the plane and then to Europe Marie's husband would do everything he could to keep the fate of Rune from her ears. In Europe, it may make the news for a day or two, than it would be quickly forgotten. As a husband, he could certainly keep her busy for the first two days. If nothing else, he would just tell her that they should shut out the world's problems and enjoy themselves. No news, no newspapers, just a carefree life. Yes sir, he figured he was a genius extraordinaire.

CHAPTER 11

Rune, Olaf and Travis mounted their bikes and visited while the traffic leaving the parking lot of the reception hall thinned out. The marriage was not on their list of things they wanted to see. The groom just did not seem to be very trustworthy. To Rune and Olaf, it was a sad union that took place. They both looked at Marie like family, and family has a basic human emotion to protect each other.

Finally, the boys started their motorcycles and headed to the reception hall. Anyone that knows Rune will readily admit that he has the biggest, softest, kindest heart in the world when it comes to animals. It does not matter what kind of animal, dog, cat, rabbit, gerbil, crow or in this case a turtle.

About half way to the reception Olaf and Travis were side by side on their motorcycles sharing a lane of the road. The large ten inch round turtle was straight ahead and dead center in the middle of their lane. They both swung out to the side and gave the poor critter a wide berth of safety.

Rune was farther back and saw what the boys had swerved their bikes to miss. Braking hard, he pulled his Goldwing to the shoulder of the road. He stopped almost even with where the turtle was trying to make its way across the warm asphalt. Cars were still coming from both directions as Rune held out his hand in a motion to stop the oncoming car in the turtle's lane. The car did stop as Rune rushed onto the road and scooped the turtle up in one hand. The other side of the road was temporarily clear as Rune carried his little hard-shelled friend to the other side of the road. He made his way down the embankment to the swampy area and gently left the non-to-smart painted turtle down on the wet weeds to swim happily away for another day of life catching minnows and eating aquatic plants.

As Rune made his way back up the embankment the earth shook, the sound of a hundred thunders and a flash of a thousand lightning bolts seemed to fill the air. A shower of melted plastic, rubber, and hot metal rained from the smoke filled sky. Rune instinctively ducked behind a large rock off to his side. On the road, Olaf and Travis witnessed the same explosive fury as Rune as they both leaped from their motorcycles and took refuge in the roadside ditch.

Cars had stopped; the area was eerily silent for a few minutes. Everyone living thing in the area was in silent shock. Rune finally peeked over the rock towards the road. His Goldwing was gone. In its place was a small pile of burning gas and derbies. The other parts of the Goldwing were spread in a quarter mile radius. Small pieces of rubber, metal and plastic still red hot and smoldering into nothingness.

Cell phones must have been buzzing into 911 at a furious rate. Already sirens of fire trucks, police, and ambulances could be heard. All converging on the spot that just a short while ago held a beautiful illusion blue Goldwing.

Olaf and Travis had located Rune and were guarding their leader for his own safety. The police and ambulance personnel were all over Rune. Was he hurt, what happened, who did this? The firefighters were spread out all over extinguishing small fires and cooling down hot pieces of metal with handheld fire extinguishers. The police were detouring traffic around the area. Yellow tape with 'keep out' was strung quickly around the perimeter of the area. A bomb squad and swat team truck were called into investigate the area.

Rune and the boys were whisked off in a police car to the local police station for questioning. What happened, a bomb? Maybe a missile like a bazooka. A malfunction on the Goldwing? What had caused the bike to explode like that? Why did Rune just happen to be off the bike when it happened? Was this a publicity stunt? An accident? Alternatively, an attempted murder?

Outside the police station, the news crews and newspaper people had already camped out. Journalist from all over the country were on their way to the scene. Everyone wanted answers. Including Rune, Olaf, and Travis.

With the Rune's sense of honesty from his campaign and local knowledge about him, the police were inclined to eliminate a publicity stunt. The chance of a Goldwing blowing up all by itself was remote to non-existent in theory. A missile also seemed farfetched. A bomb, now that seemed like a possibility. Until the answer was found, the boys were to be held in protective custody. They settled the boys into an open jail cell. No phone calls, no public contact until there were some answers. The three of them knew that Marie, Valerie, and Boone were going to be furious when they did not show up at the reception. No matter how hard the boys tried to convince the law enforcement people that they should notify their friends that they were detained, it was not going to happen. The less people that knew about this the better the chances they may have in catching them. If the culprits thought that Rune or his friends were dead, they may just make some mistake to give themselves away.

The press outside was sure that someone important was in the jail and that 'someone' had something to do with the explosion just outside of town. So far, it was only speculation. The police were doing well at keeping the identities of their voluntary prisoners secret. At least for a little while.

As Valerie and Boone left the reception hall, two men dressed in plain old everyday suits approached them. The men flashed their badges and identified themselves as police detectives. They requested that Valerie and Boone come with them to the police station. Of course, the request was more of an order; they had no choice in the matter.

Valerie and Boone of course had to with hold the anger they had about the boys missing the reception. After all, they had more than a good reason for not showing up. The police wanted to hush up the involvement of a political party member in this incident until more evidence became known. The police station had a garage entrance that the press and media were not watching. This was ideal for smuggling out individuals that the police needed to protect. Valerie and Boone had been brought into this garage entrance under cover. They would now leave the same way. Rune and Olaf were fitted with police officer uniforms and allowed to drive out on two police motorcycles. What a great disguise, and the boys loved getting to play with the two Harley Davidson police cruisers. Travis, dressed as a bum with floppy hat and oversize suit coat left with one of the officers in a private car about a half hour later.

A private meeting at Rune's home that evening consisted of the four other Common-Cents members, the state's governor, and assorted law officials. Like it or not Rune was to have twenty-four hour protection assigned to him. The party members felt this was not an expense that the taxpayers should have to borne. The officials soon convinced them that anytime a citizen was in danger that this was a necessary step, and that is what the police were there for. It was something that was built in to their emergency budget. Reluctantly Rune and his party agreed. The party now had two new members. Adam and Scotty would be Rune's pretend press agent and transportation guide. Both would be glued to Rune like a fly to flypaper.

The newlyweds were flying across the ocean on their way to their honeymoon. The groom had no knowledge that his plan had gone awry. Tomorrow all would be like normal. The local crooked nasty law breaking legal group of the grooms was in for a very nasty surprise. Rune was alive and kicking. More determined than ever to finally win this election.

The next day, work at the campaign headquarters was resumed as if nothing had happened. For the next three days, things went at a normal pace. Boone was busy watching, checking, and tabulating the latest figures from the polls. Valerie and Travis were working on more interviews and personal appearances. Adam and Scotty were busy sticking their noses into every aspect of the operation as possible. Rune and Olaf played darts and talked about the steps to be taken if they actually were to be elected to the White House.

Meanwhile the scene of the explosion looked like the Oklahoma land rush. There were people everywhere. Police officers, federal agents, bomb specialists, metallurgy experts, rubber and plastic experts, bomb sniffing German Sheppard dogs, and caterers to feed all these people. The road was temporally closed and detours were set up. From the swamp a tiny head occasionally popped to the surface to watch all the activity. Yes sir, that poor turtle had to wonder if he had been the cause of all this fuss.

At the lawyers office in town things were non-too pleasant. The word was out that Rune and company were alive and well. Their hatchet man the groom and his new bride were in Europe undercover. They had left no way to reach them in case any suspicion should be aroused. Of course, that was the plan all along to keep Marie in the dark and unaware of Runes untimely demise. The people that hired the legal group wanted answers, and they wanted answers now. All involved knew that by now, the federal agents were involved and Rune would be watched like a hawk. The chances of getting rid of the Common-Cents party were now nil to zero.

The next three days produced enough evidence from the bombsite to piece together the scenario of what had happened. Sometime from the time Rune had arrived at the church for the wedding and his leaving the parking lot a bomb had been planted. Interviews with the ushers had confirmed that all the guests and the wedding party were in the church. Of course, the ushers were all part of the legal group that was arranging the bombing in the first place. What the heck, they were all legal aids or lawyers, what is a little perjury to them, they will buy their way out of it.

The final analysis figured that someone had planted a bomb near the gas tank of the Goldwing. Residue of plastic explosive and small fragments of a timer had been located at the bombsite. This was a clear-cut case of attempted murder. The motive was yet to be ascertained. Was it personal against Rune or politically motivated, the consensus of the law enforcement people and the federal agents was confirmed after Rune told them about his close calls from the night he went to play darts. Someone wanted Rune dead. Politics seemed to be the prime suspect. Knowing how politicians worked the federal agents knew that the trail would be well concealed. Whoever was trying to eliminate Rune was most likely a local acquaintance who would know of his movements and habits. Bank accounts and phone records were being scrutinized, any possible shred of evidence had to be searched for.

As for our legal eagle group, they were smart enough to keep all money coming in on a cash basis. By promoting the new bridegroom that would account for any extra cash, he might be spending. They felt safe and secure. Only one problem was still open in their minds. They had not completed their job. The people that hired them would not by very understanding. By the time the newlyweds would return the election would be over. The bridegroom was in deep trouble from his own bosses, plus the large political organization that had paid him to complete a job.

As for Rune, he was getting a feel of what it was like to be an important politician in America. With two full time bodyguards, he started to feel like a prisoner. Progressive Insurance was very understanding about the loss of Rune's Goldwing. He had a check in his hands for the bike within five days. Rune, Scotty and Adam made a trip to Rune's old boss to purchase a new Goldwing. The old boss even got a new motorcycle for Rune at cost. It would be at least a week to install all the accessories Rune had to have. In the meantime, Rune started driving his Honda Silverwing scooter with sidecar. A rather obnoxious and visible unit on the road. Bright yellow with checkered taxicab stripes and a light up taxi sign on the cowling of the sidecar. Scotty and Adam took turns riding in the sidecar while Rune drove. Whichever agent was not with Rune was loaned a Honda 250 rebel by Rune so that he could come with and do his 'protect Rune job.'

Less than a week remained before the final election. The Common-Cents party was riding high in the polls. Like it or not the American people were lending their support to a semi-redneck, brutally honest straight up candidate. All this even in the face of a temporary downslide of living conditions, credit limits, and possible job losses. Bailing out poorly run businesses or giving out cash stimulus payments from money the county did not have was to put it mildly, 'stupid.' Some suffering from the American people to hopefully gain an independent strong United States. Depression be damned. Common-Cents made perfect sense.

CHAPTER 12

It was the eve of the election. The Dog's Breath Saloon was packed with well-wishers. Boone was in charge of monitoring the election results. A big screen television was set up on the bar so everyone could see Boones computer screen as he tallied the incoming results. SvenBrew beer and Beertzel pretzels were on the house. Rune and Olaf tried to calm down with a few games of darts. The first few hours showed the eastern states favoring the opposition. The Midwest was strong for Common-Cents. Overall, it was much too close to call for any definite party.

Finally, Rune and Olaf went outside and sat on their motorcycles to relax. The Dog's Breath Saloon was too crowded and much too stuffy. Rune looked up at a clear starry sky. Not a cloud anywhere. The moon was about three quarters out. A slight breeze stirred the air. It was the kind of night that would be nice to share with someone you loved. Not a night to be wasted on election results. For Rune and Olaf, maybe the loneliness of not having girlfriends would be overshadowed by becoming President and Vice-President of the United States of America. Ok, so they were losers in love, maybe they would be winners to the average working class Americans. If so, they would spend the next four years doing their best to rebuild this great country into something Americans could be proud of.

Valerie and Travis came out of the Dog's Breath Saloon looking for Rune and Olaf. Scotty and Adam were sitting with their backs against the fence that surrounded the parking lot. They pointed at two big lumps on the grass. Rune and Olaf had lain down on their backs to gaze at the sky and fell asleep.

Travis slowly trickled some SvenBrew from his mug onto Rune's face to awaken him. Rune sat up with a start. Olaf awoke to the noise of Rune cussing out Travis. Marie, Scotty, and Adam were teary eyed with laughter.

"Wake up you two bums. It is two in the morning and we are just over two percent in the lead. A few more hours and you guys might be in the Oval office." said Travis.

This was almost beyond the boys wildest dreams. They all went back inside to see what the next few hours would bring. The smell of stale beer and sweaty bodies in the crowded saloon made the place very appropriate to its name by this time. The crowd opened up and gave the members of the Common-Cents party a prime table in the middle of the room. Every eye was glued on the big screen TV. Boone was updating figures as fast as he could. A few more hours would give the world an answer. Just who was going to be President? The Republican Party was slipping fast. It was showdown time, Democrats or Common-cents. If nothing else, Common-Cents had certainly made its mark in history.

By six am, the streets around the Dog's Breath Saloon were jammed with traffic and people. The police were on hand trying to control the crowds. Win or lose the Common-Cents party was now a dominate factor in American politics.

Boone updated the numbers as fast as he could. Rune was making slow gains even in strong Democratic territories. The Republicans had announced a heart breaking defeat. Then in a surprise move by the Republican Party, they urged their followers who had not yet voted to support the Democrats. They urged the public to keep the country as they thought it should be, two parties only. The message was flashed across the country to any remaining voters. Both the Democrats and Republicans literally tossed money into last minute ads and messages. If you vote Common-Cents, it will "Rune" America.

To the Common-Cents party the advertisements sounded self-defeating, how could having common sense be a bad thing for the country. If only the average American citizen felt the same way.

CHAPTER 13

Not only did the average American citizen's feel right about Common-Cents, the big surprise came when the Electoral votes were counted. Common-Cents won the election. It was not a landslide, but it was enough to cinch the Presidency of the United States for Rune and company. What had started as a fun game of politics in a local bar just turned into a very serious position of responsibility for all involved.

Rune and Olaf were now the two most important people in the United States. The way Secret Service people and the media flocked towards the two reluctant heroes of the day proved that their lives would never be the same.

The Common-Cents party refused to move to more secure headquarters. All the regular customers that came to the Dog's Breath Saloon were registered and investigated by the Secret Service. Their names then were kept on a register at the Saloon so they could still come and go as they please. The party members still played darts and pool, had drinks and snacks. Now the group listened to the concerns of all that they knew. Somewhere they had to start formulating how to drastically change an overindulged selfish country into a self-supporting, out of debt respectable nation. A nation every citizen could be proud of. Cutting cost would be a top priority.

What was needed was a way to create more jobs for Americans. Boone researched some little known information that made a lot of sense. To some businesses, this would be costly; these businesses had been paying starvation wages and no taxes or insurance to millions of illegal immigrants. It was time to put a stop to this. The plan would be ready to put into action as soon as Rune and party took office. No more pussy footing around. If congress or the senate disagreed, Rune and Olaf would do fireside chats on television to garner the support of the American People. If it worked for President Reagan hopefully it would work for the Common-Cents party. If politicians wanted to keep their jobs it was time to do what the people wanted done. No kickbacks, no bribes just do what is right.

Cutting off countries with unbalanced trade would cause a hard blow for many Americans. Cheap goods from China would be almost non-existent. This would force Americans to make these items on our own shores, thus creating more jobs. It would also mean less health problems, less lead in toys and other products. No more tainted foodstuffs coming to our shores. Best of all our money could no longer help to fund the communist war machine in China or other countries.

Prisons, jails, and courts would have to become self-sufficient. Prisoners and inmates would produce what they needed to survive. A savings of millions and millions of dollars for the taxpayers. It would cost some big business' money in lost revenue, but it could be made up in supplying the prisons with the material they would need to be self-sufficient.

Gasoline would be a major obstacle. Cutting or equalizing trade with the Arab nations would be tough on everyone. It was time for gas rationing or higher prices at the pumps. For Americans that had made it through world war two this would be nothing new. For the rest of the baby boomers it was to be a hard reality to swallow. Higher gas prices and gas tax would be used to create a new system of mass transit. Monorails above ground for city-to-city travel. More and easier access to public transpiration. Many cities would return to electric trolley cars. Cheap and efficient with schedules to fit the areas rush traffic. Like the European countries, we would learn to cope with a new more efficient and cleaner world and environment.

All this information was available to the country so that it would be prepared for the changes when the Common-Cents party moved into the White house. The people would complain and grumble, it is the American thing to do. Rune and party were here to coach them and make

America a country of team players. Work together, trust each other, and weed out the bad elements. Utopia, probably not, a new safer cleaner country, "you betcha" said Rune.

CHAPTER 14

Inauguration day. Rune and Olaf were dressed in Victorian long tailed coats and clothes similar to those worn by Rune at the presidential candidate debates, only they switched the colors to light grey. Rune was never fond of flying, so a train with open observation car was dispatched to the St. Cloud, Minnesota east side Amtrak train depot. To the chagrin of the secret Service people Rune, Olaf, Travis, Valerie, and Boone all left from their home base at the Dog's Breath Saloon to the Depot on their motorcycles. Rune and Valerie shared the Goldwing, Olaf on his 'Kawasaki tribe" Indian with Boone as passenger and Travis on the Honda Spirit 750 bobber.

Along the route were crowds of cheering people. The Legal Eagles were in the crowd with their evil minions. Unfortunately for them security was better than they had been expecting. Any move by the Legal Eagles to harm Rune or his party would most likely lead to their own demise. They would have to wait for a better opportunity. Getting Marie back on the Common-Cents team at the White house would be their best bet.

The trip to Washington was pleasant and fun for all. Every whistle stop was met by crowds of cheering people. Rune looking like ex-President Ulysses S. Grant with his beard and Edwardian dress was quickly becoming the image of a new America.

As the party arrived at the White House plans were made that they would all be staying together. Rooms were set up for Rune, Olaf, Valerie, Boone, and Travis. One room left set and ready for the hopeful return of

Marie and her husband to complete the core ingredient of the new administration.

Marie's new husband finally received word of his failed plot to eliminate Rune. He had only one choice, figure out a way to infiltrate the new administration and bring it down. He and his new bride headed home as soon as possible. Marie called to congratulate her friends. Rune was only too happy to offer her the position that she held from the beginning of the campaign. Valerie needed help and Marie would be a welcome addition. Marie's husband was very supportive of Marie's wishes to return to work. The whole family could move to Washington and stay in the White House with the rest of the group. Maybe, Marie could talk to Rune and get her husband a job as legal adviser to Rune. Now wouldn't that be nice?

The inaugural ball was up next and the list of people wanting to attend was huge. Politicians, media people, movie stars, rock stars, foreign dignitaries. Where to start? Marie was now with the staff and her and Valerie started to whittle down the list of guests. Of course anytime a woman has a husband he is bound to get some input into what is happening. The legal eagle group from their old hometown somehow became invited guests. Their influence and proximity to the President could mean a quiet change of policies and pre-knowledge of actions that might just be very profitable. The big money that hired them was all for this new direction, Rune's life was safe from them, at least as long as they could use him and his staff.

Rune had final say on the movie star issue. Of course stars love to hob-nob with the president, its good publicity. Only Rune picked out the stars he wanted to be seen with, there were only two. Rune's favorite's, the king, and queen of horror, Bruce Campbell and Cassandra Peterson received personal invitations. As for the musical part of the festivities, Nancy Sinatra & Lee Hazelwood were asked to provide the great duets and fun music for the ball. Chuck Berry was to provide the Rock and Roll. For a fun musical interlude the Jack D'Johns from the east coast made a special appearance.

Only two hundred guests were invited. Tradition was broken immediately. It was to be casual, comfortable dress with buffet. A short thank you speech from Rune and Olaf then on to dinner and dancing. The media of course had a field day. The talk shows and newscasters condemned the whole affair as cheap and tawdry. The public loved it.

The first Monday after the Inaugural ball would be a day of strictly business. The Illegal immigrant issue was first thing on the list. Rune, Olaf, Marie, Valerie, Travis, Boone, and now Marie's husband as legal advisor would sit in on this decisive issue. Marie of course had asked a major favor of all her friends to allow her husband a place in the administration. Their hard heads and common sense said no. The soft spot and trust in their hearts for Marie said they should try to be nice to her new family. Anyway, Marie's new stepdaughter seemed to be a little sweetheart.

Boone had done a fantastic job of research into the illegal immigrant issue. This was not the first time the President and his administration had decided to deal with this issue.

During the Great Depression President Herbert Hoover ordered the deportation of all illegal aliens in order to make more jobs available for American Citizens who needed work.

Harry Truman deported over two million illegal aliens after World War Two to create jobs for veterans being released from the armed services.

As recently as 1954, President Dwight Eisenhower deported 13 million aliens. Giving World War Two and Korean War veterans and every other American a better chance at getting jobs.

It was time again to take our country back. Boone was put in charge of accessing computer records and start tracing down the illegals. Marie's husband was given the job of drawing up the legal paperwork to accomplish this.

Presented to congress and the Senate this bill would have no chance of passing. Marie's husband had already forwarded the minutes of the meeting to his legal eagle bosses within hours of the meetings finish. The legal eagles spread the word to their bosses immediately. This was a devastating bill to many of the filthy rich who ran companies exploiting the illegals. Congressmen and Senators were alerted. Lawyers all over the country who worked for the big business concerns went on standby.

Common-Cents or not the word was out to stop this action as soon as possible.

There was one old time White House employee who was loyal, honest, and upright. He had been on the White House staff for over thirty years. He was sort of a jack-of-all-trades doing whatever was required of him. He kept the staff informed of changes, checked to make sure everything was in its place and clean and neat. He really had no official title. He was a glorified gopher and get it done guy when it came to non-political items. He also seemed to know of everything that went on at the white House and any area even remotely connected to the political system in Washington, DC. He was just a middle-aged colored man, a shadow in the White House who heard it all and knew it all. Everyone trusted him. he was friends to the people that worked for all the higher ups on the Washington ladder. If you want to know what is happening, listen to the workers. That is what he did best. His name was Einer.

While everyone was settling in and getting down to business one important item was being over looked. The first dogs of the White House. Yes sir folks, there were first dogs. Three of them to be exact, all full bred Shih-Tzu's. If you go back to the title of this story, you will see that this is a Saga by Sven. That is me. I am one of the first dogs of the White House. There is me, my stepsister Lena and my cousin Oliver. Unfortunately, we are not the main characters in this Saga so we just get to have a cameo spot in this chapter. Enjoy us while you can. In a sad and unusual note, Marie's black dog somehow disappeared while she was on her honeymoon. No trace of the poor black mongrel was ever found. Of course we know Marie's husband was the prime suspect.

Einer was out in the yard checking to see that everything was in order when the three of us dogs started barking at him. Soon he was down on his knees and inviting us over to say hello. He seemed like a nice enough person and soon we were all wrestling and playing together. That is when Rune appeared.

Einer stood up, brushed himself off, and started to apologize for his un-professional behavior. Rune just laughed and told him no need to apologize. If the dogs liked Einer, Rune knew he was an ok guy. Rune told Einer that all three of us dogs were 'fixed' so there was no way we would 'bull Shih-Tzu.' Yes I know it sounds dumb but it was one of Rune's favorite sayings and he never missed an opportunity to use it.

Einer and Rune shook hands after a quick introduction. Then just like we were all old friends the two humans and us three dogs spent the next half an hour playing. This became a regular ritual for the next few weeks and Einer decided that Rune was a person of upright quality and morals. Finally Einer had a President as boss that he felt really cared about America and her people. He would make it a point to start funneling important information to Rune about the local happenings. With Boone monitoring the computers and Einer monitoring the people Rune was to have one of the best resources of information a President could ever hope for.

The illegal immigration issue was first on the list. Einer knew from his sources that the majority of lawmakers would kill this issue dead. Too many big business companies had invested in exploiting illegal's to let this happen. Favors were traded for votes as usual. The bill hit the house and was shot down by over a seventy-five percent majority.

It was time to reload the guns and try again. Fireside chat time. Every station in the country would carry the President's message live and directly to the people. Boone set up a web site for immediate response from the general public. It was time to sink or swim. If the public backed the Common-Cents party they were on all a roll that could last a full four years. If the public shot this down it would be an uphill battle all the way.

The big day for the fireside chat finally arrived. The President of the United States and the Common-Cents party were taking on the majority of the politicians in America. Lawyers sat eagerly ready to fight for all the big business concerns and flood the courts with lawsuits. For the lawyers it looked as if the world's biggest cash cow was about to arrive.

Rune was rightfully nervous this time. If the people did not support him, it would be political suicide. A large fire was blazing in the fireplace at one of the rooms in the White House. Rune took his place in a large brown leather chair with American eagles carved of wood on the ends of the arms. Cameras filled the room. No media people were allowed to attend. Rune's colleagues were all there except for one, which he asked not to attend. Therefore, Marie's husband had to sit this one out.

The cameras were less than a minute away from starting. Rune called Sven and Lena to his lap. He needed the moral support and love from his two dog kids. Lena curled up on his lap and Sven law along one arm of the chair. Rune now relaxed as he took turns stroking each of the dog's fur and scratching their ears. Three, two, one. Cameras rolling.

Rune, Sven and Lena the new first family of the White House. Operation jobs for Americans. The immediate deportation of millions of illegal immigrants. People who have taken the jobs that un-employed Americans not only need, they deserve to have these jobs. Americans deserve not only to have jobs but also to be paid a fair and equitable wage.

Illegals are using our roads, our services our medical care. Who is paying for all this? The American taxpayer. It is time for Americans to take back America. This means all Americans, black, white, red, yellow if you are an American take a stand. Eliminating millions of illegal's will bring down the cost of taxes by eliminating their freeloading on our systems, being it health care, insurance rates or cost to our infrastructure.

Please, all of you out there, email, call, write your legislatures. Tell them what you think. You pay their wages. You can bet the illegal immigrant does not pay any of their salaries. The American people must be heard and listened to.

Help the Common-Cents party to get this legislation passed now. Once we have won our first battle we can proceed to the next. There will then be new laws to save the American public even more money. Prisons, jails, prisoners, it is time they pay their own way and cover their cost of incarceration. Then they can start to make restitution for their wrong doings.

God Bless America.

Did the people listen? You bet they did. Telephone calls, emails, letters poured in to every lawmaker and politician in the land. The people wanted reform, the illegals must go. Of course, some of the bleeding hearts started a grass roots campaign to make everyone feel sorry for these poor down trodden illegals. Those are the same people who found out that driving a Hummer truck when gas costs $5 gallon is not to smart. Finally, after generations of keeping their mouths shut the average

American was fed up. It was time to take a stand for what was good for the country.

A special session was called for the Senate and Congress to address the situation. 'Illegal's out 'Was the title of the legislation." No add ons, no little hidden clauses, no pork barrel politics that you can have this if we can have that. Marie's husband wrote up the new legislation. The members of the Common-Cents party scrutinized every line of this new law. Marie's husband had to tell his bosses he was between a rock and a hard place. If he was to keep his inside job and spy on the Common-Cents party, he had to write this law up correctly.

It only took ten days of being hounded for the lawmakers to act. The bill was passed by a seventy percent majority. 'Illegal's Out' was now a law. The law enforcement offices and immigration had six months to enforce it and have the majority of the illegals gone. No ifs and or butts. Do your job or someone will be found that can. Those who do not like it will be welcome to visa's that will allow them to leave the United States and live elsewhere. Common-Cents wanted to be fair, if you do not like living in America, you can leave.

Once again. "God Bless America."

CHAPTER 15

The next item on the agenda was a little easier to shove through. Rune signed the documents to start bringing our American troops back home. With all the illegal's leaving, there would be lots of job openings. Sure, some would be menial jobs, but the American way has been start at the bottom and work your way up. This was true now for both the citizens and the country.

America was not at war with anyone. So why have troops out fighting. The United Nations of course was throwing a major fit over this. Our country would continue to leave troops where we were wanted in our allied countries. This troop concentration would be for passive protection. We were no longer going to fight other countries wars.

The prison issue was the next assignment. This would be another fight against big business and their lawyers. Common-Cents knew this was one issue that Americans had long been waiting to have addressed. Rune and party met again and Marie's husband drew up the legal documents. Once again, he made sure his legal eagle bosses had the information before it was made public. The word went out and the legal community and the big business boys were arming themselves for a battle. Big business verses the White House.

Marie's husband of course was the devil's advocate. Chain gangs, paying prisoners a wage, allowing prisoners outside of the prison walls were all bad things.

Rune and party had a plan though and it would address the major concerns of the new 'Cash for Incarceration' bill.

Marie's husband figured that for sure this new bill would be enough to put the big business concerns over the edge. Drastic action would be forthcoming. Most likely Rune would be back on the hit list. If so, his death could be worth millions of dollars. Certainly, a reward Marie's husband and his legal eagle associates would like to collect.

Only Rune and his associates tossed some provisions into their bill that may actually benefit the big business concerns. Prison yards would now be turned into farms, crops and animals would be raised for food. Prisoner labor would do the work. Public projects requiring menial labor would be assigned to prisoners. Chain gains would become common sights in the United States. Any business that needed low cost or temporary labor for jobs such as fruit or vegetable farms could hire prisoners at minimum wage. The earnings the prisoners make would be applied to their room, board, and restitution. Any money left over would go to the prisoner's bank account. An incentive for a prisoner to do well, work and have something to look forward to upon release. Like the rest of the United States, one important factor needed consideration. Incorrigible inmates or those on death row still did not pay for themselves. Therefore, every prisoner earning money would pay a small tax on their earnings to support the prisoners who were unable or too old to work. Big business now had no need to worry about filling jobs left by the illegals. A great asset for transient seasonal jobs. The catch was that this was only usable if the local work force was not filling those positions.

Marie's husband relayed the information to his superiors. They of course told all their cronies of the bill. Once again, a leak from the White House had the news available well before it was announced to the public. Only this time it did not matter so much. Sure, the big companies were not happy that they lost prison contracts for food, clothes, and goods. At least some of the companies would have available workers. The American public would no longer pay for people who were incarcerated. The saving for labor costs on public projects would save the taxpayers tons of money. Pros and cons aside. The new bill squeaked by the House and Senate. Rune and Party won a first great victory without having to resort to an open public fireside chat. The common person loved it. The bleeding hearts, well you know, the government is exploiting the poor prisoners. Prisoners rights are being violated, they should not be forced to work. The Common-Cents party answers with "being incarnated does not entitle anyone to a free ride."

Two wins chalked up for the new administration. No need to stop now. The next meeting of the party was going to be a tough one. This time Marie's husband would be an integral part for his legal knowledge. A moral problem would be a major issue with the new bill. Even Rune and his associates were not sure how to handle this one. The Ten Commandments and the bible's interpretation would be key issues. Right or wrong, how to punish lawbreakers was the issue at hand.

Certainly, this was a very touchy issue. Was it right that a jury of human peers had to make the decision of a person's future after they had found that person guilty of a crime. Especially in cases involving a life or death sentence. Did the government of the United States really have to force anyone to make such a moral judgment on another individual. Of course this was also true for the Judge in charge of the case, was it right to make him have to decide and rule on a person's fate.

The consensus among the Common-Cents party was that this current system of judgment was not right. It was wrong for people not even involved with the crime to have to make those judgments. On the one hand, they may be more objective by not knowing those involved. Then again, what about the rights of the victims. Should a victim or the victim's family not have a say in the sentencing of the guilty party. "Darn right they should have a say." Was agreed upon by all in the room. Well, except for Marie's husband who kept out of this conversation. It would be a step down in the lawyer's book of tricks to have this happen.

The meeting was adjourned for the night. Everyone wanted time to think out the right way to handle this situation. The next night the meeting was called to order. Down to the basement of the White House. Rune had requested the opening of a game room for meetings and at off time for the White house Staff to enjoy. A few games of bowling and some SvenBrews would help everyone to relax and get their old mind tickers working.

The matter was finally resolved about midnight. A jury would still be used in major crime cases. Twelve people would make the decision of guilty or not guilty. From this point on all evidence would be admissible, including past crimes and behavior. No more hiding facts from the jurors. No more twisting facts from lawyers. Witnesses would be able to tell all and not be cut off by some quick talking, serpent-tongued lawyers. Judges would be required to use common sense, let the truth be heard was the new law of the land.

Perjury from witnesses or lawyers would not be tolerated. Lawyers must now defend the case as it was. If the lawyer knew his client was guilty, he must enter the plea as such. The victim's lawyer, the victim, and their family would be the only ones to allow any type of plea-bargaining.

If a person were found guilty in case of bodily harm, or death, the victims and or the victim's family would make the decision of the punishment. A death for a death would be allowed. In that case, the victim or their family would be required to carry out the sentence. This way the moral judgment from God would rest on the minds and conscious of the victim and their family. Was the bible verse of 'An Eye for an Eye' literal or not. It would be between the decision makers and God.

Lesser crimes as theft would have a maximum restitution of twice the value of the item in question. Multiple offenders could serve jail time if the victims so requested. A panel of fifty average randomly chosen citizens would set up the terms of imprisonment based on number of instances and value of assets or cash involved. One citizen from each state, their name drawn in a lottery.

Lawyers and legal institutions were now to be held liable for misrepresentation of facts or hiding evidence. If a lawyer knew his client to be guilty, the client must be represented as such. The lawyer's job was now to try to convince the judge or jury that their client may deserve a lesser punishment. It was time to pay the piper. A criminal now has few rights left, the common American citizen now would once again have their rights represented and upheld.

The old saying of 'if you can't afford legal counsel it will be provided for you' was over. If you cannot afford counsel, you will represent yourself. Lawyers beware, outlandish lawsuits, class actions, hiding evidence will no longer be tolerated.

To top it off no more nuisance lawsuits. If you spill coffee on yourself, if you tip over your ATV, if you die of smoking, people are responsible for their own actions. If someone gets hurt on your property because they do something stupid, it is their fault not yours. If someone is robbing your house or threatening your family and you hurt them, it is their fault not yours. Justice for the innocent was the new rule of the land.

A kid buys alcohol with a fake ID. The kid is punished not the bar owner. A sixteen year old asks to buy tobacco, turn the kid in, the kids breaking the law, not the storeowner. The person drinks too much and smashes their car up, that person is responsible for their actions, not the person that sold or supplied the liquor. If you sell illegal drugs or buy them, both parties are guilty, treat them the same. Come on people, common sense.

Lawyers, crooks, and stupid people beware. The government for the people by the people has returned. The law of the land will prevail. Lawyers who are honest and upright have nothing to fear. The rest of them, well they will be treated like the scum of the earth that they have protected, be it a pickpocket or a big business corporate swindler, they all deserve what they get.

Marie's husband was white as a ghost. As well he should be. He knew he had to get this information to his partners and soon. Rune had now officially signed his own death warrant. Lawyers would unite to put this maniacal President to death as soon as possible. Every major dug and crime ring, every questionable big business company would donate money to put a price on the Presidents head.

When Rune was gone, Olaf would move up the ladder. If he tried to continue Rune's policies, he would be the next to disappear. Then the "Speaker of the House of Representatives" would take over as president. Whether the speaker was a Democrat or Republican would not matter. Every change that Rune and his party had accomplished could be declared un-constitutional once the crooked legal system got their hands on it. Then life would be back to normal. At least normal for the rich, the crooked and the lawyers that served them.

CHAPTER 16

Foreign trade, next on the agenda. This time Marie's husband raised red flags with his bosses even before the meeting was to happen. Money was coming in like a whirlwind with all the technology and trade that big business had set up in China. This income could not be lost. Rune had to be stopped before this next bill could be written and presented to the American public.

Marie's husband had to work fast. He had a meeting with his partners who made it clear that not only were they his partners, they were still the senior partners. They were his superiors and he must do as he is told. Marie's husband was put on a corporate legal eagle jet, of course paid for by the 'eliminate Rune contributors.' Next stop was mainland China.

Marie's husband was met at the airport by a long black Chinese built limousine. Next stop was an elaborate building that covered more land than the eye could see. Frisked, stripped and every crevice searched Marie's husband was then dressed in silk Chinese robes and placed at a seat of an enormous dining table. Most of the dignitaries at the table wore military uniforms. Others were dressed in expensive handmade Chinese outfits much like the one given to Marie's husband. Everyone was told to stand and bow as the Chinese president Hu Jintao entered the room and took his seat at the head of the table.

The President welcomed his guest from America in English. The staff of the great hall started serving the rare and elaborate courses of the meal. The head of the Chinese military was the next to address the table filled with dignitaries.

"Gentleman and our honored American guest. This is a grave time for the relationship of our two great countries. American dollars and trade has allowed us to move quickly into a new era of technology. China is now one of the two great powers in the world. Still we need the trade with the United States to continue. It is the quickest and easiest route to our ultimate goal. The trade imbalance is making the United States more dependent everyday on our manufacturing capabilities. Once we have amassed the technical information from the United States that we need, it will be time for us to flex our muscles. The debt of the United States is so great at this moment that if we were to call them to terms and demand payment we could collapse the economy of the United States. We are close now as America is already on the verge of a great depression. Today will be the day that we begin the final drive to domination."

A small round piece of metal about the size of a quarter was presented to Marie's husband. The small medallion had an intricately carved head of Rune's dog Sven on one side, the other side had Rune's little Lena dog engraved on it. It came on a velvet cushion in a hand carved wooden box with a Chinese dragon carved on the cover. The carved dragon was holding a likeness of the United States in one of its front claws. Fire spewed from the dragoon's mouth engulfing the great American continent.

Marie's husband was given his instructions as to what he should do with the medallion. It was to be given to Rune as a lucky piece. The explanation that it was to be kept close to the heart. Inside this lucky piece was a homing device. The homing device worked much like a 'smart' bomb. In this case, it would be the directional signal for a smart bullet. A rifle could be shot at the basic target from up to a mile away. The bullet contained a signal that would home in on the lucky medallion. Thus would be the end of Rune. Killed by a snipers bullet.

Marie's husband was rushed back home. No one was to know where he had been. Everything he needed to know was committed to his memory. His next step was to get Rune out in the open. Someplace where he would be venerable to attack by a sniper.

Marie's husband arrived home before midnight. He often worked late on his legal briefs so Marie was not concerned. Einer had carried up a small overnight bag for Marie's husband upon his arrival.

It did not take long for Marie's husband to convince her that Rune should really take some time to get out among the people. Forcing through all these changes in government policy may be upsetting to the public. A road trip by the president to show he was still part of the common everyday people would be a nice boost for his popularity.

Marie and Valerie were in charge of public appearances so the next day they went to work mapping out a road trip. They had never really covered the mid-west states so that would be their general plan.

Rune was receptive to the idea. Olaf and Travis of course figured this would be a great road trip. That is if they could convince the security people to let them drive their motorcycles. Before any more legislation would be planed the Common-Cents party would make a personnel tour. It would be a complete surprise. No one would be told when they were leaving or which roads or towns they would visit. Security was to be minimal. No fancy convoys or hotels. The group would stay at local little mom and pop establishments. The same for meals, eating was to be done a t the local café's. They would stop and walk the streets of small towns. Introduce themselves and maybe give a few short questions and answer speeches as they went along.

Marie, her husband, Valerie and Boone would travel in a Honda CRV for their own comfort. Motorcycle riding was not on the top of their list of fun things to do. Although occasionally the women did hitch rides behind Rune and Olaf for short distances.

Marie's husband easily found out their itinerary from Marie. He was in constant touch using text messages to his Legal Eagle cronies. They of course passed this information on to the Chinese Delegate in the United States. A town was chosen. Marie's husband was to make sure the medallion was in Rune's pocket. Than he was to have Rune in a certain area at a certain time. A sniper would do the rest. One stipulation for Marie's husband was required. Olaf was to be kept away from Rune and everyone else for at least an hour while the sniper did his job.

CHAPTER 17

Shorlty before their trip Rune was out in the yard with his dogs. Einer was keeping an eye on Sven and Lena to make sure they received enough exercise. Rune had developed a trust with Einer and asked him to take care of his 'kids' while he was away on a road trip.

Einer felt it was time that he should share some information with Rune. Einer graciously excused himself for being so inquisitive. Then he told Rune that he had carried up an overnight bag for Marie's husband a few days ago. He noticed that the bag had a recent baggage check attached to it with a Chinese destination and return destination to the United States. The time on the baggage check showed that the trip had been accomplished in less than twenty hours.

Rune pondered the information. He thanked Einer for the information and asked him to inform him of any other activities that looked to be out of place. There had been no mention of Marie's husband leaving the country. Rune hoped that it might just be something with his legal practice. Although going to China on the eve of their discussion about ending trade arrangements with countries who were not equal trade partners did seem strange. Tomorrow they would be on the road for their surprise tour. Once they returned to the White House, Rune knew he should look into this matter concerning Marie's husband.

The group all met early in the morning to begin their trip. Security personnel left first to reconnoiter the route. Then Rune, Olaf, and Travis were next in line on their motorcycles. A car filled with security agents went next, then the Honda CRV with Marie, her husband, Valerie and Boone. One final security vehicle followed the procession.

The first day went well. Meals at local eating places. Gas stops about every 120 miles. Lots of surprised reactions from each town's citizens. This was how America should be. The President and entourage being able to travel and mingle with their constituents.

When evening arrived, they picked out a little motel at the edge of a small town. Next to the motel was a local bar called Grant's Crossing. It was amazing that the pictures on the wall of Ulysses S. Grant really did resemble President Rune.

The Common Cents group played darts and pool and had SvenBrews and Beertzels for snacks. Adam and Scotty were in charge of security and had a good handle on the situation.

Rune and Marie's husband ended up in the restroom at the same time. Standing next to each other at the urinals Marie's husband began to speak.

"Rune I know you do not care much for me. That old thing with my temper and taking it out on Marie. I just want you to know I have changed, I really believe in what you are trying to accomplish. If it is ok with you, I would like you to have a little token of friendship and thanks. I had this medallion especially made for you. It has engravings of your dogs Sven and Lena. They call it a 'medallion of the heart.' That's because it is always to be kept in a pocket as close to your heart as possible."

Rune accepted the gift with some trepidation. It seemed to be a peace offering. Looking the medallion over Rune could see that it was a very expensive piece of artwork as far as the engraving was concerned. He knew he had to say something. So he did his best while trying to be polite.

"Thank you so much. It is a very nice gesture on your part. I will continue to try to accept you into the group. Marie is one of my closest friends; I wish only to look out for her welfare. You treat her well and I think things will only get better with time"

Rune then dropped the medallion into his top left shirt pocket. Marie's husband had a wicked little smile cross his lips. Part one of his current assignment was accomplished. Later that evening when he was alone Marie's husband telephoned his associates with the route for the President. A town was chosen, they should arrive there in two days. The legal eagles had good contacts in their chosen town. With the knowledge of Rune's arrival, the local lawyers were well paid to make sure that Rune would give a short speech on the morning of his departure from town. It would look to be spontaneous. Just a little speech located in the town square's small park. They would get Rune up on a park bench so everyone could see him. Including the pre-arranged sniper.

As Rune and his entourage entered town they stopped and filled their vehicles with petrol. Then they checked in to a little place called Kay's Motel. Larry's Bar and Grill was chosen for supper and a time to relax. It also just so happened that a number of local Lawyers were there having there after work drinks.

Overlooking Rune's stance against lawyers, the group of course welcomed Rune with open arms. They shook hands, bought drinks, even played darts with the Rune and his party. Scotty and Adam were rather nervous about the whole set up. Both the agents had been trained to notice strange behavior. These lawyers were just a little too nice. Being lawyers, they were already suspect in Scotty and Adams minds. Even Rune and his friends seemed to be aware that this contingent of Legal people was not on the up and up. Rune however always tried to think the best of people and let the matter slide along. What the heck, hanging out with some lawyers for a few hours would not kill him. Or would it?

The next morning Maries' husband had to fulfill the next part of his assignment. He feigned being ill and asked if he could stay at the motel for another hour or so. Rune had agreed to the lawyers request from the night before to give a short speech at the town square.

Marie offered to stay with her husband. He insisted that she should attend the gathering with Rune. Maybe Olaf would not mind staying with him for company for an hour or so. Well Olaf was not to keen on the idea. Then Rune told him maybe it would be a nice thing to do. After all Marie's husband did seem to by trying to fit in. Olaf and Marie's husband stayed in the room. the rest of the party left for a little speech giving and politicking.

The town square was only a short walk away. Rune was wearing a denim shirt with his new lucky medallion in his left shirt pocket. This was one of his favorite shirts, he had purchased it at Disneyworld, and just above the pocket was an embroidered figure of 'Tigger' from 'Winnie the Pooh.' A good size crowd had assembled. One of the lawyers from the previous night took charge of Rune and his party. He led them to a park bench and helped Rune step up onto the bench so everyone would be able to see him. The town's mayor looked rather distraught at the way the lawyers in town seemed to be taking over.

Marie's husband was working hard on faking his illness. He lay in bed doing his best to act as if he were trying to sleep. A few well placed groans and jerks of his body should keep Olaf alert enough that he would not dare leave the room.

Olaf sat reading a Louis L'Amour book called Monument Rock. Of course thinking to himself, "why me, why do I have to babysit this jerk?"

Almost three hours before Rune stepped up onto the park bench another man had made an appearance in town. The man was in the United States under a visa as a foreign exchange student. His name was On Sot Kille from China. Student of academics he was not. Crack sharpshooter with the Army of China he was.

On Sot entered the town's Catholic Church in the darkness of early morning. He silently made his way to the bell tower. Quietly he opened his duffle bag and assembled a prototype rifle, which used a new type of ammunition. Years of training allowed him to assemble and ready his weapon more by instinct then by sight.

A small box held six of the new prototype bullets. On Sot would need only one. A liquid hydrogen fluid gave the bullet the velocity of a jet-propelled rocket. Within the bullets confines was a small microscopic homing device. This homing device was set to find a lucky Medallion with an imbedded receiving chip.

On Sot took aim at the park bench in the town square. A distance of just a little over a mile. With his telescopic site and steady hand, this would be a simple shot for him. He had only to wait a few more hours until his target would appear. A silencer built into On Sot's rifle would muffle any sound. No one would have any idea where the bullet came from. On Sot and his Chinese superiors would have no connection that could be traced to them. On Sot was just doing his duty. He would finish the job and then start attending college on the eastern seaboard of the United States. Just like his Visa said he would.

The Chinese had a plan. This was only the beginning of a scheme that would affect the whole world. The blame for Rune's assassination was already decided. The person that would be blamed for this dastardly deed would open the White House to a new sphere of control. A control that would be very pro-Chinese.

Rune stood on the park bench. He raised his hands up in the air to quiet the cheering crowd. Then as if caught by a huge gust of wind Rune tumbled backwards off the park bench. Landing hard on the cement sidewalk, he hit the back of his head and it made a sickening thud as it cracked against the sidewalk.

Scotty and Adam were at Rune's side in a flash. Travis, Boone, and the security agents were busy holding back the crowd. Marie and Valerie were doing their best to keep the situation calm.

Scotty was using his suit coat as a compress to keep Rune's head from bleeding any more than necessary. Adam looked at Scotty and whispered. "Scotty, I think Rune's been shot. Look at his chest near my hand." Adam lifted his hand, which was over Rune's heart to reveal a dark stain of blood slowly discoloring Rune's denim shirt.

Out of nowhere, it seemed that Valerie's CRV had appeared. One of the Security agents had confiscated it as the nearest vehicle. They tossed everything out of the back of the truck and laid the seat down flat. Rune was hoisted into the back of the CRV and rushed to the nearest hospital. With so little room left in the CRV only Scotty, Adam and the driver were in the vehicle.

Pulling the CRV into the hospital emergency garage the boys quickly loaded Rune onto a waiting hospital gurney and rushed him to the emergency room. A team of doctors was ready and waiting. Presidential security had made sure that the hospital was on full alert before the make shift CRV ambulance arrived.

A lone figure exited the Catholic Church and walked to his rental car. He drove slowly out of town. The crowds were still on the streets. Many people looked to be in shock. Women and even some men were still crying over the disaster they had just witnessed. The driver smiled as he drove away. A job well done. On Sot Kille would receive no money for his well-done deed. The most he would get was a thanks from his superiors. Unknown to On Sot he would vanish from the world later that day. It was best for the Chinese government that no one ever know that On Sot Kille had ever existed.

CHAPTER 18

Rune's friends were gathered in a motel room awaiting word on his condition. As far as they or anyone else knew, Rune had fell and hit his head. Scotty called with a progress report and said everything that could be done was being done.

Rune's crack on the skull looked worse than it was. Diagnosis would be splitting headache for a few days. Maybe even a slight loss of balance. To Rune that was not unusual, having only nine toes his balance never was very good.

Then there was the bullet wound. The bullet had hit Rune straight in the heart. This of course tended to be much more serious than the head wound. Scotty and Adam arranged for a helicopter to transport Rune to an undisclosed Military hospital.

Rune's friends and fellow party members had all been returned to the White House. There they waited impatiently for news of their friend and the country's leader. Later that evening Scotty made the telephone call to the White House. Olaf took the call on the secured White House line. Being Olaf was Runes brother Scotty felt it best to explain the situation to Olaf first seeing he was Rune's only living relative. After a brief conversation, Olaf hung up the phone. His face had become ashen white in color. Turning to Marie and her husband, Valerie, Boone, and Travis he made the announcement. Rune was dead.

Officially, the news would be announced to the Media in the morning. The job was to fall to Olaf. A press conference was called for nine in the morning. Scotty was to stay with Rune's body until arrangements could be made for the funeral. Adam was already on a military jet and returning to the White House. He would take over as head of security for Olaf during this trying time.

Marie's husband took her to their room in the White House. He did his best to act shocked and sad. Comforting Marie with the fact that Olaf would carry on the good work that his brother had started. Of course, in the back of his mind, dollar figures were piling up faster than he could imagine. He would be a millionaire. Maybe even garner himself a high position in the administration. Power and wealth the ultimate victory.

At nine the next morning Olaf stood before a podium. The media filled the area in front of him. Behind Olaf sat Marie, her stepdaughter and husband. In addition, there was Valerie, Boone, and Travis. All dressed in somber dark clothing.

The word of Rune's fall and his hit on the head of course was world wide news by this time. Everyone was now waiting for how serious the injury actually was.

The Speaker of the House of Representatives had already been notified. She would step into the position as temporary Vice-President for the time being. Her name was Hilama. She had a reputation for being a no nonsense ruthless politician. Hilama and those behind her had much more lofty ambitions than the vice-Presidency. The wheels of a takeover were all ready well in motion.

Olaf reached up and ticked the microphone in front of him with his finger. The slight thud of noise in the room told him the microphone was on and working.

He drew a deep breath. Stood for a second, holding back his tears. Then he began to speak.

"To the American people and the world let me be the one to give you this grave and shocking announcement. As Rune's brother, and as the Vice President of the United States of America it is my duty..." a long pause of silence permeated the crowd as Olaf tried to gain his composure. "My brother the President of the United States passed away peacefully in his sleep last night. As almost all of you likely know he had been about to give a speech yesterday. Standing on a park bench he lost his balance and fell backwards hitting his head on the cement. Knowing my brother he would most likely blame this on his inherited imbalance from only have nine-toes. I mention this only because knowing him he would have to have told the world that he was not perfect, he was just one of us common everyday people, living with our own faults and phobias."

"Never the less he is gone from this earth. I will take his position as President. The Speaker of the House of Representatives, Ms. Hilama will be acting Vice-President. This is a sad time for the United States. I will do my best to continue with Rune's and our parties promises to make this country strong and self-efficient, as it should be. Thank you all for your support and God Bless."

To a large group of people, politicians, lawyers, and big business this speech was shocking. There was no mention of an assassination attempt. On Sot had already been eliminated. The question was did he actually shoot Rune or was the Presidents death really just a freak accident. Although it probably did not really matter, Rune was dead. Hilama was in place as Vice President. Soon the county would be back in the hands of the big money concerns where it belonged. Screw the common people, America was about to see a major change. A rumor was about to be planted.

The hospital that Rune was rushed to right after his injury was soon a focus point of lawyers and their minions. Scotty and Adam had done their best to swear the doctors and staff involved in Rune's quick visit to secrecy. Lawyers know that money can easily buy secrecy. Cash did the trick. Soon a half dozen witness from the hospital staff were secreted away from the public eye. Well cared for on a nice remote island and pampered like royalty.

Hilama had used her new found position to start an internal investigation into Rune's death. Was the Secret Service covering up his actual cause of death? Could Olaf or his staff been responsible. Was it really an accident? Maybe it was an assassin. Major newspapers were leaked enough information to make the national scandal sheets look like comic books. Soon every television station and radio broadcast started talking about government conspiracy. A cover up of major proportions by the Common-Cents Party.

Hilama quickly organized a major congressional hearing. Six witnesses would be called to testify. Four doctors and two nurses. All from the hospital where Rune was first treated. It was media frenzy.

Olaf, Marie, Valerie, Boone, and Travis were all busy with the funeral arrangements. As per Rune's wishes he was not to have an elaborate funeral. As the country mourned it was up to Olaf to convey the last wishes of his final resting place to the grieving nation.

Rune would lie only one day in state at the White House. Closed coffin, no viewing of the body. The casket would then be transported by train to the shores of Lake Superior in Minnesota.

Two groups were asked to help with the funeral preparations. The Ancestors of Norway and the Tribes of American Indians. Both were eager to assist in any way they could.

At the White House Hilama was quickly flexing her muscles. More security was top priority. It was also noticeable that many Chinese delegates were now visiting the White House. Not only visiting but also being allowed access to almost all areas. Einer was one person who was taking notes on the activities. Something did not look right to him.

Einer was taking Sven and Lena outside when he noticed Marie's Husband slinky his way down the hallway to Olaf's room. Marie's husband entered Olaf's room with a pass key. He carried a small duffle bag with him. Einer stayed out of sight. Sven began to growl as Einer told him to be quiet. Then Marie's husband left Olaf's room, without the duffle bag.

Einer made a quick note in his little book with the date and time of the occurrence. Later that day he would ask a favor of the security person who would have access to the video tape of this action by Marie's husband. A copy for future reference seemed to be a wise thing to have.

The day of the funeral arrive. It was late afternoon. A slight breeze stirred the air on the shores of Lake Superior. Moored to the end of a long dock was a quarter size replica of a Viking longboat complete with a carved dragons head bow. The ship had been built quickly and efficiently by the Ancestors of Norway and the American Indian Tribes. The two groups worked together to Arrange a combined Norwegian/Indian burial fit for either a King or a Chief.

The longboat was filled with dry branches. A small pedestal rose slightly above the edges of the ships sides. The same type of platform used in many American Indian burials. Being a burial at sea a Naval honor guard carried the casket to the ship and place it on board.

The sail of the ship was lowered into place. A sail of magnificent splendor. The sail was a huge American flag in its beautiful red-white and blue. The breeze soon caught the sail and the ship proceeded out into the lake.

Indian archers stood on shore with bows and arrows at the ready. Olaf picked up a flaming torch and proceed down the line of archers making sure he lit each arrow as he went by. The Minnesota National guard fired off a twenty-one gun salute. This was also the signal for the archers to let their arrows fly.

A hundred flaming arrows lit up the sky like so many falling stars. Many landed in the dry timber of the boat. Others had their flame snuffed out in the waters of the lake.

As planned the ship was soon blazing in red and yellow flames. The color of the fire dancing across the dark waters of lake Superior. A true Viking funeral for a fallen leader. The amount of mourning tears of the nation would have given a rise to the level of the lake that night. Sadness prevailed on the shores of Lake Gitchigoomie.

CHAPTER 19

With the witnesses ready for the Congressional hearing, everything was in place for the new powers to be. Soon Hilama and her cronies would have complete control of the country.

The first major blow came when Olaf, Marie, Valerie, Boone, and Travis arrived at the White House after Rune's Funeral. They were all put under house arrest. Scotty and Adam were temporally relieved of duty until an investigation into their actions after Rune's injury could be determined. A national hearing with medical witness was to begin the next morning. It would be televised to the world.

Einer managed to have himself assigned as the caretaker for the now confined Common-Cents party. He made sure to take Olaf's meals to him as a first priority. Before Einer and Olaf could begin talking there was a knock at the door.

Three security agents burst into the room. A camera person was video recording a search of the room. Hilama stood at the door to observe the proceedings. In Olaf's closet far from sight stuffed into a dark corner on the top shelf one of the agents located a duffle bag. Upon opening the bag they discovered a high powered prototype Chinese made rifle.

Hilama glared at Olaf as she said. "This will be exhibit two at tomorrow's hearing."

The agents left the room. Einer looked at Olaf and said. "Rune was my friend. We trusted each other. Eat your food. Remember that." Then he left the room.

Olaf sat dumbfounded for many minutes. None of this made sense. Why was he under House arrest? Where did the rifle come from? Exhibit two? What hearing? Eat your food?

A friend of Rune's. That is what Einer said. Why did he say eat your food? Olaf took the cover from his food. He glanced around the room. For sure the room was bugged and had hidden cameras somewhere. He noticed a piece of paper under his mashed potatoes. Sliding the paper out with his fork he read it.

"Marie's husband left a duffle bag in your room while you were away. I have contacts; you are being set up to take the blame for assassinating your brother. Is there anyone I can go to that will help you? Please eat this note for desert. Einer."

When Einer returned for the dishes, he noticed the words Scotty & Adam written in the left over mash potatoes. He quickly obliterated the mashed potato message with a napkin. Then Einer said:

"I will let them know downstairs that you really enjoyed the mash potatoes. Have a pleasant night."

Einer pulled the files for Scotty and Adam up on the one of the many computers in the White House. He was surprised to see the two agents were on mandatory leave of absence. Investigation pending. Luck was with him though; home addresses for both agents were listed in their files.

Einer left work that evening and immediately went to Scotty's house. He told Scotty about the house arrest of Olaf and the other party members. Then he proceeded to inform Scotty about the duffle bag that Marie's husband had smuggled into Olaf's room. Then Einer dropped the bombshell. Through his many contacts at the White House, that as far as he knew Vice-President Hilama had ordered Olaf's room to be searched. The duffle bag contained a rifle that would be used as positive proof that Olaf had killed his brother.

Scotty quickly explained to Einer that no one knew of the assassination except for Adam, himself and Olaf. It seems that when Scotty called about Rune's death he did tell him of the bullet to the heart. Anyway, Olaf was in a room with Marie's husband when the assassination took place so he would have an ironclad alibi. There was no way Hilama and her people could make a case against Olaf.

Scotty gave a secure telephone number to Einer for future use. If Hilama and her people were going to try to prove Olaf was involved, well than it would only be logical that Scotty and Adam would also be prime suspects.

As soon as Einer left, Scotty grabbed a few clothes and drove to Adam's house. He dared not telephone in case the phones or Adam's house might be bugged. Even when talking with Einer they had sat out on the front porch steps to keep their conversation private.

Arriving at Adams house Scotty motioned him to the door and made some hand gestures for Adam to grab a few things and to get out of the house as quickly as possible. It was best they disappear until they had more information. Einer would now be their only contact with the White House and the actions of Hilama and her associates.

At the White House, a meeting was arranged for Olaf to talk things over with Marie's husband. Olaf had now been informed that the White House had proof that he murdered his brother, the President of the United States. Marie's husband was assigned to Olaf as his attorney for the hearing, which would take place the next morning.

As for Valerie, Travis and Boone they were temporally exonerated from wrongdoing in Rune's death and ordered out of the White House. They would be sent back to Minnesota and have no further contact with Olaf or anyone else in Washington DC.

For Sven, Lena and Valerie's Oliver they had better go with the Common-Cents party members. Otherwise, Hilama said she would have them baked and basted until they were tender enough to serve to her Chinese guests for supper.

CHAPTER 20

The hearing for Olaf was a media frenzy. As acting Vice President Hilama had waived the rules of no media coverage inside the courthouse. She wanted to see Olaf and the Common-Cents party go down in flames.

Olaf and Marie's husband took their position as defendant and lawyer on the right side of the courtroom. Marie's husband had suggested to Olaf to wave a jury trial and let the judge make the decision. Olaf, knowing only about the rifle planted in his room as evidence had reason to feel that the case was still on his side. After all Marie's husband was not only Olaf's lawyer, he was Olaf's alibi. With Marie's husband in the same room as Olaf during the 'supposed' assassination there could be no doubt that Olaf could not have been the assassin.

The first witness's were the two nurses. Then three of the four doctor's that had initially treated Rune were brought to the stand. They all confirmed that beside the head injury there was blood and some type of wound near Rune's heart. The last doctor on the stand had a surprise piece of evidence that he produced from his suit coat pocket.

He asked the lawyer if it would be permissible to show an item he had taken from the emergency room. The lawyer asked the judge for a lenient decision in the matter as this item might be very crucial to the case. The judge allowed the evidence to be presented.

The doctor opened the small case and held a tiny piece of lead between his fingers. Having seen many shooting victims in the past the doctor announced that this lead had most certainly come from the bullet of a gun. Furthermore, the doctor claimed that he removed this piece of lead from the area by Olaf's heart.

The lawyer asked why the operation was stopped if there was a wound so near the heart. The Doctor replied that as soon as they started to investigate the wound near the heart the two secret Service agents stopped the proceeding and had Rune whisked away to a waiting helicopter. Supposedly, Rune was being rushed to a secret military base for further treatment.

Scotty and Adam it seemed had now disappeared. There had been warrants issued for their arrest for perpetuating a cover up in the assassination of the President. Unfortunately the pilot and medical facility that handled the next part of Rune's ordeal seemed to have been covered up by the secret service. No further records had been located at this time.

Through all of this, Marie's husband had sat quietly. He had no questions to ask any of the witness's. Olaf could not imagine how Marie's husband was going to use his strategy without cross-examining the witness. Olaf figured Marie's husband was his lawyer and he knew best. All this legal stuff always did seem to be a cat and mouse type of game. It was almost like going to Las Vegas to watch a world-class magician. You never really knew whether to believe what you saw or not.

A surprise move by Marie's husband was in order. He asked if he could address the judge with an important piece of information. The judge looked at the opposing lawyers who agreed to this rather unusual request.

Marie's husband spoke. "Judge, your honor. I would like to remove myself as lawyer from Olaf's defense. I do this in consideration of the beliefs of the Common-Cents party. They believe that a lawyer should not defend a person that he knows is guilty. With this in mind I feel I cannot morally justify my defending Olaf."

The judge looked seriously at Olaf then at Marie's Husband before speaking. "Request allowed. You are removed as legal counsel for the defendant. Mr. Olaf I now assign you as your own legal counsel for you defense."

Olaf sat in a state of shock. Marie and her stepdaughter who were in attendance also had a glazed look in their eyes. Marie could not believe her husband felt Olaf was guilty. Marie's stepdaughter whispered to her, "Marie is Olaf going to die?"

Olaf was asked if you would like to make a statement before continuing with the trial. Also, if Olaf had any witness's that may help in his defense he should give the judge a list of those people so that they could be notified and brought to the courtroom.

Olaf stood to present his statement. "Your honor. I am shocked by the behavior of my legal counsel. I have only one witness that can exonerate me from this unjust and slanderous accusation of murdering my brother. That witness is my ex-lawyer. I would like to call him to the witness box to be questioned."

"Motion denied. The prosecuting attorney still has the floor. I believe they have one more witness to call to the stand. After this next witness, Olaf, you will be allowed to present your case." Thus, the Judge allowed the trail to proceed.

The prosecuting lawyer then called Marie's husband to the stand. The bible was presented, Maries husband swore to tell the truth, the whole truth and nothing but the truth. He then took his seat in the witness box.

Prosecuting attorney to Marie's husband. "You have sworn to tell the truth. In a previous conversation with you, we have learned that Olaf planned to have you as a witness to his whereabouts during the dastardly assassination of his brother. In fact, it is believed that Olaf is going to claim he was with you when his brother was so un-mercilessly killed. Is this true?

Marie's husband answered in the affirmative. That was what Olaf planned to present as his defense.

Prosecuting attorney. "As Olaf's ex-legal counsel and part of the inner circle of the Common-Cents party would you please tell us if it is true? Were you with Olaf the whole time that he claims to have been with you? Is there any possibility that there could be a lapse in Olaf's memory? Is it possible that he may have slipped away and no one can account for his whereabouts during the cold-blooded murder of his brother?

Marie's husband. "I was very ill the morning that Rune was assassinated. It seemed to be a side effect of food poisoning. I had eaten dinner with Olaf and the other the party members the previous evening. On thinking back to the occasion I was sitting next to Olaf. It would have been very easy for him to slip something into my food to make me ill. The next morning he volunteered to stay with me while I slept and tried to recuperate. As I dozed off, I noticed he was still in the room with me. Not feeling well I was rather restless and was tossing and turning as I tried to sleep. During this time I cannot recall Olaf still being in the room."

Prosecuting attorney. "To put this simply, do you believe that Olaf would have had the time to leave the room? Shoot his brother and return without your knowledge?"

Marie's husband. "Yes, I believe this could have very well been the case. In fact, I am almost certain that Olaf drugged my food and set up the assassination so that he could usurp Rune's position as president of the United States. While I was in a drugged induced sleep it would have given Olaf more than enough time to kill his brother and return without my knowledge."

Olaf knew it was all lies. What could he do? His star witnessed had perjured himself beyond belief. Scotty and Adam were in hiding, they knew things that could clear Olaf of all charges. Without them, Olaf was a rat on a sinking ship. He made only one closing comment. "Judge, people of the United States. I loved my brother. I am innocent. Believe me, the truth will eventually prevail. God Bless America and the Common People."

The judge found Olaf guilty of murder. With consideration of Olaf's position, the judge would allow Olaf to remain under house arrest at the White House until such time as a just punishment could be decided. The verdict of punishment would be announced in the next seventy-two hours.

Olaf was handcuffed and led from the courtroom. He was then transported in an armored Swat team vehicle back to the White House. He was sequestered in his room. Two armed guards were stationed outside his door. The room's windows had been barred and two other armed soldiers stood by outside the windows as an added precaution.

The American people were left in a total state of shock. How could everything have gone so wrong? Just when it looked like America was finally re-establishing herself as the country her forefathers had meant for her to be.

CHAPTER 21

At the White House a private party was being held. Hilama and her staff were hosting this clandestine affair for the top diplomats from China. Marie and her husband were also in attendance. Much to Marie's objections. She felt betrayed and ashamed of her husband after the day's events. As a god-fearing woman who was brought up to believe in the bible and its teaching, she still felt obligated to show loyalty to her husband.

Marie's husband had a nice little legal document all written up and ready to be signed. Hilama and her people had arranged for a sweet little lease deal to be arranged between the United States of America and the Chinese Republic. The Chinese were prepared to transfer a large sum money as a loan to the United States in exchange for a lease on some property along the eastern seaboard of our great country.

Hilama would use this money to show the American public that we were gaining ground on our huge money deficit. All this was due to our new friends and allies in world peace. The Chinese. The Chinese in return would receive a small amount of unimportant military technology. As a little footnote, they would be able to lease land from the American government. This little piece of land just happened to be the now defunct Charleston, South Carolina Naval Base. Much like Guantanamo Bay in Cuba is to America, this area would be a Chinese possession. No American influence would be allowed without the approval of the Chinese government.

The lease and legal documents were presented by Marie's husband. He laid them out neatly on a table for all parties to sign. When finished he notarized the document and each of the attending parties received a copy.

Einer had himself assigned as a waiter at this clandestine little party. He witnessed the complete transaction. Right up to the toasts of a new America, a new domain for China. Once again, the American people would be taken in by crooked politics. Worse, they were now slowly being sold out to a communist government. The elimination of Rune and the Common-Cents party had now become the greatest act of traitorous villainy to ever befall the United States of America.'

The party was in full swing. A little too much alcohol in all that were in attendance was evident. Even the staid Chinese seemed to be tipping the old bubbly rather freely. Then again, the Chinese had a lot to celebrate. They now had a legal lease to a military base located on the American mainland. Certainly, they saw this as a step in their slow moving venture to eventually dominate the world. Control of the United States would put the Chinese in a position that no country in the world would dare to oppose.

The legal documents were left on the table for all in attendance to observe. Pieces of paper relinquishing land from the United States to a communist country. Hilama and her associates did not care. Greed was their ultimate goal. Therefore, they had to share a little power with the Chinese. No big deal. Hilama did not seem to realize that already she was a puppet in the communist's hands. Pull her strings and watch her dance.

Einer continued to wait on the guests in a pleasant friendly manner. He carried a large silver tray with a huge rounded cover. As he approached each group of guests, he would lift the cover to offer a large assortment of sushi. When the tray was empty, Einer exited the room for a refill. Once out in the hall he hurried to his own quarters and pulled a paper from under the silver trays lid. He had every original of the signed papers from the party upstairs. He quickly made copies of every paper and slipped them back on his tray. A stop at the kitchen to replace the sushi and he went back to the party and replaced the papers with the copies. Finally, he had made enough trips, one page at a time to replace all the papers with copies. Some day the time would come when the Chinese had to have proof of their lease. Copies from the Chinese or from

Hilama and her party would not hold up in any court in the world. Einer just had to pray that no one noticed that the original documents had been replaced by copies.

As the party ended, Einer helped the delegates roll up the signed papers and put them in sealed tubes, which then went into locked briefcases. No one was any the wiser that the papers were copies.

Later in the evening Einer went for a walk outside. He made a telephone call to Scotty and told him of the recent developments. Scotty was in Germany seeking aid for the next big move to salvage the Common-Cents party. Adam was in Japan doing the same thing as Scotty.

These three people were doing everything in their power to save America. With the Chinese intervention, Scotty and Adam had the ammunition they needed to seek help. Their allies would soon prove worthy of the task.

Scotty and Adam both went after the help they needed. Meetings were immediately arranged with the heads of state from both Germany and Japan. It took only a key phrase from Scotty and Adam to accomplish this. The real president of the United States is alive and well. His name is Rune.

Eye com's were set up to receive a broadcast from Rune himself. The assassination attempt was real and it did happen. Only Rune did not die.

There of course had to be an explanation. Up to now, only three people knew that Rune was still alive. All of them were of course sworn to secrecy. Scotty, Adam, and Olaf were the three individuals that knew exactly what had happened on the day Rune was supposed to die.

Rune had developed a peculiar habit from the old days when his business ventures had him traveling all over the United States. Carrying cash, credit cards and even a driver licenses was always a little risky to anyone who used a billfold. Rune was a tried and true billfold user for many years. Hearing horror stories from his business associates who had their pockets picked and lost everything, Rune decided to change his money and credit card habit from a billfold to a new two-option system.

Rune's front left pants pocket know contained a money clip made from a 1936 buffalo nickel. Cash was now within easy access to Rune.

Darn hard to get at for a pickpocket. Credit cards and drivers license were now kept in a special gift he had received for being a top salesman for Honda Motorcycles. It was a metal hinged credit card holder. Rune kept his two credit cards, insurance card, and drivers license in their metal hold. This particular holder was always kept in Rune's left shirt pocket. The holder was now dented and damaged, but it did stop a bullet from entering Rune's heart.

Scotty and Adam had taken the real bullet and the now damaged lucky disc to a top secret government laboratory for investigation. The lucky disc, which was a gift from Marie's husband and the bullet were found to be a nicely matched pair of homing devices set up to kill Rune. The bullet that had been presented at Olaf's trail was a fake.

Rune's death was staged so that the culprits would come into the open and show themselves. Little did anyone suspect that they would also eliminate Olaf and align themselves with the Chinese. The plot for takeover was much more devious then anyone could image.

With Scotty and Adam's help, the Germans and the Japanese soon formulated a rescue plan to free Olaf from the White House. Scotty and Adam were given all the necessary papers and documents to assume new identities. Disguises were provided to change their facial features and allow them access to areas in the United States where they might be recognized.

The next step was to get Scotty, Adam and a contingent of six trained special rescue agents into the White House. Einer arranged special guest passes for the two separate parties to get a tour of the White House. The tour would be in conjunction with a regular tourist tour that took place every day. Three extra Japanese and three German tourists would not even be noticed in the crowds of people that went on these tours. Scotty and Adam in disguise would not even be recognizable.

Everyone must go through metal scanners before taking the tour. No problem there. The clandestine group of the rescue party was armed with the few things they needed. Lock picking tools; knock out gas and a disguise kit for Olaf. Everything they had was made of plastic or ceramic derivatives so that it would not be detected by the metal sensors.

The German and Japanese military commands stationed themselves at their American consulates to provide support as needed. Transportation and housing for the Common-Cents party was arranged at these consulates. By moving the party to foreign soil, they would have protection from Hilama and the Chinese until the American People could be notified of what was taking place.

Einer telephone Travis of the recent developments with Olaf. Travis was to notify Valerie and Boone to be ready at a moment's notice to be picked up by helicopter and delivered to the Japanese consulate in Washington D.C.

With-in thirty hours the rescue mission was in the White House and supposedly enjoying their tour. Einer had mapped the whole area out for the rescue team. Every move was planned and ready.

At the first junction, Adam and two of the Japanese agents slipped out of sight and down an unmarked staircase. This allowed them into the back entrance to the video camera monitoring room. Einer had a friend on duty that day that was aware of the plan to free Olaf. The monitor's agent for the security video just backed away from his position and let Adam and the Japanese agents take over. They quickly re-routed the camera from the hallway and Olaf's room to a similar area in the White House. Just in case anyone was monitoring this area for Hilama and the Chinese, it would look as if all were normal.

Einer was standing at the junction of two hallways when he motioned Scotty and two of the Germans off to one side. One of the Germans and one of the Japanese stayed with the group to take away any suspicions that may arise in the tour group. As luck was with them, no one seemed to notice that anyone was missing.

Scotty was more than familiar with the layout of the White House and quickly led his little rescue party to the hallway near Olaf's room. Two armed guards were positioned at Olaf's door. Scotty, in disguise, approached the guards and flashed his top security clearance badge. As the two guards examined Scotty's credentials the Germans came up behind them with cloth kerchiefs filled with knock out gas. Both guards slumped to the floor. Scotty already had the lock on Olaf's door picked open and in the three of them went.

Olaf was lying on his bed reading a book as the rescue team entered the room. Scotty quickly tore of his disguise so Olaf would recognize him. After a quick explanation that this was a rescue mission, Olaf agreed to leave with Scotty and the two German agents.

One of the German agents helped Olaf shave his beard off. A blonde wig and blonde eyebrows made Olaf look like a new person. Scotty had already replaced his own disguise and was ready to go. The two guards were dragged into the room and tied together on the floor while all this was going on.

Time was running short. They had ten minutes to accomplish their task and get out. The two Germans had changed into the guards outfits and took their positions outside Olaf's door. Scotty and Olaf disappeared down the hallway and quickly re-joined the tour group. Adam and the two Japanese agents turned the security system back to its proper setting and re-joined the tour group. Olaf, now in disguise was now a new member of the tour group. All bodies would be accounted for when the tour ended.

The tour guide did a final count of people in the group. Everything looked good. The tour group dispersed and was soon on their way off the White House grounds. Scotty, Olaf, and the last German entered a Mercedes and headed to the Japanese consulate. Adam and the three Japanese agents got into a Honda Pilot truck and headed to the Japanese embassy.

The two Germans that were now guarding Olaf's room were relieved by their replacements fifteen minutes later. The two Germans left the White House with the help of Einer and were on their way. They both went straight to the airport and flew back to their home country.

The escape was picture perfect. In one hour, it would be suppertime. That was when Hilama and her cohorts would be in for a very un-usual surprise.

CHAPTER 22

Before Hilama would even know about Olaf's rescue the wheels of justice were not only turning, they were in full spin. The Japanese had a private Honda built jet whisking the Common-Cents party back to Minnesota. Once arriving at the local airport Olaf, Valerie, Boone and Travis were ushered into a black Honda Pilot truck which the local Honda dealer "by the way he was also Rune's old boss" supplied for the occasion.

Soon the truck arrived at the Dog's Breath Saloon. The occupants were rushed inside by Scotty and Adam to a darkened bar room. Standing at the throw line of a dartboard a lone figure was practicing his throw. Two small Shih-Tzu dogs rushed over to greet the new guests.

In the glow of the dartboards light, it was hard to make out who the lone player was. He threw three darts as everyone in the room silently watched. A bulls eye, another bulls eye, then a third bulls eye. Hat trick.

The figure turned to greet his guests. Scotty turned up the dimmer on the lights to brighten the room. Rune stood in front of the group. They mobbed him like teenage girls on the Beatle's first tour of the United States. Hugs, kisses, and tears spread like wildfire throughout the group.

Valerie, Travis, and Boone had a few unkind words for Rune. After all, he had to deceive them into thinking he was dead for the plan to work. The Common-Cents party had positive proof against Hilama, Marie's husband, a large percentage of politicians, big businesses, the countries association of lawyers and legal representatives, and the communist Chinese government. This huge house of cards would not only fall, it would be wiped out by a national hurricane of upheaval from the American public.

Einer had been very busy in the last hour. He called in favors from everyone that could possibly be of help. His friends at the local veterans clubs quickly volunteered to help. It seems that suddenly the White House was inundated with ex-service people from World War two, the Korean Conflict, the Viet Nam war, Operation desert Storm and even a few newcomers from the Iraqi War. Veterans were always given special treatment on White House tours and it seems that there was a flood of them wanting tours. In fact, they demanded tours immediately. Einer had prepared the leaders of these veterans who were ex-officers to be ready for anything. Most of all these veterans needed to take the White House over and secure it until regular troops would arrive to take control.

With the Chinese threatening to occupy the old Charleston navy base other veterans had been activated by their service clubs. Charleston harbor and the Charleston River were now patrolled by every imaginable civilian boat that could be located. It looked like the evacuation of Dunkirk during World War Two, sans the presence of any real Navy Ships.

This flotilla of civilian craft manned by veterans of five wars was determined to hold Charleston bay from any incoming foreign ships. An ex-Navy battleship Captain patrolled the front of the bay in a restored World War two Higgins PT boat. The veterans Navy was armed with everything from rifles, handguns and a few weapons that they conveniently borrowed from the local National Guard. These National Guard weapons of course were a formidable arsenal to be flashing at a foreign power like the Chinese.

Two Chinese battleships and one nuclear submarine were station at the harbor entrance. There signal to enter the harbor and occupy the old Navy Base was to be the announcement of Olaf's sentence to the public. Unfortunately, for this tiny Chinese fleet any action they may take to enter the harbor now could mean all out war between China and the United States. This was not part of the gradual taker-over of the United States that the Chinese ship captain had been briefed for.

Back at the White House, the discovery of a missing Olaf was a signal of a major disaster between Hilama and the Chinese. Accusations of deceit flew from both sides. The Chinese still had the Lease agreements for the old Charleston Navy Base. They insisted that they be allowed to occupy the base immediately.

Hilama and her people knew such action by the Chinese would cause panic across the land if the American public were not informed of the lease agreement before hand. Hilama called an immediate press conference to be held in the Oval Office. The Chinese would be in friendly attendance to show the new spirit of cooperation between the two nations.

As for Olaf, a bounty was put on his head. Dead, not alive, to anyone from Hilama's inner circle that could kill him. Marie's husband was notified that he should have Marie contact her friends to locate Olaf. Of course, he told Marie he just wanted to help Olaf. Have him give himself up and Hilama would be lenient with him. At the most, five years in prison or else deportation to any country that would have him. For the next hour, a now bruised and battered Marie refused to talk. Her stepdaughter witnessed the whole affair, tears and screams flowing from her poor confused little body. Marie of course could not say anything about Olaf. She knew nothing of what had happened to him.

Hilama was busy issuing warrants and death threats for any of the Common-Cents party. They must be found, arrested, or eliminated, preferably the last item on the list. Elimination, yes in Hilama's mind that was the way to end any further threat to her power.

As the media set up their equipment in the Oval room, Einer took charge. He was an ex Naval lieutenant and he delegated the ranking officers of the veterans their assigned jobs. With Einer's reputation of honesty and all his friends in the White House, the current guards and Secret Service agents who were not part of Hilama's crooked system were soon recruited to the Veteran's War of the White House.

The head of C&N had received a telephone call from Olaf and had a news crew at the Dog's Breath Saloon in less than an hour. Both press conferences were to be held with-in minutes of each other. Unbeknownst to either group.

How America or the world would react was known to no one. For C&N this was a tough call. Back the current President who was in control of the White House. On the other hand, should they support a President that the world assumed was dead? Never had such a dilemma been faced by any news organization in the history of the world.

Only a matter of minutes was left. The broadcasts were about to begin. The world was glued to television sets, radios, and the internet. What could be so important that a White House press conference was called on such short notice?

Einer made his move. He got control of the loudspeaker system through his friendly contacts and made the announcement. The veterans War was to commence immediately. The current contingent of guards and security on duty had been informed by Einer of the situation that had been developing and was about to come to a head. It was agreed that the guards and security on duty would stand by as the Veterans Army took control of the situation in the Oval room. Einer and representatives from each of the five veterans groups, which included the Navy, Army, Marines, Air Force, and the Coast Guard, entered the Oval office.

The small contingent of war veterans soon put the Cameramen and sound technicians at bay. The Chinese delegate's in the room headed for protection behind drapes, furniture, or anything else they could find. Hilama sat behind her desk, fire in her eyes. Screaming for her guards to shoot the intruders. Einer announced President Rune would be having a news conference, not Hilama.

Marie's husband who had been standing to the right of Hilama as her new appointment for Vice president was livid with rage. He had worked to long and too hard to be denied this position of power at the last moment. He rushed Einer who had made his way to the front of Hilama's desk. Marie's husband's face was red with the anger of a thousand erupting volcanoes as he lunged his out stretched hands for Einer's neck.

Einer's old Navy training came back to him more as instinct than as a controlled reaction. He sidestepped Marie's husband's lunge. Einer's right hand swung up with a closed fist to meet Marie's husbands chin. Einer was filled with an adrenaline pumped strength. His fist to the chin of Marie's husband sent the would be Vice President crashing against the wall. Marie's husband teetered for a moment. His jaw askew from being broken. Then he slumped to the floor in an unconscious heap.

The room was silent. Einer started giving instructions. "Ms. Hilama, sit still and watch the monitors. You, the Chinese delegate get on your cell phone and order your ships to leave Charleston Harbor immediately. That is unless you want to start World War Three. Everyone else in this room sit still and listen to the Press conference from the real President of the United States."

Hilama stayed in her chair sitting dead still and as white as a sheet. The Chinese delegate was busy sputtering Chinese into his telephone. The media people settled in and shut down their equipment. The war veterans and the guards in the room held their present positions. Marie's husband laid on the floor looking like a broken rag-doll. He was groggily aware of what was happening.

The television monitors in the room flashed on. C&N was broadcasting. Live from the Dog's Breath Saloon in Minnesota. The screen filled with a long shot of Valerie, Olaf, Boone, Travis, and Rune sitting at a round pub table. Dart machines in the background, bottles of SvenBrew and Summer Wine on the table. Slowly the Camera zoomed in on Rune.

Rune started speaking. "People of the United State of America. This is not a hoax. I am alive and well. Immediately I must apologize to everyone in the United States and the rest of the world for the deception, which I felt compelled to perpetrate to the world in general. As you can see, I am back. Not from the dead, but if my enemies had their choice it would be so. Acting President Hilama wanted the world to think I was killed by an assassin's bullet. Part of this statement made by her is true. I was shot in the heart by an assassin. Fortunately it was only a flesh wound. A metal credit card case saved my life. It was not my brother Olaf as Hilama and her people would have you believe. It was Hilama and her minions who perpetrated this dastardly deed."

"With the help of an insider and his friends at the White House we have every reason to believe that the assignation attempt was made by a joint effort of Hilama, the Chinese government, and the myriads of crooked lawyers, legal assistants, politicians, and big business concerns.

Their motive was strictly greed oriented. Cash in their pockets, not concern for the American public is what motivates these people."

"Now I ask for you the American public to decide. If you can forgive me for the deceptive plot to undermine these greed mongers, which want to control the United States I now ask you to go immediately to your computer and vote. Boone has set up a hot line voting system. You need only to log into rune.com to place your vote. Your choices will be."

Do you want to keep me as your president and re-instate me to my Presidential position?

Are you in favor of the Common-Cents party returning to its position in the White House?

Do you agree that Olaf is innocent?

Should Hilama and her associates be put on trial?

Instead of wasting taxpayer's money on a trail for Hilama and her associates, should we just deport them from the country? We are sure China will welcome them with open arms.

Should the Common-cents party continue with its original platform of change for the United States?

Do you wish to keep Hilama and her party in control and leave things as they currently are?

"We will close the web site for voting in twenty four hours. At that time, Boone will present the results. You the people are making this decision. Whatever the outcome we will submit to the wishes of the American public. Thank you, and God Bless."

C&N ended the broadcast and quickly switched their coverage to Charleston harbor. The Veterans Navy was still blockading the Harbor. The leader of the Veterans Navy and the Captain from the Chinese flagship agreed to a meeting at Fort Sumter in Charleston Bay. The American Civil war started here April 12th, 1861. This important meeting would hopefully avoid the staring of World War three.

By this time, Rune had set up communication with Fort Sumter. Under no circumstance were the Chinese to enter the harbor or occupy the old Charleston naval base. The Chinese on their part demanded that they had a lease signed by the acting President of the United States. Einer had informed Rune that the Chinese Lease was only a copy; Einer had the original two signed leases stored away in a safe place. The Chinese informed of this information quickly examined their lease. It was a copy and thus not valid.

This information was relayed to the Chinese ambassadors at Hilama's office. They ordered their ships to leave the United States territorial waters immediately. What they said in Chinese to Hilama and Marie's husband unfortunately cannot be put down in print. Bad words in Chinese do not translate well to the English language.

The veterans now in charge of security at the White House escorted Hilama and Marie's husband to their rooms under house arrest. Once the American people voted on Rune's proposition, the next steps would proceed. As for now, the country was without an acting President or government for the next twenty-four hours.

The United Kingdom, Germany, Japan, and Norway assumed the right as protectors of the United States until the American public proclaimed their wishes as to who the President would be. Rune or Hilama, Americans would decide.

CHAPTER 23

The Common-cents party was up early and meeting at the Dog's Breath Saloon. Boone had been up most the night monitoring the votes. An overwhelming majority wanted Rune and the Common-Cents party back in office. As for Hilama and her cronies, the votes were almost too close to make a call. Many Americans were more than willing to pick up the cost of trying her for everything from attempted murder to treason. Marie's husband fared even worse. The majority of those who wanted to punish him, well let it be said that we cannot print things like that; children might just be reading this.

A fair share of the voters also wanted her deported. The problem with that idea was that the Chinese had made it clear in a telegram to the White House, and to the allies of the United States that Hilama and her party would not be welcomed in China.

Although a breakthrough of friendship was offered by the Russians. They made a direct offer to the American public to accept Hilama and her people in Russia. It seems that a few of the gulags in Siberia were short on help. A few new bodies would be more than welcome.

Rune and his party boarded a train for the trip back to Washington. Standing on the open-air observation car Rune waved to the cheering crowds that had assembled along the way. Einer, Scotty, and Adam had followed Rune's instructions to move Hilama and those who were with her at the White House to a safe and secure place. Marie remained with her husband. Her wedding vows were a serious thing for her. For better or worse, this was certainly a case of worse. If for no other reason, Marie's stepdaughter needed an honest caring parent, Marie would fulfill her duty as a mother.

The Veterans navy and the Veterans army that kept the shores of America and the White House safe during this crisis disbanded. All involved would later be awarded a congressional medal of honor. The congress of the United States was not so eager to fulfill this request. Yet they could not deny the wishes of the American people and the President in bestowing this token of gratitude on these brave individuals that came to their countries aid in a time of need.

The allied countries that helped the United States in this crisis become closer than ever. Trade agreements were quickly and fairly worked out and put into action. A new union of nations that was working for freedom and equality was slowly but surely developing. There was even talk of a universal currency to stabilize the world's economy.

During the next month, changes were noticeable. Chain gangs were seen working on roads and fields. Prison farms were constructed by the prisoners. The inmates plowed and sowed the fields with vegetables to be harvested later. Livestock was purchased with money that the inmates earned by being jobbed out to private business. With-in a year the prisons would be paying their own way. The American public loved it. Taxes for the average citizen started to go down.

A number of large and small businesses failed. They closed their doors. Poor management was not a reason for the government to step in with loans and stimulus programs. It did not take long before other better run companies came along and rehired the displaced workers. Trade from the communist countries was now non-existent. America was forced to produce both the needed and wanted goods here on our own soil. The power of the Unions subsided; workers were now becoming loyal to their own companies. Welfare programs ceased to exist. If a person wanted to work there was a job available. If they did not want to work, they were on their own.

Everyone would pay the same amount for medical care, no big discounts to insurance companies. The public had nationwide insurance programs, the funds provided by the taxes from their paychecks. With more reforms, less legal suits and everyone working together, taxes continually decreased.

The handicapped and the old and feeble were cared for by the government. If anyone was caught defrauding the system penalties was severe. Examples of people receiving disabilities from the armed services, government or private jobs were securitized. Too many had taken advantage and held cash paying jobs or developed ways of making money on the side. The new attitude in the nation was to turn in these criminals and keep the country honest. Why should hard working taxpayers fund a bunch of freeloading bums?

Education was stepped up. No more dropping out of school. It became mandatory until the age of eighteen. State or government loans for college would be paid back automatically from the students first jobs. Each paycheck would have a percentage paid back for the loan. Small interest charges were applied. People once again learned to be responsible for themselves.

Lawyers became scarce. Innocent people had little need for their services. The guilty found that with the law enforcing lawyers to present the case in an honest way they could no longer buy their way out of trouble. If the lawyer knew his client was guilty, the most he could do was to plea for a more lenient judgment.

Million dollar contracts for athletes soon began to disappear. No state or government loans were allowed for sports stadiums. The public was tired of the bad boys of sports who could buy their way out of trouble. Some states even went so far as to recruit only local players to their teams. All fifty states now vied to have teams that were born and raised in their home states. The public was ecstatic. A rivalry between states with homegrown teams was the best medicine for sports that ever happened.

No added sales taxes to pay for a state's or politicians pet projects. In fact, within two years, sales tax on everything other than gasoline, tobacco and alcohol were abolished. The court system levied fines and judgments that included the cost of running the government and state legal system. Police departments were allowed to keep the fines that they collected. Criminals were forced to pay back the cost of loss to both their victims and to society. The days of a free ride were over.

Who benefited from all this. The common American hard working taxpayer. They took home a larger chunk of their paychecks. Social security became a viable form of retirement. People were no longer afraid that a friend, neighbor, or stranger would sue them if they happen to get hurt on their property. People were held responsible for their own actions. The cost of goods decreased as companies no longer had to carry millions of dollars of liability because someone did something stupid with their product.

It was simple common sense. Cars do not cause accidents, people do. Cigarettes do not cause caner, smoking them does. Guns do not kill people, people kill people. Alcohol does not cause drunkenness, dinking to much of it does. Talking to a stranger should not be dangerous. Hitching a ride should be a safe thing to do. Walking the streets at night should be a God given privilege.

Soon the country started to change. We became a family. We watched out for each other. Kids stated to help old ladies across the street. Neighbors helped neighbors who were sick or injured. Towns took it upon themselves to help with any local disasters. People learned to become responsible. If you could not live in the system, the government offered free visas and transportation to the country of your choice.

Gangs, drug dealers, murder's, rapists, crooks now began to fear the everyday common Americans. If someone was in trouble it would be a matter of seconds before the good people came to help. No need for them to worry about lawsuits or stepping on someone's rights. If the person they stopped was no good, then what they did was good for the people. Two cheers for right verses wrong.

It took four years. The country was rebounding from the brink of disaster. Trade balance was almost equalized. America was just about out of debt. Kids were finishing school and proud of their countries heritage. History was used as a lesson of learning about past mistakes and past triumphs. People learned to live with-in their means. Sunday blue laws were common, no business' open on Sundays. A day of rest, a day to spend with the family, a day to thank the lord, a day to be proud to be an American.

CHAPTER 24

The remaining three and a half years were busy and productive for the Common-Cents party. Of course, some bad things happened at first. The unemployment rate was high for a while. Many of the imports disappeared and caused shortages to the American public. Gas was rationed and that in turn tended to raise prices in every sector of the economic system. Some big companies closed their doors forever. They of course blamed Rune and the government for not bailing them out. Then with-in a few years' new companies sprouted and started to supply the missing goods that we had lost from importing. Two major Japanese and two German automobile companies were building cars in America. They took up the gauntlet and started to produce hybrids and more gas efficient vehicles. 80 miles per gallon was not unusual for these new vehicles. The government's policy of not paying people to junk old cars, buy new cars, not to raise crops, and no bailouts to poorly run businesses saved the taxpayers billions of dollars in only a few short months.

Rune and his party were not always well liked. Although with-in three years of the Common-Cents administration Americans could see a new future. An American team of common sense honest upright citizens was coming to the forefront. The bad seeds and the criminals suffered, along with their money hungry lawyers.

People who could not live in an honest decent America were given two choices. Prison time, which meant working full time at small wages for their keep. Alternatively, deportation to any county that would have them.

The deportation system was working well. Russia with its need for workers made a pact with the United States. They would take our un-wanted un-desirable citizens free of charge. The stipulation was that they would send these people to Siberia to work in their gulag system. The new gulag system was not really so bad. It consisted of cities in the middle of nowhere. Escape would mean death as no roads or transportation in or out of the city was available expect under strict supervision. Each gulag city ran like any other city, except that they had to produce products for the Russians. Coal, gold, silver mines or Oil field work were the most common occupations. Also large factories and menial labor types of jobs. A hard life, but they fed and clothed the people that lived in the gulags. Pay was very minimal.

Soon the advantages of the new administration started to pay off. Low taxes, public health care, guaranteed retirement benefits that actually paid enough to live comfortably. More pride in workplaces meant better productivity, which equated to better pay and a new nationwide average of four weeks paid vacation per year.

Crime dropped to almost an unbelievable low. Towns became like families watching out for each other and making strangers and newcomers feel at home. People started to leave their homes un-locked. Why you could even pick-up a hitchhiker without fear of being robbed or killed.

Children could roam the great outdoors again. People who owned property no longer had to worry if the neighbor kid might get hurt. Lawsuits became almost nonexistent as people assumed responsibly for their own actions. Everyone soon realized that sometimes accidents do occur. They also realized that accidents do not mean someone did something wrong. That is why they call it an accident.

As for the prison population. They started to take pride in their work. They learned new trades. Many of them earned early paroles. They also left prison with the knowledge that they could fit into society and be useful citizens.

When four years were up Rune and Olaf both declined re-nomination to run for office. They accomplished what they had hoped for. It was time to turn the reins over to someone else.

Leaving the White House for the last time was bittersweet. All members of the Common-Cents party refused government paid security guards. They just wanted their old lives back.

The United States now had a new President. The Common-Cents party was still leading the nation. Einer was the new Commander in chief. Boone was the new Vice President. The country was in capable hands.

Valerie and her dog Oliver returned to Minnesota where she took a job in health care. She was to an age now that her next goal in life was to have a family. Strong willed and capable she was sure to succeed with any plans she made.

Travis continued to hang around at the Dog's Breath Saloon. He took over a management position at a local business. Hard work and loyalty to his employer made him an asset wherever he might go.

Olaf decided to just hang out for a while. Play darts, ride his motorcycle, and tell tall tales to all who would listen. It seemed he always had the attention of the ladies and he enjoyed it. He was content to live on his retirement from public office for the time being. Certainly, he was not rich, but he could cover his daily expense with a little left over.

Rune shaved off his beard, lost some weight, and got his old job back selling motorcycles. With his new look no one recognized him and he continued his life just as if he had never been gone for four years. Within a few months he was back with Olaf, Travis, and occasionally Valerie at the Dog's Breath Saloon. Playing darts, shooting some pool and drinking a few SvenBrews. Any fame he had seemed to disappear with his new clean-shaven look. No one recognized him anymore and that is the way he liked it.

Scotty and Adam were now looking after Einer and Boone at the White House. They emailed Rune and Olaf once in a while just to say hello. They booth seemed to be happy in their current positions.

Marie, her husband and stepdaughter did not fare so well. Public opinion felt he should be sentenced to prison for life. It was a tough decision for Rune to make. Was Marie's husband guilty of both Treason against his county and plotting the assassination of an American President? Was the public the ones who should make the decision in his fate, or was it up to Rune as the President and the intended victim?

Rune also had Marie and the little girl to consider. How much suffering could he put them through on account of her husband and the child's father? Tough as it may be decisions had to be made. It fell to Rune and Rune alone to make this decision. Rune was alive and well, the country was on an upswing and united, as it had never been before. Maybe even the whole assassination, Hilama, Chinese debacle had helped to unite the American public. After all, there is nothing like a major threat to bring people together. A reason for the American public to unite and face a common enemy.

Many sleepless nights finally brought Rune to a decision. Marie's husband was signed over to life in Russia at a Siberian gulag. There would be no reprieve, no amnesty, Marie's husband would never see the United States again. As for Marie and her stepdaughter, they were found free of any wrongdoing. Marie had to make her own decision as to the future of her and her stepdaughter. She felt that with her religious background she had no choice but to stay with her husband.

The Russians allowed a small concession for Rune in his request as to the treatment of Marie and the little girl. Marie was assigned a job in the local hospital as a medical aid. The little girl would be attending school with the other children at the gulag. Both Marie and the little girl had open visas to leave and return to the United States anytime they wanted. Marie's husband. He was assigned work in the gulag's coal mine. A dirty, dangerous job. A punishment many Americans felt was not severe enough. Then again, what better place for lawyer then deep underground in a coal mine, this way he would be closer to his final destination. Hell.

Sven and Lena. Well this is my 'tail' "a little a dog humor there." Being a Norwegian dog this is actually know as a 'Saga" or should I say a "Sven Saga." My human Rune, Lena and I, we settled down to a comfortable life away from the White House and the crowds. We run, play, go swimming, chew bones and take naps. When the mode strikes me I tell more saga's around the outdoor fire pit. We roast hot dogs and share smores. We are just enjoying a 'dogs' life.

CHAPTER 25

As for Hilama, surely she was not forgotten. The Chinese had a change of heart and offered her amnesty in China. In fact, she was offered a free place to stay, someone to clean up after her, even free food and protection from anyone who may wish to harm her. Yes you have to hand it to the Chinese they seemed to be very forgiving under the circumstances.

Hilama was presented with her options. A gulag in Russia, which she would probably be sharing with a number of her cronies who were also going there. In fact, it would be like a little town of ex-Americans, lawyers, legal assistants, politicians, crooked big business owners, and a few other undesirables. Why would the Russians hoped to indoctrinate all this evil into a nice little communist training center. After all, every one of them had the cut throat no mercy attitude that any KGB agent would die for.

The other option was the invitation from the Chinese. Which Hilama found to be a pleasant and unexpected offer. Of course, Hilama choose the Chinese offer of free room and board plus protection from possible enemies. Certainly, it was a no brainer decision. The White house conveyed Hilama's request to the Chinese for asylum.

Hilama was ecstatic with the warm invitation that the Chinese offered her. Under heavy guard, she was exited from her room at the White House where she had remained under house arrest. Scotty and Adam took personal charge to make sure she arrived safely at the airport. She was then turned over to a Chinese military escort who had a plane waiting to fly her to China. The United States military was on full alert until the

Chinese left American soil. The United States Air Force then escorted the Chinese airplane out of United States air space.

Landing in China, Hilama exited the plane to cheers of thousands of Chinese. This was almost too good to be true. Her interrupter explained that the Chinese looked upon her as a national treasure for their country. She was right up on the scale of importance as the Giant Panda's of China.

Hilama was quickly escorted to a long black limousine, the windows dark tinted in the passenger area, the Chinese national symbol painted on the doors. Her luggage was loaded into the trunk and they were on their way. Hilama watched as the car drove by the cheering crowds. Soon she would be in her new home, safe and sound. By the looks of things, she expected to be treated like royalty. A pampered and treasured queen from America, a status symbol for these lowly Chinese peasants to cherish and honor.

Hilama settled back in her car seat and dozed. Reaching their destination, she was ushered quickly from the car to her new living quarters. It was well past midnight, no moon or stars were visible in the sky. Blackness filled the area as she was introduced to her new home. It was hard to see and the interrupter was vague about the exact location. It seemed strange that the door to her apartment was made of iron and had only a small window with bars on it. The room looked comfortable enough. It was carpeted in animal skin rugs. A single bed, dresser, nightstand, table, and chairs were of simple bamboo construction. The sink, toilet, and a shower were in the corner with no surrounding walls. To think that the Chinese would put her into such a room. In fact, the room did not have a window, television or even a telephone. In the morning, she would talk to someone of importance and remedy this living situation.

A scraping sound on the floor of Hilama's room awoke her in the morning. She looked at the clock on the wall, seven in the morning. She noticed a trap door at the bottom of the door in her room. A tray off rice, eggs, and tea had been slid through the trap door and the scraping of the tray on the floor is what she had heard. She hurried over to see who had pushed this food into her room instead of delivering it in style, as she was accustomed to. Trying the heavy metal door, she found that it was locked from the outside. She tried to see where she was but the only view from the doors small barred window seemed to be a long gray painted corridor.

With no other choice left to her, she picked up the tray and sat at her tiny table on the only chair that was in the room and had her breakfast. Two bites of rice and a bite of eggs all which were bland and unseasoned convinced her to skip her meal. The tea was room temperature but at least it had some flavor.

She took a shower, brushed her hair and opened her suitcases. At least she had brought some decent clothes with. She dressed in one of her best outfits, ready to lodge her complaints as soon as she could contact someone.

Hilama investigated the perimeter of her room. It seemed to be made of corrugated sheet metal, much like a military Quonset hut. The long wall opposite the door seemed to give some as she pushed on it. She could see that it was not sealed on the bottom like the other walls. It seemed like it might be pushed up and open, but try as she might it would not budge.

She was hearing sounds from outside. The sounds were similar to those that had kept her half-awake during the night. Wild animals and birds seemed to be close by. Most likely, that was why her hosts had locked her into this metal building. She was sure they were near the jungle and she was being locked into her little room for her own safety.

Outside of Hilama's little sanctuary of safety, the crowds had already started to gather. A stand was set up to sell to rice cakes, fruits and candy to toss to the new arrival from America. Off course the crowd of on lookers hoped that by tossing her treats maybe she would speak or do a some kind of special trick for them. After all, they had never witnessed such a distinguished and unusual creature as Hilama.

A few minutes before nine in the morning. Hilama felt the call of nature. Guess it was time for the breakfast tea to leave her body. She looked at the toilet, of course in her mind more of a porcelain throne for someone with her status. Of course having no walls around the bathroom seemed a barbaric custom to Hilama. Then again, one must do what one must do.

She carefully arranged her fancy clothes so as not to wrinkle them and took her place as queen on the shiny white porcelain throne. Suddenly she heard a grating sound. The building seemed to shake. The complete wall opposite her single entrance door began to rise into the air. It was not a wall after all. It was a large electric garage door.

Hilama gasped and tried to wipe herself clean and compose herself in one fluid motion. In horror, she looked upon a crowd of hundreds of Chinese people staring at her. Soon they were all laughing and clapping their hands. Media people in the crowed were taking movies and snapping pictures.

In the most regal manor she could muster, she smoothed the slight wrinkles from her dress and held her head high in the air. She did her best to smile. As she walked forward and out of her little room she started to wave to the crowd. As she looked around, she could see she was enclosed in a large cage like structure. There were cement benches and chairs, even a little fountain with an American eagle whose beak had a stream of water flowing from it. Iron bars surrounded her on all three sides attached to the corners of her little building. Above her was a metal mesh that completely covered her cage. In her mind, the Chinese were being embarrassingly over protective.

Small children and even the grownups were tossing rice cakes, fruits and candy through the bars and into the area she was standing in. A small 8-foot wide, twelve foot deep trench surrounded her enclosure. The slick straight up and down cement wall would allow no one to get near her, or for that matter there was no way she could escape. She noticed people pointing to a large sign mounted on the roof of her living quarters. She walked out far enough into her enclosure to see it.

It was in large Chinese letters. The Chinese symbols to Hilama of course were very strange and she could not decipher them. Then underneath the large Chinese symbols she noticed a smaller interpretation of the sign written in English.

The national Chinese zoo wishes to thank the United States for this donation

"Hilama"

North American predatory animal

END

Manufactured By: RR Donnelley
Momence, IL USA
April, 2010